M000043212

Praise for *A Rebellious Woman*

"An engaging and in places riveting story about Belle Boyd, the captivating young Confederate spy from Martinsburg, Virginia. Griffin captures Belle's indomitable, energetic, and forward-thinking spirit. She places Belle within the context of the culture and history of her era, particularly portraying everyday life during the Civil War in Martinsburg and Front Royal in a way one can see, hear, smell and feel."

—Carol J. Appenzellar, curator, Berkeley Co. Museum, Belle Boyd House

"*A Rebellious Woman* by Claire Griffin addresses a void in American history: the lack of authentic voices of women who defied social expectations from the 1840s through 1900. It focuses on Belle Boyd, a compelling historical figure who charted her own course in life. It is rare to find such a well-researched work of historical fiction of a woman who chose to be an active participant in the tumultuous events unfolding around her and who forged a uniquely independent life through four decades. Griffin's *A Rebellious Woman* brings this remarkable character to life with its attention to historical detail as well as the development of Belle's character from her early years as an irrepressible young girl in Martinsburg, Virginia, including her daring exploits as a spy, to her acting career and extensive travels throughout America, and finally, to her death while she was still performing on stage in 1900 in Kilbourne, Wisconsin. Griffin's Belle Boyd, in many ways, is a welcome antithesis to the portrayal of the stereotypical Southern belle. Her research revealed Belle's many and varied accomplishments and experiences—an expert horsewoman, a spy, a prisoner of war, a domestic and world traveler, an author, a *diseuse*, and finally, a woman who married three times and divorced twice, gaining and losing financial independence along the way. With *A Rebellious Woman*, Claire Griffin has written an American woman's story that needed to be told."

—Dr. Adeline Merrill, adjunct professor of English,
Western Connecticut State University

# A REBELLIOUS WOMAN

## Claire J. Griffin

Brandylane
Publishers, Inc.
*Publishing books since 1985*

*Though based on the life of a real person, this book is a work of fiction. References to real people and events are used fictitiously, and some characters and all the dialogue are invented. They are not to be construed as real.*

ISBN: 978-1-951565-47-3
LCCN: 2020924796

*Designed by Michael Hardison*
*Production managed by Christina Kann*

*cover photo credit: Library of Congress, Prints & Photographs Division, [reproduction number, LC-DIG-cwpbh-01988 (digital file from original neg.)]*

Printed in the United States of America

Published by
Brandylane Publishers, Inc.
5 S. 1st Street
Richmond, Virginia 23219

Brandylane
Publishers, Inc.
*Publishing books since 1985*

brandylanepublishers.com

To women who break the rules

# A Sample of Etiquette Rules for Ladies
## *Mid-1800s America*

- *Do not* sit with your legs crossed at the knees or ankles. Your feet should always rest flat on the floor.
- *Do not* lean back in your chair. Your posture must be erect at all times.
- *Do not* move your hands while seated. Unless you are sewing or knitting, your hands should rest quietly in your lap.
- *Do not* run in public. You must also *avoid* walking quickly, swinging your arms, singing, whistling, laughing, speaking in a loud voice, or calling to someone on the other side of the street. *Do not* raise your voice in conversation. Also *do not* speak quickly, gesture, shrug your shoulders, or roll your eyes.
- *Do not* make exclamations such as "Goodness gracious!" or "Mercy!" Laughter should also be avoided.
- *Do not* go up a flight of stairs in front of a gentleman. It is improper for a man to observe a lady from behind as she climbs. If you encounter a gentleman at the bottom of the stairs, you must stop, bow, and indicate that he should precede you.
- *Do not* use or listen to suggestive language. If someone uses such language in your presence, you must quickly leave the room and *avoid* that person in the future.
- *Do not* have second helpings at dinner or eat everything on your plate. A lady must display a delicate appetite.

- ***Do not*** bite your bread. Instead you should break off a single small piece, and place it in your mouth.
- ***Do not*** speak with food in your mouth. ***Avoid*** taking large mouthfuls that require lengthy chewing. An agreeable female guest must be ready for polite conversation at all times.
- ***Do not*** accept wine at dinner. If wine is poured, you should raise the glass to your lips and set it down without drinking.
- ***Do not*** address a gentleman by his first name unless he is a relative. ***Do not*** use a person's last name without adding the word "Mister."
- ***Avoid*** being alone in a room with a gentleman unless he is a family member. If you enter a room where a gentleman or group of gentlemen is, you must apologize and leave the room immediately.
- When riding, a lady must show dignity and restraint at all times. You must always ride sidesaddle, never astride. ***Do not*** ride alone. Let your companion guide you. He sets the pace and decides where you will go. ***Do not*** go faster than your escort or force him to chase you. ***Do not*** race or be the first to go over a jump.
- Your riding dress should fit snugly and have a skirt that is full but not too long. Always place yourself on the left side of your escort where the graceful flow of your skirt is seen to its best advantage. ***Remember, a lady is always on display.***

*Mount Washington Female College*
*Baltimore, Maryland*
*January 22, 1857*

## Prologue

Belle sat in her favorite window seat and stared out at the rain. A French grammar book lay open on her lap, but several minutes had passed since she had looked down at its pages. The other girls were gathered in one of the classrooms, painting pretty flowers on china plates. Belle had no patience for such feminine pursuits. Thank goodness they were not much stressed at Mt. Washington Female College.

Rain depressed Belle. It made her introspective, which she did not like at all. She would much rather *feel* her feelings than *think* about them. There seemed no reason at all to think about how you felt, as far as Belle was concerned. But a letter from her father had arrived at school that morning, asking if she was happy in her new term. And of course, dear Papa deserved an answer.

"Am I happy?" Belle wondered aloud, winding a ringlet of hair around her finger. "I suppose I am. For the moment."

Last May, when she had turned twelve, Papa offered her the chance to go away to school. It was shortly after the incident in which Dame Havens, Belle's former schoolmistress, had sent her least favorite pupil walking home through the streets of Martinsburg at ten in the morning, followed by Thomas, the dame's slave, carrying Belle's desk, schoolbook, slate, and chalk. Thomas had delivered Belle, her desk, etcetera to her surprised parents, along with a note listing Belle's transgressions. Disrespect. Disobedience. Defiance. More etceteras.

Mama had grown teary at the contents of the note and at the very notion of her oldest daughter being paraded through the streets. Surely by now the whole town was talking about Belle. Again.

Papa had taken his daughter aside for a private conversation. Belle described the tedious lessons, the strict discipline, the whiny voice, the annoying sniff.

"Her nose drips, Papa."

Ben Boyd had pressed his lips together.

Belle went on. "But mostly, it's that I can't stand being inside all day. It doesn't suit me. I need to move about. I need to *do* things."

Her father nodded. His expression was grave, lips set in a firm line. Yet when Belle searched his face, she thought she detected just the tiniest sparkle in his eyes.

After that conversation, nothing more was said. Still, something had to be done. Even Belle knew that.

A few months later, on her birthday, along with a dark blue sapphire ring that exactly matched her eyes, Papa had given Belle a brochure to read. *Mt. Washington Female College* claimed to be a forward-thinking institution whose mission was to educate young women by means of "thorough physical and intellectual training."

She remembered Mama's gifts too. A lace shawl, which Belle adored. And a copy of *The Southern Ladies' Book of Etiquette and Politeness*. Belle loved Mama, but it was Papa who understood her. She had told him that the new school would do very nicely, thank you.

And that fall, Belle had headed off to Baltimore. She was accompanied by Eliza, aged twenty-three, who was as solid and steady as her young mistress was wayward and flighty. Eliza had been with the Boyd family since—well, since always, Belle realized, although Eliza had once belonged to Mama's brother James. Papa and Mama trusted Eliza completely, and they had made it clear that among her other responsibilities, Eliza must prevent their headstrong daughter from repeating her earlier mistakes. Belle *would* be a lady!

So here she sat in the college's main building, the octagonal one pictured in the school's brochure, staring moodily through the drizzle at the damp grounds.

Belle decided she *was* happy. On the whole. She enjoyed learning history, French, literature, chemistry, and mathematics. The social arts were not neglected, and Belle was unusually accomplished at playing the piano, singing, and dancing. She took pride in being able to make conversation on a variety of topics, including current events, which she followed by reading all three of the Reverend's daily newspapers. No, Belle didn't mind in the least being hopeless at china painting, embroidery, and all the other activities reserved exclusively for ladies. She considered them pointless, stupid, and boring.

The director of the school, Reverend Staley, gave his charges considerable freedom. Belle used hers in various pursuits. Some of them forbidden. She was teaching Eliza to read! In secret, of course. It would have meant trouble for them both if they were found out. Even the Reverend's liberal views might not extend as far as teaching a slave to read. Eliza learned amazingly fast, and Belle congratulated herself on her abilities as a teacher. She still didn't know why she'd started teaching Eliza. Perhaps it was because she herself was being educated. More likely the reason was that it was forbidden. Belle was always tempted to break a rule she didn't agree with. Why shouldn't a slave know how to read?

Among all the freedoms at her school, the one Belle cared about most was being able to spend time outdoors. Reverend Staley thought the young women of his day were too prone to attacks of nerves, headaches, and fainting spells. His solution was regular physical exercise. His girls must leave the parlor and go outside to enjoy sunshine and fresh air. And so, whenever the weather was fine, there were games of croquet and badminton on the lawn. Mr. Abbott, their natural history teacher, took his students on long tramps across the fields and through the woods. Observing the changes of the seasons. Collecting specimens.

And then, of course, there was riding, which Belle loved more than anything in the world. Though one of the youngest pupils, she was the best horsewoman at the school. Unknown to her instructor, she sometimes rode astride, which delighted the few girls who were her friends and scandalized the many who were not.

Reverend Staley had proved most understanding of Belle's boundless energy. During her first week at the school, in a fit of restlessness, she had left the grounds on her horse, been caught in a rainstorm, and gotten lost, returning hours later to a frantic staff. Wrapped in a blanket, a hot mug of tea in her hand, she had stood dripping on the Reverend's carpet and been invited to explain herself. This was when she confessed to Dr. Staley that she was burdened with too much energy. She simply never grew tired! Afterward he had written her parents a letter admiring their daughter's high spirits and vigorous good health. "Unusual in a female."

Closing the book with a snap, Belle told herself she would go for a ride as soon as the weather cleared. But even that thought did little to lift her spirits, and she went back to twirling her hair.

A stray beam of sunlight broke through the clouds and flashed on her ring. Staring at the jewel, Belle's eyes lit up. She slipped the ring off her finger and turned to face the window, long skirts bunching around her knees, her white-stockinged ankles exposed. Most unladylike. But Mama was not nearby to give a gentle reprimand.

Belle leaned toward the window, scratching the name and date into one of the panes. It was harder than she expected, difficult to grip the ring tightly enough to cut into the glass. She didn't give up. Of course not. Belle never gave up. Not when she had set her mind to something.

When she finally finished and sat back to view her work, she giggled. She had done the name exactly as she intended. *Annie Bell.* Who cared if it wasn't her own! Her real name of course was Maria Isabelle, but no one had ever called her that. No, it was the date that made her laugh. That was a true mistake. She'd forgotten that a new year had arrived three weeks past. It was no longer 1856. Leaning toward the glass, she scratched a 7 on top of the 6, then replaced the ring on her finger.

Belle read the name again and tossed her head. Quite right, she thought. No one would ever tell Belle who she would be. She intended to live her own life. Exactly as she chose.

# Chapter 1

T he dressing room was filled with excited chatter as dozens of young women, this season's crop of debutantes, finished their preparations for the ball. Tweaking a stubborn curl here. Helping a friend retie a loose bow there. Sharing perfume for last minute dabs at neck and wrists. The pitch of their voices increased when dance music began filtering in from the ballroom.

In the midst of the twittering and preening, sixteen-year-old Belle stood perfectly still in front of the mirror and examined her reflection. With her arched nose and somewhat slanted eyes, she knew she was not conventionally pretty. Nonetheless, at the first ball of her debut season, she had overheard one old gentleman describe her as "nothing less than magnificent."

Belle agreed. The white dress flattered her coloring, her luxuriant chestnut curls and flashing blue eyes. The pearly gleam of satin emphasized the smooth, pale skin of her neck and shoulders. She remembered what Eliza had said earlier that evening while she knelt in front of Belle to pin a bouquet of tiny pink roses at her waist. "No man ever gonna complain 'bout the shape of you, Miss Belle."

It was true, Belle thought. She saw how men's eyes flickered over her small waist and generous bosom before coming to rest on her face. And how they were always surprised by the amusement they found there. Which amused her even more. Did they truly think she would not notice those looks? Belle noticed everything. She prided herself on it. And when an admirer saw she was not embarrassed or offended by such obvious appreciation, then he knew she was not the same as other girls. Which was exactly right.

Still watching her reflection, Belle turned sideways, inclined her head with a graceful curve of the neck, and gave herself a flirtatious glance over the top of her fan.

"Ahem!"

Behind her, a trio of young women stood together, waiting their own turn at the mirror. Without a word, Belle swept from the room with her head held high, pausing in the doorway as she pretended to consult the dance card that hung from a cord around her wrist. Twenty-two dances, and every one accounted for! She already knew this, of course, but she made sure to hold the card so the three watching girls couldn't fail to notice. She would have wagered anything that their cards were not even three-quarters full. Belle would never be one of those passive wallflowers who stood hopefully around the edges of the room, waiting to be claimed while others danced.

Belle's victory was short-lived. As she continued through the doorway, she could not help hearing the whispered comments behind her.

"Did you ever see anyone enjoy looking at herself more than Miss Belle Boyd?"

"One would think she had no mirrors at home to admire herself in."

"Perhaps that's true. I've heard her father is a storekeeper."

*Yes, Papa is a storekeeper. But on Mama's side, I am related to the Randolphs and the Lees and the Jeffersons. Thank you very much!*

Belle wanted so badly to tell them this, and then to box their ears. But of course, that would never do.

The musicians were playing the opening notes of a waltz when Belle entered the ballroom. The comments of the other girls faded from her thoughts as soon as she saw Wilfred Sprokett. His handsome face filled with relief as she walked toward him.

"There you are! I was worried we would miss our first waltz."

Without another word, Freddy took Belle's hand, led her onto the dance floor, then swept her away on a wave of music. Once she had reacquainted herself with Freddy's long strides, Belle let her body dance for her, only half listening to the music. She enjoyed dancing more than anything. Except riding, of course. Both allowed her the speed and motion she craved, when her surroundings blurred past and she felt herself to be at the exact center. Of everything.

"I thought you might have been kidnapped." Freddy said teasingly.

"What a thing to say! Surely you know that a gentleman must never comment on the time a lady spends in the dressing room."

"Forgive me, but I didn't want to miss our waltz for anything. The next two dances are on the square. You know how boring that is. Holding hands and shuffling forward and back with three other couples. I can dance those with any girl. While you, my dear, are the best waltz partner in Washington."

Belle only smiled. By now she was feeling a bit breathless, but she would never tell Freddy. He would slow down, and she wanted to spin even faster, knowing she was safe in his arms.

"You know, there are some girls you have to drag around the floor, especially late in the evening. But you never get tired. How do you manage it?"

"There's something about those other girls you don't know."

Freddy waited, smiling already. "Well?"

"Can't you guess?"

"It must be the shoes. They're too tight."

Belle hesitated, knowing what she was about to say was most improper. Then she thought of the three girls in the dressing room. Leaning close, she whispered, "Most of them have to lace their corsets so tightly they can scarcely breathe."

*There, I've actually said the word "corset" in public. And to a man! While dancing!*

Freddy laughed. "Belle, you truly are like no other girl I know. You're just the slightest bit . . ." He stopped speaking and colored with embarrassment.

Belle squeezed his shoulder gently. She had met Freddy for the first time the year before at a party hosted in Baltimore by a mutual friend. From the start, Belle and Freddy had been comfortable with each other. Playfully flirtatious, both seeming to understand without it being said that they were simply good friends. One of the things Belle liked most about Freddy was that he sometimes said things he shouldn't. Just as Belle did. It made talking to him so much more interesting.

"Really, Freddy, you must tell me."

"Well . . ." Another pause. "I have heard you called 'fast' on occasion. Or sometimes the word 'forward' is used."

"Don't forget 'bold.' I don't mind. Truly. I am all of those things. And more."

Freddy grinned hugely. "Belle, I shall miss you. Is it true you're leaving soon?"

"In the next few days. We've been gone for months. Mama and I. She's enjoyed staying with her friends. But ever since Lincoln was inaugurated, there's been so much unrest. Protests. Rioting. It's worst at night. Mama says she hasn't slept properly in weeks."

"Let's not think about that now. If this is to be your last ball, we must make it one to remember. Don't you agree?" When Belle nodded, Freddy asked, "Are you ready?"

"Always."

He grasped her more firmly about her waist, and they flew around the room even faster than before.

Belle's next dance was a perfectly satisfactory quadrille with Dickie Farnsworth, then a thrilling galop with Paul D'Orsay, followed by a polka with Earle Westbrook, whose unfortunate sense of timing caused him to stomp hard on her foot two separate times. It was Belle's own fault. She should have known better than to put him down for a polka.

At this point, Belle realized she was thirsty and checked her dance card to see what was next. A mazurka. With Evan Baird. She was fond of Evan, who was an excellent dance partner, especially considering his generous proportions. Still, she groaned inwardly when she saw him approaching. Evan was perspiring heavily, wiping his damp hands with a handkerchief, then stuffing it into his pocket. Belle was relieved when he claimed to be winded from the polka and proposed a glass of punch instead, which she had been about to suggest herself.

"How perfectly lovely."

Evan went off to the refreshment table and returned with two cups. "We'll be cooler outside," he said, nodding toward the verandah, where glass doors framed by velvet curtains stood open to the mild evening. "Lead on, Miss Boyd!"

As they neared the doors, there was a commotion on the street.

"That sounds like gunfire!" Evan exclaimed.

Even over the music, the guests heard the shots, and some surged toward the doors. Because she was in front, Belle was the first to hear the other sounds. Men shouting. The squeal of frightened horses.

Belle peeked around a curtain, and said, "Rioters again! They sound drunk."

She was about to step onto the verandah when Evan moved in front of her.

"I don't think that's a good idea."

"I want to see what's happening!"

"No, Miss Boyd. It isn't safe. Even the men are inside for the moment."

Belle hated the word "no." As she moved to pass Evan, a sudden crash made all the guests pull back. Then a confusion of screams and overlapping voices.

"Are they shooting at the house?"

"They're throwing rocks! Someone get the ladies away from the windows."

The women were pressed back, and a tense silence followed while a pair of men, armed with pistols, detached themselves from the rest of the guests and stepped outside.

One of them shouted angrily, "You there! Move along before someone gets hurt. There are ladies present."

His companion chose a friendlier tone. "If you don't like Abe Lincoln, go to *his* house. Make as much noise as you want. In fact, you can wake him up for all I care!"

With an answering roar of approval, the horsemen rode off, shooting and shouting. The two men returned from the verandah, looking pleased with themselves. For a long moment, none of the guests moved. Or spoke. The careless remark about Lincoln hung in the air.

Then something strange happened. People began to draw apart. For months now, these young people had set aside their fears of the future in shared enjoyment of another glittering Washington social season. The sons and daughters of the best families from Charleston, Richmond, and Baltimore had danced with their counterparts from Philadelphia, New York, and Boston. This was the height of the season, a time for romance and matchmaking. Even as South Carolina seceded, followed by Mississippi, Florida, Alabama, Georgia, Louisiana, and Texas, these couples from opposite sides of a looming conflict had continued to dance together, exchanging smiling looks and whispers. The men shared jokes while the young women gossiped behind their fans. After all, the states that had seceded were far away, weren't they? In fact, some of them were known to be terribly backward. And no one *wanted* war. Surely it could be prevented. It wasn't too late.

Suddenly Freddy appeared at Belle's side.

She grabbed his arm and held it tightly. "What just happened? A month ago a rude remark about Lincoln would have been shrugged off as poor manners."

Freddy said quietly, "You've heard about the standoff at Fort Sumter. That the Federal soldiers there are short of food."

"And Lincoln wants to resupply them."

"Which Jefferson Davis won't permit," Freddy said. "He claims the fort belongs to the Confederacy."

"Of course it does. Because South Carolina seceded in December. So now Fort Sumter stands on Southern soil."

Freddy nodded. "The latest news is that Jeff Davis will issue an ultimatum. If the Federals don't evacuate, he'll order an attack."

Belle felt a sudden chill. No matter what some of the papers said, it couldn't really happen, could it? She pushed the thought away.

"President Davis would never attack a Federal fort!"

"It's bound to happen at some point, Belle. Lincoln has tried to reassure the Secessionists. He promised not to interfere with slavery where it already exists. But he also said he'd fight to keep the Union together. And to protect Federal property."

Looking around the ballroom, Belle noticed that the dance

floor was empty. The orchestra labored on, but the guests were huddled in tight groups, glancing over their shoulders, as if they did not want to be overheard.

"It's started, Freddy, hasn't it?"

He nodded slowly. "Now people will have to choose."

"I must get home right away."

*Washington D.C.*
*Capital of the United States,*
*Early April 1861*

# Chapter 2

The next morning, Eliza rose hours before dawn, and soon she was everywhere at once. Down and up and down the stairs a dozen times to finish the packing, close and lock the trunks, supervise the hired men who carried the luggage down—"You best be careful of that wallpaper!"—and finally to dress Belle and her mother in their traveling outfits. While mother and daughter sat down to breakfast in the dining room, Eliza was out by the curb, a warm buttered biscuit in her hand, overseeing the loading and strapping down of trunks and boxes.

It was a quick ride to the train station, Belle and her mother in the carriage, followed by a wagon for the luggage with Eliza seated beside the driver.

At the station, Eliza followed Belle and Mrs. Boyd to a pair of first-class seats, helped them get settled, and then handed over the lunch basket the cook had prepared for the journey. Eliza shook her head inwardly, knowing they would not touch the food, Mrs. Boyd being of the firm opinion that it was unseemly for a lady to be seen chewing in public. Then Eliza went off to see to the loading of the trunks onto the baggage car.

Shortly before the train left the station, she found her own place in a second-class car. Sinking down on the wooden seat with a sigh, she blessed Mrs. Boyd for allowing her to sit alone. The hard seat was a small price to pay for having these next few hours to herself. For being able to sit. Still and quiet. No need to jump up at a moment's notice to find or fetch or carry. The next few hours were hers alone. Mrs. Boyd had no idea how precious this was. Really, Eliza thought, a second-class train ride was as close to Heaven as anything she was ever likely to experience. She planned on a nap, but first she would eat her own lunch.

She untied a small bundle and spread the cloth across her ample knees. Ham biscuits. Dried apples. Two boiled eggs. A small jug of water. She ate it all, shaking her head at the thought of Belle and her mother. The two of them would arrive in Martinsburg half-starved, and Missus Boyd would hand their basket to Eliza and tell her to deliver the food to her own family.

The Boyds were generous with food, but more was always welcome. Eliza's boy John was eleven now and growing like a weed. He never stopped being hungry, for all he was as skinny as a beanpole. *Belle and me have been gone since Christmas. Almost four months. I wonder is he starting to fill out some?*

Now that they were finally going home, Eliza could allow herself to feel her need, like an ache deep in her belly. She wanted to see them, hold them. Her boy and her man. Sam was the Boyds' yard hand, splitting firewood, carrying water from the well, tending the garden, taking care of the carriage and the horses, along with the chickens and hogs. He lived over the stable, and that's where Eliza visited him, late at night after John was asleep. *John!* It hurt sometimes how much she loved that boy. They only had the one. Sam wanted more. But Eliza was skilled in women's matters. She knew how to stop a baby from getting started. She had made a vow to herself. Just the one child. Later on, maybe that would change. She was only twenty-eight. Plenty of time yet.

Eliza put that thought out of her mind and let herself think about her family. Once in a while, when Belle was writing her sister, Eliza would ask for news of them, and get a snippet back. Sam's hound about to have puppies. John being helpful with Belle's little brother, Will. Eliza knew if anything bad happened, illness or accident, Belle would think to mention it.

Eliza's shoulders slumped, and her head dropped forward onto her chest. She slept.

*Martinsburg, Virginia*
*Early April 1861*

# Chapter 3

Belle Boyd Returns to Martinsburg read the headline of the article Papa had clipped from the newspaper. Pleased to see her name in print, Belle read the story out loud to Mary. The article briefly mentioned Belle's recent graduation from a prestigious female college in Baltimore, as well as her debut in Washington. Much space was given to describing the fashionable traveling ensemble she'd worn as she stepped from the train. A gown of deep yellow lavella cloth under a long, fitted jacket, marigold-colored and trimmed with dark blue braid. Also a fetching marigold hat with a rosette of tiny blue and green feathers. Belle's mother, Mrs. Benjamin Boyd, was reported as stylish in navy and gray but looking somewhat weary from the journey.

"'They were met at the station by Mr. Boyd and his children—Mary, age ten, and William, age four. Miss Belle Boyd was overheard to mention to her sister and brother that her baggage contained promising gifts. Altogether, a most joyful family reunion.'"

Mary clapped her hands. "May I have it, Belle? The newspaper story? I've started a memory book. There's very little in it so far. But with you home, that's sure to change."

Mary bustled from the room in search of her jar of homemade paste, and Belle turned to her father. "Where is the rest of the paper, Papa? What's happening at Fort Sumter? I'd far rather read actual news than a description of what I wore two days ago."

Papa wouldn't meet her gaze. "I didn't bring it, Belle. I'd like to avoid anyone at home discussing the rumors about Fort Sumter." He raised his eyes to the ceiling. "I'm worried about your mother. She hasn't come downstairs since you arrived."

"She's just tired, Papa. Washington was dirty and noisy. There was rioting. It was hard to sleep at night. You know how Mama likes peace and quiet. It must have unsettled her more than I knew."

"Did anything happen on the journey from Washington?"

"Only that several times the train stopped between stations and simply sat on the tracks. Once for over an hour. The conductor offered me no explanation when I asked. If I had been a man, he would have told me something."

Papa nodded and pursed his lips, his brow creased into a frown that was new to Belle, yet already growing familiar.

"Tell me, Papa!" she demanded. "Is there news about Fort Sumter? Nothing's happened, has it?"

"Just the usual talk." He reached for her hand. "I'll not try to keep the news from you, Belle, but I don't want it talked about in the house. Not until your mother feels stronger."

Belle stiffened. *This is not acceptable!* She would have to be firm.

"Papa, in case you haven't noticed, I'm no longer a child. And as for being a woman, that shouldn't matter. I'm not a delicate flower in need of protection. At school we discussed the news every day."

He looked at Belle from under bushy gray eyebrows. "You never did like being told what to do." A smile tugged at one corner of his mouth. "Remember your Mama's dinner party?"

"The one she said I wasn't old enough to attend?"

"You saddled Penny, the oldest horse in the stable, and rode him into the parlor."

"And announced to Mama's guests that surely *he* was old enough!"

"Fortunately, the guest of honor was an obliging old fellow who thought your behavior was perfectly charming." Papa's smile disappeared. "You're not a child anymore, Belle. As you rightly point out, you are a woman. Children can sometimes misbehave, but grown women are never permitted to act like children."

Belle was in no mood for a lecture and intended to tell Papa again how wrong it was of him not to bring her the paper. Before she could say anything, he squeezed her hand, stopping her from speaking.

"I've been thinking about this since you came home. I want to be honest with you. About the things that are likely to happen. It would be a relief to tell you things I can't share with your mother or sister. You're the oldest. You can help them understand."

Papa's serious look made Belle feel quite grown up.

"Let's you and I go riding tomorrow. It will give us a chance to talk. We can ride cross country. A good gallop. You'd like that, wouldn't you?"

❧

The next morning, the Boyd household was considerably more cheerful. For the first time, Mama came downstairs and presided over the breakfast table, pale but smiling. Everyone chattered happily. Belle, pleased to be surrounded by all the people she loved best, looked around the table, her eyes lingering on each face.

First there was Papa, with his kind voice and mild gray eyes. She had missed him most of all. His beloved pipe, which Mama firmly forbade him from smoking at mealtimes, sat waiting by his plate.

Mama sat at the other end, looking a bit tired but more like herself. Mary Boyd, still in her thirties, had kept her good looks and her slim figure—despite seven pregnancies. Belle pictured the sad little row of gravestones in the Boyd plot at Green Hill Cemetery. Ben, Anna, Fannie, another Annie. Poor Mama! Yet here she sat with young Will on her lap, laughing and turning her head away as he tried to feed her a damp piece of toast.

Belle's sister, Mary, was named for their mother because Papa had requested it. Mary was Belle's opposite in every way. Quiet and domestic, she had spent all of the previous day deep in a secret project that involved hours of cutting and stitching. That morning before breakfast, she had raided Mama's sewing basket. "With permission of course!" she'd assured her family, although Belle was sure no one cared. When Mary couldn't find what she wanted in Mama's bag of sewing scraps, she'd made a list of supplies for Papa to bring back from his store.

Finally there was Grandmother Glenn. Mama's mama. Because of the census the previous year, Belle knew for certain that her grandmother was fifty-seven years old. Otherwise she would never have found out, as this was one of many things Grandmother Glenn did not think it proper to discuss. Rigidly correct at all times, she sat at the table wearing a ribboned cap and lacy indoor gloves, her posture ramrod straight so as not to touch the back of the chair. That is what the etiquette books of Grandmother's day had demanded. When Belle was a little girl, always in and out of scrapes, her grandmother had terrified her. Now that Belle was a well-educated young lady with opinions of her own, she found her grandmother both irritating and amusing.

Belle was an early riser and had been the first to come down to breakfast. Grandmother had been last. Now she fixed her eyes on Belle and frowned.

"What is that you're wearing? Are you riding after breakfast?"

"With Papa. First we'll go into town to get what Mary needs from the store. And then we'll ride cross country. It will be glorious!"

"You didn't think to show me your new riding outfit?"

"I was going to wait until after breakfast." Belle rose from the table and stood before her grandmother. "I hope you approve."

The dark green riding costume had a flowing skirt and a tight-fitting jacket that showed off Belle's well-proportioned figure. She knew she created a striking impression when she was seated side-saddle, mounted on a horse even some men would not dare to ride.

"Turn around," Grandmother ordered. "Then show me your hat."

Belle found her black hat with its fetching wisp of a veil and pinned it on.

"Your riding gloves are also black?"

"Of course."

Grandmother's lips curled into a rare smile of approval. Turning to her daughter, she raised an eyebrow. "All those months in Washington, Mary, and not a single proposal of marriage?"

Mama sighed unhappily. "The whole season was upsetting. Not a bit like when you and I made our debuts. All anyone talked about was Secession and War." After a pause, she smiled and added, "Although I must say that Belle received a great deal of attention."

The subject of their discussion stood by the table, impatiently tapping her riding whip against her shiny black boot. Belle watched Grandmother pat Mama's hand. "Don't worry. She's a beauty. There's still time."

❧

Belle waited with Papa on the back porch. When she saw Sam walking up the hill with a horse on either side, her heart beat a little faster. Papa's chestnut was a fine mount, but Belle only had eyes for her own dark bay.

Fleeter was such a beauty. Sometimes it truly seemed like the horse could read her mind. When they rode, she had only to think of going faster, and they were. She would see a fence up ahead, and in two strides she'd feel Fleeter rising beneath her, lifting her into the air. Belle did not control her horse by dominating him. She merged her will with his, and then his power belonged to her. This was her secret.

Belle had begged to take Fleeter to school with her, but Papa had demurred at the expense of sending a horse back and forth between Martinsburg and Baltimore. She'd had use of a perfectly fine horse while she was away, but he'd been nothing like her Fleeter.

As the horses approached, Belle jumped lightly off the railing where she was perched and went to greet them, taking Fleeter's reins from Sam so he could help her father mount. She stroked the horse's velvet nose, watching while Papa hopped half a dozen times on his standing leg before finally swinging himself up and into the saddle.

*He didn't used to hop like that.* Belle was quick to push the thought away. Sometimes she didn't like the things she couldn't help noticing.

Then it was Belle's turn. Sam bent and held out his hands, the fingers intertwined into a living basket. Belle placed her boot there, then gave a little hop and said, "Up!" Sam lifted, Belle straightened her knee, and in one smooth motion she was balanced on Fleeter's back as securely as a sidesaddle would permit. Once she was settled in the stirrups, Sam handed her the reins.

Belle leaned forward and whispered to Fleeter. As the horse

23

cocked an ear back and tossed his head, a rush of pure delight washed over her. *We're together again. Fleeter and I!* Meanwhile Sam stood quietly, holding the horse's bridle.

"Yes?" Belle prompted.

Sam squinted up at her. "This horse ain't got much exercise since you's been gone, Miss Belle. I did what I could. But he's achin' to run." He nodded once. "Thought you should know."

"I'll keep that in mind." As the horses moved off, Fleeter dancing sideways a few steps before he settled, Belle looked back. "Thank you, Sam. He looks wonderfully fit."

The horses walked along the path that led from the back porch out to the gravel street. Here Belle stopped to look at the house. Papa followed her gaze.

"This is how I always pictured home while I was away. In spring, with everything in bloom. See Mama's roses? They reach Mary's bedroom window now. And the honeysuckle climbing the tree?" Belle took a deep breath. "My two favorite smells in all the world."

Papa breathed in too. "Both of them right here in our own front yard." He paused. "It's good to have you home, Belle. I missed you."

"I missed you too, Papa. It's fine to be back." She looked at the house one last time, then turned and asked briskly, "Where to first?"

"Let's stop at the store and give Mary's list to Mr. Meaders. He can make up a parcel while we go across the street to the train station. The telegraph office is the best place for news."

They let their horses walk at a leisurely pace to make conversation easier.

"The children were pleased with their gifts," Papa said.

"Will carries his toy locomotive everywhere. And Mary loves her garnet necklace." Belle smiled. "She's such a lady. More of one than I will ever be!"

Belle spoke lightly, trying to erase the frown from between Papa's eyebrows. Was he worried about Mama? The war? It seemed that events were reaching a crisis at Fort Sumter.

Something was bound to happen soon. Belle was irritated that Papa might know more than he was telling her. Never mind. He was taking her to find out the latest news. For the moment, she would just enjoy the pleasure of riding Fleeter with her dear Papa by her side.

Looking around at the tree-lined streets, the pleasant houses with their deep porches and well-tended flower beds, Belle smiled.

"It's a lovely morning. Isn't it, Papa?"

"And more lovely with you beside me," he said gallantly, giving her a rare, real smile.

As they drew closer to the center of town, the houses grew smaller and closer together. When they approached a place where two streets crossed, Belle slowed automatically. One often had to wait here for a wagon or carriage to pass.

She turned her head from side to side. "Shouldn't the streets be busier?" She paused, looked around again, narrowed her eyes, then said, "It's happening here, too. Isn't it?"

"What do you mean?"

"My last ball in Washington, there was a riot outside on the street. One of the guests said something rude about Abe Lincoln. And afterward, people acted differently. You could see them taking sides."

Papa's lips tightened, but he remained silent.

"I thought it would be different here. Because we're all Virginians."

An open carriage drove down the street, a well-dressed couple seated inside. Belle recognized the elegant dark blue cabriolet that belonged to Mr. Gaylord, local representative of the Baltimore and Ohio Railroad. As the carriage drove past, he nodded a greeting to Belle and her father. Mrs. Gaylord stared straight ahead.

When the carriage was out of sight, Belle looked at her father for an explanation. Mrs. Gaylord, like Grandmother, was unfailingly correct in her behavior.

Papa sighed wearily. "You may remember that Mrs. Gaylord is from Philadelphia. Such things didn't used to matter so much. But now . . . Well, everyone knows our family will stand with the South. It seems Mrs. Gaylord favors abolition. She's quite vocal in her views."

Belle had already lost interest in Mrs. Gaylord. Here was a chance to show Papa how much she knew about current events. As their horses began walking again, Belle said, "Lincoln claims he's not against slavery where it already exists. If he fights, it will be to keep the Union together. But the states that have seceded say they don't want the Federal government telling them how to grow their cotton and tobacco. It's a matter of States' Rights, Papa." When her father said nothing, she went on. "In Washington, everyone predicts Virginia will secede too. Is that what you think?"

"The situation here is more complicated than people in Washington realize."

"Because Virginia has always been divided on slavery."

Papa nodded. "You learn things owning a store, listening to the farmers talk when they come in to buy. Here in northwestern Virginia, the farms are small. They barely support a single family. The farmers work hard from dawn until dusk. They resent the rich plantation owners who have slaves to do the work for them."

Belle thought of Mama's tobacco farm that Grandfather Glenn had given her when she married. Belle had never been there. If she wanted her father to treat her like an adult, she should know more.

"Tell me about the tobacco farm. Where is it?"

"South and east. About a hundred miles. Close to Fredericksburg. Three hundred twenty acres. There's no proper house. Just a small place for the overseer and his family. And slave cabins of course, with garden plots. It's good tobacco country. The soil is rich, and the growing season is three weeks longer than here."

Belle had never thought much about soil and growing seasons. What else could she ask?

"How much help do you have, Papa?"

"Seventeen workers. All field hands, since there's no big house to look after. That's another reason the farm is profitable." After a pause, he asked, "Any other questions?"

Belle thought a moment. "What about the town? Is it divided too?"

"Right down the middle, I'd say." Papa's lips were set in a grim line. "One problem is the new railroad yard."

"But that's a grand thing!" Belle said, thinking of the day the new depot had opened and how exciting it had been. "I was a little girl, but I still remember. There was a parade with a marching band. Mr. Gaylord gave a speech. Everyone in town was there, dressed in their Sunday best. Mama bought new ribbons for my bonnet. Blue ones."

Papa nodded. "The rail yard's been good for the town. That's for certain. It's brought in a lot of business. Some folks think, with Martinsburg being so far north, that the Federals are the ones who'll be best able to keep it from being blown up."

"Blown up!" Belle exclaimed, reining in Fleeter once again. "But why?"

"Whatever side doesn't control the rail yard will try to destroy it so the other side can't use it."

Belle felt her world shift. The events in the newspaper, the endless secessions, the standoff at Fort Sumter suddenly seemed much closer to home than they had when she'd woken up that morning.

"But, Papa! Your store is right across the street. What will happen to it if the rail yard blows up?"

Her father raised his shoulders, then dropped them, shaking

his head sadly. "Hopefully nothing. But if the depot is destroyed, every business in town will suffer. Not just the store."

"Everyone says, if there is a war, it will be short. If Virginia secedes, Arkansas and Tennessee will follow. If enough States leave the Union, there won't be any Union left to fight us!"

"There are many who think the war will end quickly. And many who believe the South will win."

With a stab of fear, Belle realized that her father, always ready to see things in the best possible light, was not so optimistic.

"Ninety days is what people are saying!" she insisted. When Papa did not answer, she asked slowly, "But that's not what you think, is it?"

He shook his head, the look on his face the saddest she had ever seen. "Maybe it's because I run a store that I see things differently. If the war lasts more than a few months, it's not going to be enough that our men are brave. The North has all the factories they need to equip an army. We don't. You don't just fight a war with men and horses. Soldiers need guns. Bayonets. Bullets. Saddles. Uniforms. Knapsacks. Canteens. Tents. Blankets. Boots. Bandages." He practically spat the words. It was a voice Belle had never heard him use before. Hard, flat. Relentless. Not caring if his words hurt her or frightened her. It was almost like the words themselves were bullets. Belle forced herself to sit and listen. After the final word, she shuddered.

"You don't want me to keep things from you, Belle, so here it is. Martinsburg is just twenty miles from Pennsylvania, which will stay with the North for sure. However long the war lasts, I think the fighting will be worse here than anywhere else."

# Chapter 4

On April 12, at 4:30 in the morning, Confederate General P.G.T. Beauregard gave the order for his artillery to open fire on Fort Sumter. And the Civil War began. A day and a half later, after thirty-three hours of bombardment, the Union commander surrendered and was allowed to evacuate his men from the ruined fort.

The surrender took place on April 13. On April 15, Lincoln called for seventy-five thousand volunteers to fight for the preservation of the Union. Men enlisted in droves. On April 17, Virginia seceded.

Belle felt her world breaking apart. She had always been a patriot. On Mama's side of the family, she could count nine relatives who had fought against the British in the War for Independence. She loved the United States of America, but her home was here, in Virginia. There was not a field or forest near Martinsburg that she and Fleeter had not ridden through. Not a stone wall they hadn't jumped over on a sparkling autumn morning. Belle had only to close her eyes to imagine her favorite rocky glen two miles east of town. A place of dappled sunlight, lilting birdsong, and the sound of a stream rushing downhill toward the mighty Shenandoah River.

ლ

"Is the war over?" Mary asked a week later as they sat in the parlor after lunch.

Papa was gone, as he often was these days. So Mama nodded to Belle, giving her permission to answer.

"No, dear," said Belle. "What makes you think it's over?"

"I know there was a battle at Fort Sumter. But now whenever you and Papa come back from the telegraph office, you always say there's been no fighting. And it must be true because if there *was* fighting, Papa would look worried. More worried than he does now."

Papa had told Belle she should explain things, and Mama seemed to want her to, so she said quietly, "The war isn't ending, Mary. It's just beginning."

"But that Union major surrendered Fort Sumter. He gave it to our side. And you said there weren't any casualties. That's what you said, Belle! So there's no reason to keep on fighting."

"Right now, both sides are getting ready. Gathering up guns and ammunition and horses. Signing up soldiers. Finding officers."

"But I don't want a war! I don't want anyone to get hurt."

"Don't worry, dear," Mama said. "Hopefully the fighting will be far away. And no one we know will have to go."

Closing her eyes, she murmured a short prayer and then picked up her book again. Grandmother hemmed handkerchiefs. Will spun a top at her feet. After pouting a few minutes to show she was still angry with Belle, Mary agreed to a game of Cat's Cradle.

Belle let her mind wander as they played, thinking about what she'd told Mary, that both sides were busy preparing for war. She'd received a note the day before from Freddy Sprokett, telling her he'd enlisted in the Virginia Cavalry. With his devil-may-care attitude, she'd known he would not hesitate.

Freddy had been Belle's favorite. She didn't want anything to happen to him. Nor the others! In Washington, some of her friends were Northerners. Surely they'd fight for the Union.

In the end, everyone would fight for his home. His state. What would happen to them all?

Belle mustn't be like Mary. She must face facts. Many of her friends would be killed unless the war ended quickly. It wouldn't matter what side they were on. She hated to think of it.

Her bleak thoughts were interrupted when Eliza hurried into the parlor.

"What is it?" Mama asked.

"I was just in town, Missus. Colonel Thomas Jackson rode in with a buncha officers. They's signin' up men left and right for the Second Virginia Infantry."

"Oh dear," Mama said.

"Infantry!" Belle exclaimed. "Any man with a decent horse should join the cavalry. That's what I'd do!"

Everyone stared at her, and she felt her cheeks grow hot.

"Don't be absurd!" Grandmother said sharply. "You could never be a soldier!"

"I mean if I were a man!" Belle explained, although that wasn't what she'd meant at all. She'd give anything to ride in the cavalry. To fight for Virginia.

Mary looked at Mama accusingly. "You said the fighting would be far away!"

"I said I *hoped* it would be."

Belle had a frightening thought. "Where's Papa?"

Mama's eyes widened, as if she guessed what Belle was thinking.

"He's helping at the store. Mr. Meaders sent word there were more customers than usual."

Mama, Grandmother, and Belle exchanged glances.

"What's wrong?" Mary asked.

"Nothing." Belle held up the string from their game. "Look, it's all tangled. We shall have to start again."

The women returned to their activities—except for Eliza, who had gone back to the kitchen, where Belle knew she would share the news with Cook and Delia and Patsy. That is, if they didn't know already. Belle frowned, picturing how Eliza had looked when she told them about Colonel Jackson. Her face had been a mask, as if she was holding something in. But what? She couldn't be frightened. Eliza was never frightened. She must know the Boyds would take care of her and her family. Just as they always had.

Suddenly Papa was in the parlor with them, his step quick and energetic.

"I'm glad you're all here!" he said, rubbing his hands together, his loud voice echoing in the room.

He didn't seem to notice how still they were, like statues posed on the furniture. That was when Belle knew it had happened. The thing she feared.

Papa pushed out his chest, smiling self-consciously. "You are looking at Private Benjamin Boyd. Company D. Second Virginia Infantry. Army of the Confederacy. I joined up."

After a moment of stunned silence, Mary wailed and ran to Grandmother.

"Oh, Ben!" Mama protested. "You didn't! I was sure you wouldn't. I never dreamed . . ." She took her handkerchief out of her pocket.

In an instant, Papa was on his knees beside her chair.

"I had to, Mary."

"I suppose you did." She wiped her eyes, tried to smile. "It's just that, well, you're forty-four years old. And the infantry of all things. I'm not saying you aren't fit, dear. But couldn't you leave the job to younger men?"

"Of course I could, Mary," Papa said softly. "But that wouldn't be right, would it? So many men are joining up, you wouldn't believe it. The entire Fourth Company will be from Martinsburg. We filled a whole company! That's how many we are. Everyone must do his part."

Belle stepped forward and took his hands. "You'll make the Boyd name proud, Papa."

He gave her a grateful look and kissed her fingers.

"Why didn't you join the cavalry?" Mary asked.

"I'm not the rider I used to be. The infantry is where I'll be most useful."

"But to think of you being a private, Ben. Carrying a heavy pack. Marching wherever the army sends you."

Belle guessed what Mama was thinking. Colonel Jackson was a local hero. He'd fought in the Mexican war. Everyone in the Shenandoah Valley knew he had experience leading soldiers into battle. That's why so many had joined his company. But the rumor was that he used his men hard. How could Belle's father keep up with soldiers half his age?

Papa pulled Mama to her feet and put his arms around her. Mary joined them, hugging Papa's waist. Belle watched with her hands clenched into tight fists.

"I wish I could go!" The words burst out before she could stop them.

"Oh, Belle!" Mama said. "You mustn't say such things. It's not ladylike."

"Not the infantry. The cavalry. I'm a good shot. I ride better than most men."

Ben Boyd gave his daughter a hard look and spoke in a voice that was uncharacteristically stern. "Yes, you do. But going to war is not the same as a day shooting rabbits with your Papa." He thrust out his jaw. "Don't even think of it, Belle. Not for a moment. Women don't go to war. No matter how well they ride and shoot."

"I want to be useful!"

Grandmother said, "There are ways to be useful and remain a lady."

"We can knit socks!" said Mary.

"And collect money and supplies," Mama added.

"Yes, of course," Belle said absently, thinking, *I must find a way to do more!*

Papa went on to tell them he would be sent to Harpers Ferry for training. "It's close by. I might be able to come home from time to time." He rubbed his hands together again. "I report in two weeks. So I'll need you ladies to start my uniform right away. Later on, if the war lasts long enough . . ."

"Which we all pray it does *not*," Mama interrupted.

He squeezed her shoulder gently as he continued. "Later on, we will be issued standard uniforms, but for now, Jackson has asked each man to supply his own."

"I'm sure there's plenty of cloth at the store," said Grandmother.

"Mr. Meaders has been selling cloth all day long. And a lot of it is dark blue. Don't forget Martinsburg is split. A man can sign up with Jackson right here in Martinsburg. But joining the Union Army just means crossing into Pennsylvania. It's a day's ride. Two days walking."

The room was silent again, everyone looking at Papa, now staring into the distance. He gave himself a shake, looked at their worried faces and spoke in that hearty voice again.

"At least for now, war is good for business. I had Meaders cut a nice length of gray wool. I'll bring it home this afternoon."

"What about the store, Ben? Is Mr. Meaders enlisting too?"

Papa shook his head. "He really *is* too old. Lucky for us. Before long there's going to be a shortage of men in this town." He patted Mama's arm. "Not to worry. Old Meaders knows the store better than I do. He'll keep things going."

"Papa, I don't want you to go!" Mary said, her lip trembling.

He knelt in front of her. Taking her chin in his hand, he said gently, "We must all be brave soldiers now, little one."

He was still on his knees when there was a knock at the door. Belle answered and accepted a folded piece of paper from the small black boy she found on the porch. She saw the name on the outside and brought the note to Mama, who unfolded it, then read it out loud.

*Dear Mary,*

*Ellis and Avery have decided to join up. I wish they would wait. Especially Avery. He's so young. But of course, he must do everything his brother does. I pray God keeps them safe. Felix tells me not to worry. But I tell him that is what a mother is for.*

*Eugenie Osbourne*

*P.S. It's Jeb Stuart's First Virginia Cavalry for the both of them.*

When she had finished reading, Mama pressed the paper against her heart.

"Poor Eugenie. I must write to her. I would visit, but there's too much to do. She will have her hands full too. Two uniforms to sew. How dreadful!"

"How old is Avery now?" Grandmother asked.

"Barely eighteen," said Belle. "The minimum. If you do pay a visit, Mama, may I come? I would like to say good-bye and wish both boys good luck. Before I left for school, Avery and I were close."

Mama nodded, her lips pressed tightly together, her eyes closed. Papa put his hand on her cheek. She tilted her head toward him, but her eyes stayed closed and she did not speak. The room filled with unhappy silence.

*Martinsburg, Virginia*
*May and June 1861*

# Chapter 5

The morning that Papa was to leave for Harper's Ferry, he came to Belle's room, something he hadn't done since she was a little girl. When Belle opened the door, he was standing in the hall, looking uncomfortable. Without a word, he held something out to her, knotted inside a dirty rag.

"I want you to have this. Just in case." As Belle reached for it, he said, "Careful. It's heavy."

She lifted it from his palm, already knowing what it was. The sharp smell of gun oil told her. As well as the weight of it. Papa's Colt pocket pistol.

"Don't bother to unwrap it. I cleaned it last night. I hope to God you don't need to use it, but at least you know how." The words came out in jerks, like they were being pulled out of him against his will. "Your nerves are steady enough. So's your aim. It's a good gun at close quarters." He blinked a few times, as if hearing his own words. His mouth hung open, ready to say more. Instead he closed it, shook his head, and walked away.

That was on May 2. On May 9, Belle turned seventeen. Mama gave her a brooch of coral beads and tiny seed pearls. There was cake and elderberry wine after dinner. At the head of the table, Papa's chair sat empty.

Belle missed talking things over with her father. May 23 was scheduled to be Voting Day, when the property-owning men of the state would decide whether they agreed with Virginia's vote for secession or instead wanted to break away from Virginia and remain with the Union. The day before the voting, Colonel Jackson, anticipating a riot in Martinsburg, sent a hundred soldiers from Harpers Ferry to keep the peace. Unfortunately, Papa was not among them.

"It would have been nice to see his dear face," Belle sighed. "To have a chance to speak with him. And find out what camp life is like."

"His letters are always cheerful," Mary said, placidly knitting another pair of socks.

"To be sure," said Mama, "but seeing him would tell us more than any letter."

Belle agreed. One look would tell them everything. How was his health? Did the food agree with him? Was he exhausted by Jackson's endless drilling? Was he able to get enough rest? She had so many questions that only seeing him could answer.

છ્ય

Voting Day was filled with shouted speeches, angry crowds, raised fists, shots fired in the air. A few days later, when the votes throughout the state had been tallied, the results were just as Papa predicted. Most Virginians supported secession. They did not want the Federal government telling them what to do. But *western* Virginians, many of them poor farmers, did not want rich plantation owners in eastern Virginia telling *them* what to do. So they favored staying with the Union. And western Virginia included Martinsburg.

When Belle told her family that Martinsburg would stay with the Union, no one could believe it.

"I don't understand! We favor the South!" Mary cried angrily before running out of the room.

Mama had sat down quickly. Eliza hurried to fetch a glass of water from the kitchen, where Belle knew she would tell Cook and her boy, along with Delia and Patsy. She'd find Sam and John and tell them too.

*I wonder what they're saying among themselves. Eliza used to talk to me. I used to know what she was thinking. But she's quiet lately. Ever since Papa joined up.*

Mary was gone a long while. She returned with a square of folded cloth, which she thrust into Mama's hands.

"Here's the surprise I've been working on. There wasn't time to finish it, because of helping with Papa's uniform. And there's another reason. You'll see when you open it."

Mary sat beside Mama, sniffling a little as she watched her mother unfold her gift. A Confederate flag. Poor Mary! Each star was meant to represent one of the states in the Confederacy. And the one that was supposed to stand for Virginia hadn't been added—because Martinsburg had just voted to stay with the Union!

"I hear there's talk of forming a new state," Grandmother said, her voice rich with disapproval. "To be called West Virginia. That means we won't even live in Virginia anymore. Nothing makes sense these days."

"Thank you for the flag, dear one." Mama kissed her daughter's cheek.

"Everything is so confusing," Mary complained. "Even when Belle explains it. I know what she says is true, but the truth keeps changing!"

Belle sat on Mary's other side to admire the flag and praise her sister's needlework.

Grandmother spoke again. "How can anyone tell us we no longer live in Virginia? It's ridiculous."

"It's just a vote," Belle said. "Everything will be decided by the fighting anyway."

Mama sat up straighter. "Our family has always stood with the South. There are Boyds throughout Virginia. We are related to Robert E. Lee and Thomas Jefferson. The last is a distant connection, to be sure, but a connection nonetheless."

Belle smiled at her mother's show of spirit.

"You're right, Mama. I'm sure our boys will fight valiantly. That will decide everything."

"And we pray it will all be over soon," Mama sighed, shoulders drooping again.

"So Papa can come home," whispered Mary.

℘

June 20 brought more mayhem to Martinsburg. The day began normally with their neighbor Petey Higbee coming over after breakfast. Although he was Mary's friend, he worshipped Belle. The three of them had played together for so many years that Mama didn't protest now at her grown daughter sitting on the parlor floor playing pick-up-sticks with her skirts bunched up and petticoats showing. Belle might want to be treated as an adult, but she sometimes relished the chance to act like a child.

Suddenly her head went up, and she sniffed the air.

"Smoke!"

Showing a calmness she did not feel, Belle went to the front door, opened it, and saw a slave boy running past, bare feet pounding the dirt.

Belle called out, "You there! What's happening?"

The boy looked around and stopped when he saw her standing on the porch.

"Jackson's men is wreckin' the train yard, missus. Ain't nobody there to stop 'em!"

The rail terminal was on the south edge of Martinsburg. Colonel Jackson's men must have marched from Harpers Ferry, which lay to the southeast, so his soldiers didn't have to go through town to reach it. Which is why the attack had taken everyone by surprise.

*It doesn't make sense for Jackson to destroy the rail yard. No matter the results of Voting Day, the town is still in Confederate hands.*

Belle wanted to see for herself what was going on. She hurried to her room to get her parasol, hat, and gloves while Mary did the same. Petey dashed outside and waited for them, dancing with impatience on the brick sidewalk, stretching his neck in the direction of town as people rushed by.

When they reached Papa's store, right across from the depot, there was a small crowd gathered on the porch, viewing the confusion from a safe distance. Belle recognized each face, all of them Southern sympathizers. Without a word, they made room, the men lifting their hats, the women giving quick nods before turning back to watch the destruction. No one spoke. There were no words to describe what was happening.

It was the flames that Belle noticed first. Fed by coal, and oil, and kerosene, and tar, all the flammables stored in the various buildings, the flames grew taller even as she watched. She could pick out dark figures moving in and out of the smoke, soldiers in gray lighting more fires, setting off small explosions of gunpowder under the locomotives to wreck their giant rods and pistons, swinging sledgehammers and crowbars to tear up the tracks.

They seemed bent on destroying everything. Buildings, water tanks, every piece of machinery. Anything the enemy could use. The air was filled with roiling clouds of choking black smoke.

An angry mob had gathered between the inferno and the porch. Many were railroad employees who shook their fists as they watched their jobs go up in smoke. There were women in the crowd too, silently weeping. Belle knew that these men bought their tobacco in Papa's store. Their wives came in for cloth and buttons, needles and thread, or a stick of candy to be broken up and shared among the children. These were Martinsburg's citizens. And now the men, their faces twisted in anger, yelled curses while their women wept.

One voice rose above the others. "Those damned Rebels!"

A ripple went through the crowd on the porch, and Mary shrank against her sister. Belle was as shocked by the word "rebel," as she was by "damned." She sided with the Confederacy. She was a Secessionist, but that did not make her a rebel! Abe Lincoln had declared her one. When all she wanted was to see her town protected. Her beloved Shenandoah Valley. So life could go on as it always had.

The look on Petey's face was also a shock. Belle knew how much he loved the trains.

Now his face was red, his eyes wide, mouth hanging loose. A mix of outrage and fascination. Glancing around the porch, she saw the same look on other faces, the young men especially. They stared greedily at the orange flames and billows of smoke. She watched them jump when a new explosion sent showers of sparks high against the churning clouds. She saw their noses wrinkle at the stench in the air. She could almost hear them thinking, *Now isn't this something?*

Once Belle had taken the children back home, Petey turned mournful.

"It was *our* soldiers that did the burning and tore up the tracks. Did you hear what the men were saying? All the engines and cars smashed and burned. Or tipped in the river." He was close to tears.

"They say they're going to blow up the bridges too," Mary whispered.

Belle tried to explain. "Jackson had orders. The Baltimore and Ohio railroad is based in Maryland, which tried to stay neutral. But the Federals wouldn't let them. Now the whole state is filled with Union troops. Jackson can't let the cars and engines fall into their hands!"

"I suppose," Petey said grudgingly, wiping his nose on his sleeve, which earned him a frown from Belle. "It's a lot quicker to move things by train than by road."

"Especially when it rains and the wagons get stuck in the mud," Mary added.

"That's right," Belle said, still hoping that the winter rains wouldn't matter, hoping the war would be over by then. That everyone in town could work together to rebuild the depot. That Martinsburg would return to normal. That Papa would come home.

*Martinsburg, Virginia*
*June 1861*

# Chapter 6

'Liza slipped from under the blanket she shared with her son John and padded down the attic stairs in bare feet. As she walked downhill to the stable, she felt herself grow taller. It happened every time she turned her back on the house and started down the hill. She'd stopped wondering if she actually got any taller or not. Didn't make any difference. What mattered was climbing the stairs to the loft and Sam's straw-filled pallet on the floor. In warm weather he would drag it next to the door so 'Liza could look out and see the sky.

Sam received her without comment—he wasn't much for words—and then she received him. Afterward, they lay side by side under the faded quilt and watched lightning play behind the clouds.

"Storm's comin." Sam's voice was a deep rumble, like the thunder in the distance.

"Comin' every which way. Master Boyd joined up. Old as he is. And now Colonel Jackson's burned the train yard, and ever'body in town is fightin' each other. Virginia's for the South, but Martinsburg favors the North. What's that s'posed to mean?"

'Liza didn't expect Sam to answer, but she could feel him thinking, lying there beside her, staring up at the rafters, his hands behind his head. She could see the shine of his eyes when the nearly-full moon peeked out from behind racing clouds.

"Do you think this war could mean . . ." Sam drew a deep breath and held it. When he exhaled, the word came along with it, sweet as honey, "Freedom?"

In the darkness, 'Liza found Sam's hand and squeezed hard.

# Chapter 7

Following the destruction at the rail yard, the atmosphere in town was more oppressive than ever. Jackson's soldiers had gone, but the air still stank of burning. And betrayal. The town had favored the Union partly to save the train depot, which Jackson destroyed anyway. Depending on where their loyalties lay, the townspeople were either angry or defensive. Everyone knew how important the yard was to the town, and now it lay in ruins.

To raise their spirits, Mama gave a small party to celebrate finishing Mary's flag. In the end, all the Boyd women worked on it together, with Mary having the honor of sewing Virginia's star into its proper place. When it was finished, Mama had Sam hang it over the mantel in the parlor. Then she invited the Osbournes, along with Petey and his parents, Mr. and Mrs. Higbee, to come and admire it.

Eliza passed cookies, and there was wine, with Mr. Osbourne doing the pouring in Papa's absence. Once everyone's glass was filled, he proposed a toast.

"To Benjamin Boyd. To Ellis and Avery. To the men of Martinsburg. To all the brave men and boys willing to fight against Northern Tyranny."

"May God preserve them!" they all said.

The party distracted Belle for only a day. Then her restlessness returned.

She felt as if she might explode with it and went on long cross-country rides in a vain attempt to tire herself out. Perched high on Fleeter's back, she noticed things, as she always did. But this time she found herself looking at them the way a soldier might. She examined the terrain, deciding where an officer might set up an ambush. Where a unit of men could hide if they were being pursued. She thought of Papa. Of keeping him safe. She should make a map! That would be useful, wouldn't it? But whom would she give it to? Never mind. She'd worry about that later.

Working late at night after everyone was asleep, Belle soon realized that mapmaking was harder than she'd thought. She couldn't get the spacing to come out right and was forced to throw away her first two attempts. A terrible waste of good paper, which Papa had warned her would soon be in short supply.

Undeterred, she tried a more systematic approach. First she made a list of all the features she wanted to include. Then she pasted four pieces of paper together and lightly penciled in the features on the map with a series of x's. She marked a piece of string with ink dots to represent each hundred yards, then used the string to adjust the spacing between features and get the distances right.

Was this how proper maps were made? Belle had no idea but was totally engrossed in the challenge she had set herself. Ravines and streams and forests. Farms and barns. Outbuildings and orchards. Roads and stone walls and fences. Everything must be placed accurately or the map would be useless.

Finally Belle was satisfied. Tomorrow she would take the map with her when she rode and check it for mistakes. Then she'd be ready to go over her pencil markings with pen and label everything. Perhaps she'd take out her box of watercolors. Add green and blue and brown and gray. It would be quite pretty when she was finished. Someone would find a use for it. She was sure.

Because Belle had worked so late, when she finally went to bed she fell into a deep sleep. She dreamed she was back at school, in a class taught by Mr. Abbott, the natural history instructor who had been interested in moths and butterflies. The school's director thought lepidoptery was an ideal subject for his students, as it combined physical exercise with scientific observation.

Belle had been good at capturing butterflies, happy to traipse through fields and meadows with her collecting net, a white linen duster covering her clothes, a veiled sunhat sheltering her complexion, a pair of canvas gloves protecting her hands. She enjoyed the subject less in the classroom, where she and the other girls were shown how to impale the lovely butterflies on small pins and display them in glass cases above neatly lettered labels.

In her dream, Belle was a butterfly trapped inside a glass case. With her wings spread wide and pinned on either side, she called out in a tiny threadlike voice, begging for release. On the other side of the glass, Mr. Abbott leaned close. His enormous eyes stared at her as his plump, rosy lips curved into a grotesque smile.

"Ah yes. A magnificent specimen."

Belle woke with her heart hammering. The room was hot and airless. She slid out of bed, damp sheets dragging onto the floor, and went to sit in the rocker near her window. She would not return to bed. The view of moonlit trees calmed her, but when dawn came she still shivered at the images in her dream.

೧

The next morning at breakfast, Mama had news that made Belle forget all about her nightmare. The Osbournes were planning a trip to visit their boys at Harpers Ferry, and they had asked if Belle and Mary would like to go with them. Mama had already given permission, and she spent the rest of the morning in the kitchen consulting with Cook about filling a hamper of food for Papa.

Three days later, Belle, Mary, and the Obsournes left for Harpers Ferry. Because Mr. Osbourne's large landau was rather heavy for two horses over a distance of twenty miles, he decided to avoid the added weight of a separate driver. He would drive the carriage himself. He also insisted that the ladies restrict themselves to two small trunks each.

Inside the carriage, there was plenty of room for three passengers, even with the women bundled into their traveling cloaks. It was a warm day, but overcast, with the sun mostly hidden behind clouds, so Mrs. Osbourne insisted that the top be left down. This was a great relief to Belle, who hated a closed carriage more than anything.

By early afternoon, they had reached the Bolton house on the outskirts of Harpers Ferry. They were greeted at the door by George Bolton, Mrs. Osbourne's widowed brother. As soon as the trunks were unloaded and carried upstairs, and the ladies had been helped to shed their cloaks and brush their skirts, and everyone had drunk chilled water to wash the dust from their throats, Mr. Bolton proposed they all get back in the carriage and drive into camp.

Belle said she would rather walk. "If I don't, I'll never sleep tonight."

"I'll stay too," Mary said. "It wouldn't be proper for her to walk into camp alone with so many soldiers about."

Mrs. Osbourne smiled at Belle. "Some might disapprove of you, my dear, but I have always admired your spirit."

After the others left, Mary sat on the stairs, sighing impatiently, while Belle had a lengthy consultation with the hall mirror, taking time to adjust her new hat to its most flattering angle. There would be dozens of people she knew in camp, and she must look her best!

She gave herself an approving final glance. Mama was right. The hat was very becoming. And it was generous of Papa to buy it. At the time, he'd explained that soon there would be a shortage of pretty hats. Belle pushed that thought away, preferring to think it was because Papa liked to spoil her.

She turned and pulled Mary to her feet. "What are you waiting for? Let's go."

Her sister's indignant protest was interrupted by a knock at the door. For some peculiar reason, no one was around to answer it, so Belle took the liberty of opening it herself. After all, she was about to go out anyway.

There, on the front porch, stood Papa. Papa! For a moment, during which she could scarcely breathe, Belle was afraid he wasn't real. For weeks now, she had imagined seeing him again. And now here he was. Her darling Papa!

She reached for his hand. He took it and held it for a few moments, squeezing tightly. Then he let go and executed a smart salute, announcing, "Private Boyd reporting for duty!"

Belle threw herself into his arms, and Papa lifted her off her feet, something he hadn't done in years.

"Papa's here!" Mary cried, running onto the porch.

He repeated his greeting for his younger daughter, swinging Mary in a circle before setting her down.

"How did you know we were here?" Mary asked, clinging to his hand.

"Word spreads quickly."

Belle led the way to the parlor, hoping the Boltons wouldn't mind this further liberty.

Papa looked around. "Where is everyone?"

"They all drove into camp. Mr. Bolton too. Mary and I decided to walk."

When her father lifted the tails of his coat, preparing to lower himself into a chair, Belle said, "No, don't sit yet. I must inspect you, so I can put everything in a letter to Mama. First impressions are often the truest." She tilted her head to one side, her habit when composing a letter. "Let me see. I'll tell her Private Ben Boyd is looking strong and trim, if a bit thin. In fact, his uniform fits better than when he left us. As you will recall, Mama, we all thought it somewhat snug but didn't want to hurt his feelings by saying so."

"I'm sad without you, Papa," Mary said, crawling into his lap. "I want you to come home."

He said nothing, just held her while she played with the buttons of his coat as if she were still a little girl.

Belle gave her father news of Mama and Will and Grandmother. And reported how upset everyone was by the devastation at the rail depot.

"It's certainly a blow to the town," Papa said. "But Jackson had to do it."

"I know," Belle sighed. "Worst of all is how it's made people turn against each other. Even more than before. The other day I saw Petey's mother start to leave her house. When she saw Mrs. Hutchinson coming down the sidewalk, she went back inside. They both go to the same church!"

"It can't be helped," Papa said matter-of-factly, eying the lidded basket that stood in the corner. "Is that for me, I hope?"

Belle nodded. "There's a good-sized ham, plus bacon, flour, and molasses. A big crock of cheese. Also pickles and peach jam and butter. The biscuits are fresh. Mama had Cook make them this morning. You'll want to eat them right away."

"I can't tell you how pleased my tentmates will be. We share everything. There's plenty of food in camp. But home cooking, now that's something special. I'll take it with me, if you don't mind.

They'd never forgive me if I came back without it."

"You can't carry that yourself! It's much too heavy."

"As you said, your Papa is fit as a fiddle." He lifted the square basket easily and placed it on his shoulder. "Open the door, my dear."

Passing through the doorway, he stooped so Mary could kiss his cheek. Then Belle.

"I'll come again tomorrow for a longer visit. Today I more or less had to sneak off." He gave a quick smile. "My plan is to invite one or two officers to this evening's feast. That way I'll have no trouble getting permission for tomorrow."

&#8485;

Belle found the atmosphere at Harpers Ferry unexpectedly cheerful. The men in the camp seemed almost lighthearted. Despite constant rumors of imminent action, they had not seen battle. Yet. When they weren't being drilled, they played like schoolboys—racing, wrestling, singing and fiddle playing.

The visitors too seemed able to push dark thoughts from their minds in the fragile happiness of spending this short time with sons, brothers, fathers, husbands, sweethearts. To entertain the guests, there were dances almost every evening and occasional picnics. Belle and Mary saw Papa every day. While most of the soldiers continued marching and drilling, those with visitors had been relieved of their duties. For once Colonel Jackson relaxed his famous discipline. The men from Martinsburg had enlisted early and already endured weeks of training. It helped that the Colonel knew many of these families personally. He could hardly deny them the pleasure of being together while they still could.

⁀

One day, a pair of cavalry officers invited Belle and Mary for a horseback tour of the camp. When the men tried to hurry past one practice area, Belle protested. So the four of them sat on their horses and watched clumsy recruits obey bellowed orders to "Fix bayonets!" then run full speed to plunge the wicked points into human-shaped bales of hay.

Belle was sorry she had insisted on watching, especially when she saw her sister's chalk white face. The reins trembled in Mary's hands, making the mare she was mounted on toss its head in irritation. Before either of their escorts could react, Belle grabbed the bridle on Mary's horse, steadying the animal. Then she looked at the two officers, her eyes flashing.

"Sirs, I understand why you tried to protect us from seeing this. Especially my sister. But if this is what war is, we women should know. It's our war too!" She turned to Mary, now slumped in the saddle. In a changed voice, Belle cooed, "Come darling. I have the reins. Just sit, and I'll lead you home."

When they reached the Boltons', the house was empty, everyone at the camp as usual. Belle took Mary upstairs, undressed her, and put her to bed with a cool wet cloth folded over her eyes.

"Shall I lie down with you until you fall asleep?"

"Yes, please." When they were side by side, Mary groped for Belle's hand and held it tightly. "Will you sing to me?"

In her low, sweet voice, Belle crooned the Scottish folksongs Mama had taught them long ago. When she was sure Mary was sleeping, she got up, smoothed her dress, and headed back to camp. There was someone she wanted to see.

During her visit, Belle had become reacquainted with an old friend, Henry Kyd Douglas. He lived near Martinsburg and had enlisted as a private in the Second Virginia Infantry. Henry was a lawyer and a preacher's son. Belle had once heard him say that slavery was a curse. Yet when Virginia seceded, he had enlisted in the Confederate Army.

She found Henry singing hymns with a group of men seated on a circle of logs. She watched for a while, then joined in, her voice soaring above the others. Afterward, the men applauded and asked her to sing again. Belle declined with a smile, nodding to Henry, inviting him to walk with her.

"I have made a map," she said without introduction, placing it in his hand. "Of the countryside around Martinsburg. I marked everything of military interest. Afterward I rode over the area again to check it for accuracy."

When Henry unrolled it, he let out a low whistle. "Belle, this is quite impressive."

She smiled, remembering the hours she had spent on it.

"To think you could have drawn this with no help. Or instruction. I do like the way you've colored in all the details. It's very pretty."

Belle held up her hand to stop the stream of silly compliments. She *would* be taken seriously. "I'd like you to give it to one of Colonel Jackson's aides."

Henry blushed. "Well." He paused. "I suppose I could find someone to give it to."

"I wish Jackson himself to see it. I'm sure he'd be interested in a map drawn by someone who knows the terrain as well as I do."

"I'll do what I can," was all Henry would say.

Belle smiled prettily through her clenched jaw. It would not do to show how angry she was. A lady must never express strong emotion. There was no point. Her good friend Henry would think it nothing more than a female temper tantrum.

*Why is it that no one—no man—will let me be of use?*

*Harpers Ferry, Virginia*
*July 2, 1861*

# Chapter 8

T hen came a morning when the camp visitors were abruptly ordered to pack their things and leave. The army was moving out within the hour.

It broke Belle's heart to watch Mary cling to Papa, sobbing frantically as they said their good-byes. Belle cursed herself for insisting on viewing that blasted bayonet practice. She was often too stubborn for her own good. Making a point that women did not have to be protected from unpleasantness. And what did she accomplish? Nothing except to make her sister half hysterical. And Mary didn't know, as Belle did, that Papa was going into battle.

ↄ

They arrived back in Martinsburg to find Patsy, Delia, Eliza, Sam, and John washing all the windows, closely supervised by Mama and Grandmother.

"We weren't expecting you!" Mama said, flustered at having to greet the Osbournes' carriage while wearing her kerchief and canvas work apron.

"Never mind. Belle will tell you everything!" Mrs. Osbourne said.

Sam and Eliza worked quickly to unload the trunks, and the Osbournes' carriage sped away.

"Why are they in such a hurry?" Mama asked.

Belle realized then that Mama and Grandmother hadn't heard about the battle to be fought at Hoke's Run that very day. Less than ten miles from where they were standing. Surely everyone else in town must know what was about to happen.

*Why didn't Eliza keep Mama informed as I told her to?* Belle gave Eliza a hard look, and Eliza stared back, her face unreadable. *As it always is these days,* Belle thought.

Mama stood and stared after the Osbournes' carriage, oblivious to Mary, who had buried her face in her mother's apron. Finally, Mama noticed Mary's distress and looked at Belle in alarm. "What's happened? Is it your father?"

"He's fine. Perfectly fine. Fit as a fiddle. Those were his exact words. Fit as a fiddle." Belle's nerves were strung tight after everything that had already happened that morning. She heard herself babbling and took a deep breath to calm herself. "There's going to be a battle."

Grandmother immediately took charge of Mary and led them all inside.

"Why didn't you tell them?" Belle hissed as Eliza lifted the dusty cloak from her shoulders. "You were supposed to keep them safe."

"I tol' her and tol' her. All 'bout that Hoke's Run place. Didn't keep nothin' from her. She won't listen. Wants ever'thing to go on just the same as always. Your grandma's just as bad."

Grandmother ordered Eliza to bring two wooden chairs into the parlor so she and Mama could sit down in their work clothes.

"What's happening?" Mama asked, holding Mary in her lap.

"As I said in my letters, it was a fine visit. Papa looks well. Everyone in camp is cheerful. But this morning all the visitors were told to leave. Henry Douglas said General Patterson and three thousand Federal troops have crossed the Potomac River into Virginia. Colonel Jackson has orders to engage them at Hoke's Run."

Grandmother gasped. "Why, that's no distance at all."

"Will Ben be in the fighting?" Mama asked.

"That's what we were told."

Grandmother told Eliza and Sam to empty the window washing buckets while she and Mama went upstairs to dress properly. Afterward they all sat in the parlor with the shades drawn, hands folded quietly in their laps, backs straight, and waited. That was what war meant for women, Belle realized. Sitting and waiting. Always waiting. It made her want to scream.

Then, without warning, the battle began. Even with the windows closed, they could hear it. The blast of cannon fire rattled the glass. The sharp reports of rifles stabbed the air. Mama sat in her rocker and read aloud from the Bible, Psalm twenty-three, over and over.

"The Lord is my shepherd, I shall not want. He maketh me to lie down …"

Eliza stood in the doorway with Sam. Clustered behind them were Delia, Patsy, Cook, and Cook's son, Joshua. They whispered the words along with Mama, who never faltered except to close her eyes when an especially loud explosion shook the windows.

Grandmother took young Will onto her lap, and he sat against her, his thumb in his mouth, clutching his beloved train. Belle wrapped her arms around Mary, who pressed her hands over her ears as the noise grew in intensity. But there was no shutting it out.

"It must be bad, right Belle?" Mary had to shout to make herself heard. "If it's getting louder, our boys are retreating. It means we're losing. Isn't that what it means?"

"It's all part of Jackson's plan," Belle said soothingly, glad to have some real information, the result of listening closely to the men's talk at Harpers Ferry. "In the camp, they said Patterson has more men than our side. So Jackson isn't trying to win. He just wants to slow them down. It's called a delaying action."

"Does that mean there won't be so many casualties?"

"That's right, dear."

Eliza's son, John, appeared in the doorway and squeezed close to his mother. Belle hadn't missed him until now. He was a small, darting boy of nine or ten. Maybe eleven. Belle couldn't remember exactly. It didn't matter. She saw him tug his mother's sleeve and Eliza bend close to hear, then stand up, frowning.

"What is it?" Belle asked.

"This boy of mine's been up on the roof, Miss Belle." Eliza put her hand on his shoulder. "He says there's men comin'. They's wearin' gray coats."

"John?" Belle called softly, beckoning the child to her. The boy's bare feet shuffled forward a few steps. "Can you tell me how far away they are? A mile? More?"

One shoulder lifted shyly. A whisper Belle had to lean forward to catch. "Maybe a mile." He narrowed his eyes, thinking hard. "If I ran the whole way, I'd have to stop and rest two or three times."

"Are they running or marching?" Belle asked. In the camp she had learned that such details mattered.

"They's marchin'."

"Ah, good. That means an orderly retreat. Thank you, John."

And suddenly there was silence. A silence so complete, it seemed almost like sound.

Belle's ears strained, reaching into the distance, but heard nothing. Belle, Mama, Mary, and Grandmother exchanged looks, filled with questions no one dared ask out loud.

*What's happening? Is it over? Are we safe? Is Papa alive? Unhurt?*

Mama closed her Bible. She smoothed the front of her dress and said to Cook, "Bring us something cool to drink. It's hot with the windows closed."

Cook left. So did the others, returning to their work in various parts of the house and yard. The family remained in the parlor, sitting perfectly still. The eerie silence seemed fragile, precarious, as if any movement might start the noise of battle again. They sat and waited, taking slow sips of the chilled water Eliza brought on a tray.

A short while later, they heard flutes and drums in the distance. Moving like a sleepwalker, Mary walked to the door and opened it. A lilting tune trickled into the room, feeling somehow like a blessing. Belle uttered a silent prayer for Papa and the boys. The ones from Martinsburg she'd known all her life. The ones she'd just met at Harpers Ferry. Mama's eyes were closed, her lips moving. Slowly the music grew louder.

"Is that the retreat, Belle?" Mary asked.

"It must be. They'll be marching through town. It'll be our boys first. With the Union Army following, I would imagine."

"Let's go up to the square," Mama said, "and watch our men go by. Maybe we'll see your father. We wouldn't want him to be looking for us in the crowd and us not there to wave to him." Her voice broke on the last words. She looked at Eliza and the other slaves. They had all drifted back into the doorway, along with the music. "You may all come. Eliza, fetch our parasols and gloves and bonnets."

In a few minutes they were hurrying toward the town square, joining a steady stream of people headed in the same direction. Young boys ran down the middle of the street, yelling. Most people looked excited rather than frightened. For the moment, it didn't seem to matter which side of the conflict people were on. The war was right here, on their very doorstep, and everyone wanted to see what it looked like.

The gray-clad men came through town at a quick march but in orderly ranks. It turned out Papa's company had not been in the battle. Belle looked in vain for his regimental flag, with its proud message, *Our God, Our Country, Our Women.*

Even so, she saw plenty of familiar Martinsburg faces. Belle called out to one of them, "Where's Company D?" ignoring several disapproving looks. A lady was not supposed to raise her voice on the street.

She was rewarded with the decisive but unhelpful answer, "Not here!" delivered with a proud grin. At first Belle was disappointed not to see Papa. Then she scolded herself. She should be grateful! He'd missed the fight. He was safe.

After the briskly marching soldiers came the cavalry, their job being to protect the rear from the Union advance. Belle's heart lifted at the sight of the horses and their riders, the mingled sound of stamping hooves, creaking saddles, jingling spurs. She was surprised to recognize the officer riding in front of the mounted men. Captain Turner Ashby and Belle had danced together at Harpers Ferry the night before last. He must have remembered her too. He nodded and touched his hat as he passed.

Then, almost within sight of Ashby's last riders, came the Union ranks. If Belle's heart had thrilled to see her own boys march by, she despaired at the sight of the boys in blue. There were so many! Each one bent on destroying everything she knew, everyone she loved.

With piping flutes, snapping drums, rippling flags, prancing horses, with clumsy cannon carriages rumbling behind teams of mules, the men came and came and came, singing in their triumph and relief. They had met the enemy, and the enemy had run. Their expressions proclaimed confidence and pride. The rest would be easy.

Belle wanted to yell at them. "They were meant to retreat. Jackson's boys. They didn't run away! They were following orders."

Instead she stood and watched as wave after wave of blue soldiers marched past. How could she stop them?

# Chapter 9

General Patterson's thirty-five hundred men spent the next day taking possession of the town, their loud voices and harsh accents setting everyone's nerves on edge. When the Federals first marched into Martinsburg, Belle had noticed all the different regimental flags. Most of the men were their neighbors from nearby Pennsylvania, but there were real Yankees too. From places like New York, Connecticut, even Massachusetts. Belle had never realized there were so many different ways of speaking Northern.

Everywhere she looked, the town bustled with activity. Infantrymen set up a city of tents on the edge of town, cavalrymen fed and watered their horses, the general and his staff established their headquarters in the county courthouse. A problem arose at the small hotel that had served as a makeshift Confederate hospital during yesterday's battle. There had been just a handful of wounded, and the doctors had evacuated them during the orderly retreat. But two soldiers had been left behind, too ill with fever to leave with the rest. Now Federal doctors had taken over the hospital, and the sick soldiers had to be moved. Soon enough, they would be prisoners of war, but for now they were patients and would be treated with compassion.

Eugenie Osbourne was sitting in the parlor, explaining all this to Mama when Belle walked in.

"Since we are just around the corner from the hospital, a Yankee officer has told us we must make room for the two sick boys."

"But Eugenie, you said it was fever. Is it safe to bring them into your home?"

"I'm not worried about that. The doctor says it's not serious, but he insists they are too ill to travel just now. Anyway, Felix has sent me to you for help."

"What kind of help?" Mama asked. "I don't understand."

"Apparently, as they are *our* soldiers, we must move them ourselves, with no help whatever from the Federals!" Eugenie declared indignantly. "We have only Chester and Eva. They're both quite old now. Felix can help, but he asks that you lend us Sam. And isn't your Cook's boy nearly grown? That's three. Who else do you have?"

"I'll come," Belle said.

"You can't carry a stretcher!" Mama said.

"Of course not. I'll bring Eliza. She's very strong."

A short time later, the rescue party arrived at the hotel to move the soldiers. Sam and Mr. Osbourne led the way with the first stretcher. Eliza and Joshua, Cook's fourteen-year-old son, followed with the other. Two Federal soldiers walked alongside them, not to help with their burdens or to clear the crowded streets. It seemed they were there only to ensure the safe return of the stretchers.

Mrs. Osbourne walked beside the first patient, angling her parasol to shade him from the sun. Belle did the same for the second man. If not for his pale and hollow cheeks, he would be quite handsome. She placed her hand lightly on his shoulder.

The street outside the hotel was mobbed with Union soldiers. It looked to Belle like they were just milling about with no purpose. As their slow procession inched its way along, blue uniformed men pressed close to see what was happening. Mr. and Mrs. Osbournes' expressions of outraged dignity meant the Federals kept a distance from the first patient, but this made them crowd the second stretcher all the more. Belle was relieved to be walking beside Eliza as the soldiers jeered at her and jostled the sick man. Her hand trembled around the handle of her parasol, but she kept her expression calm. She wasn't frightened as much as angry.

*Why are they acting this way? You'd almost think they'd been drinking.* Belle spotted three Federal officers sitting on their fine horses near the edge of the crowd. *Surely they can see what's happening. Why don't they control their men? Such behavior toward women and the sick would never be tolerated among Southern troops.*

In the end it was Eliza who came to her defense. Her hands gripping the stretcher's wooden handles, she loudly complained, "Let us pass, you good-for-nothings! Where's your manners? Can't you see my mistress is a rebel lady?"

Just a month ago, Belle had objected to the term "damned rebel." Now Eliza's words filled her with pride. So much had happened since the war's beginning. Papa enlisting. Belle's trip to Harpers Ferry, where she'd seen those brave men and boys larking about the camp. Where she'd watched that dreadful bayonet practice. Yesterday she'd sat in the airless parlor, listening to the battle, believing Papa was there. Now these smug men in their blue coats were strutting all over town, ordering everyone about. She couldn't bear it!

In the last few months, she had come to love Virginia more than ever. Her beautiful Shenandoah Valley was in danger. It was agony that she hadn't yet found a way to help. Eliza's words had been exactly right. Belle was proud to be called a *Rebel Lady.*

Belle and Eliza stayed at the Osbournes' to help settle the sick men. Later, on their way home, Belle was thoughtful.

Finally she said, "Yesterday I told you to keep Mama informed.

But let's not say anything about what happened today. It will only worry her. If this is how the Federal officers are going to let their men behave, with no respect or decency, she will find out soon enough."

Eliza said, "I been hearin' things 'bout them soldiers."

Belle gave her a sharp sideways glance. "What have you heard?"

After a pause, Eliza said, "Most of 'em is volunteers and their time is 'bout up. They's goin' home soon, so they's happy. And feelin' like they whupped … us … yestaday."

Not noticing how Eliza had hesitated over her words, Belle was indignant. "They didn't whup us! Jackson gave orders to retreat. In the face of superior numbers."

Eliza pressed her lips together and stayed silent. Belle barely noticed, as her thoughts returned to the Union soldiers who jeered and jostled her. And the Union officers who watched and did nothing.

After another minute of walking, Belle touched Eliza's arm lightly. "Thank you for defending me against those ruffians."

"It wasn't right. Those boys was sick and helpless. Anyways, I never could stand seein' a man disrespeck a lady. It riles me up."

❧

That evening, the Osbournes stopped by the house on their af-ter-dinner walk. Mama, Mary, Grandmother, and Belle were on the porch enjoying the cool night air. They all sat together for a while, sipping chilled water, discussing the battle, the Federals marching into town, the two sick Confederates.

"How are they?" Mama asked Eugenie.

"Better, I think. And as sweet as lambs. So grateful to be in real beds. With clean sheets." Mrs. Osbourne's voice trembled. "I only hope, that if . . . anything . . . were to happen to our own two boys, there would be some kind woman who would take care of them. Oh dear!" She covered her eyes with her handkerchief while her husband patted her arm.

Mr. Osbourne turned to Mama. "Mrs. Boyd, today we witnessed some poor behavior among the Union soldiers. Their officers did little to control them." He paused. "As you know, tomorrow is the Fourth of July. We should be prepared for more rowdiness. I suggest you keep your family inside and lock the doors. As a precaution."

With that he stood up—rather abruptly, Belle thought—and walked to the gate, leaving his wife to say good-bye to Mama and the others. When he turned in the middle of the path to glance back at Belle, she quickly joined him. It wasn't until she'd opened the gate and Mr. Osbourne had passed through that he turned back to speak to her. It would appear to those on the porch that what he said was of little consequence.

"I didn't want to mention this in front of your sister, but I've heard stories of Union soldiers forcing their way into the homes of families like ours and frightening women whose men are away fighting." As he spoke, he began stabbing the point of his walking stick into the dirt. Harder and harder. When Belle reached out to stop him, he gave a start and looked over his shoulder to see if anyone on the porch had noticed. After an awkward smile at Belle, he said, "I'm told these Yankees go into a rage whenever they see a Confederate flag. Mary's flag is hanging in your parlor. Tell your mother to hide it away." He lowered his voice. "And keep that pistol handy."

After the Osbournes left and everyone went inside, Belle suggested to Grandmother that she and Mary go upstairs for the night. Then she told her mother what Mr. Osbourne had said about Mary's flag.

Mama's mouth tightened, then smoothed again. "Of course." She took Belle's hand. "Come. We'll do it together."

Mother and daughter took a moment to stand side by side

in the parlor looking at the flag. Then, with Mama steadying her, Belle stood on a chair and took it down. Mary had sewn two neat loops at the corners, so it was easy to lift off the nails.

"I shan't hide it though. Like it was something shameful. I'll hang it in my room."

"Do that, Belle. It seems cowardly to put it away. Your room should be safe enough."

After Mama went upstairs, Belle stayed in the parlor. She was often the last to go to bed those days. She liked to sit in Mama's rocker and stare out the front window into the dark. It calmed her. Her nerves were pulled taut these days. She could hardly bear just sitting and waiting for whatever might happen next.

She reached into her pocket and took out the pistol Papa had given her. She held the gun on her lap, the weight of it making her feel safe. At some point, she must have dozed off because she was startled awake by a soft knocking.

Belle went and stood by the door, afraid to unlock it. Afraid! She'd never in her life felt afraid before.

"Who is it?"

"Message for Miss Belle Boyd," came a child's voice.

She opened the door, saw no one at first, then looked down at the small dark boy standing on the porch. "From Mista Osbourne," the child whispered, thrusting the note into her hand and scampering off.

*Miss Boyd,*

*I'm told that a bunch of Federals broke into Mr. Nadenbousch's whiskey factory and carried off nearly a hundred kegs of whiskey. If these Yankee officers can't control their men when they are sober, there will be no hope at all once they are drunk. I pray that the first Fourth of July of our newly divided*

*nation will pass without incident. But I fear the worst. Tell your*
*mother to hide that flag!*

*—Yours, Felix Osbourne*

When Belle finally went upstairs, she was surprised to find
Eliza waiting for her.

"I said you didn't need to stay up. I can undress myself."

"I knows that, but it's better if I helps you get yourself settled."

Eliza was right, as usual. Belle found the nighttime rituals
soothing—being unlaced from her corset, slipping on a clean
nightgown, having her hair brushed and braided. But once Eliza
had left, once Belle had slid between the sheets, the restlessness returned. She turned her pillow again and again, searching for a cool
spot to lay her head. It was hot, the evening breezes having died
away. In the still air, sounds traveled a long distance. She could hear
yelling, singing, gunshots coming from the Union camps.

Belle looked over at the place on the wall where she'd removed
a picture and replaced it with Mary's flag, its bright colors dim in
the moonlight. She was glad it was there. It would have been so
wrong to hide it. She meant to honor her new flag as she had hon-
ored her old one. Until it had ceased to honor her. It still seemed
strange that the Stars and Stripes had become the symbol of her
enemy. Her own country had turned against her. No, she had no
intention of hiding the flag. After all, Belle was a true Rebel Lady.

Her mind tumbled with images of the day. Swaggering Union
soldiers. The two sick Confederate boys on their stretchers. Belle
standing on a chair to take down Mary's flag. The drunken uproar
she could hear coming from the camps outside town.

*What will tomorrow be like? Can we really be in danger from*
*drunken Federals? Mr. Osbourne thinks so. If soldiers try to force their*
*way into the house, is the front door strong enough to stop them?*

Belle took a mental inventory of everyone Papa had asked her to protect. Surely that was why he had given her his gun. She counted on her fingers. One old woman. One child. Three women. Seven slaves. Twelve souls all together. Her responsibility.

If Belle needed help, she'd have Sam arm himself with the axe from the woodpile. Joshua too. Cook could use a fry pan. Belle would give Patsy and Delia pokers from the fireplace. And Eliza? She could scold those soldiers until they turned tail and ran.

Belle's lips twitched in a smile. She'd make sure everyone was ready.

# Chapter 10

S ometime after midnight, 'Liza carried John down the stairs and out to the stable. Sam must have seen her coming. He hurried out and took the boy, giving his wife a puzzled look.

When she heard his slow inhale, she answered his unspoken question. "I don't know why. I just thought we should be together tonight. The three of us."

Sam carried John up the loft stairs and laid him on the thin pallet. 'Liza sat on a hay bale near the wide-open door and watched her husband stretch himself on the floor beside their son.

Staring up at the sky, she said, "Can you hear those soldiers outside town? They's carryin' on somethin' fierce. At least Belle took down that flag and put it in her room. That's a better place for it. Not out in plain sight where anybody comin' in the house can see it right off. Where *I* can see it whenever I walks into the parlor. Remindin' me of that party with them starin' at it all moony faced while I passed cookies." She paused. "And you were the one had to hang it on the wall."

"It's just a piece of cloth, 'Liza."

"No it ain't. It stands for somethin'. Somethin' they's willin' to fight for. Same as Mr. Lincoln's flag stands for somethin'. At least Mr. Lincoln hisself does. He says slavery should be abolished."

"That's what he *used* to say," Sam reminded her. "That's not what he said in his 'naugration speech. You brought a copy home from Washington. Cut from the newspaper."

'Liza had read the speech to Sam over and over until the paper was so worn it fell apart. It didn't matter. She had the words memorized. She closed her eyes and recited them.

"'I have no purpose, directly or indirectly, to interfere with the institution of slavery in the States where it exists.'"

"'In the states where it exists,'" Sam repeated softly. "See?"

'Liza shook her head stubbornly. "I believe in the President. He talked anti-slavery before. He'll find a way."

"All's we can do is wait anyways. And work. Same as always."

There was silence. Then Sam spoke from the bed where John was sleeping.

"Come over here, 'Liza. Look at our boy. See how he's growin'."

He reached out and put his big hand on John's chest, soft as a leaf floating to the ground.

"I am lookin' at him, Sam. That's just what I'm doin'."

*Martinsburg, Virginia*
*Union controlled*
*July 4, 1861*

# Chapter 11

Independence Day dawned hot and bright. Breakfast was soon over, everyone too worried to eat. An unspoken question hung in the air: *What will today bring?* In other years the town had celebrated with parades and speeches, picnics, music, dancing, fireworks. Even most of the slaves were given a few hours off. This Fourth of July would be different though. Belle's hand kept straying to her pocket and the reassuring lump of Papa's pistol.

*I promised to keep everyone safe.*

As they had done during the battle, just two days earlier, everyone sat in the parlor with the windows closed, the shades drawn. The room was stifling, but Mama insisted and Grandmother agreed, so that was the end of it. Belle and Mary tried to distract themselves with a game of Old Maid, but the cards were as limp and damp as they were. Young Will and John had gone to the stable to play with Sam's beagle and her new puppies. John could be a bit of a scamp, but Belle knew he was completely trustworthy where Will was concerned. When John was in charge of the little boy, he never let him out of his sight.

Suddenly Eliza was in the room with them. "Union soldiers is comin' down the street. Just as drunk as they can be."

They could hear commotion in the distance, coming closer. Yelling. Gunfire. Rough voices singing. "Yankee Doodle."

Before anyone could move, they heard a crash from the house next door. Their neighbors had fled south weeks ago. Belle peeked around the window shade. Mrs. Vance's favorite settee sat lop-sided in the street, one leg broken off, the carved back split right up the middle. It must have been thrown out the window.

Stamping boots and rough voices on the Boyds' porch. "Open up! Orders of the Union Army!" Fists pounding the door, and the door giving way. The house suddenly filled with shouting, shoving men, their blue uniforms sweat-stained and foul smelling. They prowled the room, stumbling against chairs and tables, sending one of Mama's prized vases crashing to the floor. Grandmother sat frozen on the settee, her arms around Mary, who was crying with her eyes squeezed shut.

A young soldier confronted Mama, slurring, "We hear ya got a Rebel flag!"

Belle watched as the other men circled her mother, crowding close. There were five of them. The young one thrust a Union flag under her nose and yelled, "We'll make ya look like loyal Unionists, whether y'are or not! We'll raise the Stars and Stripes right over this house. What d'ya say to that?"

Lifting her chin, Mama said, "Sirs, I will never allow you to raise that flag over us."

Belle felt a rush of pride as her mother faced the men. *Who knew Mama would be so brave?* The soldiers pressed nearer, one of them close enough to touch her. Now the one with the flag was shouting and shaking his fist at Mama, his spit spraying her face.

A wave of rage swept over Belle. The men were drunk. Heaven only knew what they'd do next. She had to make them stop.

Unnoticed by anyone but Eliza, watching in horror from the doorway, Belle took the pistol from her pocket. When the crowd of men jostling Mama shifted for an instant, she pulled the trigger.

The young soldier fell to the ground, bleeding from his neck. The other men stared at Belle in stunned amazement, then crowded close to their companion. It was obvious, even to them, that he was seriously hurt. Suddenly sober, they picked him up and carried him away, all the while casting dark looks at Belle.

"He wasn't gonna touch yer mama," one of them snarled over his shoulder.

Eliza opened the door for them and leaned back against it after it closed.

Belle stood as if frozen, her arm hanging limp at her side, the gun almost slipping from her fingers.

Mama took the pistol and placed it on the table. "What have you done?" she whispered as she led Belle to Papa's armchair and made her sit.

Belle said nothing. What *had* she done? She let her head drop against the back of the chair and closed her eyes. She felt numb.

Grandmother held Mary, the girl too shocked even to cry. No one spoke, their eyes focused on the blood slowly seeping into the floor.

Sam rushed in shouting. "They's sojers takin' straw out the stable and layin' it 'gainst the back of the house. They found some kerosene. They's gonna set the house . . ."

When he noticed his four mistresses sitting perfectly still, looking at a pool of blood on the floor, his voice trailed away. He searched the room until he found Eliza, still with her back pressed against the door. She crossed to him, touched his hand.

"What happened here, 'Liza?" he whispered.

Instead of answering, she asked, "Where's Young Will?"

Sam blinked twice before answering, "John and him is in the kitchen with Cook and ever'body else. I been down in the stable, keepin' the horses quiet."

"That's alright then." Eliza took a deep breath. "You need to run right up the courthouse fast as you can. That's Federal headquarters. Tell 'em there's been a bad accident and to send some officers right away. Tell 'em their soldiers is mad drunk and fixin' to do somethin' turrible!"

Sam left but returned almost immediately, followed by a colonel and several mounted officers. They'd seen the wounded private being carried up the street, heard a garbled report of what happened, and were already on their way. The colonel ordered his men to remove the kindling piled against the house, then he mounted the front steps and knocked on the door.

Eliza answered and led him into the parlor, where he found the occupants much as they had been when Sam left. Grandmother still sat on the settee, her arms curled around Mary. Belle sat with her eyes closed, her head resting against the cushioned back of Papa's chair. She might have been asleep except for the pulse racing at her throat. Mama stood behind Belle, her hand on her daughter's shoulder.

The colonel had removed his hat and gloves when he entered the house. Now he bowed politely to Mama and Grandmother, introducing himself as Colonel Compton.

"I am sorry for your troubles, Mrs. Boyd. As soon as I heard the news, I came to assure you that your family is not in danger. And to find out how such a thing could have happened."

Belle did not hear the colonel's words or Mama's murmured response. Belle did not even lift her head. It was much, much too heavy. She felt as if she were made of stone.

The officer now bowed to Belle. "The man you shot is severely wounded, Miss Boyd. He will almost certainly die."

Whether it was due to the colonel's words or Mama's gasp, Belle finally opened her eyes. Her mind was filled with a strange, gray mist, but a thought slowly formed. *A Union officer is standing in my parlor. And wonder of wonders, he appears to be a gentleman.*

Colonel Compton watched Belle closely as one corner of her mouth lifted in a slight smile followed by a weary sideways shake of her head.

"I will question you ladies in the dining room one by one," he informed Mama. "You must all remain here until I have finished. I will start with you, Mrs. Boyd. You may give yourself a moment and come to me when you are ready." Turning to his lieutenant, he said, "You may send the rest in any order, but save Miss Belle Boyd for last."

One at a time, the women followed each other into the dining room to speak to the colonel—Mama, Grandmother, Mary. When they were not being questioned, they sat in the parlor under the watchful eye of the lieutenant, with strict instructions not to speak to one another. The heavy silence was broken only by the sound of Mary's whispered prayers.

When it was Belle's turn, she walked into the dining room, her feet dragging as if they belonged to someone else. She groped for the chair the colonel indicated and sank into it, her shoulders drooping. Minutes passed and her senses slowly returned, until finally she was aware of the colonel studying her.

"What happened here, Miss Boyd?"

Belle closed her eyes and spoke in a flat voice. "Last night, there was so much noise from the camps. Our neighbor said the soldiers had stolen whiskey. There were rumors of them breaking into people's houses and being rough with the women. Then this morning we heard them coming down the street. They sounded drunk, and they broke into the house next door. We heard glass breaking. They threw Mrs. Vance's settee out the window. And then they were pounding on *our* door . . ."

Belle had opened her eyes as she spoke, her words tumbling out faster and faster. Now she stopped, breathless, chest heaving, eyes wide and staring. The colonel waited. When she did not continue, he prompted, "And then?"

"They were all around Mama, shaking their fists and yelling. She looked so small. I was afraid they might hurt her. I just wanted them to stop."

"Yes?"

"I don't remember pulling the trigger. But I did, didn't I? I must have. I remember aiming the gun. And then Mama taking it from me. Then you. Standing in the parlor." Belle paused, then said, "That's all."

When Colonel Compton had finished his questions, he and Belle returned to the parlor together. She sat down while he wandered the room, seeming to take note of the furniture that had been shoved out of place, the broken vase, the rucked-up carpet, the gun sitting on the table where Mama had laid it. The blood that had been on the floor was gone. Mama must have told Eliza to scrub it away while Belle was being questioned. Now only a damp spot remained, slowly drying.

Finally the officer turned to Mrs. Boyd. "Madam, I regret that your introduction to Union troops was so unpleasant. They are better men than this. But many of them are volunteers and unused to discipline. I have seen evidence throughout the town of their poor behavior these past two days. And this in a divided town, where many have Union sentiments. Even if you do not share those feelings, you should never have been subjected to this behavior. Please accept my apologies." He bowed to Mama, then fixed his eye on Belle. "As for you, Miss Boyd. You were frightened for your mother and believed you needed to protect her. That is what I will write in my report. We do not need to worsen hostilities by punishing the foolish and regrettable actions of nervous young girls."

Still dazed, all Belle understood was that she would not be punished.

Turning again to Mama, the colonel said, "This unfortunate incident is over." He waited for her nod before continuing. "For your protection, I will post sentries outside your door. Officers will visit regularly to be sure all is in order. As long as the town is under my command, I wish you to feel safe." He raised his chin to indicate the gun on the table. "Put the firearm away, if you please."

As Mama walked the colonel to the door, he said in a voice Belle knew she was meant to hear, "It will be difficult to guarantee your daughter's safety if she leaves the house. It seems she is known as a young woman of some spirit. I fear this incident will not make her popular with my men."

*Martinsburg, Virginia*
*Union controlled*
*Early July 1861*

# Chapter 12

Belle's shooting of a Union solder made her an instant sensation. Some people in town thought she was brave. Others said she was reckless. The most charitable called it high spirits, though everyone knew she'd been allowed to run wild as a child.

She was nearly silent for the next few days, refusing to speak to anyone about what had happened. She sat lost in thought for hours at a time, her mother and sister and grandmother always nearby, but respecting her silence. Mama allowed no visitors.

Belle still couldn't remember events clearly. She had trouble believing she had killed a man. She did remember Mama taking the gun from her, and the relief she felt when the colonel said she wouldn't be punished. She recalled his exact words.

*We do not need to worsen hostilities by punishing the foolish and regrettable actions of nervous young girls.*

She was most definitely *not* a nervous young girl! Nor was her action foolish, though she supposed it was regrettable. Yes, of course it was regrettable. But the soldiers were drunk. They threatened her mother. Who knows what might have happened next? She'd been frightened. If a woman was frightened, didn't she have the right to defend herself?

Of course, Mama had sent a letter to Papa, and a few days later he wrote to Belle, offering her comfort, praising her bravery. More than anything he begged her to be careful.

*You live in an occupied town, my dear. Don't call further*
*attention to yourself. Try to be more like your sister, Mary.*

Papa would have been surprised at how much Belle's view of
her situation differed from his. She had made a decision. If she now
lived in occupied territory, she would make the most of it. Whether
the men guarding her front door were there for her protection or
some other reason, she saw her forced proximity to the enemy as
an opportunity.

At intervals throughout the day, Belle would appear on the
front porch carrying glasses of chilled water or a plate of Cook's
hot buttered biscuits, with Mary trailing reluctantly behind. The
sentries made Mary nervous, and she quickly found an excuse to
go inside, but Belle would stay and arrange herself on the porch
swing, her pretty ankles showing just a little as she pushed herself
back and forth.

In Belle, the soldiers discovered not the cold-hearted murder-
ess they had expected but a flirtatious, seemingly empty-headed
young girl. A welcome distraction from the boredom of standing at
attention on either side of the front door and staring at the empty
street.

Belle clearly enjoyed passing time with her guards. She would
ask questions in her melodious voice. "Where is home? Your poor
mama (or wife or sweetheart) must be terribly worried about where
you'll be sent next. Have you *any* idea where that might be?"

It was laughably easy. Belle knew these snippets of information
might have little value. Might already be known. Even so, several
times a day she went to her room and wrote everything down. She
had an excellent memory. Still it was important to record information while the details were fresh in her mind. When she judged that

she had learned enough, she gave the messages to Eliza to carry to the nearest Confederate camp.

Eliza tried to refuse the first time, much to Belle's surprise. Standing stolidly in her battered men's shoes, the ones that had once belonged to Belle's father, Eliza kept her hands by her sides and would not take the folded note. Belle couldn't understand why she didn't want to go when Belle so badly wished to go herself.

"There's a Confederate camp near Shepherdstown. Less than nine miles. No one will stop you. People barely notice slaves. They're just always there."

The stubborn look on Eliza's face did not change.

"I'm sure it's quite safe. And if anything happens, you'll think of something. Tell them you're lost. Pretend you're simple-minded." Eliza's scowl stopped Belle, who smiled. "Alright. Not simple-minded." She changed tactics. "Please, Eliza. In all the years I've known you, well at least ever since I stopped being a spoiled child, you've never denied me anything outright."

Eliza sighed and took the note. "I'll fill a food basket. If I gets stopped, I'll say it's for your father—Private Benjamin Boyd—and is this the way to Harpers Ferry."

"See? I knew you'd think of something. You're very clever."

"It's best to have a plan, Miss Belle," Eliza said sternly.

"Yes, yes! Just hurry!"

Eliza didn't move.

"I's not finished yet." She had her hands on her hips now, her speechifying pose. "I'll do it. But only because if I don't, you'll figure some way to go yourself. And then, if anythin' happened to you, what would your Mama do?"

Belle was in such an agony of impatience, she barely listened.

"If you don't go downstairs, pack up that basket and leave quickly, I *will* go myself. I cannot abide just sitting. One of us has to do something! We must always be finding ways to help our boys!"

Eliza muttered, "Far as I can see, there's boys on both sides."

"Speak up. I can't hear you."

Eliza did not repeat herself. After a moment she said, "Write a note to your papa. There oughta be a note in the basket. Say somethin' like, 'I'm sendin' you this food with my . . . my trusty Eliza.' And then when I tells 'em I'm Eliza, that makes it more convincible like."

Belle was already writing at her desk when Eliza left the room.

~

Eliza returned hours later, weary from her walk, and Belle was still awake, eager to hear every detail.

"Were you challenged?"

"No, ma'am. I walked along the edge of the road, so's I could duck in the woods if anybody come along. Things was real quiet. The one time somebody did come, a coupla Federals on horseback, they barely looked at me. One of 'em said, 'Who's that?' and the other one said, 'No one. Just a slave.' So it was like you said."

"Did you find someone to give the letter to?"

"When I got near the camp, there was sentries posted. They axed me who I was and where I was goin' in the middle of the night. Because it was . . . our side, I just said I had a message for the camp commander. And I handed over the paper."

"You gave it to the commander himself?"

Eliza sniffed. "Not likely. I give it to one of the sentries. He said he'd give it to someone who'd give it to someone who'd see the commander got it. It was like that."

"I see," Belle said, her disappointment obvious.

"What was you expectin'? The general or colonel or whatever to make a big fuss 'bout your note? Maybe send a thank you letter to Miss Belle Boyd personal like?"

"Yes, Eliza. I know it's foolish, but that's exactly what I was hoping for."

"You wants to be a spy, right?"

Belle nodded.

"Spyin's s'posed to be secret, ain't it?"

"Of course," Belle's shoulders sagged. "Did anything else happen, after you handed over my message?"

"What happened next was I turned 'round and walked nine miles back home."

*Martinsburg, Virginia*
*Union controlled*
*Mid-July 1861*

# Chapter 13

Belle continued to gather bits of information and send Eliza to deliver messages. It became a game. How clever could Belle be at wheedling information from an unsuspecting soldier? At hiding what she was doing from the rest of her family? It might not have been real spying. It might only have been playing at spying. Still, it amused her. And at least she felt like she was doing something. Her only disappointment was that Eliza never brought back a response from the Confederate camps. Not even an acknowledgement that Belle's notes had been received. Was Eliza even delivering the messages? Of course she was. She would never disobey.

Mama did not notice, or at least did not question, Eliza's mysterious errands, and after a few days had passed, Belle was satisfied that her activities were undetected. Until the morning a Union captain presented himself at the door and demanded that she accompany him to headquarters. She treated this as a simple request, gave Mama the most cheerful assurances, and told the officer—Captain Gwyn—that she would be delighted to walk with him.

Beneath her carefree manner, her mind was a whirl as she walked beside the captain. Was he taking her to the same officer who had investigated the shooting? Belle hoped so. She remembered his name. Colonel Compton. He'd been quite lenient. And surely murder—for that was what some people in town were calling it!—was far more serious than passing notes. She didn't think she would be severely punished, but at the very least, being caught would mean she would have to stop.

Belle tried to calm herself. Perhaps the interview was about something else entirely. It could be anything. Anything at all. She struggled to make conversation with Captain Gwyn so she could find out more. However, the captain proved resistant to her charms. *Grim Gwyn*, Belle thought. And smiled, and felt better when she realized her spirit had not deserted her. Perhaps the fact that the information in her messages was so inconsequential, just snippets really, perhaps this would work in her favor.

When they reached headquarters, Belle saw that it was in fact the same colonel who had questioned her after the shooting. He stood behind a desk in a large room humming with purposeful activity. Groups of officers hovered over maps spread across tables, pointing here and there. Some sat at desks writing out orders. Couriers stood about in dusty boots, impatiently slapping their gloves on their thighs, waiting for messages to be written so they could be on their way.

Yes, it was the same colonel, but a different man entirely. Not apologizing for his men's invasion of her home. Not excusing Belle's panic. Not worried about her safety and posting sentries by the door.

He glanced down at the papers strewn across his desk, then up at her.

"I know of your messages."

Belle's heart gave a jolt. How had it happened? Had Eliza dropped one of her notes? Surely she would have said something. Belle had heard that real spies wrote in code, but she had no idea how that was done. Her own messages had been written out in her distinctive handwriting. At school she had worked hard to develop an individual style. Now she regretted it. She leaned closer, trying to get a better view of the top of the colonel's desk. He narrowed his eyes at her, slid some papers into a drawer, and continued his lecture.

"Miss Boyd, you do not seem to realize the seriousness of your offense." He picked up a densely printed document and waved it under her nose, saying loudly, "This paper is called *The Articles of War*. No doubt a young girl like you has never heard if it, but it was approved by Congress fifty years ago and is an important document to this day. 'Why?' you might ask. Because, Miss Boyd, it lists all the rules the United States Army must follow in times of war. Including," he went on as he leaned across the desk, his voice getting even louder, "including how enemy civilians should be treated. You will now listen while I read Article 57 as it pertains particularly to your situation."

When the colonel read the penalty for passing information to the enemy, when Belle heard the phrase "shall suffer death," she found it hard to breathe, as if her corset were laced too tightly. The constriction reminded her that she was a woman and expected to be weak. It was this thought that revived her.

*If he wants to see me swoon, he will be disappointed!*

Belle straightened her spine, inhaled so deeply that her ribs pressed painfully against her corset. The dizziness passed. She looked the colonel in the eye. And said nothing.

All the while, Colonel Compton was watching her, his face growing redder and redder. Finally he growled, "Miss Boyd, don't you understand?" He threw the document back on his desk. "Passing information to the enemy, however trivial that information might be, is treason. Punishable by death!"

*It's not treason*, she thought, remembering the stories of her grandfather—Mama's father, James Glenn, who had fought in the

American Revolution. *Didn't the British call that treason? He wasn't a traitor! He was a patriot. And so am I! A patriot of my new nation. I am a loyal citizen of the Confederacy.*

Belle noticed the other men in the room watching her conversation with the colonel as if it were a scene in a play. Very well. If it was drama they wanted, she was happy to provide it.

"Thank you for your attention, gentlemen," Belle said, curtseying deeply. "If we have finished our business, Colonel, I will take my leave." And with an icy look at Captain Gwyn, standing stiffly at attention, "I will see myself home."

ॐ

When Mama inquired about her interview with the colonel, Belle said she had asked to see him, to request permission to go riding, but that he had refused. Belle told Eliza the truth about what had happened, adding that their espionage activities must be suspended for the time being.

She never knew if Eliza said anything to Mama about *The Articles of War*, but two days later, her mother announced that Belle had been invited for an extended stay with Mama's sister, Fannie Stewart, who lived with her husband and two daughters in Front Royal. It was forty-three miles further south, hopefully far enough from Martinsburg to keep Belle out of trouble.

Front Royal was smaller than Martinsburg, a village really. Until recently the Stewarts had lived in Washington, but, like so many others, they had fled the capital when the war began. After all, to any loyal Confederate, Washington D.C. was now the capital of an enemy state. Aunt Fannie and Uncle James had moved to Front Royal and taken over an inn on High Street called the Fishback Hotel.

Belle was rather pleased at the idea of visiting Front Royal. There would likely be constant comings and goings at the hotel. Travelers always brought news. Who knew what spying opportunities might come her way?

# Chapter 14

As they lay on their pallet in the hayloft, Sam said slowly, "You know, 'Liza, you could stay in the Union camps. When you take those messages. There's others run off already. Then at least one of us would be free."

'Liza twisted around in his arms to see his face. She put her hand on his cheek. "I could never do that, Sam. Leave you and John. Never. We's a family. We belongs together."

"Things is different now though."

"Not so different. The war's only been goin' on three months. We don't know how it will turn out."

"Still . . ."

He rolled onto his back, put his hands behind his head, and stared up at the rafters. His thinking position.

"Why's she do it, 'Liza?"

"The spyin'?"

"Everything. Shootin' that poor boy. Sittin' on the porch with Union sojers where anybody can see. Writin' stuff down. Sendin' messages." He paused, frowning. "She 'minds me of a bumblebee in a jar."

'Liza smiled. Quiet as he was, Sam could still surprise her.

"It seems like she's got somethin' inside won't let her rest," she said. "And just like a bumblebee, she don't even know why she does half the things she do. She just always gotta be goin' and doin'. Like that foolish bee." She sighed. "I try an' discourage her most outlandish notions. Try an' keep her safe. I owe it to Missus Boyd, don't I?"

"I s'pose."

"Who knows where I'd be if she hadn't let me stay all those years ago when I run off from her brother's place? I was just a girl. Fifteen years old. I never was so scared as when I heard Master Glenn might sell me South. I coulda ended up a field hand in Loosiana. Or somewhere worse. I ran here 'cause I remembered Missus Boyd. She was always kind to me when she visited her brother. I took a turrible chance, but I was right about her. 'Cause when I got here, she told Mr. Boyd right off that he had to pay her brother for me. So's I could stay. I never was so scared in all my life till he paid that money."

When Sam heard the tremble in her voice, he took her in his arms again. His 'Liza, always so strong.

# Chapter 15

After a long dusty journey in a public coach, Belle arrived at the Fishback Hotel, where Aunt Fannie, Uncle James, and Belle's cousins Alice and Frances were lined up outside to greet her. Belle descended into a sea of welcoming arms and joyful greetings, her uncle supervising the unloading of Belle's baggage, and her cousins claiming Belle herself, spiriting her off to the room they would all share during her visit.

"You didn't bring Eliza?" Franny asked.

Belle removed her gloves and cloak and bonnet and veil, sighing with relief to be rid of them. "One of the reasons Eliza travels with me is to ensure I behave 'in ladylike fashion,' as Grandmother likes to say. But since I was coming here to be with family, I was allowed to make the trip alone. Anyway, it's better for Eliza to stay at home. Mama depends on her, and Papa always says she has more sense than the rest of us put together."

"We'll make sure your behavior is the utmost in decorum," Alice promised, holding her hand over her heart and sending herself into peals of laughter. Belle gazed fondly at her favorite cousin.

There was a loud knock at the door, and Uncle James entered, followed by two slaves, each bearing a trunk.

"Two trunks?" Franny exclaimed, eyes round with excitement.

"Gracious! How many dresses did your papa buy for your debut? When can we see them?"

"We'll have Lettie unpack them later, Franny," said Alice. "Right now, our cousin needs rest. Let's unpin her hair and comb it out. She'll be happy to get rid of those awful hairpins. Won't you, Belle?"

The girls helped Belle undress down to her chemise and drawers. Then they set to work with sponge and comb.

"Doesn't our lovely cousin look comfortable lying on her bed with no corset or petticoats?" Alice asked. Snapping her fingers, she said, "I have an idea. Let's tell Mama that tomorrow none of us intends to get dressed until suppertime!"

"Don't do that!" Belle protested. "She'll think I'm a bad influence and send me home."

"Mama won't care. I'll tell her we wish to stay in our rooms all day and do nothing but bathe and lotion and powder ourselves." Alice arranged her pretty face into a pout. "Life is so much less interesting here than in Washington. Especially now with all the men away." She sighed dramatically. "I do hope the fighting ends soon."

"I have a recipe for skin lightening cream," Franny said happily. "You do know, Belle darling, that you're quite brown?" She asked her question timidly, so as not to hurt her cousin's feelings. "I've another recipe for getting rid of freckles, the very bane of my existence." Franny was like Mary. Her view of the world limited to needlework patterns and skin-improving recipes. And like Mary, Franny was quite sweet.

"It does sound like fun."

"Belle is such a . . . celebrity," Franny prattled. "Everyone will want to meet her."

"Perhaps not everyone," Alice said.

There was an awkward silence. Belle guessed why. Her shooting of a Union soldier had been widely reported. Everyone in Front Royal would know of it. And, just as in Martinsburg, not everyone would approve.

"I'm sorry, Belle. That was thoughtless of me," Franny said, then fell silent.

"I think, to start with, we will have a small party here," Alice said, taking Belle's hand and stroking it. "To welcome our beautiful cousin to the village. I've already spoken to Mama, and we have agreed it's best to invite only those people we particularly wish to see."

"I'll go speak to her about it now, shall I?" Franny said and fled the room.

Once the door had closed behind her cousin, Belle began to pluck nervously at a loose thread on the coverlet.

Without looking at Alice, she said, "I don't want to talk about it."

"There's no need." Alice took Belle's hand again, keeping it still. "You did what you had to. I wonder if I would have been so brave."

"I don't remember anything very clearly. There was no moment when I thought to myself, 'I intend to shoot this man.' They were all around Mama, pushing her." Belle sighed tiredly. "Even though I don't remember, I can't forget. I don't suppose that makes any sense, does it?"

"You poor dear." Alice put her arms around Belle. "When I heard from Mama what happened, I was so relieved that all of you were safe. And that you weren't punished. I never thought how difficult it would be for you, thinking about it afterward."

There was a knock, and the door opened, Franny peering around it, her face sunny once more. Still holding Belle, Alice shook her head slightly over her cousin's shoulder and watched as Franny held her finger to her lips and quietly withdrew.

"You needn't talk about it anymore," Alice murmured. "Unless talking will make you feel better."

Belle pulled away and said, "I already feel better. It was a mistake not to speak of it. But whom could I tell? Mary's too young, and Mama believes the whole thing was her fault. That it was her defiance that made the soldiers angry. But it might have happened anyway. The men were horribly drunk."

There was another quiet knock, this time Aunt Fannie opening the door and asking, "May we come in?"

Belle nodded, and her aunt swept into the room. Franny followed, carrying a tray that she set carefully on a table. A plate of sliced chicken and two pieces of buttered bread. A small pitcher of milk.

"You must eat," Aunt Fannie ordered.

Belle sat, poured a glass of cold milk, and drank it down. Delicious! She hadn't realized she was hungry. The cousins sat on the edge of Belle's bed and watched her eat.

"Alice said you needed rest," Aunt Fannie said, "but I find food is very restorative."

The cousins giggled. Their mother really was quite plump.

"Is there enough? Would you like more?"

"Please don't tell Mama about my appetite. She says I eat much too heartily."

"I disagree. A young woman should not deny herself food if she's hungry. It makes no sense at all. You should eat whatever you like. That's what I do."

The girls giggled again. Meanwhile, Franny had started bouncing on the bed. Her mother raised her eyebrows at this. "I believe that a healthy appetite is entirely acceptable, as long as one's table manners are elegant. However, I regret to say, Frances, that bouncing has never been considered the mark of a lady."

"It's just that I'm so pleased to have Belle visiting."

"So am I, my dear, but do you see me engaging in bouncing?"

"Oh no, Mama. You would never bounce!"

"My point exactly."

Dear Aunt Fannie could never be stern for long. Now she was saying, "Why don't you tell Belle the news that is giving you such a strong desire to bounce?"

"Mama says we may have our beauty party tomorrow and spend the day in our unmentionables!" Then Franny's face fell. "Unfortunately, though, the real party must be delayed."

"Why is that?"

"Because it would not be correct to have an entertainment at such a time," Aunt Fannie explained. "The rumor is that, in the next few days, there will be fighting at a place called Manassas. It's between here and Washington. General Beauregard is camped there with nearly twenty thousand of our boys."

"But the Union General," Alice broke in, "someone named McDowell, who also has twenty thousand men, is marching to meet him. Only it seems he's going very slowly. And General Beauregard knows he's coming."

"I remember hearing about this before I left home. But then I became so busy packing I forgot."

"A little forgetting can be a good thing," Aunt Fannie said in her soothing way.

"Forty thousand men," Belle said. "Counting both sides. It's hard to imagine a battle with so many." She had a dreadful thought. "Will Papa be in the fighting this time?"

"There is talk of Jackson going," Alice said gently. "But no one knows for sure."

"We mustn't worry or brood," Aunt Fannie declared. "We must be strong, no matter what."

"I should be home with Mama. It was wrong of me to leave her!"

"Nonsense! Your mother wants you here. Out of harm's way. As any mother would. Manassas is forty miles away." Aunt Fannie's eyes flashed, and her chins quivered. "But since there will be many Front Royal boys in the fighting, a party would be in poor taste."

"There's a chance that some of the wounded will be sent here," Alice added. "The ladies are organizing a hospital. Just in case."

"But you said it's forty miles. Why would they be sent so far?"

Aunt Fannie looked unhappy again. "With so many men, it's bound to be a major battle. In the event that there are many casualties, the wounded will be moved by wagon train. All the towns between here and Manassas have been alerted. We must be ready."

Franny stopped bouncing.

"Therefore a hospital is being prepared," Aunt Fannie explained. "We will all help. I'm sure there will be much to do. Organizing supplies, rolling bandages, and so forth. It will be good for Belle to be seen. It will put a stop to the silly talk in town. There must be no more . . ." She paused to find the proper word. "Unpleasantness." Another nod trembled Aunt Fannie's chins. "And now I won't say anything more about that!" She gave her niece one last long look.

"Of course we'll help!" said Belle. "There needn't be a party at all. I'm happy just to be here with all of you."

*Front Royal, Virginia*
*Confederate Controlled*
*Late July to Late August 1861*

# Chapter 16

The cousins had their beauty party, as Franny called it, and the following day they went with Aunt Fannie to help set up the hospital, working alongside the other women of the village. A hospital steward and several assistants arrived to supervise their efforts, commandeering an empty tobacco warehouse on the edge of town for use as a hospital. Throughout the day, slaves appeared at its wide doors, carrying bundles of donated sheets and blankets, as well as any other useful items their mistresses could spare or collect from their neighbors. Pitchers, basins, buckets, bowls, brandy, whiskey, candles, kerosene, ladles, rags, lanterns, spoons of all sizes. Wagons loaded with fresh straw from nearby farms also arrived, and slaves pitched the straw onto canvas cloths so it could be carried inside, where more slaves spread it over the floor.

"About ten inches deep should do it," the steward instructed.

"The men won't have proper mattresses?" Franny asked.

"They'll be comfortable enough on the straw. It must be replaced fairly often, you see."

Franny did not see, though Belle understood instantly that the blood soaked straw would need to be replaced again and again.

Later, the steward drew Belle aside and suggested that her young cousin not return the next day. "I'd like it if you came, though," he said. "You seem to be made of sterner stuff."

This was not at all the sort of compliment Belle was used to, yet his words pleased her enormously. The steward took her seriously. He wanted her help. She would not let him down.

"Will the battle be tomorrow for certain? Does anyone know?"

"There is little certainty in war, but yes, I believe so."

Belle bit her lip. "When the wounded arrive, will it be very difficult?"

"I'm afraid it will be." The steward looked away for a moment, then returned her gaze. "That much, at least, is certain."

❧

The following day, before the Stewart household stirred, the Battle of Manassas began. Just past 5:30 in the morning, the telegraph lines hummed with the news, which then spread through the village. After breakfast, which Belle and Alice forced themselves to eat, they walked to the hospital in their dark, sensible dresses with bibbed aprons on top, keeping tight hold of each other's hands. Belle realized she didn't have any clear idea *what* they were walking toward.

When they reached the hospital, the first wounded had yet to arrive. Belle and Alice and the other volunteers must sit and wait. *Of course!* Belle thought bitterly. To keep their hands busy, they rolled the last of the bandages. Seated in a circle, they tried to talk of other things, but it was impossible. Eventually they fell silent. No one could think of anything but the conflict raging forty miles away. Every so often, an orderly would stop to report the most recent news. The casualty numbers kept climbing, and soon everyone knew that the losses on both sides were horrifying. And the day was not yet half over.

After one soldier reported the latest numbers and hurried off, the women sat, their hands now still. One by one, they bowed their heads. Some of them prayed in silence. Others murmured softly. Belle felt Alice's hand reaching for hers and clutched it tightly. Her prayer was brief. Five words, over and over. *Please God. Keep Papa safe.*

Late in the afternoon, the wounded started coming. And kept coming. Even after the battle was over, they kept on coming.

Belle quickly learned never to look around at the whole awful room. With its row after row of bloody, bandaged, groaning men, some with ragged bayonet slashes across their faces and chests, others wounded by the new-style Minié balls, which shattered bones and shredded flesh. She must never look up. Only down. At her hands. Hands that carried tangles of used bandages soaked with pus, bundles of bloody sheets, bowls of vomit or piss or excrement. Her dazed mind could hardly believe the things she carried!

Sometimes she was told to walk around with a water bucket and ladle, her assignment to go to each soldier in turn and help him drink. The men were pitifully grateful for the water. For some reason, their wounds made them terribly thirsty. This task was less sickening, but more heartbreaking. Because it meant looking directly into their eyes. It meant holding each one—"Gently but firmly!" the matron instructed—so he could raise his head and sip without adding to his pain. It meant seeing the men's fear close up. Most of them clutched at Belle's hand, croaking their thanks, sometimes closing their eyes in relief as the water slid down their parched throats. But when their eyes opened again, they were wide and staring. Each face silently asking the same question. *How did I get here, to this hellish place?*

At the end of each day, Belle and Alice trudged home side by side, their blood-spattered aprons rolled up under their arms. Two silent ghosts. They did not speak to each other. There were no words for what they had witnessed.

Back home at the Stewarts', the two girls were fed and put to bed early as if they were children, Aunt Fannie issuing orders, Franny fluttering helplessly, Uncle James watching with a worried frown. Every evening when Aunt Fannie tucked them in for the night, she would try to persuade them not to return next day. Every evening they insisted they must.

༄

On the fourth day, when Belle took her turn with water duty, she saw someone she knew. At first she couldn't believe it. She didn't want it to be true. It was easier if she didn't recognize them. Didn't know the names of these boys lying side by side on the straw-covered floor, calling for their mamas. Even grown men called out. Belle was no one's mama. She was just an exhausted seventeen-year-old girl with a ladle and a bucket.

Yet here was Wilfred Sprockett, second row, third patient from the left. A bloody bandage covered one side of his face, and he was unconscious. But it was Freddy.

Belle dragged Alice over. "I know him!" she said. "It's Freddy Sprockett. My dancing partner in Washington."

Alice stared. "You must tell Mrs. Bailey. She always knows what to do."

"He's no one I recognize," the woman said when she came to look. "Are you sure you know him?" She nodded at the man. "He still has his jacket. No one would take it amiss if you went through his pockets, dear. Just to be sure."

Belle hesitated. "It doesn't seem right."

Before Mrs. Bailey walked away, she said, "If he is your friend, seeing a familiar face could help. With that head wound, he might not know who he is himself when he wakes up."

The two cousins knelt by the man's side. The sleeve of his jacket showed three captain's stripes on a yellow cuff. Yellow meant cavalry. When Freddy had written to Belle, he'd told her he'd enlisted in the Virginia cavalry.

"I had a letter from him a month ago, saying he'd been made captain."

"Look," Alice said, pointing to the buttons on his jacket. "They show the Virginia Seal."

"It has to be him."

Passing by again, Mrs. Bailey asked, "Did you go through his pockets? He's probably carrying a letter from his sweetheart or his mother. Most of them do."

Belle shook her head frantically. *Dear God! I don't want to find one of my letters in Freddy's pocket!*

"No, we mustn't! I know it's him."

Alice returned to her duties, leaving Belle with Freddy, murmuring softly, stroking the uninjured side of his face. Until Mrs. Bailey came and gently reminded her that there were other men needing her attention. Belle nodded, but first she searched out the steward and asked if Freddy was likely to recover.

"It's difficult to know with a head injury." The doctor was pale, with dark circles beneath his eyes. His words were blunt. "He might recover completely. Or he could recover physically but not mentally. He might need to be fed with a spoon for the rest of his life." After a pause he added. "He'll lose that eye for certain."

He turned to leave, but Belle put her hand on his arm. "Will he live?"

"Only God can say."

Belle made a habit of stopping by Freddy's side between her other chores. She never lingered. He remained unconscious, and there was so much work to do.

Sometimes a soldier asked her to write a letter home. Letters were important, especially if death seemed close. Then she would hurry to fetch paper and pen and sit on a stool to take down the man's last words to his family. And look right at him, and smile without flinching, even when part of his face was missing. Because what boy needed to know that about himself as he was busy dying?

There was one bright spot in the middle of all the horror. Four days after the battle, a letter came from Mama. Ben Boyd, who *had* been in the fighting, had survived without a scratch.

After a while, almost without Belle noticing, the work became easier. Most of the soldiers who were going to die had done so. It seemed heartless to think it, but for most of them, death came as a blessing. The rest of the men were on the mend. More or less. So brave and cheerful, even those with dreadful injuries. Still they knew they were done with the war. They were going home.

Those soldiers whose wounds were less serious were sent back to their regiments, except for a few that the steward kept to help with the more demanding chores. As the need grew less desperate, Alice stopped coming, but Belle continued day after day.

And then one morning, when she went to Freddy's bedside as she always did first thing, his place was empty. A coldness swept through her. She felt as empty as the space where Freddy had been lying only the day before.

When Belle's knees buckled, Mrs. Bailey was at her side in an instant. She beckoned for an orderly to carry Belle to the makeshift kitchen and place her on a bench, where she slumped limply, Mrs. Bailey's arm the only thing keeping her from sliding to the floor.

"I'm so sorry, Belle," the woman said gently. "It's a terrible shock. I had hoped to see you when you came in. To prepare you." She took a cup that the orderly had filled with an inch of brandy. "Here, my dear. Drink this." Mrs. Bailey held the cup to Belle's lips. "Your friend died quite peacefully. He never woke up, you see. No pain. No fear. Just drifted away."

Belle still did not speak.

Turning to the orderly, Mrs. Bailey said, "Find someone to drive her to her uncle's. She can't walk home in this condition."

☙

Belle was moved from her cousins' room into the guestroom where she could rest undisturbed. She slept for a day and a half. It was the following afternoon when she awoke with Aunt Fannie's cool hand pressed against her cheek.

"How do you feel, dear?"

Belle shook her head, unaware of the tears streaming onto her pillow.

"She'll be all right, won't she?" Alice asked, standing at the foot of the bed.

"Of course. She just needs rest." Aunt Fannie wiped Belle's tears and said, "I've written to Mrs. Bailey to say you won't be coming anymore."

Belle nodded, eyes closed.

"I blame myself. I should have done a better job of looking after you. But I was so proud. Your mother will be cross with me."

Aunt Fannie gave Belle's hand a final pat and stood up. "I'll send up some bread and butter. And a nice cold glass of milk. After you've eaten, you must sleep. Frances, find a bell to put by the bed so she can ring if she wants anything." She paused in the doorway. "Total rest! If you're not feeling better soon, we'll find a doctor to look at you."

Aunt Fannie was right. Belle's collapse was due to exhaustion as much as shock. As she rested, her strong young body began to recover. Her mind was another matter. Whenever the image of the empty space where Freddy had laid—and died—appeared in her mind, she felt again the creeping coldness that left her numb and unable to move. Non-existence. How was such a thing even possible? She couldn't bear thinking about it. And so she decided she wouldn't.

Instead she repeated what Mrs. Bailey had told her. *Freddy didn't suffer. He wasn't afraid. He didn't suffer.*

One morning, Aunt Fannie appeared after breakfast, took one look at Belle, and said, "You're starting to brood. We can't have that." She bustled about the room, raising the shades and opening the windows. "I've ordered a long, hot bath. Lettie will be up with the tub shortly." Soft grunts and a clanging of metal made her turn around. "Ah, here they are."

Lettie and Dido appeared, lugging a copper tub between them. They set it on the floor and arranged a folding screen in front for privacy. Then they began a series of trips up and down the stairs, each of them carrying two buckets of hot water, emptying it into the tub, then going back for more.

Once Belle was soaking in the bath, Alice arrived with a sponge, soap, and towels. She scrubbed Belle's back and washed her hair, pouring pitchers of clean water over her for a final rinse. When Belle was dressed in a fresh nightgown and back in bed, Franny arrived with her creams and lotions. The cousins spent the rest of the morning pampering Belle in every way.

After lunch, Uncle James knocked and stuck his head into the room. "I want to see how Belle is feeling. There you are! Why, you look better already." He sniffed the air. "I can tell that Franny has been busy with her recipes. It smells like a French lady's *boo-dwah* in here!" He cleared his throat. "What I mean to say is, these smells would make a fine French lady turn green with jealousy."

"James!" This from Aunt Fannie, standing behind him.

"Come in, my dear," Uncle James stepped aside for his wife to pass.

"Such a way to talk in front of the girls! And what do you know about fine French ladies and their boudoirs? That's what I'd like to know."

"We had a French lady from Baton Rouge here last month. Don't you remember?"

"Perhaps I do. But I don't wish you to remember!"

James grinned at Belle. "So much beauty in one room. My eyes can't stand it."

He turned and groped his way to the door, one hand partly covering his face. Aunt Fannie plumped down on a soft chair and sighed as he left.

"Though he is a proper gentleman, your uncle is rather colorful in his speech. It must be from his time in the newspaper business. And now of course he runs a hotel, which puts one in touch with all kinds of people. Please don't mention this to your mother."

"He was only trying to cheer me up. Anyway, Mama adores Uncle James."

"I must say, you do look better. There's some color in your cheeks." Aunt Fannie stroked Belle's still damp curls. "James and I agree you ought to go home as soon as you feel strong enough."

The thought of another journey made Belle want to weep.

"Whatever you think, Aunt Fannie. I'm sure I'll feel up to it soon."

"Don't worry. Not in a public coach this time. James will drive you. It's all settled."

"It would be lovely to ride with Uncle James. Just the two of us."

"He's a wonderful traveling companion. The stories he tells to pass the time! And he is an excellent driver."

A wave of homesickness washed over Belle. Suddenly she longed to be back in Martinsburg.

# Chapter 17

Under the care of Mama and Eliza, Belle's strength slowly returned. She was too weak to ride, but she went on long walks, often for hours at a time. While she walked, she thought about the war. Over thirty-six thousand men from the North and the South had fought at Manassas, and almost five thousand had been killed or wounded. Although Confederate soldiers had routed the Union troops, they had not been able to finish the job, and the soldiers in blue managed to stagger back to the safety of Washington. A day of carnage had proved one thing only. That the War Between the States would be long and costly. There would be no easy victory for either side.

Belle thought often of Freddy Sprockett and how she had adored dancing with him. Their conversations were always lively and interesting. Looking back, she realized she was never bored or restless when they were together. How could she not have recognized what he meant to her? She'd never even kissed him. She could be so foolish sometimes. Not knowing what her true feelings were until it was too late.

Now that she was feeling stronger, she let herself think about Freddy's death. Just a little. She wondered if he had somehow known on the day of the battle that it would be his last. Was it a beautiful summer morning, the last morning he would ever have?

Did he stop to notice the sun rising? The birds going about their business? No one would ever know about Freddy Sprockett's last morning.

It still didn't seem possible that he was dead. That this very moment, Freddy was lying in a grave in Front Royal. She tried to imagine him in the cold ground, darkness all around. His smiling lips stiff and silent. His eyes closed and sunken. His long legs still. Forever. Only now did she understand that she might have married Freddy and been a happy wife. Instead she wrote to his mother, wanting her to know that it had been a friend who helped nurse her son. And that he had not suffered.

Which still left Belle to face the question of her future. She had always assumed that like almost every woman she knew, she would one day marry and have children, but that was not possible in the here and now. All the men her age were fighting. Or dead. To think of marriage seemed selfish. How could her life go on in a normal way while such awful things were happening?

Even though Belle was a woman, she too was part of history. She was young, strong, and intelligent. She had to find a way to help. She was not suited for nursing, although she was grimly proud of herself for doing it. If anything, the horrors of the hospital had hardened her resolve to somehow be of use.

Every day she walked and thought, walked and thought. She could feel herself getting stronger, but her future remained blank. Then she received a letter from Alice.

*Dearest Cousin,*

*I know you are still recovering, but has your mother let you see the newspapers? It is being widely reported that Mrs. Rose Greenhow, a Washington hostess with important connections—on both sides!—has been charged with spying and is under house arrest. Papa says there's more to the story than that. His newspaper friends told him that a few days before Manassas, Mrs. Greenhow sent a girl named Bettie Duvall to General Beauregard with information about Union troop movements that helped him win the battle! So far only Rose has been charged. But Papa's friends say that Miss D. carried the message written in code and pinned up in her hair. Can you imagine?*

Belle could imagine all too well, and the thought left her breathless. Alice's writing seemed breathless too, her excitement carrying into the next paragraph.

*And I said to Franny and Mama that you were friends with Bettie Duvall when you had your coming out in Washington. They didn't believe me. But it's true, isn't it?*

"Not friends exactly," Belle murmured, as if Alice were at her side. "But we did sometimes speak at parties. She was always cordial to me."

Belle paced the room, still talking to herself. "Imagine Bettie Duvall being a spy!" She stopped walking. "Of course, if one were lucky enough to be an actual spy, one wouldn't talk about it. Especially not to casual acquaintances." Her pacing resumed. "Now if I were a spy, a real one, I'd want everyone to know. I do see how foolish that is. Eliza told me as much when I was passing those scraps of information I got from the sentries guarding the house. What if I could be a real spy, though? I'd be just as good as Miss Duvall. And anyway, now every Confederate seems to know what she did, how brave and clever she was. That might have been me. It should have been me!"

Belle went back to reading the letter. The next part was as interesting as the first. Alice explained that Allan Pinkerton, the head of Lincoln's new Secret Service, had been watching Mrs. Greenhow for months. When he finally searched her house, he found letters, diary entries, coded messages, proof that the lovely widow had used her connections with Northern senators, generals, and cabinet members to collect information, which she passed to her Southern friends. Lincoln had authorized further investigation, and Mrs. Greenhow would almost surely go to prison.

Belle longed to be back in Washington. To serve the Confederate cause. What could she accomplish in Martinsburg? For one thing, the town was still controlled by the Federal Army. In addition, Belle was sure she was being watched. Her dedication to the South was well known. Anyone who might recruit her would hesitate because of reasons one and two.

*Never mind.* She would think of something.

However, after weeks of fretful pacing, of long walks and longer rides, of untouched meals and sleepless nights, she still had not found a way.

Then Mama announced that the two of them were going to visit Papa near Manassas, where he and his regiment were still camped after the battle. It would be a double treat, for Mama's brother was also posted there. William James Glenn was a lieutenant in Jackson's Twelfth Virginia Cavalry. He and Belle had always been close. She would ask him if there was any way the Confederate Army could use her.

വ

This camp visit was not like the one Belle and Mary had made to Harpers Ferry in the first days of the war. That visit took place before a single battle had been fought in the Shenandoah Valley. But now Papa had survived Manassas. Now Freddy was dead. How many others would die before the war ended? These days, Belle had trouble keeping such dark thoughts away. Her time as a nurse, the suffering she'd witnessed, made the costs of war so much more real. This camp visit was different because Belle herself was changed. They all were.

Belle and Mama stayed in a large house with other wives and daughters who were having their own bittersweet reunions. It was heart-warming to see Mama and Papa together. After all these years, there was still so much affection between them. Belle hoped that someday she would have a marriage as loving and tender.

When she observed whispers and caresses between other married couples or sweethearts, she quickly turned away to give them privacy. She was surprised to discover that for once she was not interested in pursuing a flirtation of her own. She told herself there was no time for that. This was a historic moment! She must find a way to help end the war. Before hundreds more were killed or maimed. This was now her obsession.

Uncle William and Belle were alike in temperament. When she was a little girl, in trouble for climbing onto the roof or throwing acorns at passersby, Uncle William would sometimes send her a cheering note, telling her of all the mischief he'd gotten into as a boy. Now Belle had a better understanding that the rules for high-spirited boys were different than those for girls. Even so, she saw her uncle as a kindred soul and felt free to confess her eagerness to serve.

On the day they arrived, when Mama and Papa had gone for a stroll, Belle invited her uncle to sit with her on the porch, saying she wished to speak with him about an important private matter. She began formally, reminding him of her work at the hospital in Front Royal, which she knew he had admired. When she saw him nod, she took a deep breath and continued.

"While I was there, I heard some soldiers talking. They said

General Jackson always wants to know where the Union forces in the Valley are. So he can attack without warning. Or sneak away if they're trying to trap him. The men I overheard said there's going to be an intelligence system."

William raised his eyebrows. "Yes, we're putting together a network, using civilians to gather information and pass it to the generals. Especially Jackson, who makes the best use of it."

Belle's pulse raced at this, but she said nothing. She reminded herself that sometimes it was better to listen. But Uncle William didn't say anything else. He just sat with his long legs stretched out in front of him, staring gloomily at his boots.

Just when she thought she couldn't wait another second, he asked, "Do you know the name Turner Ashby?"

This seemed like a strange question, but Belle answered anyway. "I presume you mean the lieutenant colonel? I saw him march through Martinsburg after the battle at Hoke's Run. His men covered the retreat."

She stopped herself from adding that she had danced with Ashby at Harpers Ferry two nights before the battle. She did not want to remind her uncle that most young women were happy with a life of parties and dances. They did not ask to become spies!

"The colonel is a gifted cavalry commander, but he has other duties as well. He's the one who supplies Jackson with the information he needs. It's important work."

When Uncle William stopped again, Belle couldn't help saying, "And?"

For a moment her uncle's face twisted, as if he were struggling with himself. "And Ashby uses civilian couriers to carry messages, especially in areas where the Federals are active. Some of them smuggle medicines too. Or guns. Ammunition. We're always running out of what we need."

"Uncle William, let me help! I've seen firsthand how soldiers suffer when there's no morphine to ease their pain. I do so want to carry medicines. And messages. Whatever you need."

William rubbed his eyes.

"You know I can ride, Uncle. And I'm brave. Plus I'm good at memorizing. I can carry messages in my head." Despite her vow to listen more than speak, Belle plunged on. "I've ridden all over the Shenandoah Valley. Martinsburg. Shepherdstown. Harpers Ferry. Front Royal. Not just the roads, but paths and open country. I know every tumble-down shack, every cave, every hiding place."

Her uncle held up his hand. "Stop, Belle."

But she couldn't stop, not now that she was speaking her dreams out loud. "Everyone is saying that if not for Rose Greenhow and Bettie Duvall, we might have lost Manassas. Isn't that true? Well, isn't it?"

William sighed, a weary sound. "This is difficult for me, Belle. Surely you see that. I serve the South, but I also have a loyalty to your parents. They will not thank me."

This time Belle knew enough to hold her tongue.

Her uncle sighed again. "I will mention you to Colonel Ashby and let him decide."

⁂

Within a few weeks, Belle had joined Ashby's network and begun work as a courier, carrying messages between the three generals who were active in the area: P.G.T. Beauregard, Jeb Stuart, and Thomas Jackson, known as "Stonewall" since the victory at Manassas.

Belle was thrilled with her new life. She was trusted with information of real military value. Even better, she no longer had to depend on Eliza to carry messages for her. Belle's old enemy, Colonel Compton, the officer who had read her *The Articles of War*, was no longer administering Martinsburg. The Union Commander who replaced him viewed Belle with no suspicion at all. She could ride whenever and wherever she pleased.

She preferred to deliver her messages in the daytime. There were several reasons for this. First, it was easier to avoid getting lost. Although she usually rode over familiar ground, Belle had learned early on that moonlight, scudding clouds, rain, and fluttering leaves could make even well-known terrain confusing. Second, the Yankees had couriers too, and they were mostly active at night, since much of the country hereabouts was held by Rebels. It was always best to avoid running into enemy messengers.

The third reason was that Belle had not been able to come up with a single plausible explanation for why a well-bred young lady on a fast horse would ride for miles across open country in the dead of night. No, it was much better to go out boldly, in broad daylight, wearing her pretty green riding habit with the matching hat. No one would give it a second thought. At least that was what she hoped.

She rode nearly every day. Sometimes for pleasure, sometimes with a message concealed in her clothing. She knew the countryside well, and most of the time she managed to avoid the sentries when she passed between Union and Confederate territory. If she was challenged, she would simply laugh and flirt. A pretty girl out for a ride. What harm could there be?

Belle's only regret was that she had yet to see any of her heroes face to face. The general she most wished to meet was Stonewall, of course, because he commanded Papa's brigade. According to Belle's father, Jackson was a stern officer, but a brilliant leader, never taking risks that might put his men in unnecessary danger. They trusted him completely. Unfortunately for Belle, whenever she arrived at the headquarters of any of the generals in the area, she was expected to give her information to one of their subordinates. Sometimes the message was a simple one, which she committed to memory and recited perfectly while an adjutant wrote it down. Other orders were more complicated and would be written either in code or in plain text, though Belle was sure she could have memorized and recited the longer messages as well.

Eliza and Sam knew what Belle was doing. It was Eliza who helped her change into her riding habit. And helped her take it off when she returned home hours later, her face chafed by the wind, her skirts splattered with mud. It was Sam who saddled and unsaddled Fleeter each time she went out. He knew exactly how far the horse had been ridden. How hard. Of course they knew. Belle counted on them to say nothing.

Eliza, being Eliza, found other ways to express her disapproval. She often made a point of bringing the newspaper to Belle's room and handing it to her. There were times when Belle almost regretted teaching her to read. The paper reported arrests almost weekly, some poor messenger carrying dispatches or driving a farm wagon with a few smuggled rifles hidden under a load of potatoes. Someone who had the bad luck to be in the wrong place at the wrong time.

Belle glanced at the headline in the paper Eliza gave her.

Boy Smuggler Caught!

"I read it this morning."

"Did you read how he's goin' to prison?"

Belle waved her hand. "He's a boy. This is one situation where a woman has advantages over a man."

"That Colonel Compton, he threatened you with hangin', didn't he? No matter if you's a woman or not. And that was before you joined this here *network*, that no one even knows exackly what it is. Only that a fourteen-year-old boy goes to prison if he's caught."

Belle took the paper and found a different story. "Did you see this one?" she demanded, jabbing it with her finger, then reading it out loud. "'A deputation of Winchester ladies drove their carriage to Colonel Ashby's camp to report that the Federals had left the town and moved on to Berryville.'" Another jab. "The article calls them 'respectable matrons of the town.' You've seen them, haven't you? The women who stand on their porches, taking note of which way the enemy is marching. They keep count. This many men. This many horses. This many cannon. Do the men seem tired or are they singing? Are the horses thin or do they look well-fed? They send reports to the Rebel camps. Farm women do it too. They deliver information along with a cartload of turnips. I'm not the only one."

"You're the only one that's carryin' *papers*! Papers is different."

Belle ignored this. "Stonewall needs local citizens to report whatever we can find out."

"But the risks…"

"The risks aren't the same for a woman."

"Anyone can have bad luck," Eliza insisted.

"I'm cleverer than most couriers. I don't sneak about. I go out in broad daylight, whenever the weather is fine. And I never, ever act afraid. That's my secret."

"Even you can make a mistake, Miss Belle."

"I'm not stopping. The work is too important."

*And too exciting.*

Eliza would not give in. She stood and glared at Belle, as unmovable as a fence post.

"If you don't stop, I'm gonna tell your Mama."

In an instant, Belle was across the room and had pushed her face close to Eliza's. They were the same height, mistress and slave. Belle narrowed her eyes. Eliza raised her chin.

"Don't you dare. If you do, I'll—I'll . . ." *What would she do?*

Belle had no idea. But she had to make Eliza understand that this work meant everything to her. The words burst out. "I'd sell Sam. I'd sell John too. That's what I'd do!"

Eliza didn't move, but somehow her body changed. She grew denser, as if she had turned from flesh into stone. In an instant, she seemed to withdraw to a place that was completely closed off from Belle.

Eliza turned and left the room. She did not see her mistress standing there, eyes wide, her hand clamped over her mouth. The words echoed through the room. Belle could still hear them, but she could not take them back. She didn't mean what she'd said. She would never sell John. Or Sam. Surely Eliza knew that.

# Chapter 18

"She won't do it," Sam said, when 'Liza went to him that night. She had refused to lie down, choosing instead to sit on his one stool, wrapped in a ragged shawl against the cold. Her back was rigid with anger, her hands balled into fists. Sam stood behind her, gently kneading the muscles in her neck and shoulders.

"I know she won't. For one thing, her mama wouldn't let her." She banged her fist on her thigh. "But that she would say it. That she would even think it."

"She ain't her mama. That's for sure."

"No, she's not. The missus is a lady. She would never speak or act from anger. She's never even raised her voice to me."

Sam's strong hands kept rubbing.

"It doesn't change nothin'," he said. "You still have to go on helpin' Miss Belle. Try an' keep her from gettin' caught. Because of the Missus."

'Liza nodded, then leaned her head back until it rested against Sam's belly. "I do. But I'm gonna be more careful from now on."

# Chapter 19

W eeks passed, during which Eliza would not talk to Belle or even look at her. Eliza did everything she was told and left the room. When Belle asked her to stay, she stood with her hands clasped in front of her and stared at the floor. When Belle told her to raise her eyes, she did so but still would not speak. When Belle ordered her to talk, she said things like, "Cook's havin' trouble with the pastry for this bunch of pies." Or "Sam says somethin's been gettin' at the cabbage plants. They's all et up."

Finally Belle couldn't stand it anymore.

"I wouldn't do it, Eliza. You know I wouldn't."

Eliza turned her head away. "Still . . ."

"I shouldn't have said it."

No answer.

"I can't unsay it!"

"That's maybe somethin' to remember."

&

Riding as a courier, Belle had only one close call that autumn. It happened at night, when she was carrying a dispatch to General Jeb Stuart and took a short-cut through the woods. When she emerged onto the road, a group of Union soldiers was waiting for her. They must have heard Fleeter picking his way among the trees. Before Belle could react, one of the Yanks stepped forward and grabbed the horse's bridle. Their officer didn't speak at first. His eyes swept over Belle's outfit, glanced up at the moon and looked back at her, all the while scratching his beard in mock puzzlement. He didn't bother to play out the charade of asking what she was doing. With Yankee directness, he went straight to the point.

"Where are you going?" he demanded, and before Belle could answer, "Are you carrying any papers?"

The message she carried contained important details about repairing a nearby section of railroad and sabotaging the telegraph wires that ran beside it. It had been written on the thinnest possible paper and folded into a long strip, so she could hide it in the side seam of her jacket. If the paper was found and decoded, not only would it reveal Confederate plans and result in Confederate deaths, but things would go very badly for Belle. It was undeniable proof of treason. This was not the kind of message farm women delivered to Confederate camps along with a load of fresh vegetables. This was information between commanders about a planned military action.

By concentrating on controlling Fleeter, Belle managed to resist the urge to touch the paper's hiding place. The officer continued to look at her, waiting for an answer.

In a steady voice, she said, "I have no papers."

"Give them up," the captain urged. "Or we'll have to search you."

The soldiers elbowed each other.

Belle might not have hidden the message well, but she did have one trick to play. Uncle William had told her it might be effective. Under just these circumstances.

"I only have this one little paper," she said, handing the soldier a small leather bag, "that my uncle told me never to give up except to save myself from death or dishonor."

Inside the bag the officer found a piece of paper folded around a small silver cross with flared ends. The cross and the paper identified the bearer as the niece of a Mason. The captain studied it while Belle prayed that, like her uncle, he too was a Mason, a member of the national brotherhood whose members are sworn to aid each other. And their families.

The captain looked at Belle and seemed to make a decision, one that did not make him happy. "I don't know what you're about," he growled. "But don't ever let me see you again."

As soon as he gestured at his man to release Fleeter, Belle gripped the reins, snapped her riding whip, and sped away, her heart outracing her horse. By the time she reached home, she had recovered her composure. In fact, she felt exhilarated. She had been in danger, *real danger*, and she had escaped punishment. Again!

A few days later, Belle's feelings about her adventure changed. Instead of relief, she began to feel sorry that she hadn't been detained. She was desperate to make a name for herself and thought often of Bettie Duvall. According to the Washington newspapers, the lovely Miss Duvall had still not been arrested, yet everyone spoke openly of how she had delivered the information that helped win Manassas. Belle fell asleep at night dreaming of ways to make herself famous.

❧

At the end of November, she visited a Confederate camp in Centreville. Belle was fond of experimenting with different outfits, and today she was dressed in a short jacket with large brass buttons and a skirt she had had Eliza shorten to a daring length halfway between her knees and her ankles. Into her belt she had thrust a

Bowie knife, as well as Papa's pistol, which she now carried with her everywhere. Below the hem of the shortened skirt, a pair of woolen pantaloons showed, and below that her high buttoned riding boots. In between, several inches of her legs were revealed, encased in white woolen stockings.

It was an unflattering but practical outfit of her own design. The pantaloons allowed her to ride astride. The shortened skirt permitted longer steps. Today she was smuggling whiskey, and she had eight pint bottles hidden under her clothing. The Army seemed to have an endless thirst for spirits. Doctors gave it to their patients as a comfort and a painkiller. Officers doled it out as a reward after a long, cold march. And to dose them with courage before battle.

As Belle walked through camp, searching for the quartermaster's tent, she could sense the men's despondence. Despite the bright November sun, it hung in the air, a gray heaviness that kept them grim and silent. There was no music. No fiddle playing or singing. No joking. After the hard-won victory at Manassas, the Rebel Army had sunk into a kind of paralysis. Belle had heard that President Jefferson Davis was impatient with his generals, who couldn't agree on a plan of action.

Meanwhile, the Union blockade was having an effect. Belle saw evidence of shortages everywhere she looked. Some of the men had wrapped blankets around their shoulders to keep out the cold. Many were without shoes or boots and had tied burlap sacks around their feet.

*This with winter coming on!* Belle paused to listen when she overheard a conversation about deserters. Two men had been caught and were to be hanged that very day! Troubled by what she observed, she decided not to linger in camp. She would find the quartermaster's supply tent, make her delivery, and leave.

With eight glass bottles dangling from a sturdy ribbon that

circled her waist, Belle had to move slowly and carefully. There were a few other women in camp, there to visit loved ones or deliver food. Belle tried to blend in, but her strange outfit and awkward gait caught one soldier's attention. Or perhaps it was the weapons she carried in her belt.

"Got any whiskey, Miss?" a rough voice asked.

Belle knew that soldiers weren't allowed alcohol of their own. She should ignore the man, but instead she said, "Two dollars."

"One."

Right away she regretted admitting she had whiskey. She didn't like the look of the man. He was slouching and unshaven. When she turned away without answering, he grabbed her arm and held her, groping under her skirt, his hand brushing her legs, finally tugging a bottle free and raising it in the air. It all happened so quickly she couldn't stop him. He was very strong.

For a moment Belle was stunned, then frightened, and finally a boiling rage washed through her, the same white-hot anger she'd felt when the Yankees threatened Mama on July Fourth.

Snatching the knife from her belt, she snarled, "Give it back!"

She didn't care about the whiskey. What she hated was being made to feel helpless. She would punish him for that.

The soldier threw the bottle on the ground, where it smashed and puddled, the smell of cheap whiskey filling the air. He reached for his own knife and crouched low, his hand making slow circles in the air. A crowd gathered, and Belle heard her name whispered, the last thing she was aware of before fighting erupted all around her.

In seconds, someone had grabbed her and pulled her out of the brawl. When she joined the crowd of onlookers, she recognized a few of the rioters and realized some of the men were fighting for her personally. Others had come to the defense of a woman. The rest were just hungry for a fight.

❧

A few days later, the newspaper reported the incident. Belle had been hoping for a small amount of publicity, but not the story Grandmother read out loud in the parlor after sending Mary from the room.

"'A fight occurred in Beauregard's army at the Centreville encampment, with more than thirty soldiers badly wounded in the rioting. The fracas arose in consequence of a woman, named Belle Boyd, refusing to sell a bottle of whiskey to a soldier.'"

Mama made a small sound of distress and pressed her handkerchief to her lips.

Grandmother too, said nothing for a moment. Then, her pale eyes flashing, she snapped, "You will explain."

Belle was relieved that some of the more sensational details were missing from the story. Her exposed legs. Her own drawn knife. The man's groping hands. She tried to justify herself.

"It was just like the Fourth of July. I was frightened and had to defend myself."

"You were carrying whiskey."

"The army needs whiskey. They use it in the hospitals and to warm the soldiers on wet nights." Grandmother's expression did not change. "The story is exaggerated." And finally, "You don't understand."

"You are correct. I do not."

❧

Later Belle tried to make at least Eliza realize what it was like to have a man hold her helpless and reach under her skirt. Eliza was the one she could talk to. At least she used to be.

"When he put his hands on me, I felt . . ."

"I ain't innerested in how you felt. That skirt you was wearin' was scandalous. What was you thinkin', goin' into camp lookin' like that? Carryin' whiskey? You wanna 'splain yourself, go tell your Mama 'bout your feelin's. She's always ready to 'scuse whatever foolishness you do. It pains me seein' how she suffers on account of you."

Belle knew she should care more about hurting Mama and Mary. Grandmother. Papa. She *did* care. In the end, though, the one thought that kept running through her mind was, *What will Colonel Ashby say?*

*Martinsburg, Virginia*
*Confederate Controlled*
*Late January to Mid-April 1862*

# Chapter 20

Two months later, Papa was given permission to return to Martinsburg for the rest of the winter. He needed to regain his health. December had been an especially grueling time for Jackson's troops. After marching them all over the Valley, Stonewall launched an expedition to Berkeley Springs on December 31. Men and horses labored for days in the foulest weather imaginable, through water, mud, sleet, and slush. When it was over, Belle's father, stooped and gray faced, was sent home with a wrenching cough that rattled through his chest.

With a regimen of rest, healthy food, and Eliza's strange tasting teas, Papa's health slowly improved. Soon he was telling stories like every battle-hardened soldier. The winter campaign that had nearly killed him became a tale he told with gusto, praising Stonewall Jackson's brilliant leadership and his men's unflagging devotion. He told how the soldiers would harness themselves to the cannons or supply wagons when there weren't enough horses to pull them. How, when they slept, their blankets, if they were lucky enough to have one, froze to the ground. How near the end of an especially cold and miserable night, one of the men complained that Stonewall was no doubt sleeping in a warm, dry bed in a local farmhouse.

"All of a sudden," Papa said, "there was movement under a

blanket nearby, and up rose a tall, stalwart figure. It was Stonewall! He'd slept out there through all that sleet storm with his boys. There was no more grumbling after that."

ℰ℘

Papa's poor health was not the only reason he was home. Belle overheard him say to Mama that he intended once and for all to put a stop to their daughter's dangerous activities.

For once, Belle didn't care. The deepening cold had brought a lull in the fighting, and Martinsburg was in Confederate hands again, which meant there were many handsome officers in town. Everyone knew hostilities would resume in the spring. Until then, the young men and women threw themselves into a feverish round of dances, musical evenings, ice skating parties, and sleigh rides. On Sundays, the churches were filled with inspired sermons, heart-felt hymns, fervent prayers, but for the younger set, the remaining six days were devoted to the pure pleasure of being young and alive. Belle received invitations daily. The report of a camp brawl over a pint of whiskey had been so hard to believe that people seemed willing to dismiss it, apparently deciding that even Belle Boyd would not go so far.

With the arrival of March, the days grew warmer, the snows melted, and Belle could resume riding. She fell in love with the Valley all over again as the trees put out soft green leaves, and drifts of purple violets filled the woods. She loved these flowers best of all and brought baskets of them home to Mama and Mary and Grandmother. To Belle, these modest blooms symbolized the perfection of a Virginia spring. But it wasn't long before she grew fidgety, itching to return to work as a courier. Assuming Colonel Ashby would still use her.

Then, without warning, Papa derailed all her plans. "Your mother and I are sending you to Front Royal," he announced one morning at breakfast. "You leave in two weeks."

For over month, Belle had been eavesdropping on her parents whenever she had the chance, but she'd had no inkling of this. She tried at first to make a joke of it.

"Papa! Are you banishing me?"

His voice was firm when he said, "If that is how you choose to see it."

"But why?" Although she knew perfectly well.

"Because you have called unwelcome attention to yourself. And you will be in trouble if the Union army takes the town again. Front Royal is deeper in Southern territory. You'll be safer there."

When Belle tried wheedling Mama into allowing her to stay, her mother never wavered.

"It's not just for your sake, Belle. Uncle James and Aunt Fannie need your help. They are taking Franny to a friend's farm near Richmond. The poor girl has always been high-strung, and they think she should be in a quieter place. They're leaving soon. Alice is staying behind to manage the hotel. They can't find anyone to buy it, and they dare not leave it empty. They want you to help her." Mama added, "We're sending Eliza too."

Belle stopped protesting about leaving Martinsburg when Colonel Ashby wrote to tell her she would be useful as a courier wherever she was. She decided she liked the idea of helping to run the hotel, especially with no adult supervision.

એટ

Belle and Eliza's all-day journey to Front Royal was long and tiring, but uneventful. After Colonel Ashby's note, Belle had been eager to go. She did not ask Eliza what her feelings were.

Almost as soon as Belle and Eliza arrived, the Stewarts left, their hurried departure full of tearful embraces and last-minute instructions. No one had any idea how long they would stay in Richmond.

"Look after the place as best you can," Uncle James said. "We can't afford to lose it."

Aunt Fannie kept reminding Alice and Belle where the silver was hidden.

"All the breakables are packed in the attic. The crystal. My good china. The furniture can't be put away of course, but try to take care of it. It was my mother's. I would hate for it to be ruined."

Poor Franny was in a state of nervous collapse at the thought of leaving her sister behind. She sat in the carriage and sobbed, comforted by the ever-faithful Lettie, whose own eyes were wide with alarm at the thought of leaving Front Royal.

In the last moments, Aunt Fannie clung to her oldest daughter, saying, "I don't think we should leave Alice, James. She ought to come with us."

"This is our property, Fannie. One of us needs to stay."

"I don't think we're doing the right thing."

Rarely short-tempered, Uncle James said sharply, "We've been over this time and again. It's the best we can do." His tone softened when he saw her face and Alice's, both streaked with tears. "Think of little Franny in the carriage. We mustn't drag this out any longer. One more hug, and then we go."

∽

With her aunt and uncle gone, Belle had more freedom than ever before. It was so easy to hide what she was doing from her unsuspecting cousin, and even Eliza seemed resigned to letting Belle do as she pleased. No one questioned her about the messages she received almost daily. They could come in any number of ways. A slave child knocking at the front door with a message folded inside an invitation or other innocent piece of writing. A note passed to her when she greeted an acquaintance on the street. It might be about something trivial, a few stolen muskets or a box of Union ammunition needing to be smuggled to the nearest Rebel camp. Or it could be an official dispatch from Confederate headquarters to one of the generals based nearby.

Belle read everything that passed through her hands, even the dispatches, if they were carelessly sealed. That's how she learned that several Union generals were gathering their armies twenty-five miles away. A place called Kernstown. There would be another battle soon.

 

"Out of the fry pan, into the fire," Eliza said gloomily one night. She was helping Belle unlace and remove her clothing—dress, two petticoats, hoopskirt, corset, chemise, pantaloons, stockings—before putting on her nightdress. "Though I 'speck you's gettin' to feel right at home in that fry pan."

"I'm glad Grandmother decided to come," Belle said, changing the subject. She was tired of Eliza's dark moods. "She's good at getting things done."

"Good at givin' orders, you mean."

"I can't spend all my time helping Alice. I have important work to do."

"That reminds me. I got somethin' for you."

Eliza reached into her apron pocket and handed Belle a small bundle wrapped in oilcloth. "A boy brought this to the kitchen after supper. Don't know what's in it."

Unwrapping the package, Belle saw twenty small square envelopes of heavy folded paper. Each packet was tied with string and labeled in clear bold handwriting. *Sulphate of Quinine. Morphine Sulphate. Powdered Opium.*

"It's medicine, right? That don't seem like such a bad thing to be carryin'."

"It's still smuggling. These powders are made in Boston, see?" Belle turned one of the packets over. "There's an ink stamp on the back of each one. Both armies need medicine. But only the Yanks can get it. They aim to keep it that way."

She sat back in the chair and stared at the rug, remembering. After a few moments, she began to speak in a low voice. "You weren't at the hospital in Front Royal. All those wounded soldiers." Her voice wavered. "Sometimes we ran out of medicine. Even at the beginning of the war. Poor Freddy Sprockett was one of the lucky ones. He never woke up. It's a terrible thing to die in pain." Her voice dropped to a whisper. "To hear a grown man crying for his Mama."

Eliza's look softened. "I guess that was hard."

Giving herself a shake, Belle jumped to her feet. "Think of all the soldiers we'll be helping if I can get these medicines through. How will we do it?"

"You can't carry them this way."

"No. They're powders and have to stay dry. You must cut up the oilcloth and sew a waterproof case for each envelope. Then I can slip them into the hem of my riding skirt." A glance out the window. "It's not going to rain, is it? What excuse could I give for riding in poor weather?"

Eliza had brought out Belle's sewing basket and was collecting scissors, thimble, needle, and thread.

"You must have everything ready by morning," Belle said. "The nearest camp is quite far. But Colonel Ashby always says, 'What's important is to move supplies further down the line.' There's a certain farmhouse I've been told about. I'll head there."

Eliza had already plumped Belle's pillows and turned back the covers.

"Will you go to bed now?"

"I should be able to ride there and back in a few hours. No one will think anything of it. Even here people know I like to ride early."

Eliza asked again.

"What?" Belle glanced at her bed. "I suppose I should try to sleep. Heaven only knows I am no good at sewing. Wake me before first light. And tell Thomas—he's the one who takes care of the horses, isn't he?" Belle didn't wait for an answer. "Tell Thomas to saddle the chestnut mare so I can be gone by sun-up."

❧

Stonewall lost the Battle of Kernstown, his first defeat of the war. Afterward it was said that he had inaccurate information about the number of Federal soldiers he faced. Colonel Kimball, commander of the Union forces, had almost three times as many men as Jackson. Even so, the Confederates fought from nine in the morning until six at night. Finally, with his men exhausted and out of ammunition, Stonewall ordered a retreat up the Valley.

Belle felt partly to blame. "We should have given him better reports. This shows how important our work is!"

A "Hmph!" from Eliza.

They were sitting together on the kitchen porch, stringing beans for supper. Once they would have been chatting easily, but it seemed those days were past. Eliza stayed silent, and Belle let her mind wander. She daydreamed of meeting her idol Stonewall, but that seemed unlikely. Jackson was based in Winchester, only thirty miles north of Front Royal, but Belle's job as a courier was to carry messages in the opposite direction, to the commanders further south.

Sometimes when she thought of Jackson, she indulged in romantic fantasies about fighting at his side, sharing his privations as a comrade-in-arms. And maybe something more. Her feelings were confused, and as usual she did not inspect them too closely. First and foremost, Jackson was her father's commanding officer, and she looked to him to keep Papa safe. But what she felt was more than gratitude and respect. Even though Papa had told her that the general's uniform was often filthy, and his boots unpolished, she had seen the newspaper portraits that showed his noble features, the high forehead, penetrating eyes, and curling beard.

Belle's pleasant thoughts were interrupted by Grandmother coming out onto the porch. She held a note whose contents clearly annoyed her.

"This message was just delivered by a Union soldier. Who, by the way, did not bother to remove his hat or wipe his boots when he came inside."

"What does it say, Grandmother?"

"It seems that General Shields will be arriving tomorrow. He intends to make the hotel into his headquarters. Imagine having Union soldiers under our roof! Except it won't be our roof. The letter says that we—you and Alice and I—must move into the guest cottage." Grandmother quivered with indignation. "There are only two bedrooms in the cottage, and both of them are quite small. Such presumption!"

"Ours is the only hotel in town," Belle said soothingly. "So it's logical they would want to stay here. Perhaps we should take it as a compliment."

"I'm sure I don't understand what you mean. The point is, what with getting Fannie and James and Frances off to Richmond, I've just gotten myself settled. It will be most inconvenient to move my things again. And I do not wish to have the house and yard overrun with Union soldiers. Such poor manners. Even the officers do not know how to behave."

Belle hid a smile. Grandmother could be amusing when she was angry, like a furious old hen. But what she said was true. Belle and this general would soon be living practically under the same roof. *Really, what could be better?* Belle and Alice had keys to every room in the hotel, plus an excuse for being wherever they wanted. Fresh towels. Hot water for shaving. Such things were delivered daily. This put Belle in an ideal position to collect information, not just relay it. She'd make sure that next time, Jackson had reports he could trust.

Jumping to her feet, she said, "Grandmother, I will be happy to help you move your things. Shall we start right away?"

᠀

General James Shields arrived at the hotel with a broken arm. He'd been hit by an artillery fragment so early in the battle that he'd had to retire from the field, ceding command to Colonel Kimball. Which meant that it was Kimball, not General Shields, who was the official commander of the battle. It was Kimball, not Shields, who had handed the legendary Jackson his first defeat of the war. This, plus the constantly throbbing pain in his arm, made the general very cranky indeed.

Belle made it her mission to soothe the officer's battered ego as well as his wounded arm. She became his special friend, attending to every need and offering every kindness. Her seemingly endless supply of whiskey helped dull the general's pain. She also gave him some of her precious Virginia cigars. She had only a half dozen left but decided it would be worth it if he smoked every one. As long as she got the information she was after.

Before long, Belle and General Shields were spending entire evenings closeted in the hotel parlor, she pouring generous servings of whiskey into the best of Aunt Fannie's remaining glasses, he loosening his tongue along with his coat buttons. He was in his fifties and, like many Irishmen, a gifted storyteller. It was easy to encourage him. Belle had only to ask a single question, and he would launch into a story that lasted half an hour. About his time as a general in the Mexican War. Or being elected the first U.S. Senator from the State of Minnesota. Or serving as Governor of the Oregon Territory. Belle's interest was genuine. The general was a remarkable individual. The fact that she truly admired him only made her job easier.

"General, I can hardly believe all the places you've been and the important positions you've held!"

He chuckled. "I haven't told you yet how I nearly fought a duel with Abe Lincoln."

"My goodness! What happened?"

The general sipped his whiskey, sighed in appreciation. "Obviously we both survived," he said with a wink.

Belle risked a joke of her own. "It couldn't have been that you were both poor shots?"

"Not a bit!" he blustered. "It was years ago. Out in Missouri. Lincoln had written some unflattering articles about me, having to do with a political issue on which we disagreed. As we did on everything. In the end I decided his scribbling was not worth a duel. I never liked the man."

As interesting as this story was, Belle wanted to steer the conversation back toward the war.

"Tell me more about fighting in Mexico. Was it so different from here?"

From there it was just a hop, skip, and a jump to get the general talking about plans to defeat Stonewall. However, after a month of charming and flattering the old war-horse, Belle finally decided there was a reason why Shields gave nothing more than vague hints and suggestions. There *were* no Union plans to defeat Jackson!

With no spying to do in Front Royal, Belle decided to return to Martinsburg for a visit. The Federals were in charge again, but she didn't care.

# Chapter 21

T he railroad buildings in Martinsburg were still in ruins, but the tracks had been repaired. Belle and Eliza were able to ride the train, a much easier journey than traveling in a public coach. When they arrived, Mary and Sam were waiting for them, their faces lit up with nearly identical smiles.

Mary threw herself into Belle's arms. Eliza could only nod at Sam. Later she found a chance to squeeze his hand when she gave him the ticket for Belle's trunk.

While Sam was off retrieving her luggage, Belle asked Mary, "How is Mama?"

"I don't think she's well, but she won't say what's wrong." Her sister's lips trembled. "It's been hard with you and Grandmother and Eliza all gone at the same time."

Belle felt a pang of guilt. It wasn't like Mary to complain. While Belle had been off having adventures, flirting with generals, smuggling medicine and information, her dutiful sister had stayed in war-battered Martinsburg, caring for their ailing mother and helping to run the household. It was no life for an eleven-year-old.

"Do you still play with Petey?"

"Sometimes. But he's a boy. He gets to go places now that Mama won't let me. She worries all the time."

"We'll plan an outing. You and me and Petey. A picnic. It will be like old times."

For a moment Mary's face brightened, then fell. "We can't all ride one horse the way we used to. Petey and I are too big. We just have Fleeter now. The Confederates took the rest. They only left Fleeter because they know he's yours."

"My goodness! I never dreamed our side might take Fleeter. But now that the Federals are back in charge, why don't they take him?"

"I don't think they know about him. No one rides him when you're not here. So they've never seen him."

"We only need two horses for our picnic. We'll just have to borrow one more."

Mary stamped her foot, something Belle thought she would never see.

"You don't understand! There's practically no horses in the whole entire town. They're all gone."

Belle leaned close to Mary and said gently, "You are perfectly right, dear. I don't understand. Because I've been away. That means I need you to explain things to me." She straightened Mary's bonnet, retying the ribbon under her chin. "May I depend on you for that?" Mary bit her lip and nodded. "I am fairly certain someone in town will loan us a horse."

Meanwhile, Sam had arrived with Belle's trunk loaded on a handcart, and they set out for home, Mary and Belle walking ahead, Eliza and Sam following behind, him pulling the cart.

Mary slipped her hand into Belle's. "May I tell Petey about the picnic?"

"Yes, dear. We'll go for certain. It's a promise."

❧

When they reached the house, Mama was not waiting in her customary place on the porch. Belle found her in the parlor. Even then, her mother did not rise from her rocking chair when they walked through the door. Belle was shocked to see her looking so pale, and she ran across the room to kneel at her mother's feet.

"Mama, I should never have left you!"

Her mother did not cry, but she pressed her lips together and her eyes glistened with unshed tears. Somehow, though, she kept her voice steady when she said, "I wanted you to go. Remember? But it doesn't matter, now that you're here." She smiled. "I'm pleased to see you looking so well."

"I shan't leave you again. I promise."

Belle said it even though she knew it wasn't true. It was so easy to make a promise and so hard to keep one. But her mother probably didn't believe her anyway.

Mama unpinned Belle's hat and placed it on a table so she could stroke her hair. "Such lovely curls!" After a long pause, she added, "Now as to whether you stay or go, we can discuss that later."

Something in her voice made Belle raise her head. Mama's eyes shifted toward Belle's younger sister, sitting attentively nearby, hands quiet in her lap.

"There you are, Mary!" Belle said. "I've just had a good idea. Sam has to return the cart to the station. If you find him quickly, I think you could persuade him to give you a ride in it. Wouldn't that be fun?" Belle looked around for her drawstring purse. "Now that I'm back, you need not stay by Mama's side every minute.

Although you've been very good to do so." She found her purse and located a penny. "On the way back, you can stop at Papa's store and see if there are any peppermint sticks. On second thought, buy two." She held the coins out. "Find your brother. I'm sure Will would like to go."

Mary took the pennies but said, "I am much too old to ride in a cart, you know. Though I am sure Will would like it." She glanced from Belle to her mother. "And I'm also old enough to know when you are getting rid of me."

"Oh dear," Belle said once Mary had left the room, stomping her feet in a most unladylike way. "That's the second time I've made her angry. In less than half an hour."

Mama looked after her younger daughter and sighed. "I'm afraid your sister has changed. I try to be understanding. Mary is such a help, but she is easy to offend. I don't mean that unkindly. It is just a simple fact." She smiled at Belle. "Don't let her spoil your homecoming, though. You'll find a way to make it up to her. You've always been good at winning people over." She reached for the bell sitting on the table. "I'll have Cook bring us tea. You must be parched from your journey."

Belle stood and removed her gloves and cloak, dropping both carelessly on the sofa. She pulled a side chair over to face her mother, so they could sit knee to knee.

"I want to hear all about James and Fannie leaving," Mama said. "Was it very hard for them to go? How was Franny?"

Belle clasped her mother's hands. "First tell me about yourself."

Mama blushed, and for a moment resembled her younger, prettier self. "I was suffering from women's problems. I think I was just tired and worried. It was difficult, though. The people I might have talked to about it were all gone. I missed Eliza especially. She knows about these things." Mama closed her eyes for a moment.

"I'm sorry you were alone."

"Cook was helpful. And Mary does whatever I ask, though I could not tell her what the trouble was."

"I promised her a picnic. If I can find a spare horse."

"Sam will find one."

"I worry about her."

"I worry about *you*!" Mama squeezed Belle's hands in a surprisingly strong grip. "The town is in Union control again. It's not safe for you."

Eliza arrived with a tray of tea, along with biscuits and jam.

"I brought enough for Mary and Will when they gets back from the station. Cook said she woulda made gingerbread, but we's all outta ginger. Pro'bly 'til the war ends."

"Eliza!" Mama said with a smile. "How nice to see you. I was just telling Belle that I missed you. How have you been?"

"Just fine, missus."

"And how do you find Sam and John? They must be happy to have you home again."

"We's all happy 'bout that," Eliza said, giving Belle a sideways glance before she left the room.

Mama accepted the cup Belle handed her, took a sip of tea, and said, "Another thing that worries me is the latest news about Rose Greenhow."

"Please don't say anything against her, Mama. You know I admire her."

"So do I. At least I admire her patriotism, if not her actions. Still I'm worried about her. She's been in Old Carroll Prison since January. The papers say she doesn't get enough to eat. Imagine! And Little Rose is with her. Just eight years old. I'm sure the Yankees have done it on purpose, to add to Mrs. Greenhow's suffering. They can be very wicked."

Mama had grown teary again. Belle patted her hand and gave a low laugh. "From what I've read of Mrs. Greenhow, she is well able to take care of herself." She cast around for something else to talk about. "How are things at the store with the Federals in charge again?"

"You must go see for yourself. The store itself is in a shocking state, the shelves nearly empty. Hardly a length of fabric, a button, or a pair of shoes in the entire place. But Mr. Meaders tells me we are making more money than ever."

"How is that possible?"

"Tobacco and whiskey," Mama said primly, or tried to, for her mouth turned up at the corners. "It's rather funny, isn't it?"

"Tobacco from your farm?"

"Of course."

"And the whiskey?"

"Homemade. Mr. Meaders buys it from the local farmers. Well, the farmers' granddads, since the farmers are all gone. Most of them have some sort of distilling operation hidden behind a shed somewhere. It helps their families make ends meet."

"Moonshine!" Belle said, laughing.

"Of the highest quality, according to Mr. Meaders. And he charges double when the customer is wearing a blue uniform."

"Well that's one good things about the Yankees, isn't it, Mama?"

# Chapter 22

To celebrate being together, that night 'Liza spread an old horse blanket on the floor of the hayloft for a strawberry picnic. She and Sam and John sat together in a patch of moonlight and took turns reaching into the basket of berries and passing around a small jug of cream 'Liza had snuck from the kitchen.

"Belle complains how I don't talk to her like I used to. Says I's grumpy. She never asks why though. Never thinks how I could never forgive what she said that one time." A glance at John, who knew nothing of Belle's threat to sell him and Sam. "Never thinks what it's like for me, leavin' my family alla time. All these years goin' off to Baltimore. Washington. Front Royal."

Sam said, "Miss Belle's got no sense. No matter she just turned eighteen."

"How come I always needs to be watchin' over her like she's a little girl? Why can't she watch over her own self? She never listens to me anyways." 'Liza shook her head. "I do it for the missus. She's the one asked how I been keepin' soon as she saw me. She's the one said how it must be nice for me to be home."

"Then sends you away again. You tol' me it's already decided."

"I'll be real sorry if you has to go, Mama," John said. "You just got here."

'Liza reached over and wiped a smear of cream from John's

cheek with her thumb, let her hand linger. "I can't blame the Missus for wantin' to keep her child safe. Any mother would do the same." She turned to Sam. "You think it's true? That it's dangerous for Miss Belle to stay?"

"Might be. I been stopped a buncha times by Union soldiers askin' where she's at. When she might be comin' back."

"What do you say?"

"Same as what I always say. I don't know nothin'. It's gen'rally the truth anyways. I aim to keep it that way."

"The missus says this time she wants Belle to go all the way to Richmond. 'Cause it's further south."

John had been watching and listening carefully. Now he said, "Mama? I heard somebody say Richmond's the capital now. Is that true?"

'Liza put her hand on his head. "Abe Lincoln lives in Washington. So I guess that's the only capital we care about. Richmond is the capital of the Confederacy."

Sam held up both hands, like he was pushing her words away.

"Don't talk to him 'bout this, 'Liza. He don't need to know."

"Yes he does."

They stared at each other a moment, their disagreement a surprise to both of them.

"Miss Belle's not on the same side as us, is she?" John asked.

Sam leaned back against a hay bale and gave 'Liza an "I told you so" kind of look over his folded arms.

"Not exackly." She cupped the boy's chin. "Remember, John. The Boyd fam'ly is decent enough folks. But Abe Lincoln is the man we love."

# Chapter 23

T wo days after the picnic outing with her sister, Belle returned to Front Royal with Eliza. Belle moved back into the cottage bedroom she shared with Alice, and Eliza rejoined the slaves
who slept together in the hotel attic.

"Come and help me put these sheets away," Alice said on Belle's
first morning back. She seemed oddly excited but would say nothing more until they had gone to fetch freshly laundered sheets from
the three girls who labored all day long in the wash house.

"Here! Carry these," Alice said, handing Belle a pile of folded
sheets, then leading her up the back stairs of the hotel, finally stopping outside the large linen closet in the hallway. Balancing the
sheets in one arm and placing a finger to her lips, Alice opened the
door and stepped inside, motioning Belle to follow.

"What is it, Alice? You're being quite mysterious."

Instead of answering, her cousin closed the door, then used
the toe of her shoe to push aside an old braided rug that lay on the
floor. Alice pointed at a circle of bright light shining in the dimness
of the closet. Bending over, Belle saw a hole, about two inches in
diameter.

"My goodness! I wonder who put it there."

"You can use it in your spying, can't you?"

Belle straightened quickly, giving Alice a hard stare and

receiving an easy smile in return. There was obviously more to her cousin than Belle had realized. Or perhaps Belle had not been as careful as she thought.

"It wasn't hard to figure out. People stopping by the kitchen at odd hours. Thomas saying something about how often you ride. How far." Alice nodded at the spy-hole, gave another smile. "It looks right into the parlor. Where the Federal officers have their meetings."

"This will be very useful indeed." Belle smiled at her cousin and kissed her cheek. "Thank you, Alice." She lifted her armful of sheets. "Let's put these away. Then I will slide my visiting card under General Shields' door. I want him to know I'm back and that I need papers to travel to Richmond."

ಌ

That very evening, the general crossed the yard that separated the hotel from the cottage and paid the ladies a visit. He was courtly with Grandmother and genially flirtatious with Belle and Alice. Once again, Belle kept the general's cigar lit and his whiskey glass full. She enjoyed the chance to show Alice and Grandmother the feminine charm she wielded so skillfully. It was similar to a military campaign, she thought. In this case, her objective was a travel pass, her weapons were beauty and wit. Seated in the tiny cottage parlor, she felt like she was performing on a stage, both the author and heroine of her own drama. She was sure her cousin and grandmother were as fascinated by her performance as her hapless victim. When the moment was right, she pounced.

"Because you are a general," she purred, "and surely you know everything, you must be aware that my aunt and uncle, the Stewarts, formerly of this hotel, are now residing near Richmond.

I have heard that you recently issued new travel restrictions, but if I were to ask for permission to visit my relatives, would you truly deny *me* a pass? You have only to look at me, General, to know I am no danger whatsoever."

The general did look and was clearly pleased by what he saw. He smiled, drank some whiskey and took a pull on his cigar.

"That is precisely why I would have to deny your request," he said. "We have recently received word that Jackson's forces are totally demoralized. What if you were to fall into their hands? As you so rightly point out, you are just a girl. I dare not trust you to their tender mercies."

Belle batted her eyes.

"In any case, soon the Rebels will be wiped out for good. Then you may go wherever you please."

He took another puff on his cigar and exhaled, adding to the pungent cloud hanging over their heads, too content to notice the appalled silence that had fallen over the room.

*Soon. Wiped out for good.* The words echoed in Belle's head. This sounded like far more than a single battle. Yet the general had not told her anything specific. There was no "actionable intelligence" she could relay to Colonel Ashby. She needed details. Times, places, numbers of troops. She must find out more.

By the following morning, Belle had decided to delay her trip to Richmond. No matter Mama's fears for her safety, she had to learn more about the plan to wipe out Stonewall's army. It would be the last thing she did before leaving Front Royal. So she turned her attention to the general's new aide-de-camp, Captain Daniel Keily, and soon he was making daily presentations of flowers and poetry.

∾

"Listen to this, Alice." Belle unfolded a note. "It's the captain's latest. Written this afternoon." She cleared her throat and read.

> *Everything beautiful that I see*
> *Reminds me, dearest one, of thee.*
> *The setting sun, a twinkling star*
> *Reminds me of how fair thou are.*

"I think it's rather sweet," Alice said.

"At any rate, it's better than the one he sent early this morning. The verses he writes at night are the worst. It seems I interfere with the captain's repose, whereas I sleep like a babe." Belle reached into her pocket and pulled out more folded bits of paper. "Let's see, where is it? The one from last night. Ah, here. My favorite so far." She assumed a formal recital pose, her hand pressed over her heart.

> *My heart! It burns.*
> *My soul! It yearns.*
> *Dare I hope for affection in return?*

Alice smiled. "Oh dear. That one *is* a trifle . . ."

When she hesitated, Belle supplied the word, "Overheated?"

The girls were still laughing when Grandmother came into the parlor.

"What is so entertaining?" She looked at the notes in Belle's hand. "Ah, another *billet doux* from the poor captain?"

"What on earth is a *bee-yay doo*?" asked Alice.

"I'm surprised you would ask," Grandmother admonished.

"A girl your age ought to know. It is from the French language, and it means a love note." She paused and tilted her head to one side, smiling as if at a pleasant memory. She looked at Alice again. "Most words having to do with love seem to be French. I have no idea why." Her eyes sharpening again, she glanced at Belle. "Captain Keily's notes are amusing?"

With a glance at Alice, Belle passed over the verse.

Grandmother's eyebrows lifted as she read. "Ah yes. There is always something faintly ridiculous about a young man suffering the pangs of love." She smiled. "Perhaps you should show some sympathy. The poor man is evidently suffering greatly."

"What do you suggest?" Belle asked.

"I should think it's obvious. He tells you his heart is on fire. Next time you see him, without saying a word, you must offer him a glass of water. If he blushes, it will show he understands your meaning. And there may be some hope for the poor man after all."

With that, Grandmother made a dignified exit, while the two cousins burst into laughter.

Alice exclaimed, "I do believe that's the most unladylike suggestion I have ever heard from Grandmother. We're seeing a side of her we never knew existed."

Belle nodded. "It seems that little by little, this war is changing us all."

∾

Although she was unmoved by Captain Keily's poetry, Belle was very interested in anything he had to say of a military nature. When the captain did not have duties elsewhere, Belle arranged for them to go on long walks. One day he mentioned that there would soon be an important meeting at the hotel. A war council, he called it.

*At last!* When he confirmed that the meeting would take place in the parlor, Belle thought, *God bless Cousin Alice!*

Just two days later, a number of officers and aides arrived on horseback to join General Shields and his staff. After dinner, when the men were gathered in the parlor, Belle slipped into the closet. Curling herself into the narrow space, she peeked through the hole at a depressing sea of dark blue uniforms. The angle of her vantage point allowed her to see only about two-thirds of the room. However, when she put her ear to the hole, she found she could hear everything. Officers greeting each other, the clank of sabers being removed, chairs shifting on the wooden floor, the rustle of papers unfolded, maps unrolled. Belle hardly breathed as General Shields announced the evening's topic. Tonight they would finalize the details of their campaign to defeat the rebels in the Shenandoah Valley.

The meeting went on until nearly midnight. Orders were issued for every commander in the Valley. Finally the visitors departed for their camps, and the general and his staff retired for the night. They went to their rooms, boots thumping along the hallway just inches from Belle's hiding place. When all was quiet, she stood up, holding onto the wall, afraid her numb legs wouldn't support her. What would happen if she toppled over and was discovered? She shook her head to clear such a thought and focused instead on what she must do next. When her legs stopped tingling, she crept out of hiding and down the stairs. As she crossed the yard to the cottage, she whispered to herself, repeating what she'd heard. She must write it all down while she still remembered.

"The Devil is in the details," Ashby had once told her. "You must get them right. It often means the difference between victory and disaster."

*I will get them right!*

Alice groaned and turned over when Belle slipped into their room, lit a candle, and sat down at the desk.

"I tried to wait up," her cousin said sleepily. "Do you need help?"

"No, dear. I'll tell you everything in the morning."

Belle felt a desperate need for speed, not wanting to waste any time getting this report on its way. The information was vital, but she took time to write in code, a lengthy process for such a long message. Belle was grateful for the hours she'd spent practicing, so she could work quickly but still be sure she was enciphering correctly. After a minute or two, Alice stopped muttering, rolled over, and fell back to sleep. Now it was easier for Belle to concentrate. In less than an hour, she was finished.

*But how to get the message to Colonel Ashby?*

Belle knew the colonel's general location, and she thought she might know just where to find him. It was only fifteen miles away. But she did not like riding at night. There were others in the village besides Belle who aided the rebel cause. A loosely organized group of boys, women, and old men, they had to be careful about making contact. But it was much too late to find another rider. Belle would have to go herself. She knew she should wait until morning, and she also knew she wouldn't. The information was too important. Ashby might be gone tomorrow. She had worked hard to gather this intelligence and wanted to deliver it to him personally.

Once she had decided to go, a series of other decisions quickly followed. She would disguise herself as a boy. She could go faster if she rode astride. Hurriedly pinning up her hair, she set a broad brimmed hat on her head. Her generous figure was only partly hidden by her belted trousers, loose shirt and riding boots. No one who looked closely would ever mistake her for a boy, but she hoped no one would look closely. At this hour, there was a chance that some of the Union sentries would have fallen asleep at their posts. As insurance, she took an unused pass written days ago by the obliging Captain Keily. A pass from Divisional Headquarters would not be easily ignored.

Dressed now, she slipped out to the stable, quickly saddled her horse, and headed into the hills outside of town. Twice she was challenged by Union sentries. Each time she wordlessly produced her pass and was allowed to continue. The moon was just past full, but there were heavy clouds, and she rode as fast as she dared over rough terrain, through woods and fields, high ground and low. She judged that two hours had passed when she arrived at the farm of someone she knew only as Mr. M. The house sat dark and quiet as she jumped from her horse and raced up the front steps to pound her fist on the door.

A moment later, an upstairs window opened and a man's voice called down, "Who's there?"

"Belle Boyd," she said, between gasping breaths. "With important intelligence. For Colonel Ashby. Is he here?"

"Wait a minute. I'll come down."

The front door opened, and Mr. M. pulled her inside with one hand, holding a lantern overhead with the other. He peered into her face, peppering her with questions, but Belle would talk to no one but Ashby.

"Tell me where to find him."

"In the woods. About a quarter mile up the road."

Belle had already turned to leave when a door opened, one she hadn't noticed before, and Ashby himself appeared.

"Good God! Miss Boyd, where did you come from?"

"There was a meeting in Front Royal. I heard everything. They mean to trap Jackson." She handed him the message. "Here's my report. The Union positions and their strength. Who is to advance where and when. What route they'll take."

The war had changed Turner Ashby, as it had so many others. Gallant and carefree when the conflict began, he'd become bitter and vengeful since the brutal bayonet stabbing of his brother at the hands of six Union soldiers. He said nothing as his hand tightened over Belle's message, but she saw the sudden fire in his eyes. That was thanks enough.

The ride home was exhausting, but by now the Yankee sentries were indeed sound asleep. At one point, when her route took her down a short stretch of road, the hoof beats of her horse woke a guard. As she neared, he challenged her and raised his rifle, but she flashed by at a gallop and reached a turn in the road before he could get off a shot.

Just before sunrise, she reached the outskirts of Front Royal where she slowed to a walk, partly to rest her horse and partly to avoid making any noise. It would not do to be seen now. What if poor Captain Keily was having another sleepless night? What would he make of his beloved, if he saw her at this moment? Returning from a mission. Dressed as a man. Belle almost laughed out loud.

When she reached the stable, she took time rubbing her horse down, giving him water and oats, tired as she was. Normally the stable boy would take care of these chores, but she didn't want to wake him. It was better if no one knew she had been out. She hummed while she worked. Her horse had done well tonight.

And so had Belle! She had managed to collect valuable information and ridden thirty miles over rough country to deliver it. She was tired but oh so pleased with her night's work.

At last she was a real spy.

# Chapter 24

Without warning, General Shields instituted a travel ban, which Belle took as a sign that the campaign to eliminate Stonewall would soon begin. Then he and his staff left Front Royal. Another sign. Unfortunately for Belle, there was no way to get a message to Jackson. The village was locked up as tight as a miser's purse. Not a single person allowed to enter or leave. Even young boys caught sneaking off to their favorite fishing holes were turned back by patrolling soldiers. Belle prayed there were others who lived beyond the village who would pass along the news of these latest developments.

On the morning of May 23, the weather in Front Royal was hot and oppressive, the air thick with humidity and an expectant waiting that frayed nerves and shortened tempers.

After breakfast, Belle was sitting by the window reading aloud to Grandmother and Alice when she heard a commotion on the street and went outside to investigate. In front of the hotel, Union soldiers were hurrying every which way, their mounted officers bellowing orders from horses that danced in agitated circles. Belle caught at the sleeve of one soldier and asked what was happening. He shouldn't have told her as much as he did, but he seemed stunned, loudly repeating the news as if he were trying to make himself believe it.

"The Rebels are a mile away!" he shouted. "Somehow they snuck up on us. We never even knew they were there! They say it's Stonewall himself!"

Belle's heart leapt. Her hero! And Papa was surely with him.

"What are your orders, with the Rebels so close?"

"We're getting out! And taking the guns and ammunition. We'll blow them up if we have to. The bridges too."

In the voice of a frightened girl, Belle said, "Goodness! Are we in any danger?"

Instantly the officer's manner changed from alarm to reassurance. He had, of course, misunderstood her completely.

"No need to worry, miss. We're leaving three hundred men behind. All of them seasoned fighters." Faced with a frail and delicate female, he had forgotten that most people in town would be hoping for a Rebel victory. "You will be perfectly safe."

Belle returned to the cottage, where Alice and Grandmother were standing in the doorway. She told them what she'd learned.

"Jackson's here?"

"In Front Royal?"

"It seems he has surprised the Yanks. They're making plans for an orderly retreat. If they have enough time."

"Hallelujah!" Grandmother said.

"I'm going upstairs to fetch my opera glasses and see what I can from the balcony of the hotel."

Alice followed Belle, and they took turns looking through the glasses. Even without them, it was easy to see a small group of mounted Rebels stopped on the low rise of Prospect Hill, as if to survey the situation in the village below.

"Our boys are moving quickly. That's good, isn't it?" Alice turned to Belle. "I wonder where the other Union forces are. Didn't you say there are several nearby?"

Belle knew for a fact that there were four Union generals near Front Royal: Banks, White, Shields, and Geary. She was sure Jackson knew it too. She herself had handed the report to Ashby containing everything she'd heard through the spy-hole. Now she knew even more. The day before the travel ban went into effect, she had received a note from a trusted source in Winchester with the latest information on each general's current location as well as the size of his army. Added together, their forces outnumbered Jackson's, but Belle guessed it would not be easy to coordinate four different armies.

The Union generals were still a safe distance away. If Stonewall attacked Front Royal immediately, he could overcome the small force left behind, gain vital arms and supplies, and still have time to escape before the Union generals could even form a battle plan.

"I have to get a message to Stonewall!" Belle said as she rushed down the stairs and out to the crowded street. There were no longer any women about. They had rounded up their children and fled indoors. A scattering of men remained, watching from a safe distance, some of them talking excitedly, unsure what to do. Most of the villagers were loyal Confederates and happy the Yanks were leaving. Still, the prospect of a battle so close to Front Royal, or even inside it, was alarming. If there were fighting in the streets, if the town were shelled with artillery, civilian lives could be lost and property damaged. This had already happened in Winchester and other nearby towns.

Belle approached three men in civilian clothes standing together in a tight knot. She knew them slightly but usually avoided them. They were of age to serve but had not enlisted, claiming that work or business or poor health kept them from following their hearts' desire and joining up. *Now is their chance to prove their loyalty!* Belle showed them her note and said she had other information that would help Jackson win the day.

"I need someone to carry a message. It could save the town. Will one of you go?"

The men stammered three different excuses for refusing. Belle turned away in disgust before the last had even finished speaking. There was no time for this! Any man who was unwilling to go would be useless anyway, turning back at the first difficulty or forgetting what he was supposed to say. She would have to go herself.

Running into the cottage for her sunbonnet, she faced Grandmother and Alice and their questions. What was she doing? Where was she going? She didn't answer. There was no point telling them. It would have worried them more, not less.

Wordlessly waving her arm in the direction of Jackson's troops, she raced back to the street. Though still filled with Federal officers and men, the chaos was over. Infantry units marched by, quickstepping in orderly ranks. Heavy wagons trundled past, loaded with weapons, food, supplies. The Union soldiers at the edge of town would have orders to resist, so as to give as much time as possible to these soldiers intent on emptying Front Royal of anything the enemy could use.

None of the blue-clad men paid any attention to the young woman walking briskly in the opposite direction, headed for the hills outside the village. Soon she had left the last houses behind and was running across open fields, already regretting her choice of a white bonnet. Even at a distance she would be all too visible.

From her brief view off the balcony, Belle tried to keep a rough map in her head. If she was going to reach the Confederate officers, she had to avoid blundering into Federal troops.

Her reconnaissance had shown the Union cannons strung along one of the ridges that surrounded the town. A bird's eye view was one thing. Up close, the cannons were terrifying. They squatted on the heights like giant spiders, leaping backward when they were fired. The sound was a deafening boom she could feel right through her shoes. The guns had been placed to overlook the road which the main body of Rebels would be using. If she continued running in this direction, they would soon be overlooking her too.

As she ran, between her panting breaths and the roar of the cannons, she heard the sharp rattle of small arms fire and knew there must be Union soldiers in some of the buildings on the edge of the village. The Confederate's advance guard was finally close enough to exchange fire with the Yanks. When Belle realized she could be hit by a stray bullet, a thrill of fear rippled through her, then left her completely calm. She knew she was in danger, yet her mind stayed clear, allowing her to make decisions about which way to go, how to use small obstacles to give herself a few extra seconds of protection. A tree, a stone wall, a small depression in the ground became precious goals along the way. She felt like she was looking down at herself from above, a steadying voice inside her head issuing orders. *Go there! Now over there! Change direction! Don't run in a straight line!*

The danger increased when the retreating Union soldiers spotted her. Before, she had been in danger from crossfire. Now she was their target. They began aiming for the small figure in the white bonnet zigzagging across the fields like a frightened rabbit. She had to keep running, hearing bullets whine past, feeling the tugs as they tore through her skirts. Once, the force of an exploding shell threw her to the ground, pelting her with clods of earth and stone and mortar fragments. She was grateful to lie in the dirt for a few moments, even more grateful when she raised her head and saw that the small ravine where she'd fallen was filled with gray haze.

The smoke from cannons, rifles, and musket fire had combined to form a swirling cloud eight feet off the ground that kept her hidden. She allowed herself to lie still, her breath like fire in her chest. Then she jumped up and ran on. As she drew even with the first Rebel soldiers, she took off her bonnet and waved it to draw their attention, urging them toward the village. She didn't stop. These men were the advance guard. It was the officers Belle needed to reach.

Bullets were no longer whizzing past, and she prayed she was out of range as she ran up a small hill, fully exposed again. She crested the top, and as soon as she was safely on the other side, fell to her knees, chest heaving, her emotions a mix of gratitude, exhilaration, exhaustion. Catching sight of the main body of Confederate troops a short distance away, she knew she had made it.

A lone figure cantered toward Belle, and she rose to her feet. As the rider drew close, she recognized her friend Henry Douglas, now a major on Jackson's staff.

"Belle! What are you doing here?"

She wasn't yet steady on her feet, and he slid to the ground, grabbing her arm to keep her from falling.

"Oh, Henry! Give me a moment."

For the next minute, Belle did nothing but breathe, taking great gulps of air that pressed her ribs against her corset while Henry kept a firm grip on her arm. Finally she handed him the message she'd received from Winchester. Then, between gasping breaths, she told him what she'd seen in the village with her own eyes and ears.

"You've surprised the Yanks completely. The force in the village is small. Just three hundred infantry. Less cavalry. A few cannon. They're destroying supplies. If Stonewall attacks now, he can save most of it, the bridges too. But he must be quick!"

Without another word, Henry jumped on his horse and galloped off to deliver Belle's report. Looking after him, she could see Jackson himself a few hundred yards away, waiting for his major to return. The general sat astride a reddish horse, with a stiff brimmed cap pulled low over his forehead in his usual way. Belle felt a thrill. General "Stonewall" Jackson, together with his short-legged mount, Little Sorrel, created a distinctive and well-loved silhouette that had been printed again and again in newspapers throughout the Valley. It was an image that was carefully clipped out and slipped into diaries or between the pages of family Bibles. This was the leader that families trusted to bring their men back home. Just as they prayed for husbands and sons every night, they prayed for Stonewall Jackson.

Belle remained near the crest of the hill and waited to see Henry hand her message to General Jackson. Then she turned and ran back to the village.

∽

"Going there, I had to run flat out. Coming back was more like a scamper. The Yanks have gone, but they did manage to fire the bridges. Our men are trying to save them, except for those who are chasing the Yanks. I hear General Banks hasn't stopped running yet!"

Belle was in the bedroom changing her clothes and reporting her adventures to Eliza.

"Mmm-hmm," Eliza said for the fourth time. Her voice sharpened. "Look here! Is these what I think they is?"

Belle turned to see Eliza poking her fingers through two holes in Belle's petticoats.

"These is bullet holes, right? You got shot at? You skipped that part of your story."

Angrily, she grabbed Belle's dress off the floor and held it up. "Course you got holes in your dress too. No wonder you came up to change. Wouldn't want Grandma and Alice to see none o' this." She wheeled on Belle. "What was you thinkin'?"

"I was thinking about helping Stonewall win a glorious victory. I was thinking about saving the bridges. And the cannons and gunpowder and food he so desperately needs. I was thinking about keeping Papa safe. And I've already received news from Henry that he *is* safe. So I have successfully completed my mission."

"Your mission," Eliza said with a sniff, gathering Belle's clothing in her arms. "I reckon I can patch the petticoats. The dress, I don't know how it'll turn out."

"Not the dress. I'll keep that as a souvenir. Of my most daring exploit. People might wish to see it. They won't believe about the bullet holes otherwise. Passing right through my skirts."

Belle was already rehearsing how she would tell the story. Now she would be truly famous. Hundreds of men had seen a woman run across the battlefield. Who else would it be but Belle Boyd? Soldiers on both sides knew she was staying in Front Royal. Henry Douglas had taken her message—how fortunate that was!—and, with her own eyes, Belle had seen him hand it to General Jackson. Not like the map she'd given Henry at Harper's Ferry, which she was sure he'd never delivered.

None of that mattered now. Not after what she'd just done. Even though it already seemed like a dream. As if it were some other girl who'd run through gunfire to deliver an important message in the middle of a battle. Belle might not believe it had happened except for the bullet torn dress. She needed to keep it for that reason alone, even if no one else was interested. But she was quite certain that would never happen. She wouldn't allow it.

"This dress all right to put on?" Eliza held up a brown calico print. "You've noticed they's bringing in wounded over at the hotel, right?"

Belle nodded. "As soon as I'm dressed, I'll go down to help Grandmother and Alice."

ʚ৹

Working among the wounded, Belle quickly fell into her once-familiar routine of closing her eyes and ears to everything except the task directly in front of her.

Alice found a chance to squeeze her hand and whisper, "Everyone is talking about what you did!"

Grandmother looked her up and down, saying, "I cannot decide which I feel more strongly. Relief or anger. Think what it would do to your mother if anything happened to you."

When the work grew overwhelming, Belle and Alice would find each other and step out onto the hotel porch for a breath of fresh air. There was always a crowd on the street, soldiers and civilians waiting for battle reports or the sight of a loved one. For the moment, the Fishback was a home, hotel, hospital, and military headquarters all rolled into one. Whenever Belle went outside and was spotted by someone in the crowd, a small cheer went up. Word had spread of what she'd done.

It was a strange afternoon. Misery and suffering inside the hotel, the praise she craved out on the street. After a while Belle felt the beginnings of a headache. Her run to Jackson had tired her more than she realized. Her feet were cut and bruised. She'd worn holes in the soles of her shoes. It was Grandmother who noticed her standing in a corner of the parlor, now crammed with injured men, pressing her fingers against her temples.

"Go upstairs and rest, child! There's enough help here."

Belle nodded gratefully, then a clatter of hooves outside drew her to the window. A courier jumped from his horse and pushed his way through the onlookers.

"More news?" someone asked.

The soldier shook his head. "A message for Miss Belle Boyd."

She opened the door, and the rider stepped inside. He handed her the note, grinned, gave a smart salute, and was back on his horse and riding away in a matter of seconds.

Headache forgotten, Belle unsealed the envelope and read the message.

*May 23, 1862*
*Miss Belle Boyd,*

*I thank you, for myself and for the army, for the immense service that you have rendered your country to-day.*

*Hastily, I am your friend,*
*T. J. Jackson, C.S.A.*

General Jackson must have written it right after the battle. With so many details surely clamoring for his attention, he had taken the time to sit down and write her a note. In his own handwriting. Belle pressed the paper over her heart and felt the beginnings of a warm glow that started beneath her hand and spread through her exhausted body.

Eliza came up to her room a short time later and found her sitting by her desk in a kind of daze, the letter held loosely in her lap. Eliza undressed her and put her to bed, pulling the covers up to her chin. Belle's eyes were already closed. In a few minutes, she was breathing deeply.

Eliza crossed to the desk and picked up the letter, read it, then put it back.

"She ain't never gone stop now."

# Chapter 25

T he morning after Belle received Jackson's note, she woke refreshed. She felt proud and happy remembering her courageous run, the cheering soldiers, Jackson's note of thanks, the knowledge that Papa was safe. Yet, she also recalled waking during the night to troubled thoughts. Why hadn't she felt any fear? How had she been able to run so far, so fast? It seemed—unnatural.

Like the shooting on the Fourth of July and the knife brawl in Centreville, Belle had felt something take possession of her. She didn't understand it. She didn't think she would ever understand. After a while, she sighed and pushed away the covers. No more dark thoughts! She was a heroine now. With a letter from Stonewall Jackson to prove it.

Alice tapped on the door, then bustled in.

"Good, you're up. There's so much news. First, all the wounded have been moved to a proper army hospital with a full staff. They don't need us anymore, which is a great relief to me and I'm sure to you too. You looked perfectly wretched yesterday before Grandmother sent you up to bed."

"Where is Jackson now? Does anyone know?"

"The word is that the Federals are retreating further north. Maybe they'll leave the Valley entirely. Jackson and his men are in hot pursuit. He left a regiment behind to defend the town."

"A few hundred men won't be enough to hold Front Royal. Not if the Yanks really mean to have it," Belle said.

Alice smiled at her cousin. "You're always a step ahead of everyone else, Belle."

"They could be back before we know it."

Alice sat on the bed. "There's one Federal under our roof right now, which is why I came to talk to you."

"Is he wounded?"

"Not wounded, and not a 'he' either," Alice said. "During the battle, General Ewell's men caught up with some Federals in a camp across the river. Mostly escaped slaves, non-combatants, and a few women. One of them is here. Her name is Mrs. Annie Jones. Apparently her husband is a cavalryman from Michigan, and she has no idea where he is. Anyway, the general didn't know what to do with her. So he sent her here. Technically she's a prisoner, but he's asked us to look after her."

"Well then, we'll follow the general's orders." Belle began dressing hurriedly. "I want to hear her story."

છ૭

"Here you are," Belle said, handing Mrs. Jones a neatly folded pile of clothing. "Dress, underthings, stockings, a shawl. I think everything will fit."

The woman from Michigan took the clothing but barely looked at it.

Belle frowned. She had picked out a dark green dress sprigged with white flowers. It was much nicer than what Mrs. Jones was currently wearing, an ugly maroon plaid much stained around the hem.

"Thank you."

Belle waited for more, but the woman just stood and looked at her. Finally, after a long silence, Belle said, "At some point I would like to hear your story, Mrs. Jones. How you were captured. How you come to be here with us. Under our roof."

Belle's bald hint to this woman that she was an unexpected and perhaps even unwelcome guest had no effect whatsoever. Mrs. Jones stood there with all the poise and grace of a butter churn, wearing her ugly dress, staring at Belle out of a pinched, unsmiling face. Apparently she was unwilling or unable to recognize the awkwardness of her position. Really, the woman was infuriating! Unsure what rude words might fly out of her own mouth if she stayed any longer, Belle accepted defeat and left.

She turned in the doorway and asked, "Would you like me to send Eliza to help you dress?"

"I can manage."

"Very well. I will leave you now."

Belle went into the parlor, looking for Alice, so she could give full expression to her feelings about Mrs. Annie Jones.

"How is our female prisoner?" asked Alice. "You look vexed."

This was just the opening Belle wanted. "Mrs. Jones is as cold a Yankee as I have ever met. I expected to feel a bond with her. A woman following her soldier husband into war and being trapped behind enemy lines. So daring and romantic. It was something I could imagine doing myself. At the very least, I felt she owed us an explanation of how she came to be stranded under such dramatic circumstances."

Belle had been pacing while she complained. Now she threw herself onto the sofa and punched one of the cushions.

"Had I known how difficult she was, I would not have given her the green dress. I'd have chosen the yellow one with the awkward mend at the elbow. All I wanted was a little bit of gratitude.

And to hear her story. I expected to find a kindred spirit."

Grandmother, who had followed Belle into the room and heard the end of her speech, said, "Perhaps she's embarrassed to accept charity from the enemy. She's in a difficult position."

"All the more reason to be pleasant!" Belle said. "Here she is sleeping under our roof, eating our food, wearing my clothes. Why she can't be bothered to make herself agreeable is more than I can understand."

"She is a bit odd," Alice said.

"I hope she won't be with us long."

"She won't," Grandmother said. "A captain has just informed me that the Union General Kimball will reach Front Royal in two days. There's not enough of our men here. They won't try to hold the town."

"So, another orderly retreat," Belle finished. "I'm sorry the Federals are coming back, but when Kimball gets here, at least Mrs. Jones will be released. That's something anyway. I find her most irritating."

❧

Three days later, General Kimball had still not arrived, but some newspapers had. Eager to see if there was mention of her recent heroism, Belle commandeered the papers and dragged Alice upstairs to their room so they could read them together. The stories about Belle's "Front Royal Dash" that appeared in the Southern papers were somewhat exaggerated but mostly accurate and, of course, highly flattering. The Southern papers had also reprinted reports from a few of the Northern journals. Some of these bordered on the ridiculous.

"This one says I directed the firing of our cannons during the battle. And here that I led the cavalry attack, riding across the field on my spirited steed while waving a sword! Really, it's too silly. The Northern papers will print anything. Truth or lies."

When Alice did not answer, Belle looked up. Her cousin was sitting quite still, cheeks pink, mouth open, apparently unable to speak.

"Oh dear. Let me see."

Alice handed Belle the paper and pointed to the article. It began with a detailed summary of Jackson's unexpected success in the battle. Belle scanned this part quickly. The second paragraph made her breath catch in her throat. She read it out loud, word by terrible word.

"'At the hotel in Front Royal, on the night of the 18th, your correspondent saw an accomplished prostitute who has figured largely in the rebel cause; and having seen her but a short time previously at Martinsburg, her presence in Front Royal, at a time when the rebels were surrounding it, induced suspicions that she meant mischief.'"

Belle could hardly take in the meaning of the words.

*Accomplished prostitute!*

Was he talking about her? Fighting for calm, she read on.

"'It is now known that Belle Boyd was the bearer of an extensive correspondence between the rebels, inside and outside of our lines, and regularly received messages from other Confederate sympathizers in Winchester. She has been questioned by the military authorities more than once, but, with her usual adroitness and assumed innocence, she has always avoided being formally charged with treachery . . .'"

"Do you see?" Alice asked tearfully. "Some of it is true. You *have* received messages from Winchester. You *have* been questioned."

"They've mixed facts with lies, so what is only partly true will seem entirely so."

Belle turned back to the story, the pages trembling in her hands.

"'Your correspondent cannot vouch for the strict accuracy of all the foregoing—but undeniable proof exists here of her treason.'"

Belle gave a harsh laugh. "The so-called 'correspondent' is a coward. He won't stand behind his words but says them just the same! Puts them down in black and white for everyone to see."

Everyone. Not just here in Front Royal, but at home in Martinsburg. Belle imagined Mama and Mary sitting in the parlor and reading these words. She thought of them going out and being snubbed. Or having to endure people whispering behind their backs. Once again, Belle had hurt them. She closed her eyes and shook her head.

Belle was torn between anger and shame. Anger at the lies that had been printed about her. Shame because she knew the lies would be believed. Her heroic dash to alert the Southern troops, the cheering of the soldiers and later the townspeople, a personal note from Stonewall Jackson, all of it had been tainted by two words—*accomplished prostitute.*

Dinner that night was a sad affair, food untouched, barely a word from Alice or Grandmother. Mrs. Annie Jones said little as usual, though she ate with a hearty appetite.

Belle went to her room early, endured a silent hair brushing from Eliza, then climbed into bed. She stared into the darkness, wanting more than anything to talk to her mother, to beg forgiveness, to try and explain. Her last clear thought, before falling into a fitful sleep, was a wish that tomorrow would be a better day.

It was worse.

❧

The next morning, Belle left the cottage immediately after breakfast and went for a long walk. She felt she would go mad if she had to be inside a moment longer—with Grandmother's disapproving silences, Eliza's frowns, Alice's worried looks. And it wasn't just them. Belle herself was agitated. That newspaper story was quite unfair! And she'd felt so proud of helping Stonewall.

Realizing her ramble was doing nothing to calm her feelings, after a few miles, Belle turned and headed back to the hotel. She walked with her head bowed, unaware of her surroundings, until she looked up and saw Union soldiers in the distance marching into town.

Belle sighed wearily. *It must be General Kimball, the only Union leader to defeat Stonewall Jackson. But at least we shall soon be rid of Mrs. Annie Jones! That's something anyway.*

When Belle reached the hotel, she found that the Federals had already taken it over. She and Alice would be run off their feet for the rest of the day—helping make beds, find clean towels, carry pitchers of fresh water for washing. Grandmother would take care of talking to Lucy in the kitchen about feeding them all. At least Belle would be busy. That might keep her from brooding.

Belle opened the door and walked into the cottage's tiny parlor, surprised to find a young Union officer sitting there, talking to Grandmother. He had removed his hat and gloves and placed them on his knee, so at least he had decent manners. But Grandmother's expression told Belle that something was wrong. As soon as he saw Belle, the officer jumped to his feet, his hat tumbling to the floor.

In his confusion, he saluted Belle, then turned red and began with a stammer. "It is my d-d-duty to inf-f-form you, Miss Boyd, that you are u-u-under house arrest. Orders of General Kimball. You are to remain on the premises at all times. Either the cottage or the hotel. A guard has been posted to observe your movements when you pass through the yard from one building to the other."

Belle was not surprised. It was partly because of her that the Federals had missed their chance to corner Jackson. However, the officer's next words came as a shock. He had noticed Belle looking out the window at the crowd gathered in the yard. Mrs. Annie Jones was there, talking with a Union officer. She was waving her hands about with a level of animation that Belle had not seen from her before.

"That woman denounced you. As a dangerous rebel and an enemy to the Federal Government."

"That woman is wearing my dress!"

"I don't know anything about that, miss. Only that I am to arrest you and post sentries outside." The young lieutenant scratched his head. "You were probably going to be arrested anyway, Miss Boyd. Everyone knows what you did for Stonewall."

&

After a few days of house arrest, Belle's old friend General Shields arrived. The general had a great fondness for Belle due to the tender attention, not to mention the whiskey and cigars, she had lavished on him when he was nursing a broken arm.

In the Union hierarchy, he was senior to General Kimball and immediately ordered Belle's release. However, General Shields' time in Front Royal was short-lived. Several days later, he received orders to leave the town. He was soon followed by a third general, Nathaniel Banks.

"What a lot of generals coming and going!" Alice remarked one evening as the two cousins got ready to go out.

Now that General Shields had released Belle, she was free to go where she pleased. Once again, she was a popular guest. Her Confederate friends had chosen not to believe the papers and their scandalous remarks. They knew better. Belle was wild, headstrong, but a *prostitute*? Ridiculous! If anything, the outlandish accusation reprinted from a Yankee newspaper had made the townspeople more indulgent of Belle. Even protective.

This newest crop of Union officers, members of General Banks' staff, all wanted to meet the famously charming Miss Belle Boyd. One of her most ardent admirers was Major Arthur Maginnis, the Union Army's provost in Front Royal. His main duty was to act as a kind of military policeman of the town. In addition, he supplied safe conduct papers to parolees and issued travel passes.

He also employed a number of spies. Or so Belle believed. She had noticed certain characters hanging about the major's large tent, which nearly filled the yard between the cottage and the hotel. The men she noticed weren't soldiers. She was sure of that. From their lounging posture and civilian dress, she guessed they were agents of the new Union Intelligence Service, run by Allan Pinkerton. It was rumored that Mr. Pinkerton reported directly to Edwin Stanton, Lincoln's Secretary of War.

ल

A few days after Stonewall's victory at Port Republic on June 9, as Belle sat in her customary observation post by the window, she saw a different kind of person near the provost's tent. A tall man with admirable posture and a well-trimmed beard, he did credit to his Confederate uniform. There was no insignia to give his rank. A parolee? Eager to meet this stranger, Belle sallied forth to introduce herself.

When the soldier heard Belle's name, he bowed and said, "C.W.D. Smitley, at your service, Miss Boyd."

"May I ask your business with the provost?"

"I was captured at Port Republic, and I've been paroled to Richmond. Of course, I had to promise not to re-enlist when I get there. With any luck I'll have my pass by tomorrow."

"I hope you get your pass, but not too soon."

Belle stressed the last two words with a smile and a flirtatious tilt of her head. She was being much too forward, but she didn't care. She liked the look of this stranger. Very much.

"If you have time before you leave, would you care to accompany me and my cousin to a small dinner party this evening? It's at the home of a Confederate friend. You would be most welcome."

"That would give me great pleasure," came the reply, along with a smile that revealed straight white teeth between rosy lips.

"Until this evening, then," Belle said. She returned, humming, to the cottage.

∾

"You invited a stranger to dinner?" Alice asked when Belle told her. "That was bold."

"Not a stranger. A handsome Confederate soldier."

"Whom you did not even know existed when you woke up this morning."

"Oh pish! Rules aren't as strict as they were before the war, Alice. Anyway, it's not like you to be such a stick in the mud."

So it was that Belle, Alice, and Mr. Smitley passed a pleasant evening at the home of Mr. and Mrs. Sherwood. After dinner, other guests arrived, including a group of local girls. Though they were all loyal Confederates, each was escorted by a Union officer. These were the only men available, saving those who claimed they favored the South yet refused to fight. These young women preferred to be escorted by a brave foe than a cowardly friend.

The crush of guests was due entirely to Belle. She reigned supreme, telling stories and playing the piano. When she struck the first chords of the popular new song *Aura Lee,* she smiled and nodded at Mr. Smitley, inviting him to accompany her. Their voices blended well together, earning them a round of applause.

After this triumphant evening, Belle regarded Mr. Smitley with special favor. For some reason, his travel papers kept being delayed, but he didn't seem to mind. In fact, he appeared in no hurry whatever to leave for Richmond.

ल

One morning as she helped Belle dress, Eliza said, "Us'ally it just takes a coupla days to get travelin' papers. You don't think it's s'picious this Smitley's been waitin' almost a month? Why you think that is?"

Belle chose to think it was because of her, but she said nothing.

"I don't trust him. Just 'cause he wears gray, that don't make him a Rebel. I seen him talkin' with Yankees in the street, Miss Belle. Handsome or not, that man's a spy. I guarantees it."

"He's nothing of the sort!" Belle said hotly. "Anyway, I've just given him a letter to carry to Stonewall, for when he does get to Richmond. I wish to tell the general how I am faring after our shared victory. And to report on developments here. I'm sure he'll be interested in knowing what the Yankees are up to."

Eliza shook her head. "You shoulda axed me first. You make

fun when a man trusts you just 'cause you's pretty. Well you's exackly the same. You never think poorly of a nice lookin' man."

With a pang, Belle realized that what Eliza said was true. Belle knew nothing about Smitley. She began to grow uneasy.

A few hours later, Mr. Smitley knocked on the door of the cottage and told Belle his papers had come through. He would leave for Richmond that very day. Belle asked him to walk with her.

As they strolled down Main Street, she leaned her head toward his and whispered, "They say you're a spy, but I do not believe it."

Smitley stopped walking. "A spy!" He seemed amused. "I am what you see. A poor soldier trying to get to Richmond. Where I'll do all I can in the cause of justice."

"I believe you," Belle said as they began walking again. "It's just that there are stories going around. About why a parolee would have to wait so many weeks for a pass."

"That I couldn't say. You must ask your friend Major Maginnis, whom I've found to be a very nice fellow. Except for the business with the pass." He leaned closer. *That smile again!* "But waiting has allowed me to know you better. May I write to you, Miss Boyd?"

"Of course. But the letter I gave you. The one to General Jackson. Will you promise faithfully to deliver it to him? And no one else?" She paused. "Otherwise I shall have to ask for it back."

Smitley's face darkened into a scowl. It disappeared in less than a moment, but Belle was afraid she had offended him.

"You have my word, Miss Boyd, that I will deliver your letter where it should go. On my honor as a soldier." Later, Belle would remember his choice of words.

"Very well, then."

They turned back toward the cottage, talking of this and that, the way couples do when they are about to say good-bye and know they will not meet again. At the door of the cottage, Smitley turned and took her hands in his.

"Good luck, Miss Boyd. May your future be as bright as you deserve."

Ɛͻ

That evening, Belle and Alice attended another party, the previous one having been such a success. This gathering was less so. Belle missed her gallant Smitley. In his absence, a Union officer, aide to General Schenck, and a former favorite of Belle's, followed her about like a lost puppy. Finally she led him into the front hall, where she told him gently but firmly that his attentions were no longer welcome.

The officer's response amazed her. Slapping his hand against the wall to prevent her from moving away, he asked, "Have you heard from Officer Smitley?"

"I fail to see how that it is any of your business."

"You fail to see a lot of things, Miss Boyd." Said with a sneering curl of the lips. "Smitley is a Union agent. Hired by General Schenck to trap you. He's got your letter to Jackson. He's taking it to Secretary Stanton. You're so clever you've been caught communicating with the enemy."

# Chapter 26

Eliza suddenly came awake, without knowing why. Usually she was a sound sleeper, even in the hotel attic, which was still strange to her. She lay on her straw pallet, her eyes wide open, and listened. All she could hear was the soft breathing of a half-dozen sleeping women. The laundry girls, Susan, Pearl, and Esther. Lucy, the cook, and Nettie, her daughter and helper.

A slight movement drew Eliza's eyes to one end of the attic, where she saw Belle standing in her fine gown, its hem dragging on the floor. She must have taken off her shoes to climb the steep ladder. Eliza was not surprised to see her. Not really. This was about Smitley. It had to be. Belle had gone all swoony for him, and now something had gone wrong. So here she was. Coming to her trusty Eliza. Expecting her to help. Same as always.

Eliza gave a deep sigh, stood up, pushed her feet into her broken-down men's shoes, and followed her mistress down the ladder.

When they reached the kitchen, Belle turned and grabbed her arm. "You were right!" she wailed. "Smitley's a spy. I should have listened. All the things he said about his honor as a soldier. All lies! He beat me at my own game."

Eliza poured a glass of water and handed it to her.

"Sit down and drink this."

Belle sat. "I've been trying to remember his exact words. I

realize now that he never quite lied about being a spy. He chose his words so carefully that I could believe whatever I wanted." She pounded her fist on the table. "I let myself care for him! How could I have been such a fool?"

"What d'you want me to do?"

Eliza's practical words seemed to steady Belle, as she knew they would.

After a moment Belle said, "I'll write a note describing Smitley. Maybe they can get word to all the Confederate sentries, stop him before he gets too far. I want you to find that old man, the one who carries messages in his broken pocket watch."

Without being asked, Eliza lit a lantern, fetched paper and pen and ink, then left to find the old man. As she walked out the kitchen door, she looked back and saw Belle at the table writing in a circle of lamplight.

Eliza shook her head, thinking of the old man with the pocket watch. In her mind's eye, she saw him slowly creeping through the dark. Then she imagined Smitley's long strides eating up the miles. They would never catch him. *She's in so much trouble now, can't no one help her.*

*Front Royal, Virginia*
*Union Controlled*
*Middle to Late July 1862*

# Chapter 27

Next morning, Belle chose a plain gray dress with a high collar, not at all the sort of thing she usually wore. She and Eliza did not exchange a word while she dressed. Alice, arranging her hair in front of the mirror, watched them anxiously. She knew Belle had left the party early, but her cousin had refused to say why.

"What's happening, Belle? Are you ill?" After asking twice and getting no answer, Alice said somewhat sharply, "I'm going down to breakfast. Are you coming?"

Belle shook her head, then said quietly, "Cousin?" Alice turned in the doorway. "No matter what happens, you must stay calm."

Alice's eyes grew wide. She opened her mouth as if to speak, then closed it. Finally, she took a deep breath, and with one last look at Belle, left the room

Belle sent Eliza after her. "Please tell Grandmother I have a headache. I'll be down shortly."

Alone now, Belle waited in her room, her head cocked to one side, listening for the sound of knocking at the front door. When it came, she heard Eliza answer, then a murmur of voices and Eliza's heavy footsteps on the stairs.

"That Union major, Maginnis is axin' you to attend him in the parlor."

When Belle walked into the drawing room, the major stood and gave her a tight smile.

"Please sit, Miss Boyd," he said formally, pulling out a chair.

Belle sank into it, her knees suddenly loose, like an unstrung marionette.

"You've been up to your old tricks, haven't you?"

Maginnis spoke in a kindly tone, like an uncle, even though he was not much older than Belle herself. "As I think you know by now, Officer Smitley is a Yankee. Like me. Not a Confederate soldier. Nor a parolee. You do know what the word *parolee* means, do you not?"

Belle nodded.

"Actually, Miss Boyd, from your actions, I'm not sure you understand the term at all. A parolee is an enemy prisoner who is released after giving a promise not to engage in any future hostile behavior. Whether it be fighting or smuggling—or spying." He cleared his throat. "*You* are a parolee. Allowed to stay with your grandmother and go about town as you please. On condition that you do not pass information to the enemy. If it had been up to General Kimball, you would have remained under house arrest after you gave so much help to Stonewall Jackson. It was your friend General Shields who ordered him to release you. But General Shields can't protect you indefinitely. I suspect he's in hot water at the moment, after what you've done. Writing to Jackson, indeed!"

*There is no point denying it.*

"The letter contained no secrets. It was just a note to a friend."

"You mean a note to the commander of an enemy army."

Belle bowed her head.

"I must ask you a question. Look at me please." Maginnis waited for her to raise her eyes. "How long do you expect to be indulged?" For once Belle had nothing to say. "Your activities have come to the attention of the War Department."

*The War Department! That's who arrested Rose.*

"How do you think Secretary Stanton feels about what you've been up to?" He leaned forward. "A friend of your father's, Ward Hill Lamon, is close to President Lincoln. A member of his staff. They see each other daily. He has spoken several times to the President on your behalf. Did you know that?" Belle shook her head. "I thought not. All this time you've been skating on thin ice. If you continue this way, eventually you will do something that will result in your arrest. You may have done so already."

"Where?" she whispered.

"Pardon?"

"Where will I be sent? If I'm arrested."

"Most likely it will be Old Capitol Prison in Washington D.C. The same as Mrs. Greenhow. Although she herself has now been paroled. Exiled to Richmond. It seems her imprisonment with her young daughter created too much sympathy for the Confederate cause. So now she is banished."

Head bowed again, Belle waited for the rest.

After a pause, he continued. "However . . ."

It was not the word, but the change in the major's voice that made Belle look up.

"However," he repeated, "after careful thought, I've decided to send you to Richmond as well."

*Is this another Yankee trick?*

In a voice whose evenness surprised her, Belle asked, "Do you have that authority?"

"As provost, I may do as I see fit."

*He's letting me go!*

"I will write out your papers and give you an escort. Be ready to leave in two weeks. I don't think Secretary Stanton will act before then. It seems, after what happened with Rose Greenhow, President Lincoln is reluctant to imprison women. It's too easy for the newspapers to turn them into heroines."

&

"I don't understand," Grandmother protested. "You're leaving? Just like that?"

Alice stood in the corner of the parlor, one hand pressed to her lips. Seeing her cousin so overcome filled Belle with resolve. She would take control of her future as best she could. If there was still time.

"I'm afraid I have been somewhat indiscreet, Grandmother. I gave a letter to Mr. Smitley that has fallen into the wrong hands. Major Maginnis advises me to proceed to Richmond. He will give me a safe-conduct."

That was all she was willing to say.

"What shall I tell your mother?"

"It was always her plan that I travel to Richmond. Now I will do so."

Strange how the right words, said in the right way, could shape events, change them from one thing into another. Belle no longer felt like she was clutching the reins of a runaway horse, in danger of being thrown from the saddle. Instead, she rode in perfect safety, at a reasonable speed, on a horse that obeyed her every command. Once more she was in control of her destiny. Or so she hoped.

&

Days of sorting, washing, packing followed. Belle had lost track of the number of times this scene had been played out. Helping

Papa get ready to join Jackson's regiment; helping the Stewarts pack up their household; packing her own things for seemingly endless trips back and forth between Martinsburg and Front Royal. It made her tired just to think of it.

"Mama and Papa and Franny are outside Richmond." Alice spoke from her seat by the window, where she was mending one of Belle's stockings. "Maybe you can visit them. I wish I could go with you."

"I wish it too. With all my heart!"

"I shall miss you. Grandmother says life is never dull when you're around."

"Perhaps a little dullness might be a welcome change."

Alice was about to answer when noises on the street made her turn and look outside. "Something's going on. The street is full of soldiers. A whole troop of cavalry."

Belle came to stand beside her. "I wonder if it's a scouting party. Major Gilmore has a small Rebel force not far away. I should write to him."

As she turned toward her desk, Alice laid a hand on her arm. "Don't, Belle. This is what's gotten you into so much trouble. You must stop!"

Eliza had appeared behind them. "Try and talk some sense to her, Miss Alice."

Belle turned back to the window. "Very well. That's interesting though. There's a carriage parked out front with no one in it. I wonder who it's for."

There was a knock at the front door. A loud, official sort of knock. Eliza left to answer it while Belle and Alice looked at each other. They heard the sound of the door opening, then Grandmother's voice demanding, "What is the meaning of this?"

Eliza stomped back up the stairs and stuck her head into the room. "The provo', Major Maginnis, wants to see you in the drawing room right away. There's two men with him I don't reckanize."

☙

Walking into the parlor, Belle remembered her last talk with the major. Two weeks earlier, he had been stern but kind. Now the atmosphere in the room was different. The major seemed nervous. There were two men with him, as Eliza had said. One introduced himself as Major Francis Sherman, clearly a gentleman. The other was an individual Belle identified immediately as one of those rough sorts she saw coming and going from the provost's tent all day long. The type of person who would do anything for money. In other words, one of Stanton's spies. His name was Detective Cridge.

His face reddening slightly, Major Maginnis said, "Miss Boyd, I am afraid Major Sherman has orders to arrest you."

Belle felt a wave of dizziness. *If only I had left yesterday!*

Major Sherman stepped forward. "I can assure you this gives me no pleasure, Miss Boyd. However, I have no choice but to execute Secretary Stanton's orders."

*What difference do his regrets make? He has to obey. And so do I.*

Major Maginnis opened the door into the hall, then turned away in embarrassment when he saw Grandmother, Alice, and Eliza huddled outside.

"What is it? Tell me what's happening!" Grandmother's usually commanding tones were suddenly reduced to the feeble fretting of an old woman.

Whenever Belle saw others being weak, it gave her strength. She kept her voice steady as she said, "It seems Secretary Stanton has ordered my arrest."

She felt an unexpected flush of pride as she spoke. She had been brought to the attention of the Secretary of War, who saw her as a serious enough threat that he wanted to lock her away.

*Very well then!* She would bravely follow in the footsteps of Rose Greenhow.

When Grandmother and Alice cried out and reached for Belle, the slouching detective stepped between them and spoke for the first time.

"There's no time for that. Go to your room and pack."

Belle's resolve nearly crumbled when Detective Cridge followed her up the stairs. She tried to keep him from entering her bedroom, but he pushed past her, saying, "I got orders to conduct a search!" and began to yank her dresses out of the trunks Eliza had packed so carefully. He shook each dress, turned it inside out to examine the seams and stitching, tossed it aside, and grabbed the next one. Belle watched in horror as he moved on to her petticoats. Then her most intimate undergarments. Next her shoes, shawls, purses, bonnets, gloves. Until every pretty thing she owned lay heaped on the floor at his feet.

Striding to the door, not caring where he set his filthy boots, he snarled, "You have half an hour. One small trunk." He looked around the room a final time. "You won't need all this fancy stuff where you're goin'."

They worked quickly this time, Eliza handing Belle her plainest dresses, everything in sturdy fabrics and dark colors. Serviceable clothes that wouldn't show the dirt. Clothes that would last. Who knew how long Belle would be in prison?

"I don't think I need this third shawl. It's summer," Belle protested, handing it back.

"Best be safe than sorry. Won't be summer forever."

"Oh Eliza!"

Belle turned to her, clinging tightly for a moment. Eliza patted her back.

"I guess you'll be fine. You're foolish a lotta the time, but you're stubborn as all get out." Then, picking up Belle's travel cloak, she added, "There's some of us has been livin' our whole lives without freedom."

Belle barely registered what Eliza said, though she would have reason to remember it later.

Walking down the stairs, Belle's legs felt like they belonged to someone else. She held tightly onto Eliza's arm on one side and the railing on the other, and she took careful steps. Everyone was standing in the hall below, looking up at her. Two blue-clad officers, the scowling detective, the pale upturned faces of Grandmother and Alice.

Belle had to say her good-byes under the detective's watchful eye. Alice wept, but Grandmother had regained her composure. Belle too managed to stay calm. She would not give that odious creature the satisfaction of showing how frightened she was.

"I will write to your mother right away," Grandmother said. "She mustn't learn of this from the newspapers."

"And you'll write to me, won't you? Both of you? Every day?" Belle turned to Detective Cridge. "I will be able to receive mail, won't I?"

He nodded curtly. "It will be opened, of course."

Belle took a deep breath. "I'm ready."

*Washington D.C.*
*Union Controlled*
*July 29, 1862*

# Chapter 28

It was a two-day journey to the Federal Capital. First a closed carriage from Front Royal, the stuffiness of the small space made worse by the forced proximity of the repellant detective. Belle could hardly stand it. Then a night spent on a general's cot in a tent at a Union camp near Winchester. Finally a train to the Capital. And prison.

Belle arrived in the station at five in the evening. As she stepped from the train, her arm tightly gripped by the detective, a small cheer went up, along with cries of, "There she is. Belle Boyd, our favorite rebel!" Her spirits lifted immediately. It seemed that word of her arrest had reached the Capital by telegraph, and a small crowd had gathered to greet her. Once again, Belle was news.

An unfamiliar voice hissed in her ear, "Come on. I'll attend to you," as a different hand grabbed her and yanked her away from Cridge. She noticed her supporters staring in shock as she was pulled between the two men like a rag doll.

She would soon learn that this second man was Lafayette Baker, Chief Detective of Lincoln's Secret Service. For now he was yet another unknown enemy, pulling her through the crowd and bundling her into a carriage. The driver took off at speed, and before long, Belle saw her future home looming in the distance. A dark, brooding red brick building with tall windows, the Old Capitol

Prison lived up to its fearsome reputation.

Belle was an admirer of the writer Charles Dickens, and the menacing title "prison superintendent" could not help but conjure up villainous images. Mr. Wood, however, was not at all what she expected. His manner was almost welcoming as he greeted her in the prison's arched doorway.

"Miss Boyd. Now that Mrs. Greenhow has left us, you will replace her as our most famous resident." He rubbed his hands together and continued in a hearty voice. "Unlike our former guest, I plan to make you as comfortable as I can. Whatever you wish, you must ask for it."

Belle was too confused to speak. *The man acts like he's running a hotel rather than a prison!* Without another word, the superintendent led her across a dusty courtyard, through a dimly lit hall, up a flight of stairs, and finally down a short passage.

"Here we are," he said when they had reached a closed door on which NUMBER 6 appeared in flaking paint.

Nodding at the sentry who stood nearby, Mr. Wood pushed the door open. Belle walked in and saw her new home. Number 6. Her small trunk had been placed at the foot of the bed. It pained her to see it there. *Her* things in *this* place made imprisonment seem all too real.

Mr. Wood gestured at the room and said, "During the War of 1812, Congress met in this building, which is why it's known as the Old Capitol. Since that time, it's been a school and then a boarding house. For a long while it stood empty. Now we've added bars, and it's become a jail."

When Belle gave no reply, he rubbed his hands together again, saying, "We've given you our best room. I'm sure you want to get settled. I'll send a servant to help you unpack. Whenever you need her, just ask the sentry."

Belle gazed about, only half listening. Mr. Wood cleared his throat to get her attention. "There is to be no communication between you and the other prisoners," he said. "If you obey that rule, your door will stay unlocked."

After he left, Belle stood in the middle of the small room, afraid to move. She had heard stories about Old Capitol Prison, as this was a place where spies were often sent. She had been told about its filthy, crowded cells and bug-infested bedding, its half-rotted food and bullying guards. Perhaps that's what the rest of the jail was like.

She walked over to the iron bedstead and gingerly pulled back a sheet, then lifted the pillow. The bed linens were coarse homespun but seemed clean enough. When she sniffed the sheets, she could smell soap. A good beginning, at least! She sat on the edge of the bed and took an inventory of the room. A washstand with bowl, pitcher and rough cotton towel; a mirror; table; two chairs; the bed she sat on. Also a fireplace on one wall and two barred windows on another. Checking under the bed, she spied the chamber pot.

Belle was tempted to ask the sentry if she could speak with Mr. Wood. She wanted to know why she was being treated so well. She was determined to suffer the same privations as Rose Greenhow, who had been fed a starvation diet and kept under lock and key. Why wasn't Belle being treated as badly? Wasn't she as important as Rose?

After further thought, she decided on a different strategy. The superintendent had said to ask for anything she wanted. Very well then! Belle would wear him down with her demands. Perhaps then he would decide to punish her properly.

"Guard!" she called. "Guard!" When he appeared, she said, "Tell the superintendent I require a rocking chair and a fire. The room is much too gloomy."

The chair arrived promptly, and soon a black woman came to lay a fire and light it. Belle asked her name. She would need a friend here.

"Mary Deane," the woman said, standing up from the fireplace. "Do you wish anything further?"

Mary stood very erect and had a dignified way of speaking that Belle suspected was meant to let the listener know she was not a slave. She must have escaped from somewhere, then joined herself to the Union cause. The Federals called these free people "intelligent contrabands." Belle had heard of them but had never met one.

"My name is Belle Boyd."

"I know who you are. Call the sentry when you need me."

Mary went out and closed the door, leaving a chill behind her, despite the room's crackling fire. Belle sank into the rocker and buried her face in her hands.

*Eliza!*

જી

Toward evening, Belle heard a whispered conversation in the hall, her guard asking, "What's all this? I heard she was gettin' bread and water."

Mary's calm voice replied, "Bread and water is what Secretary Stanton ordered, but Mr. Wood said I should bring this. Guess he has his reasons."

"He just wants to avoid trouble. The newspapers raised a ruckus over how that other one was treated. That Rose who had the little girl with her."

The guard opened the door for Mary, who came in and set a tray on the table. She turned to Belle and recited, "Soup. And beef. Only sometimes it's chicken. Boiled corn. Tomatoes. Bread and butter. Melon. Sometimes it's apples or grapes. It's pretty much the same every day. But there's only apples come winter."

Winter! Belle could hardly bear to consider this room in winter.

Still, it was best to be prepared. She was determined to make this woman a friend. She would start by using her name.

"Please tell me, Mary. How am I supposed to eat all this food?"

The woman shrugged, "Eat it or not. Doesn't matter to me." On her way out the door, she spoke over her shoulder, "My name is Mary Deane."

With her effort at friendship firmly rejected, Belle sat and picked at her dinner. An hour later, Mary Deane returned and removed the tray, and then Mr. Wood arrived, along with Mr. Baker. When Belle saw the chief detective, her hand involuntarily began to stroke her upper arm where he had grabbed her at the station.

It seemed that Mr. Baker was in charge of the interview. He was a Yankee—from New York, Belle guessed when she heard him speak. At any rate, he wasted no time in preliminaries.

"Mr. Stanton wishes me to welcome you to Old Capitol Prison." Here he gave a sneering smile and looked around the room. "We don't like keeping a woman in prison. So I've come to hear your confession. You might as well admit what you've done, as we've got plenty of proof already."

Belle's Front Royal uncle, James Stewart, had trained as a lawyer, and she had learned a thing or two from him.

"I have nothing to say. When you give me a copy of the charges against me, I will make my statement."

"You must at least take the Oath of Allegiance. Remember, Mr. Stanton will hear of this."

Belle drew herself up to her full height. She dearly hoped that what she was about to say would be repeated to Mr. Stanton. Word for word!

"If it is a crime to love the South, its cause, and its president, then I am a criminal. Do with me as you please. I would rather die in this prison than leave it owing allegiance to such a government as yours."

Belle had a strong voice, and when she had finished her speech, she heard faint cheers. Until that moment she hadn't known the rooms near hers were occupied. Baker looked regretfully at the door which he had left open because of the overheated room. Belle was glad she had asked for a fire and even gladder she had been overheard. Clearly this interview was not going the way the detective intended.

In the end, it was Mr. Wood who took charge. "The lady is tired," he announced abruptly and pulled Mr. Baker from the room.

When she was alone once more, Belle dragged a chair over to the open door. The room really was most dreadfully warm. She smiled to herself, pleased with the results of her interview. It could not have gone better! Sitting there, basking in her success, she heard a quiet cough and looked up. The door almost opposite was slightly ajar. She could see no one, but a small round object was rolling across the floor toward her. Instinctively, she checked that the sentry's back was turned, and when the ball reached her doorway, she placed her foot on top of it. When she checked again, the guard was facing her, so she waited for him to turn away before picking up the ball.

Someone had painstakingly carved a peach pit into a basket and decorated it with a tiny Confederate flag. Such a cheerful little thing, clearly created to while away the long prison hours. A scrap of paper was wrapped around the basket and tied with thread. It bore a short note. "Bravo Belle. Welcome!"

When she looked up, she was disappointed to see that the door across the hallway was now closed. Still, she was comforted by her first contact with a fellow prisoner. It helped keep her spirits steady as she prepared for bed, managing without the help of the icy Mary Deane.

The night seemed endless. Belle had never felt so alone. Unable to bear the sight of the cheerless room, she rolled over and faced the wall, but this was worse. The stained and crumbling plaster was just inches from her face. She closed her eyes to shut it out. Her head ached. The sheets scratched. The blanket had a bad smell.

*Belle Boyd, don't you dare cry!*

℘

Life quickly settled into a routine, with Superintendent Wood indulging all of Belle's requests for extra comforts. Her recent arrest had revived the public's interest in her, and reporters came to interview her several times a week. Now that she was safely behind bars, she was no longer referred to as a prostitute. These days she was written about in more sympathetic terms, as being blindly devoted to the Confederate cause without having "lost the crowning virtue of a woman."

*That should comfort Mama,* Belle thought, but an instant later she dropped the newspaper into her lap. Mama! Belle had written her just one short note to tell of her arrival, and nothing since. It had been ten days. She wasn't sure why she couldn't bring herself to write. Today she would try again. She called to the sentry to call for Mary Deane to remove the breakfast tray from the table. How she missed the convenience of a desk!

Before she began writing, Belle took a moment to admire her stationery. She wrote many letters and prided herself on the quality of her note paper. Someday she intended to have engraved stationery. Perhaps she should ask Mr. Wood to have some made for her, as if the prison truly were a fine hotel. At the top it could read *Old Capitol Prison, Room Number 6.* She smiled at the notion and decided to use it to begin her letter.

*Dear Mama,*

*I write to you from Room 6 of Old Capitol Prison. Despite its reputation as being poorly run, my room here is not unpleasant. Mr. Wood, the hotel manager, seems anxious that I be comfortable, and I have no cause for complaint. As you know, until recently I was in the hotel business myself and can appreciate a well-run establishment. The food is plain but nourishing, and there is plenty of it.*

*Word that I am lodging here has reached friendly ears. Every day I receive gifts from Southern supporters, including such luxuries as ripe peaches, newspapers, and magazines. I have even received money! I do not need it at the moment but save it for the proverbial rainy day.*

*I send you my love and hope you and Mary and Will are well. I am getting your letters. Please do continue to write. Sometimes my spirits are low. I will write Papa and Grandmother separately, but please tell them that I am well.*

*I remain as ever,*
*Your Belle*

*P.S. I hear you have not received permission to visit. Mr. Wood is not the friend he pretends to be!*

As usual Belle put the best possible face on things. Mr. Wood treated her reasonably well, and when she talked to reporters, she claimed to be content. She told them her schedule. She breakfasted at nine, then read her newspapers and opened her mail. In the afternoon, she wrote letters and looked through her magazines. After dinner, she liked to stand in the doorway of her room and sing for the prisoners. The chaplain had told her this cheered them immensely. She knew these newspaper interviews were read by Mr.

Wood, Mr. Baker, and Mr. Stanton. She would not give them the satisfaction of knowing they were wearing down her spirit.

The truth was she felt weary to the bone. Except for singing in the evening, which she did as much for herself as for the other prisoners, and pacing her cell, she did nothing but sit all day. Being locked inside made her want to weep. She, who needed the outdoors more than anyone! It was torture not to be able to ride. Or go for a long walk, striding across open country. Never to take a breath of fresh air. Never to look up and see the stars. Or feel the rain against her cheek.

Sometimes, when Belle sat listlessly in her rocking chair staring into space, she found herself recalling Eliza's parting words. *There's some of us has been livin' our whole lives without freedom.*

# Chapter 29

A month after her arrival at Old Capitol Prison, when Belle was beginning to think that confinement indoors and lack of exercise would drive her mad, Mr. Wood announced she was to be included in a prisoner exchange.

"Two hundred Rebels for two hundred Federals." He rubbed his hands together, something Belle had noticed he did when pleased. "It will help ease the overcrowded conditions on both sides."

"I am being released?"

"Paroled," Mr. Wood corrected her. "The usual terms. You must give a promise of good behavior. Will you do that?"

Belle nodded. She would promise anything to be free of this dreary place. She glanced at her barred windows. How many hours had she spent staring at the people coming and going on the streets below? It was hard to believe she would soon be free again.

"Where will I be sent?"

"Richmond."

Belle's heart leapt at the thought of seeing Uncle James, Aunt Fannie, and Franny, then sank when she remembered they had moved further south, to Atlanta.

"You'll travel by ship. The *Juniata,*" Mr. Woods was saying. "A river steamer. It will sail south along the coast, then up the James River to Richmond."

❧

The following day, Belle joined the stream of prisoners who were hustled out to the street, where carriages waited to deliver them to the riverside. The prisoner exchange had been announced in the papers, and Belle expected a large crowd, so she put on her one good traveling dress. A gown of dark brown broadcloth with a fitted jacket trimmed in black, and a matching hat. *I will use the money I've been given to buy new things when I get to Richmond. People there will want to see me looking my best.*

She stepped through the doorway of the prison, then stopped to look around, not at the cheering people, but at the trees and the wide arching sky. She took a deep breath of fresh air, then smiled, waved at the crowd, and climbed into the waiting carriage.

❧

That night, the *Juniata* dropped anchor at the mouth of the Potomac River, the captain having evidently decided it was wiser to complete the journey in daylight when the ship's white flag of truce would be visible. Though still technically prisoners, the two hundred men on board were nearly drunk with the prospect of freedom. They spent the night waving Rebel flags out the windows, singing boisterously, and cheering Jeff Davis. Belle circulated among them, flirting continuously and singing when asked. After she retired to her stateroom, she barely slept, but not because of the commotion.

The sudden change in her circumstances, the uncertainty regarding her future, even traveling on a boat for the first time, all gave an air of unreality to her situation. Belle felt unmoored. At eighteen, she was adrift in a hostile world cut off from family and friends. Forbidden to return home. With no one to guide her, no one who truly knew her or cared what happened to her. Again and again, her thoughts returned to Eliza. Her anchor.

જી

The next morning, when the *Juniata* reached Richmond, Belle was escorted to the elegant Ballard House, only to discover that Mrs. Greenhow was also a guest. The older woman's greeting to Belle could not have been more gracious.

"When I heard you were coming to join me, I was so pleased. I'm very happy to finally meet you, my dear. It seems you and I have much in common."

All day long, the two ladies received visitors in the hotel lobby, seated side by side on the same plum colored settee. Throughout the day and evening, Belle felt like she was living in a dream. How often had she fantasized about being seen in the same light as the famous Rose Greenhow!

When the last of the well-wishers and reporters had finally departed, Belle stood, suddenly weary. As she turned to go to her room, Mrs. Greenhow pressed a heavy purse of coins into her hand.

"That is kind of you," Belle said, "but Mama has sent me money. And I received many gifts from Southern sympathizers while I was in prison."

"You must never refuse a gift," Mrs. Greenhow advised. "I am simply passing along money I myself have received. This is one way our friends support the Southern Cause. We must not deprive them of the pleasure they derive from doing so." She paused. "You and I are forced to lead a gypsy life, Miss Boyd. Dependent on the kindness of strangers. But our circumstances are somewhat different. Forgive me for speaking frankly, dear. I am a wealthy woman, but you I believe are not. I am a widow. You are young and unmarried. You might believe you have a great deal of money, and perhaps you do, but at some point your funds will run out. Then where will you be? That is why you must always accept such gifts as are offered. Provided of course, if the giver is a man, that there is no suggestion of ungentlemanly intention."

Belle took the purse, thinking, *I have so much to learn!*

⁓

For a week, the two women toured the city together, attending receptions, visiting wounded soldiers, and talking to reporters. Then Mrs. Greenhow left for England. Now that she had been released from Federal prison onto Southern soil, the Union government had no power to stop her. According to rumor, she carried secret papers from Jefferson Davis that were intended to help gain support for the Confederate cause overseas.

Alone again and homesick, Belle thought she might perhaps risk a visit to Martinsburg. She knew it was dangerous. Mr. Wood had made it clear she was to remain in Southern territory for the rest of the war. Those were the terms of her parole. But at the moment, Martinsburg was in Confederate hands. The danger would come if it changed hands again—as had already happened more than a dozen times. If she was sent to prison a second time, she might not be released until the end of the war. But she was desperate to go home. She just had to see Papa, who had finally been permanently discharged from the Army because of his failing health. How sick was he? She needed to see for herself. She needed to see them all. Mama. Mary. Eliza!

As always, when Belle struggled between her heart and her head, it was her heart that won. She left for Martinsburg the next day.

❧

"You're such a lady now!" Belle exclaimed to Mary, who blushed happily. The whole family was gathered around the dining room table, Eliza trudging in and out with tea and slices of currant cake. A party to welcome Belle home.

"And you're famous!" Mary replied. "The Rebel Joan of Arc! That's what the papers call you. I've had to start a whole new scrapbook."

Belle put on a frown, "Some of the things the newspapers said about me weren't very nice. Nor true, either! Those Union papers will print anything."

Mama reached out to pat Belle's cheek. "Now that you're home, it doesn't matter. We worried every minute you were in that dreadful place. Your letters were cheerful, but we never knew whether to believe them or not."

"We thought you were just being brave," Papa said.

"I *am* brave," Belle said. "It says so in the papers!"

While everyone laughed, Belle studied Papa. She was still getting used to his worn, gray face, the stooped back, the leg that dragged slightly when he walked. His war was over.

Before Papa could feel her gaze, Belle scooped up her brother, Will, and set him on her knee. The sturdy five-year-old continued eating cake, spilling crumbs and currants into her lap.

"Look, it's snowing!" she exclaimed, brushing herself off. "Finish eating, and I will give you a present."

Will stuffed the cake into his mouth. Belle reached into her pocket, then placed something small into his hands.

"What is it?" Mary asked as they all leaned forward to see.

"A gift I received my first night in prison." Here Mama and Mary shivered. "A tiny basket carved from a peach pit. It was rolled across the floor to me, with a note tied around it. It's how we sent messages, except most of the time we used marbles. It was our Post Office."

Belle set Will on his feet and handed him a spoon. "You can use this to push it along the floor. The same as you would with a hoop and stick."

"Thank you, Miss!" Will said and ran off.

Belle looked after him. "Oh dear. I've been away so long he hardly remembers me."

"You're here now," Mama said, eyes shining with pride and affection. "That's all that matters."

# Chapter 30

"She ain't s'posed to be here," Sam said in the loft that night.

"I tol' her that. Tol' her she's got to be ready to leave as soon as we hear the Yanks is comin'. And they's always comin'. Less they's here already."

"Her mama and papa been through enough."

"She says she done it for them. Says they needed to see her in person, so's they'd know for sure she hadn't suffered none in prison. Guess I can't blame her for that."

"How's she seem? Did prison knock some of the foolishness outta her head?"

"I can't tell. Maybe. She gave me this." 'Liza reached into her pocket and handed Sam a thin, flat package, wrapped in brown paper. "She got it in Richmond."

Sam unwrapped it. His head snapped up. "'Liza, you ain't s'posed to have this!" He looked down at it, resting on his knees. "Still . . ." His face softened. "Imagine you havin' a book."

With one finger he traced the shape of the letters on the front. They were black. The rest of the cover was dark yellow. More like a golden color.

"Why'd she give it to you?"

"I think it's her way of sayin' she's sorry. I think she wants ever'thing to go back the way it was. Before she said she'd sell my fam'ly away."

"I can't believe this is yours, 'Liza." Sam paused, then asked, "Books has names, right?"

'Liza nodded. "This one's called *The Southern Primer*. That's what those letters say on the front. It's a special kinda book for learnin' to read."

"You already know how to read."

"I think maybe she was thinkin' I could teach John. Go ahead. Open it, Sam. There's pitchers inside."

He frowned at his hands, then wiped them on his pants. When he still hesitated, 'Liza said, "Here," and opened to the first page.

"An apple?"

'Liza nodded, then pointed. "This here's the letter A. There's two ways to write it. The word 'apple' starts with A."

"A. Apple." Sam shook his head in wonder, then turned another page. "That word must say 'ball.' But I just know that from the pitcher."

"That's right. The letter is B, and the word is 'ball.' You see, after a while John will be able to remember the letter and the word without lookin' at the pitcher."

"Did Miss Belle have a book like this for teachin' you?"

"No, we did it with a slate and chalk. Later on we read newspapers. This way's better."

"You better keep it here, 'Liza. Nobody ever comes up here 'cept you and me and John. It would be bad if somebody found it. We don't want trouble."

"First I have to 'splain to John 'bout readin'. Make sure he understands he can't let on once he knows how. Can't spend too much time lookin' at somethin' that's writ down, tryna figure out what it says. His eyes just has to pass right over it. Same as lookin' at a ax or a bucket."

Sam took a deep breath, then asked, "'Liza, do you think I can learn? I never wanted to before. It was enough that you could read." He gazed at the wall, like he was looking into a great distance. "But now . . . things is changin'. I think now readin' is gonna be important."

'Liza leaned into his side, felt the solid warmth of him.

"Anybody can learn to read, somebody shows 'em how."

Sam laughed out loud, put his arm around her and hugged her so hard her ribs hurt.

"We gonna be a whole readin' fam'ly, 'Liza!"

"Wouldn't that be somethin'?"

*Martinsburg, Virginia*
*Confederate controlled*
*October 1862 to June 1863*

# Chapter 31

All through that fall, the Union Army moved closer to Martinsburg. Once they took possession of the town, Belle would be in violation of her parole. She had no wish to be dragged from her home and imprisoned a second time. She would not put herself or her family through that again. So she accepted an invitation to visit Papa's relatives in Knoxville, Tennessee. From there she continued south and then west, her tour including Augusta and Atlanta, Mobile and Montgomery, and ending in New Orleans, which Belle decided she liked more than any city she had ever visited.

She was gone more than half a year, returning to Martinsburg in early summer. For the moment it was safe, the Confederates once again in charge. Even if the Union had been in control, Belle would have gone anyway. Mama had written that she was pregnant—at thirty-eight!—and wanted Belle home.

By June of 1863, Martinsburg was a shadow of itself. Although the railroad tracks had been repaired, the depot was a ruined shell. Most of the businesses were closed, and nearly half the houses were boarded up, roof shingles missing, shutters dangling from their hinges, fences broken, gardens trampled. Papa's store continued to make a profit, dealing almost exclusively in tobacco and whiskey. The Confederate currency that had been printed at the beginning of the war was now worthless, so the store often accepted food as payment. Eggs sometimes, or a sack of potatoes, a slab of bacon. The newspapers reported food shortages deeper south, but that was not the case in the Shenandoah Valley. It was the breadbasket of Virginia, with both sides willing to protect the fertile fields that could so easily fall into their own hands.

Papa too was just a shadow.

"It's all the marching Jackson had us do. The boots never did fit right."

Belle fingered the black crepe armband she wore on her sleeve, a sign of mourning for Stonewall Jackson, tragically shot by his own men in the Battle of Chancellorsville a month earlier. Wounded in three places, he had lingered for more than a week while the entire Confederacy prayed. Belle remembered her own prayers, kneeling by her bed in her nightdress like a little girl.

For a moment, she allowed herself to blame her hero. He had been a brilliant commander, but hard on his men. By now his record was well-known. In his Valley Campaign which lasted just over three months, Jackson's army marched four hundred miles, fighting minor skirmishes almost daily. His troops had been in five major battles and defeated four armies. All with less than a thousand Confederate soldiers killed. And yet so many of the men who served under Jackson were broken. Not just Papa. Even many of the young ones had been used up. They might not have died on the battlefield, but they had given their lives for the Confederacy just the same.

*It wasn't Jackson's fault. He was just trying to win a war. A war that has been going on for much too long.*

Belle, too, had done what she could to end the war. Now Jackson was dead. And Belle herself felt defeated. But ever so happy to be back home.

❦

During the weeks that followed Belle's return, Papa spent his days in the parlor with his pipe and newspaper, leaving Mr. Meaders to tend the store. On her good days, Mama was there too, reclining on a long chair with her feet propped on a pillow.

Mama had always been one of those fortunate women who did not suffer much during pregnancy. And thank goodness, for she was pregnant so often! This time was different, though. She never complained, but her hands and feet were puffy, and she was short of breath even lying down. Mary, now twelve and more domestic than ever, happily assumed the role of Mama's nurse. She bustled in and out of the parlor, Will trailing behind her like a puppy, delivering the herbal remedies Eliza prepared in the kitchen.

*Mama is much too old to be having a baby!* Belle looked with fresh eyes at her exhausted Papa. *However did they manage it?* Her cheeks grew warm at the thought. She supposed she should be happy for them. She would have been if she wasn't worried about Mama.

The days went by, everyone performing their assigned role. Eliza concocted, Mary bustled, and Belle helped her parents pass the time. Mama liked it most when she read out loud.

"I can never decide what pleases me more. To look at you while you read, or to lie back and close my eyes so I can enjoy your lovely voice."

The book Belle was reading had just been published and was extremely popular. Called *Two Months in the Confederate States: An Englishman's Travels Through the South*, it gave a moving portrayal of Southern determination in the face of the war's hardship and predicted that the Confederacy would ultimately win.

"You've just come back from your own tour of the South," Papa observed. "Knoxville. New Orleans. And everywhere in between. Do you think you might write a book someday, Belle?"

"Perhaps. But not a travel book. I'd rather write about my wartime adventures."

"You've always been a good storyteller," Papa said.

Mama had been lying back, but now her eyes popped open. "If you ever do write about your adventures, need you tell everything? There are certain parts you might consider leaving out."

❧

Soon after Belle's arrival, Eliza came to her room and asked to speak with her. Her tone of voice was almost formal, and Belle wondered what this could be about. Their relations had never gone back to the way they were before Belle's "unfortunate remark."

Eliza handed Belle a newspaper clipping that was limp from repeated readings, and asked, "Does this say what I think it says?"

"'Willey Amendment to West Virginia Statehood Bill,'" Belle read. "'The children of slaves born within the limits of this State after the fourth day of July, eighteen hundred and sixty-three, shall be free; and all slaves within this state who shall, at the time aforesaid, be under the age of ten years, shall be free when they arrive at the age of twenty-one years; and all slaves over ten and under twenty-one years shall be free when they arrive at the age of twenty-five years.'"

"It don't cover me and Sam, do it?" Belle noticed that Eliza hands were clenched into fists. "There's nothing in it 'bout me and Sam. No matter how many times I read it. On account of we're over twenty-one."

Belle nodded. "This man Willey, he wants to free the slaves

gradually. It doesn't start right away. And it doesn't include anybody over twenty-one."

"They think folks over twenty-one don't wanna be free? That if you were born a slave, if you've been a slave your whole life, what difference does it make if you *die* a slave?"

Eliza's normally calm face was twisted in anger, her voice very nearly a snarl. Belle was stunned. She had never forgotten the words Eliza had said when Belle was taken off to prison—that some people live their whole lives without freedom. It was *her* people Eliza was talking about. Sam and John and Eliza herself. Delia. Patsy. Cook. And her son Joshua. *These* were Eliza's people. Not Belle and her family. Not at all. She had always assumed Eliza would be loyal to the Boyds no matter what. *How foolish I was!*

Still, Eliza had asked Belle to explain the Willey Amendment, and this is what Belle would do. She felt she owed Eliza that at least. For the first time in her life, Belle heard herself stammering as she said, "They needed a compromise. Before West Virginia could be accepted as a new state, they had to write a constitution, and Congress had to approve it. Some of the senators in Washington wanted West Virginia to be a free state. But the West Virginia politicians wouldn't agree."

Eliza waited.

"They needed a compromise," Belle said again.

"Seems like a trick, don't it? We lives in West Virginia, but this Willey Amendment don't include me and Sam. And President Lincoln's Emancipation Proclamation, that didn't cover us neither."

"No. It only freed slaves in the states that seceded. And West Virginia didn't secede. It stayed Union."

Eliza shook her head. "It don't make sense. Two papers ever'body says is 'bout freein' the slaves and neither one of 'em is gonna free us."

"That's right," Belle softly.

"If Lincoln wins this war, then his Emancipation Proclamation would apply to ever'body, right?"

"Is that what you want? For the Union to win? Have you thought about who would take care of you?"

Eliza put her hands on her hips. "I reckon we knows how to look after ourselves. Sam and me has plans. He wants to open a barbershop. I'll be a midwife. I helped birth all your mama's babies. Just like I'm gonna birth this one. I help other ladies too. When they give me money, I put it away. Your mama knows all about it."

"My goodness!"

They stood and stared at each other. It was like Belle was seeing Eliza for the first time. Her plain, wide face. Her sturdy body. Her feet planted underneath her like they'd taken root in the floor. Eliza was a rock. Belle's rock. Belle couldn't imagine the Boyd family without her. They stared at each other. And for the first time, Belle truly understood that there was a gulf between them as wide as the ocean.

"The Willey Amendment does free John," Belle said.

"In twelve years," Eliza answered, her voice dripping bitterness.

In the long silence that followed, Belle asked, "How is John's reading?"

Some of the tension trickled out of the room, and Eliza's posture relaxed a little.

"He's real quick. Knows his numbers too."

"The amendment says children of West Virginia slaves born after this July are free," Belle reminded her. "If you and Sam have other children, they will never be slaves. No matter how the war ends, freedom is coming."

As Eliza left the room, Belle heard her mutter, "Can't come too soon for me."

*Martinsburg, West Virginia*
*Confederate Controlled*
*Early July to early December 1863*

# Chapter 32

On July 1, the Battle of Gettysburg began and raged for three awful days, the tide of events favoring first one side, then the other. Both armies fought valiantly, but in the end the Confederates were defeated. An estimated fifty-one thousand soldiers were killed, wounded, captured, or listed as missing.

Gettysburg, Pennsylvania, was less than sixty miles from Martinsburg. In the days following the battle, thousands of wounded Confederate soldiers made their slow, painful way south to towns and villages in Maryland, Virginia, and West Virginia.

Like other homes in Martinsburg, Belle's became a makeshift hospital, the parlor and hallways crowded with perhaps a dozen men lying on the floor on beds made of folded quilts and blankets. Eliza, Sam, Belle, and Mary were busy from morning to night replacing bandages, washing laundry, changing sheets. John helped with feeding, washing, wiping. Young Will ran errands, trotting up to the main hospital to fetch medicine or whatever else might be needed. Sometimes he returned empty-handed, his blue eyes filled with tears.

"The doctor says there isn't any more morphine, Belle. But maybe tomorrow."

"Never you mind. Mr. Meaders has given us three jugs of whiskey. Why don't you go to the pantry and bring me one."

The boy's mouth dropped open, and he leaned forward to whisper, "We're not going to make the soldiers drunk, are we, Belle?"

"Of course not, though I would if we had enough." Belle smiled and tousled her brother's hair. "We'll give them just enough to make them comfortable. You'll see."

Will nodded wisely, attempted a wink, and ran off to follow orders.

❧

When Mama's birth pains began, Belle and Eliza helped her, while Mary and Sam and John continued to tend the wounded. The soldiers knew what was happening. They were full of concern for Mrs. Boyd. And hope. Even in the aftermath of so much horror as a three-day battle, a baby being born was a wonderful event. Afterward, while Mama rested with Papa sitting next to her bed, Belle took the baby downstairs to the parlor and handed her to Mary.

"It's a girl!" Mary announced from the doorway. The men cheered quietly as she stood there, looking down at her baby sister, blinking as if to keep back her tears. Belle squeezed her shoulder, gave her a gentle push, and watched her walk through the rooms, tilting left and right toward the wounded men, showing off the tiny bundle in her arms. Unnoticed, Belle brushed her own tears away. They were all just so damned tired.

❧

Several days later, the Rebels abandoned Martinsburg, taking their wounded with them. A week after that, the Union Army arrived, and soon there was a major on the doorstep with an order for Belle's arrest. She knew she shouldn't have stayed. Technically she had been in violation of her parole since June 20, the day West Virginia officially became a Northern state. She had known she should leave, but her family had never needed her more. The baby, named Nina, had lived only two days. Afterward, Mama grew so ill she could not even sit up. Papa was frantic with worry. No, she couldn't possibly leave.

The major didn't care about Mama's health. Or her dead baby. Orders were orders!

On August 28, Belle was returned to Old Capitol Prison, where the formerly agreeable Superintendent Wood was extremely irritated to see her again. He barely spoke a word when he escorted her to her room. It was not Number 6 this time, and it lacked not just a number on the door but much else besides. There was no fireplace or comfortable rocker. The furniture consisted of a rusty iron bed, a chair with uneven legs, and a table in danger of collapse. The washbowl was chipped, and the cracked mirror was barely held together by its wooden frame. When Belle walked into the room and Mr. Wood closed the door behind her, she spent long minutes gazing at her reflection in the murky glass, wondering if her famous luck had finally deserted her.

Apparently believing she had learned nothing from her first incarceration, the superintendent found a dozen ways to punish her. Breakfast was moldy bread spread with lard. At noon, cold cornmeal mush. In the evening, a slimy stew whose ingredients Belle could only guess at. Every week, a different contraband was assigned to bring her meals or help her dress. She was allowed no visitors. No newspapers. No gifts of fruit or magazines. Everything about this imprisonment was drearier than the first. Perhaps it was because the war had dragged on so long, with both sides having lost so much. The country still reeled from Gettysburg, the costliest battle of the war.

After a month's imprisonment, Belle hoped she would be released, as she had been the first time. But she was not. In October she grew ill, suffering from excruciating headaches and double vision. She had fainting spells and was sometimes too weak to get out of bed. The prison doctor examined her and said it was typhoid fever, but since he had no medicine to give her, she grew steadily worse. Papa asked permission to visit her but was denied.

On a dreary day in November, as she was lying in bed, she overheard two guards talking outside her door.

"That doctor who's s'posed to be treatin' her, he's no good. Weren't he takin' care of that Miss McDonough? And she died, didn't she? Right here in the very same room as this one. Don't know as it's the same sickness, but it's the same doctor and the same room. Seems strange. That's all I'm sayin'."

Feeling she might actually be dying, Belle penned a note to Mr. Wood. He did not respond. She languished in her dirty cell, lying on the same mattress where another woman had recently died. She was a prisoner, sick and alone. And no one cared.

ϾϿ

Finally, on December 1, Belle was released. History repeated itself as once again she made the journey by boat to Richmond. This time, though, instead of meeting Rose Greenhow and being celebrated throughout the city, she was greeted with a black bordered telegram.

Papa was dead.

Belle collapsed. For days she stayed in her hotel room, heavy drapes pulled across the windows. She did not weep. She was beyond weeping.

*How can it be that I'll never see Papa again? Or feel the tickle of his moustache when he kisses my cheek? I can't even go home and comfort Mama. She's lost her husband. And her baby. Her daughter imprisoned. Papa's health was poor ever since he joined the army, but I do believe that in the end it was worry about me that killed him. I know Mama doesn't blame me, but it's my fault. I always thought I could do as I pleased, despite everyone warning me to be careful. I never thought it would be someone I loved who paid the price.*

*Richmond, Virginia*
*Confederate Controlled*
*Early February to early May 1864*

# Chapter 33

Belle remained in Richmond for several months while she slowly regained her strength. She wrote to Mary and Mama every day, only hinting at her various complaints. The persistent headaches and shortness of breath. The trembling weakness in her legs that made even climbing stairs a challenge.

Sometimes she daydreamed about talking to Eliza. The way she used to before the war. There were things Belle could tell Eliza that she would never share with Mary or Mama. For fear of worrying them. Or having them judge her. It was Eliza who knew her best. Belle understood now that she had never really known what Eliza was thinking, and yet, even now, Belle wanted to pour her heart out to her. She didn't have to pretend with Eliza or try to impress her. Belle was free to be herself. *I wasn't judged. Or was I? It doesn't matter. For years, she felt like a friend. Sometimes my only friend.* Belle hated remembering their last conversation. The Willey Amendment. How angry Eliza had been!

Meanwhile, Mama was not answering her letters. Belle had not heard from her since learning the sad details of Papa's death. She would have been frantic with worry but for the fact that Mary was such a diligent correspondent. Her sister described in detail how everyone was. *Mama, doing fair, considering the sorrowful circumstances. Eliza, bossy as ever. Will, our constant joy. Me, bearing up.*

Finally Belle received a letter from Mary that said:

> *But Mama does write you! Every day. And always sends a little money. Is it possible her letters don't reach you?*

That was when Belle knew for certain that her mother's letters were being intercepted. She didn't know if it was because Secretary Stanton wanted to keep her from receiving funds or to deprive her of a mother's comfort. Either way, she knew him to be the very Devil.

Fortunately, Belle was not short of cash, for she never failed to follow Mrs. Greenhow's advice about accepting gifts. No indeed!

As soon as her strength returned, she planned to travel. Although she was forbidden to return to Martinsburg, there were other places she could go. Finally she felt well enough to write Mama about her plans.

> *Since I can't come home—which breaks my heart! —and since I do not wish to remain in the South any longer, I will go to England until the war ends. It must end soon! Then I'll return to Martinsburg, where you know I yearn to be, more than anywhere on Earth.*

Belle did not mention that once again she intended to follow the example of Rose Greenhow. When the older woman left for Europe, she had travelled as an official representative of the Confederacy. Her assignment was to persuade influential men in England and France to convince their governments to support the Confederacy with money and arms.

The Southern papers always wrote about Mrs. Greenhow with great admiration, while Belle was sometimes still portrayed as flighty or trivial or worse. She was determined to gain the same respect as her idol. She, too, would travel to Europe in an official capacity.

Belle wrote a note to Jefferson Davis offering to carry dispatches to London. Within days, a young clerk was standing in the parlor of her hotel suite.

"I'm Hutchins, Miss Boyd. Here with official papers from Judah Benjamin. He's the Confederate Secretary of State, you know."

Belle suppressed a smile. The boy must have been all of fifteen. When he said nothing more, but simply stood and gazed at her in admiration, she nodded toward the bundle he held.

"Are those the papers?"

"Oh, yes! I'm instructed to go over them with you. Is that alright?"

"Yes indeed." Belle indicated her desk. "Please sit."

"This case contains correspondence from the Confederate States of America. See? There's an official seal on the outside. And here are your instructions." He handed her a slim envelope. "I'm supposed to wait while you read it, in case you have questions."

Belle scanned the letter quickly. She was much more interested in reading the dispatches themselves, which she intended to do as soon as her messenger left.

"When I reach London, I am to contact someone named Henry Hotze at this address. He's a Confederate propagandist. I will give him the papers and follow any instructions he has for me. This seems perfectly clear."

Hutchins set a leather purse on the table. "Here is money to cover your expenses. Five hundred dollars in gold."

Pleased to be entrusted with an official mission and excited about traveling to Europe, Belle hurried to complete her preparations. She would need a maid, of course. She placed an advertisement in the newspaper and found an Irish girl named Margaret who agreed to travel with Belle to England. After six months, Margaret would be free to return to her village and collect her younger sister, who she planned to bring back to America.

Belle was eager to publicize her journey and invited reporters to interview her about her plans. She told them how her health had suffered during her imprisonment and mentioned the tragedy of her father's death. She intended to visit London, Paris, and Rome, and then go to Switzerland for a rest-cure. Wishing to end any lingering criticism of her actions, she made sure reporters knew she traveled as a trusted courier on an important diplomatic mission.

ல

Being banned from travel in Union territory meant that Belle had to sail from a Southern port. She chose Wilmington, North Carolina as her point of departure. Of course, she would have to travel on a blockade runner. These fast, nimble vessels were the only ones that stood a chance of slipping past the Union warships that patrolled the Southern coast.

The sole function of a blockade runner was to transport Southern cotton and tobacco to European ports, where it would be sold. The captain was trusted to use the proceeds to purchase guns and ammunition for the Confederacy. This type of vessel sacrificed everything for cargo space and speed. There were no cabins for passengers and no heavy cannons for protection. If spotted by a Union ship, a blockade runner had only one hope. It must outrun its pursuer. A captured ship would have its cargo confiscated, its captain and crew thrown in prison.

Belle booked passage for herself and Margaret on the *Greyhound* and was delighted to find out that it was captained by an old friend of Papa's. The white-whiskered gentleman told her to call him Captain Henry, though this was not the name she knew him by. It seemed that when he left the U.S. Navy and switched his allegiance to the Confederate cause, a name change had been necessary.

Captain Henry showed Belle the tiny cabin where she and Margaret would sleep. "These are my own quarters, though still quite small, as you can see." When Belle protested at displacing him, the captain said, "There is really no other place for you, my dear. Don't worry about me. I'll bunk with the first mate." Holding the door for her, he said, "Now let's go up on deck, and I'll show you the rest of the ship."

Captain Henry was proud of his vessel. "They called her the *Greyhound* because of her speed. She was built expressly for the blockade," he explained, pointing to the smokestack. "She has both sails and steam so she can make good speed under any conditions. That's crucial. Blockade running is only profitable if you make it through. That means your ship must be the fastest."

There were two other passengers on board, Mr. Pollard and Mr. Newell. Belle met them at dinner the first night. Dressed in mourning for the death of her father, and wearing a wedding ring, she introduced herself as Mrs. Lewis, a widow bound for a European health-cure. Mr. Pollard, whom Belle recognized as the editor of a Richmond newspaper, gave her a sly wink as he bowed over her hand and pronounced himself delighted to make the acquaintance of "Mrs. Lewis."

The *Greyhound* set sail after sunset, then dropped anchor near the sandbar that stood at the mouth of the Cape Fear River, waiting for the new moon to fall below the horizon. While Captain Henry made last minute arrangements for their run, the three passengers stood at the rail in the balmy night air and watched the Federal fleet patrolling several miles out to sea. The Union ships moved slowly and silently, not venturing close to shore because of the Confederate cannons bristling from the ramparts of nearby Fort Fisher.

Belle gave a soft laugh. "I am not sure the *Greyhound* is so well named after all. I feel it is *they* who are the hounds and we the fox!"

A strange mood had settled over the passengers. Here they were, three strangers, bound together by circumstance, facing danger together. Never taking their eyes off the circling boats, they chatted quietly about small matters. A trivial but essential form of bravery that kept everyone from thinking about what was to come. For, as soon as the moon set and darkness settled on the water, the *Greyhound*, with no running lights and trusting only to the skills of Captain Henry and his crew, would run the gauntlet past those ships. Ships whose own skilled captains would try to intercept her, board her, sink her, even burn her, calamities that had befallen dozens of other blockade runners.

Around 10 p.m., with the night as dark as it would ever be, Captain Henry paused by the rail to speak with his passengers. He had changed into a dark suit. He wore not a single shiny button or length of gold braid that might catch a stray beam of light.

"We are about to begin our run!" he announced, a quiver of excitement in his voice. Turning away, he gave whispered commands which were quietly relayed to his crew. "Dowse all lights!" "Raise anchor." "More steam!" "Steady ahead!"

The ship glided in a silence so complete that Belle swore she could hear the sound of the bow cutting through the waves. She noticed that some of the officers had climbed onto cotton bales piled high on the deck, straining their eyes into the darkness, trying to spot the enemy ships before those ships spotted them.

The whole night, the captain, crew, and passengers stayed on the deck of the slowly moving vessel. No one spoke. Belle stood by the rail, her body as taut as the string of a drawn bow. Hours later, the sun began to rise, a rosy glow in the east that turned the waves to molten silver. Belle thought she had never seen anything so beautiful. A tired cheer went up from the men. There was not an enemy ship in sight.

Belle calculated the date so she could enter it into her journal after breakfast. May 9. *My twentieth birthday! A beautiful morning and safely on my way to England.* The thought pleased her immensely. A new year, a new decade, a new chapter to her life.

Later in the day, a thick haze settled on the water and the ship began to roll. Belle had sailed on river steamers, but never the open sea. With no shoreline on which to fix her eyes, she began to feel wretchedly ill. All the passengers were suffering, with the exception of Belle's maid, who had grown up in a fishing village on the stormy Irish Sea. Margaret did what she could to assist Belle as she clutched the rail and leaned over the side, wrapped in misery but determined to keep her dignity.

A sudden cry of "Sail ho!" caused all the passengers to slowly raise their eyes. A Union ship had appeared out of the fog less than a mile away. Captain Henry swore and barked out his orders.

"Full steam. Hard a-lee!"

As the crewmen scrambled to obey, an officer with a spyglass said, "Damn our luck, sir! It's the *Connecticut*. They can't have known we were here. The fog's like soup!"

Margaret took a step closer to Belle, and the small cluster of passengers watched in horror as the enemy ship began to gain on them.

"I thought Captain Henry said we're faster!" Belle exclaimed.

Mr. Pollard answered. "The *Connecticut* is one of their largest ships. And very fast. I doubt we'll be able to outrun her."

The *Greyhound* picked up speed, her sails bellying in the wind, but it was not enough. The other ship continued to gain. However quick and nimble the blockade runner, she was no match for the more powerful engines and bigger sails of the *Connecticut*.

One of the officers said, "They're still closing on us, sir." A pause. "Your orders?"

"Toss the cargo overboard! We'll run lighter that way. Keep giving me more steam. More steam!"

Captain Henry approached the passengers, their faces now pale with fear rather than seasickness.

"Barring a miracle, they'll board us within the hour. The only way to prevent it would be to burn the ship. But I shan't do that with a lady on board."

The *Greyhound* was newly built, sleek and fast. From talking to Captain Henry, Belle understood what a prize the ship would be if the *Connecticut* managed to capture her. *The Federals must not have her—or me!*

"You mustn't hesitate on my account, Captain."

He shook his head. "Burning her would endanger the crew as well. We'd be relying on our enemies to rescue us even as we snatched a great prize from their grasp. I can't take the risk. They'd be quite happy if we drowned." Looking at his passengers one by one, he said, "If any of you has documents that should not fall into enemy hands, now is the time to destroy them."

Mr. Pollard disappeared, returning in moments with a leather satchel which he upended over the side, sending a cascade of papers into the sea. Belle ran to her cabin, found the dispatch case with its Confederate seal, and hurried below decks to the engine room. She was glad she had studied the letters it contained enough to remember their contents.

At the bottom of the ladder, she was stopped by a wall of deafening noise and scorching heat. The furnace's doors were open, and the whole room glowed orange.

Silhouetted against the flames, two black figures took turns shoveling coal as if they were possessed by demons. She clutched her burning throat, stumbling backward.

*It's like Hell!* Belle thought, understanding now why Mr. Pollard had tossed his papers overboard. *This is what "full steam ahead" means!*

The chief engineer happened to glance over his shoulder, then rushed toward her waving his arms. Only then did Belle notice the red sparks arcing through the air and realize how foolish she was to be down here in her wide skirts. The roaring din made speech impossible, so she thrust the case at the officer and pointed toward the furnace, then retreated up the ladder. Turning at the top, she saw a coal-smeared stoker toss the case into the flames. In seconds all evidence of her treason was gone.

As she climbed up from the throbbing noise below decks, Belle was gradually able to hear other sounds. Loud explosions in the distance, followed by a low-pitched humming that grew steadily louder. The *Greyhound* was being fired upon! She braced for the impact, but there was none, just the sharp slap of cannonballs hitting the water in front of the ship and the feeling of the bow lifting high over the resulting swell. She guessed that the Union gunners did not want to damage the valuable ship. But they were determined to stop her.

When Belle reached the main deck, she saw the *Connecticut* almost upon them. At the same moment, she felt the vibration of the *Greyhound*'s engines die away under her feet.

Captain Henry shook his fist. "Why are they still firing at us? I've surrendered."

*Surrendered! What happens now?*

From the *Connecticut,* a Yankee voice boomed through a megaphone. "Haul down that British flag. We know you're a Confederate ship."

Captain Henry ordered the false colors pulled down, then watched gloomily as two small boats were lowered off the side of the Union ship and rowed rapidly toward them. In less than five minutes, the Union captain had boarded the Greyhound and was looking around at his prize with a satisfied smile.

"A fine ship." He addressed Captain Henry. "I'm not surprised you were reluctant to burn her."

By now there were Federals swarming all over the *Greyhound*, some corralling the crew, others the officers. Still others pounded down the stairs to search the ship. Belle watched all this activity with narrowed eyes, her senses as alert as an animal's.

*What is going to happen to me? Who is in charge?*

A pair of blue-clad officers approached the rail where the passengers stood in a tight knot, awaiting their fate. Belle's glance was drawn to another officer, a late arrival, just now stepping on board. Dark, shoulder-length hair and intense, light eyes. Blue or gray, she couldn't tell. He reminded her of Stonewall Jackson, the same steely gaze and quiet authority. The man looked swiftly around the ship, his eyes passing over Belle without a flicker of interest. He approached the officer who was speaking with Captain Henry and saluted.

"I am Captain Hardinge, sir. I've been ordered to take over the ship. As prize master."

There was further conversation between them, but Belle did not stay. She had heard what she needed to know. She turned to the Union officers who stood with the passengers.

"I'm tired. Please tell your captain that if he wishes to speak with me, I will be in my cabin."

# Chapter 34

"Come in," Belle called when she heard the tapping on her door.

She had decided in advance that she would remain lying on her narrow bed. Quite improper, but it was such a tiny cabin, there was barely room to stand anyway. She thought the black silk gown she wore in Papa's memory gave her an air of respectability. *As well as mystery!* A satisfying thought. And Margaret was standing in the corner, hands clasped in front of her, eyes wide.

The door swung open. The captain's gaze swept the room, but this time his eyes came to rest on Belle. He smiled.

"Captain Samuel Hardinge," he murmured, removing his hat and bowing. "At your service."

"How can that be?" Belle cried, her voice full of distress. "When I am your captive." She refused to use the word "prisoner." She would never be a prisoner again.

"Madam, I beg you will consider yourself a passenger, not a prisoner."

"As you wish." A demure smile. "I was afraid out on deck that you had overlooked me. Your captive." Repeating the word gave Belle a delightful shiver.

"Only a blind man would fail to notice one such as you, Miss Boyd."

*How did he discover my identity so soon?* But when Belle looked into his eyes, she found she didn't care.

"And the first moment I saw you, I knew you for a gentleman."

Captain Hardinge bowed again, dark hair sweeping his shoulders as he leaned forward.

"I wanted to inform you that the *Connecticut* is going to tow the *Greyhound*. I must go and see that the lines are properly placed. Please excuse me. After the ropes are secure, all the crew and passengers will go aboard the *Connecticut*. All save Captain Henry and yourself."

"Where are we going? Not to England surely!"

"I believe our next stop is New York City."

"Then I really am a captive. Or I soon will be."

The captain gave Belle a reassuring smile.

"Who will see to the ship while Captain Henry and I remain on board?"

"A skeleton crew. Also your maid, the steward, the cook, and a cabin boy. You'll be well looked after."

"I see," Belle said. "And you, sir?"

"I will remain on the *Greyhound* as well."

"Ahh," Belle sighed, with no attempt to hide the pleasure in her voice.

"As prize master."

"What does that mean precisely?"

"When a ship is captured, it becomes a prize of war. The enemy captain who takes command of the ship is therefore called the prize master."

"I see."

A flare of the captain's brilliant blue eyes. Another smile, a bow.

"Your servant, madam."

Before turning to go, he gave Belle a final glance, as if trying to fix in his mind the image of the young woman in black silk reclining gracefully on her bed.

As soon as the door closed behind him, Margaret stepped forward. Belle looked at her, remembering that her new maid was just fifteen.

"Well?"

Margaret eyes were perfectly round as she said, "I saw a play once. In Dublin. When I were on my way to America. Cheap tup'ny seats. I'd never seen a proper play before. On the stage were a most beautiful lady. And then a gennleman walks in and they talks to each other, just like you and that captain were after doin'. And somehow everyone watchin' knew right off that those two was going ter fall in love. But whether it would be a happy or sad thing, that's what you didn't know. Cause that's what the play was about. See?" Margaret's long speech left her breathless, but she wasn't finished. "And here you are, doing the same thing. I didn't know it could happen in real life."

Belle smiled. "There are some people who can *make* it happen. And I am one of them." A pause. "There will be times, Margaret, when I will need your help to make my play turn out as I wish. So that means you will get to be in the play too. Would you like that?"

"Oh yes, Miss!" Margaret bobbed a bouncing curtsey. "I would be proud to help you. In fact, it would be Heaven."

⁘

During the days that followed, Belle didn't feel like a captive at all. The cook prepared delicious meals that the steward served in the captain's cabin. Just as on the night they sailed, there were candles and silver, fine china, a snowy white tablecloth. As with his earlier Confederate passengers, Captain Henry was more than generous with his wine.

"I have every reason to be," he declared, filling their glasses, then raising his own. "The kinship between ships' captains is a thing apart! So let us drink to new friends in the midst of conflict. An unexpected pleasure."

After the toast, Belle said, "It was gallant of you, Captain Hardinge, not to displace me from Captain Henry's cabin. There is so little space on board."

Gazing into her eyes, he replied, "Anything for you, dear lady." A nod toward the older man. "As it turns out, Mr. Henry and I are compatible bunk mates."

"You might be interested to know, Miss Boyd, that our Union captain's Southern sympathies are surprisingly strong for one who hails from the city of Brooklyn."

Captain Henry leaned across the table toward Belle, then spoke in a loud whisper. "He's been asking lots of questions about you." Leaning closer, "I think perhaps he is a spy!"

Belle laughed delightedly. "And what else have you told the captain about me?"

"That I knew your Papa. That he is recently passed away and you are still suffering from his loss. That you are indeed the same Belle Boyd he has read about in the Northern papers. That for your service to the South you have been imprisoned twice and now banished. And I think I mentioned that you just had a birthday."

"How did you come to know that?"

"Your charming Margaret has been visiting the kitchen. I believe she may have said something to the cook. So it seems there will be cake for dessert."

In addition to spending time in the kitchen, Margaret had

also been talking to the small crew, her orders from Belle to find out whatever she could about the handsome captain.

"It seems as he's a real gennleman, Miss. The crew say there's not a finer feller in the whole Union Navy."

With that knowledge and Captain Henry as chaperone, Belle embarked on a shipboard romance. It seemed unreal even to her, although, as ever, she loved playing the lead role. Their courtship proceeded at a breathless pace, each of them confessing deeper feelings almost every hour. It really was like a play, Belle thought, everything compressed into the shortest possible time and space. The *Greyhound*, practically deserted, was towed at a steady speed across a smooth sea. It seemed like an enchanted ship from the pages of a fairy tale. Belle was the damsel in distress and Captain Hardinge— another Sam! —was her rescuer. Or so she hoped.

The three of them spent most of every day together, with Captain Henry at well-timed intervals finding an excuse to attend to ship's business elsewhere. Nights were the best. They sat on deck, under the waxing moon, and told stories or recited poetry. Belle sang. When Sam took her hand for the first time, she trembled all over. She had never felt so alive! After that, they were constantly touching each other in small, hidden ways. His fingers pressed lightly against her back. Her fingers accidentally brushing his thigh. His strong hands at her waist lifting her over a coil of rope left on deck. Belle found it thrilling. Their own secret language of desire.

In a matter of days, Sam asked her to be his wife, claiming it was destiny for them to meet this way, at the last possible moment, just as she was fleeing her home.

Belle's heart leaped. She loved him. Didn't she? It wasn't just that she was his captive? It was so difficult sometimes for her to know her own heart.

"Your question involves serious consequences, Captain

Hardinge, which I must consider carefully, for both our sakes. I promise you an answer by the time we reach our destination. Wherever that may be."

&

The *Greyhound* spent its last night tethered to the *Connecticut* in the harbor of Norfolk, Virginia, where gloomy Fort Monroe squatted on the shore. The next morning, Captain Hardinge was rowed over to the Union flagship. There he was told that a full crew would now board the *Greyhound*. His new orders were to captain the ship under her own power up to Boston, where he would officially deliver her into the care of the Union Navy, and where Belle and Captain Henry would be handed over to the appropriate authorities. Margaret was to accompany Belle.

When Sam told her the news, Belle asked, "What authorities? What will happen to me? To Captain Henry? Did they say nothing more?"

Sam shook his head. "Not a word."

Belle was quite sure *she* could have learned something, but maybe Sam was right, and there was nothing to learn.

"Part of the difficulty is confusion over who has charge of you. It seems that Secretary Stanton would like to decide your fate personally. But you are not a prisoner of the War Department. You were captured by the Navy. Stanton has no authority."

"Secretary Stanton has no great love for me. I have been a thorn in his side for years."

"If the Navy decides your case, I don't see how your punishment can be too severe. You were just a passenger. You were trying to leave the country, not break your parole and travel North."

Belle nodded. Sam, of course, knew nothing about the

Confederate papers she had been carrying, letters addressed to European leaders. That *was* treason. But the papers had been destroyed.

# Chapter 35

The *Greyhound* continued up the coast, stopping in New York for a load of coal and fresh provisions. Captain Hardinge and Belle stood by the rail as the ship sailed into New York harbor and up the East River. He looked eagerly at the shore and finally pointed.

"There's Brooklyn. Where I was born. Someday I will take you there." His voice shifted from a young boy's excitement to a lover's gentleness. "Have you decided, Belle? Will you marry me?"

She stared at the shoreline, brick warehouses crowded close together, docks bristling with masts, long lines of men, their backs bent low with the weight of their burdens, endlessly loading and unloading ships of every shape and size. She knew that a short distance away from the docks, there would be streets of fine houses just as in Baltimore, Wilmington, Charleston, and all the other ports she had visited. Sam's parents lived in one of those houses.

"What will your family think of me?"

Sam's face clouded, then cleared. "I joined the Union Navy only to please Father. It was a mistake. My sentiments are as much with the South as the North. The Constitution says the Union of the states is voluntary. So if a state wishes to leave the Union, I believe they should be allowed to do so."

"You haven't answered my question, Sam."

Captain Hardinge took both her hands. "Just say you'll be my wife, and you'll make me the happiest man in the world."

෴

As the *Greyhound* continued north to deliver its prisoners to the "appropriate authorities" in Boston, Belle felt no fear for herself—though perhaps she should have. She was far more worried for Captain Henry. She advised him to keep his money with him at all times, so he would be ready to seize any chance to escape. "With no blame attached to Sam, of course."

Captain Henry got his chance as soon as they arrived. The ship had just dropped anchor in the busy harbor and was moored a short distance from the dock. Small boats came and went in all directions, their skillful rowers threading their way around the larger vessels. Needing to go ashore and make his report, Captain Hardinge had ordered one of these rowers to stand by with his boat tied to the *Greyhound*. However, just as Hardinge was about to leave, he realized he was missing some papers and went back to his cabin to get them.

Meanwhile, Belle and Captain Henry were in her cabin, entertaining the two harbor pilots who had just guided the ship through the crowded waters of Boston Harbor to their anchorage. Belle offered the pilots some wine to celebrate their role in delivering the valuable *Greyhound* to the Union Navy. When they accepted, she gave a small nod to Captain Henry, who picked up his hat and left the cabin.

With Captain Hardinge still below decks, Captain Henry strolled to the stern rail and saw that his timing could not be better. Below him in the water, was the boat Hardinge had ordered. Captain Henry stepped into the boat and ordered the rower to make for shore. Thinking this was the passenger he was waiting for, the oarsman rowed away.

When Hardinge reappeared, the harbor boat was gone, Captain Henry with it.

Captain Hardinge decided the boatman must have grown tired of waiting, so he signaled for another vessel, went ashore, and made his report. Several hours later, he returned to the *Greyhound* accompanied by a U.S. marshal and his men.

Marshal Keyes wore a long-tailed blue coat with large pewter buttons and an air of self-importance, which ordinarily Belle would have found irritating. But not today. Not when Captain Henry had just made his escape, a fact that so far only she and Margaret knew. Not when Belle was anxious that no blame whatsoever should come to *her* captain, Sam Hardinge.

After waiting a few minutes for Captain Henry to appear, Mr. Keyes took out an enormous pocket watch and frowned at it.

"Search the ship," he ordered.

"I'll look too," Hardinge said with a worried glance at Belle.

Mr. Keyes muttered to himself while he waited, tapping his foot impatiently. Belle smiled encouragingly at Margaret, who stood nearby, the whiteness of her tightly clasped hands a clue to her nervousness. Belle herself was gracious and charming, trying to engage the marshal in polite conversation about the busy-ness of the port in wartime.

The searchers returned and shook their heads. They had looked all over the ship. Captain Henry was not on board. Sam looked at Belle, who gave a slight shrug, her eyebrows raised in innocent surprise.

After that, things happened quickly. Keyes ordered his men to begin a search on shore. He was determined to find the captain before he had a chance to leave the city. The description Belle gave

Keyes was woefully inaccurate. Fortunately, Captain Hardinge had gone off to search again and was not there to contradict her.

Once he had passed along Belle's description to his men, Marshal Keyes said, "Miss Boyd, I've been instructed to take a suite for you at the Tremont House, where you will remain until your fate is determined."

*So I am to be a sort of prisoner, but in a fashionable hotel! What will happen to me? And what about Sam? Where will he be? How much will the Navy blame him for this?*

Belle kept her face smooth and unconcerned. It was important that the marshal not suspect that anyone else had aided Captain Henry in his escape.

"In a few days, Miss Boyd, I will either escort you to Canada so you may continue your interrupted journey to England, or I will have the unpleasant duty of delivering you into Union custody at Fort Warren. Meanwhile, Captain Hardinge will also be staying at the Tremont. He will accompany you whenever you leave the hotel."

*If Sam is my jailer, then they must still trust him!*

⁊

After a few days touring the city with Sam at her side, Belle still had no idea what her fate would be. It was Sam who ran out of patience first. One evening, in the hotel dining room, he pushed away his half-eaten food and lit a small cigar.

"I'm afraid we're being foolish to wait for your case to be decided. We don't even know who's in charge. The Navy or the War Department? I want to go to Washington and find out. Maybe I can influence the outcome in your favor before it's too late."

"I've been thinking the same thing," Belle said. "I'll write a letter for you to deliver to Gideon Welles, Secretary of the Union Navy. Ultimately I am *his* prisoner, since it is you who captured me. I'll appeal to his pride, that he should not give in to Stanton's demands to hand me over."

"And you must tell Welles that all you want is to be allowed to continue on to Canada. As so many other Confederates have done."

"I'll promise never to return to the North or the South as long as the War lasts. If I do leave Canada, it will only be to go to Europe." Belle had grown hopeful as she spoke, but now her shoulders sagged. "What about you, Sam? I can't bear to leave you behind."

"I'll ask for a leave. So we can be married. Later I'll resign my commission and join you. Wherever you are. But first, we need to ensure you won't be imprisoned again. I'll leave tomorrow."

❧

Two days later, Marshal Keyes received a telegram ordering him to escort Belle to Montreal on the earliest possible train.

*Canada! Could this be Sam's doing? Does he even know?*

Belle gave herself a moment to absorb the good news, then began to think of what needed to be done.

"Margaret, start packing! And I must send a telegram to Sam. We talked about being married in Montreal. The train leaves tomorrow evening, so he must be quick if he plans to come with us."

As Belle wrote out her message, she heard Margaret opening dresser drawers in the bedroom, all the while humming a wedding tune under her breath. It was at times like these that Belle most missed Eliza's steadying hand. Although Belle usually ignored her warnings, she'd relied on them just the same. Margaret was often so excited by events that she kept Belle spinning like a top. What she needed was an anchor. Belle hoped Sam would be that anchor. She was very tired.

Belle's telegram never reached Sam. Instead, she got a message from him. He was already on his way to Boston and would arrive that evening. He was scheduled to meet Admiral Stringham, the Navy Commandant, the next day and hoped to get his leave then. If necessary, he would follow on a later train.

Margaret had almost finished packing and Belle was writing a last letter to Mama when Sam came through the door. Belle flew into his arms.

"Canada! Such wonderful news, my darling," he murmured into her hair. "The best we could have hoped for."

"Have you met with the Admiral?"

He stepped away from Belle to explain. "First thing tomorrow. I'll ask for a leave to go to Canada so we can marry. Then I'll come back to formally resign my commission. We'll be separated for a short while, but I'll join you in England, or wherever you go, just as soon as I can. You know I'd follow you anywhere, darling! But I can't just go off. That would be desertion. I must get them to accept my resignation."

Sam pulled Belle back into his arms. She let herself lay her head on his chest, listening to the steady beat of his heart, while he stroked her hair and called her "my dear" and told her she would soon be able to rest. A tender moment that Belle wished could last forever.

She forced herself to pull away. There was so much to do! "Off you go, darling. You must pack. And telegram your parents with our news. Tell them I look forward to meeting them when this dreadful war is over."

Sam tried to pull Belle close again, but she wiggled out of his arms.

"No more of that, sir! Soon we'll have all the time in the world."

☙

Getting off the train in Montreal, Belle's foot reached down to touch foreign soil for the first time in her life—although it was not truly soil, but rather the concrete surface of the railroad platform. She almost pulled her foot back. She did not want to be here. Not without Sam. Instead of granting him leave, Admiral Stringham had ordered his arrest, charged with complicity in the escape of Captain Henry. Belle blamed herself. Once again someone she loved was being punished for her actions. The harsh reality was that Sam was in prison, and Belle was an exile. She took a deep breath and made herself step down.

Belle checked into the hotel that Captain Henry had mentioned before his escape. When she asked for him, she was told that he and his wife had departed for Niagara Falls the previous day. Captain Henry had left Belle a note inviting her to join them there, at the Clifton House.

Five days later, she met the captain and his wife in the lobby of the hotel.

"What a happy circumstance that we should meet again!" Belle cried, taking both their hands at once.

"Thank you so much, my dear, for what you did to aid my husband's escape. He says he couldn't have done it without your help."

Over dinner, Captain Henry told of his adventures in reaching Canada and being reunited with his wife. Then Belle recounted the sad tale of Sam's imprisonment. When she had finished, the captain said, "We can only hope that there will be no serious charges made against him. He did not aid in my escape. And there is no one to say that he did."

Despite her worry about Sam, as the meal went on, Belle couldn't help feeling somewhat cheerful. For the first time in years, she was not a prisoner, nor in danger of being arrested. She was not watched or followed or escorted by her enemies. The Union had no power over her anymore.

Captain Henry might have been reading her thoughts. Raising his glass, he said, "To freedom!"

*Martinsburg, West Virginia*

*Dear Miss Belle,*

*I hope this note reaches you before you leaves Canada. I know a slave has no bizness writing a letter, but I decided to anyways. When I told Miss Mary, she gave me a look. But I don't think she was surprised. She told me she'd put it inside one of her letters. Your sister's just as stiff-necked as ever, but I know I can trust her to do what she says.*

*I miss you too, Miss Belle. Looks like your life ain't slowed down none since you left home. First you gets kidnapped and almost sent back to prison. Then you ends up in Canada. And now you say you's sailing for England. And getting married! But the man you's marrying—Captain Sam Hardinge—he's in prison. I hope you're right and he gets out soon. Hard to marry a man that's in jail.*

*I pray that your captain is the right man for you. I wish I could meet him. You're not a good judge of a man, Miss Belle. Especially if he's handsome. Like that Yankee Smitley. And this one's a Yankee too. I just hope he's strong enough for you. And not too good looking.*

*I remember how when you was little I always used to say, "Slow down before you takes a fall!" You didn't listen to me then. So most probably, you won't listen now. But it makes me feel better to say it.*

*I think of you every day and remember you in my prayers.*

*Eliza Hopewell*

# Chapter 36

The mild summer weather ensured an easy crossing to England. This time, Belle was installed in a comfortable cabin, paid for with Confederate gold. Margaret slept on a padded bench beneath the porthole. Since Belle still traveled as Mrs. Lewis and was dressed in mourning, the other passengers assumed she was a young widow of the war and left her in peace. For once, she was grateful not to be the center of attention.

Belle carried Eliza's letter in her purse and often took it out to read. Eliza was right that Belle needed to slow down and think. She and Sam would marry once he was released from prison, but afterward, she would slow down. She would.

So much had happened in the past seven months, that even Belle felt breathless. She, who was always ready for the next challenge, wanted nothing at all to happen. She needed time to adjust to her new situation. She craved peace and quiet. And what could be better for that than a two-week transatlantic voyage on a luxurious passenger ship where no one asked anything more of her than which delicious pastry Madam wished to have with her tea?

Belle spent her days reclining on a deck chair with a book, or strolling with Margaret, or standing at the rail and staring out at the endless sea, feeling the sea breeze wash away the last taint of prison and illness. Although she was unhappy to be exiled from her family and her beloved Shenandoah Valley, it was a great relief to leave the war behind.

As the voyage neared its end, she began to feel her energy return. And a thrill of excitement. She was headed to London, the most sophisticated city in the world! A place she'd always dreamed of visiting. Really, she could hardly believe her good fortune. She was a free woman! She had faith that Sam would soon be free too. They would marry and start a new life together.

☙

In London, Belle checked into the elegant Hotel Bushwick, then wasted no time in contacting Mr. Hotze, part-time propagandist for the Confederacy. The official letters she had been given in Richmond were long gone, burned aboard the *Greyhound*. Belle remembered most of what was in them and recited their contents for Mr. Hotze, adding further information about the progress of the war and the situation in Richmond when she left. She apologized that her information was not more up to date. Her voyage had taken months longer than expected. Without going into details, she claimed to have been "overtaken by events."

Belle was disappointed that Mr. Hotze had no further instructions for her, a disappointment she quickly forgot when he handed her a letter from Sam. He had been there before her! After more than a month in a navy prison, he had been released and traveled immediately to London and contacted Mr. Hotze, whose name he remembered. But Belle had lingered in Canada with Captain and Mrs. Henry and had not yet arrived. Sam went off to Paris, for some reason thinking he might find her there. In the letter Mr. Hotze gave Belle, Sam told her the name of his hotel and she immediately sent off a telegram to Paris.

❧

Two days later, Sam was in the parlor of Belle's suite, and she was in his arms.

"All through my ordeal, I dreamed of nothing else but holding you like this."

Belle touched his cheek. "That ordeal is now over. Here we are. Together at last."

She sat and pulled him down beside her, then touched his cheek again. "Tell me what happened. I want to hear everything." Without waiting for his answer, she went on, "Are you hungry? Shall I ring for lunch?"

"No."

"You should eat. You're very thin, my dear."

"That's what five weeks in prison will do."

She pushed a lock of hair off his forehead. *Touching makes him real!*

"It's not just that. You look different."

"No uniform," Sam said shortly, and for a moment his face wore an expression Belle couldn't quite name. Then it was gone. "I didn't like wearing it, but that does not mean it was easy to put off."

"I like you better this way. Taking off that uniform is proof of your love."

Sam reached into his pocket and handed her a folded paper.

*For your neglect of duty, in permitting the Captain of the prize steamer GREYHOUND under your charge to escape, you are hereby dismissed from the Navy of the United States . . .*

Belle looked up. "It's the best you could have hoped for, isn't it?" she said gently. You're not in prison, and it's not a dishonorable discharge. They have released you, which is what you wanted. You are no longer a Yankee. I say, Hurrah!" She tried to coax a smile.

"I didn't expect it to feel like this."

Belle looked at his bowed head.

"Did you expect to feel this?" She moved closer and gave him a lingering kiss on the lips, of a type she had never given before, to anyone. He made a sound in his throat, part groan and part laugh, and leaned in for more. As for Belle, if her first real kiss was not quite what she had expected, still she was thrilled by Captain Hardinge's response.

*Not a captain anymore,* she reminded herself. *He's plain Mister Hardinge now.*

⁊

With Sam safely returned, Belle threw herself into exploring London. She wanted to see everything. Westminster Abbey. Buckingham Palace. The Houses of Parliament.

One afternoon, she begged Sam to take her for a ride on the new London Underground.

"Imagine it! Three miles of tracks in a tunnel beneath the streets. Traveling in gas lit carriages pulled by a steam engine. Everyone says it's perfectly safe."

When they arrived at Paddington Station and Belle looked at the elevator that descended underground, her courage failed her. Her dislike of closed spaces was worse than ever since her time in prison. As their turn came to step into the lift, she froze, not caring about the growing line of people behind them.

"I can't do it, Sam!" Belle's voice was panicked. "It will be like being buried alive. Down there in the dark." She had a fleeting, irrational image of Freddy Sprockett rotting in his grave.

"Noffinck to it, Madam," the lift operator assured her in his comical accent. "You'll see once you're down there on the platform. It's only twelve feet underground. And everythink lit up pretty as you please."

Sam put his arm around her, whispered in her ear. Belle closed her eyes and leaned on him, allowed herself to be guided into the elevator. And when she opened her eyes moments later, and stepped onto the platform, it was as bright as a summer's day. The train cars were roomy and comfortable. The whole business was splendid, she decided afterward, remembering how patient Sam had been when she had lost her nerve. It was comforting to know she could depend on him so completely.

At other times, Sam was not enough for her, and she craved a larger audience. Her arrival in London had been reported in the press—Sam's had not!—and she was warmly welcomed into the large Confederate community. They had so much in common. Not just that they were Southerners and living in London. Belle had traveled throughout the Confederacy and could talk to them for hours about people and places they knew.

Determined to entertain, Belle arranged small dinner parties, which Sam never seemed to enjoy. When the inevitable question was asked—"What will you do now, Mr. Hardinge?"—he would give a tight smile and reach for his wineglass. Belle had to answer for him. First the wedding. Then a brief return to America to deal with financial matters. Family obligations were mentioned. Possible service in the Confederate Navy. Enough to silence, if not satisfy, their curiosity.

When they weren't going to the theater, or horseback riding in Victoria Park, or entertaining or being entertained, Belle planned their wedding. Since neither of their families could attend, Sam wanted something small and intimate. He no longer had his pay as a Navy captain, and thought Belle's dress should be simple, their rings plain gold bands, and the reception limited to a dozen of Belle's closest friends.

"I've been here six weeks. I have many more friends than that," Belle insisted. "They will expect a stylish wedding."

Belle had been given five hundred dollars in Richmond to meet her expenses while abroad. She felt perfectly justified in using some of it to pay for her white silk dress, delicate veil, and bouquet of orange blossoms. Elegant invitations were printed on white ribbon and hand-delivered to a host of friends.

The ceremony took place in the morning of August 25, at St. James Church in Piccadilly, followed by a lavish wedding breakfast for their guests at the Brunswick Hotel. Later in the day, bride and groom left by train for a honeymoon at the seaside.

*London*
*Late August 1864 to Early January 1865*

# Chapter 37

Their suite at Brighton's Grand Hotel was everything Belle could wish for, with bright airy rooms and French doors leading to a balcony overlooking the beach. After the porter had left their luggage and softly closed the door, Belle stood gazing at the strolling couples, the children playing in the sand, a few intrepid bathers in the surf. Sam came and slid his arms around her waist.

"We should go for a walk," she said.

He nuzzled her neck. "Not now."

Laughing, Belle said, "What? You would deny your wife?"

"You are not my wife yet," he reminded her.

Somehow Belle had managed to think very little of this moment. Mama would have given her good advice. Her many pregnancies and the steadfast affection between her and Papa attested to their compatibility in the bedroom. And now Belle's own marriage bed awaited.

"Come," Sam said and tugged her gently from the window. Her body was rigid with tension, but she willed herself to relax and be led to the bedroom.

Thinking about it afterward, she decided that she liked best having Sam's arms around her, or when he stroked her skin, or looked at her in the lamplight and told her how beautiful she was. She liked seeing herself the way Sam saw her, the adoration in his eyes. And she was surprised to discover that she enjoyed the feeling of surrender. For so many years she had been in charge of her own fate—except, of course, when she was in prison. She liked being guided by his touch.

When they were not in the bedroom, which was Sam's preference, they were strolling the promenade, which was Belle's. She had never been to a seaside resort and loved the wildness of the endless gray-blue water, the crashing waves, the screaming gulls. She could not get enough of it. Then there was the wind that snatched her breath away and crushed her skirts against her legs so that she would have fallen if Sam hadn't kept his arms around her. His strong arms.

On the last day of their honeymoon, Belle told Sam she was still disappointed that Mama had not been able to attend the wedding. She said she wanted him to travel to West Virginia to meet her family and deliver her wedding album, which was something Mama would treasure forever. It would include their formal wedding photograph, along with newspaper articles about the ceremony, as well as one of the invitations, the beautifully engraved menu from the wedding breakfast, some notes of congratulation, and an envelope of orange blossom petals from Belle's bouquet. She wanted him to leave as soon as the album was complete. Since Martinsburg remained in Union hands, unfortunately Belle would be unable to go.

There was another reason for the trip. Belle had realized she would soon be out of money. Mama was now selling her tobacco directly to the Union Army and receiving Federal Reserve banknotes in payment. She wrote that she had been sending Belle funds, but none of the bank drafts had reached her in London, proof that her mail was still being intercepted.

"Let's just enjoy being together," Sam begged. "We have both sacrificed so much to be man and wife. Mr. and Mrs. Hardinge. I *will* go, my love. Only not right away. I want to see my parents too, as well as your family. But not yet."

After they returned to London, Sam began slow preparations for his trip, while Belle found herself at loose ends. She had no one to spy on. No secret dispatches to deliver. No wedding to plan.

With little to do, she spent hours studying the newspapers. One day, she was shocked to read that Rose Greenhow had drowned. The widow had been a well-known figure in London, and her death was written about in gruesome detail.

Rose had been returning from Europe to America aboard a blockade runner called the *Condor*. It was reported that she was carrying secret papers and had a leather purse of gold coins around her neck. The wreck happened in heavy weather off the coast of Cape Fear, not far from where the *Greyhound* had been captured. The ship carrying Rose had almost reached the safety of the harbor when, just three hundred yards from shore, in darkness, violent surf, and a lashing storm, hounded by Union ships, the blockade runner hit a sandbar. A few passengers, Rose among them, were put in a lifeboat with two sailors to row them to safety. The lifeboat flipped in the rough waves, and though the male passengers were able to swim to shore, Rose drowned.

Belle could see it all, the darkness, the rain, the wind, the pounding surf, and Rose, her long skirts tangling her legs, struggling to keep her head above the waves, the purse of gold around her neck weighing her down. Belle had worshipped Mrs. Greenhow and patterned her life on that of the older woman. Not quite willing to believe the story, she read the report again and again, unconsciously stroking her neck.

That evening in the hotel dining room, Sam asked, "Is everything all right, Belle? You're quiet."

A sigh. "Yes."

"The death of your friend is a blow."

"Mrs. Greenhow was not quite a friend, but certainly she was someone I admired."

"A terrible way to lose your life. Drowning like that, within sight of land."

Belle was toying with her wineglass. She noticed Sam's was empty. Was that his fourth or fifth? She'd lost count.

"You know, I've been thinking. Rose wrote a book about her adventures and had it published here in London. It was a quite successful. In fact, the money she was wearing when she . . ." Belle could not make herself say the word. "The money was from royalties she had earned. She was going to donate it to the Southern cause."

"Let me guess," Sam leaned forward into the candlelight, a half-smile on his face. "*You* want to write a book too."

"Don't you think I should? I'm sure people would be interested in my story. I may not have been quite so valuable to the Confederacy as Rose, but my adventures were more varied and more colorful. They say she invited men into her bed, important men, to steal their secrets, so she could pass them to Confederate generals." Now it was Belle who leaned into the light. "But I was the one who galloped over the countryside at night. I was the one who ran across a battlefield with bullets whizzing past. I was the one who ended up marrying the man who held me prisoner."

Sam settled back in his chair and raised his glass to her.

"You always were an excellent storyteller."

⁊

Belle began working on her book at once and produced thirty pages by the time Sam was ready to leave. It seemed that as soon as she stopped pushing, he decided he actually *did* want to go. He was especially keen on seeing his parents, a mother to whom he was closer than Belle had realized, and a father whose good opinion was important to him, no matter that Sam wriggled like a worm on a hook whenever he spoke of him.

Sam's plan changed many times before he left. The Union blockade was proving fatal to Confederate shipping. Nine ships out of ten were sunk or captured. They agreed it was safer for Sam to sail into a Northern port, although this posed its own risks, since there were rumors that the Federal government had issued a warrant for his arrest. However, he was determined to see his family in Brooklyn as well as Belle's in Martinsburg, and so finally they decided New York should be his port of entry.

While he was away, Sam was a faithful correspondent. He wrote that his visit with his parents was amicable. Somehow, despite his hasty marriage to a woman of dubious reputation whom they had never met, and his imprisonment and dismissal from the Union Navy, he claimed that he had managed to reassure them that all was well. He then proceeded by train to Martinsburg, where he met Mama, Mary, and Grandmother, and delivered Belle's precious album. He stayed just a single night, but even that was too long. The next day on the train headed north, he was arrested and charged with being a deserter.

"Which is hardly fair," Belle said to Margaret, Sam's letter still in her hand. "The Navy *dismissed* him, so he can't be a deserter. They must want him for something else."

"Do they think he's a spy?"

"They are perfectly capable of thinking any idiotic thing they please!" Belle said hotly, burying her fears under indignation, as she so often did.

# Chapter 38

In Sam's absence, Belle's situation grew desperate. Another letter from her mother containing a bank draft failed to reach her. The money Belle had spent so freely from the moment she arrived in London was almost gone. She started pawning bits of jewelry, as well as the silver bowls and spoons and pitchers she had received as wedding gifts.

Worse still, she was pregnant. She calculated that the baby would be born sometime in May. How she wished Eliza could be with her! It seemed horribly unfair to be so far from home and family at such a time. Sam being gone—in prison—made things even worse.

*Never mind.* She couldn't afford to dwell on either of those problems. There was nothing she could do to help Sam, and the baby wasn't due for another four months. Her immediate problem was money. Despite all her difficulties, her book was finished, and she had made an appointment to show it to a publisher.

The day before the appointment was a Sunday, and Margaret went to church, leaving Belle with no one to talk to. She decided to go for a walk and was pinning on her hat when there was a knock at the door.

The hotel manager stood in the hallway, carrying an envelope and smiling awkwardly.

"May I come in?"

"Of course," Belle said, standing aside.

He entered, casting an admiring look around him. "I have always particularly liked this suite of rooms."

Belle was exceedingly short-tempered these days. She knew why the man was here and had no patience for his clumsy maneuvering.

"Rooms which will shortly belong to someone else. Since you are here to ask me to leave. Due to the unpaid bill which you hold in your hand." To the manager's startled look, she snapped, "Am I correct?" and snatched the bill from his hand.

"Y-yes. Quite correct. I must say I admire your directness, Mrs. Hardinge. Quite—dare I say it? —American."

Belle ripped open the envelope and read the amount without an outward flinch.

"Can you pay it?"

It seemed that the manager could also be direct.

"I shall pay some of it now, and the rest I shall pay later. Ample funds have been wired to me. You have no cause for worry. Meanwhile, I will vacate these rooms so you can rent them to someone else. Will tomorrow be soon enough? If that is all, I believe we have concluded our business."

Once again, the manager was gaping like a caught fish. When he did not move, Belle said firmly, "Good-day, sir," and opened the door.

෴

When Margaret returned, she too gaped when Belle told her they were moving.

"Where will we go?"

Belle laughed shortly. "London is full of hotels."

"That's true. And there's a number as is quite nice, and not so dear as this one."

"Then I shall find one of those. This afternoon, in fact. And you must start packing."

"Please, ma'am." It seemed Margaret was not ready to be dismissed. "I know the news from Mr. Hardinge has not been good. And so I was wondering . . ." Belle waited. Margaret was rarely at a loss for words, but evidently her wheels had stopped.

"You were wondering if you'll be receiving this month's wages on time," Belle said, trying not to show her irritation, as Margaret had every right to ask. "The answer is, of course you will."

A bobbing curtsey. "Thank you, ma'am!" Belle waited for Margaret to leave, but she had more to say. "Please forgive me for speaking out of turn." A pause. "You said once as how we're in a play. So I wanted to ask. About the play. It isn't going to end badly, is it?"

"Not for us."

"Us?"

"You and me and the baby." Then, to Margaret's look of surprise, "Oh yes! There's going to be a baby."

∽

Taking action always raised Belle's spirits. She could never abide just sitting and waiting for things to happen. The following morning, leaving Margaret to unpack their things in the new hotel, Belle went to the offices of George Augusta Sala, a well-respected London editor known to be a friend of the South. Her friends had told her he might be interested in publishing her memoir.

Mr. Sala was expecting her. Still, he was visibly startled when Belle held her manuscript out, saying, "Will you take my life?" She had planned ahead of time what she would say, purposely choosing her words for dramatic effect.

Mr. Sala took the pages from her, a neat stack written in Belle's distinctive script and tied with a red silk ribbon. Then he invited her to sit and proceeded to make polite conversation along the theme of Belle's adventures. Like so many others, he seemed to think her many escapes indicated a charmed life. She tried to persuade him that courage and intelligence had also played their part.

"Regardless, it seems that my luck has run out at present."

Belle told him of her present difficulties. A young lady of charm, education, and accomplishment, alone and nearly penniless, exiled to a foreign land, thousands of miles from husband or family. Intercepted letters containing much-needed funds were mentioned. A lace handkerchief artfully deployed.

Mr. Sala—"Call me George"—promised to read her memoir right away. He told her he would write a letter at once to one of the London newspapers and make Belle's situation known to her friends in the city. The handkerchief was put away. Tea was taken.

The next day, the *Morning Herald* featured an article hinting at Belle's reduced circumstances. Soon there were generous gifts and offers of assistance from friends and supporters. Belle was delighted. Her immediate money problems were over.

Four weeks later, "Call me George" wrote that he had finished her manuscript and was sure readers would find it fascinating. Not only that, he pronounced it nearly ready for publication. Belle was delighted. Her book would be published in just three months! Mr. Sala felt that her story should remain just as she had written it, "The unambitious narrative of an enthusiastic and intrepid school-girl."

Belle, of course, liked being called "intrepid" but was less fond of being described as a schoolgirl. However, it was true that when her adventures began on that long-ago July 4 of 1861, she was only seventeen and just out of school. In any case, she had been presenting herself to the public in different guises for years now. She was desperate for her book to sell and readily agreed to all Mr. Sala's suggestions.

*London*
*Late February to Late May 1865*

# Chapter 39

S am was released from prison at the end of February and immediately took passage on a transatlantic steamer. He was back in London by the middle of March. For a second time, he had rushed to Belle straight from prison. However, this time, their reunion was less affectionate.

He was not the same man who had left just a few months before. His eyes were sunken, his face thin, his skin an unhealthy grey. He suffered from tooth pain. He complained of a tightness in his chest which could be relieved only by copious amounts of strong red claret. He expressed little interest in the imminent birth of his first child.

By now Belle was in her seventh month of pregnancy and suffering her own discomforts. They seemed trivial, though, compared to the fact that her friends no longer visited her. She was not sure why they had stopped. Belle herself could not go out. No woman so obviously pregnant could be seen in public. Nor could she go out to dinner or attend the theater or ride in a carriage or take a walk in the park.

How she longed to stretch her legs. To breathe fresh air, to tire herself out. To move! The endless days indoors were an unwelcome reminder of her time in prison. Admittedly, her surroundings were more pleasant, and she could choose whatever food she wanted to be sent up from the hotel kitchen. But this time she was confined not just in her rooms, but also inside her own body. She had always been vain about her figure, but now she avoided looking at herself in the mirror. When she did, she couldn't help feeling that this swollen, distorted shape must surely belong to someone else.

Belle passed the time as best she could in games of solitaire or reading novels she sent Margaret out to buy. She even tried knitting a baby blanket, thinking resentfully that this was the sort of ridiculous thing a woman was expected to do when pregnant. Belle had neither the talent nor the patience for knitting. She dropped stitches. She lost track of how many rows she'd done. Somehow she managed to make knots in the yarn. Her feelings were as snarled as the mess she was making. Knitting did not relax her. It put her in a rage.

And so did Sam. He was rarely home. Not only did he make no attempt to keep her company in her confinement, he went off and did all the things Belle wished to do. When the weather was too cold for riding or walking, he liked to spend time in the hotel lobby with its soft chairs and wide selection of newspapers. Belle thought of him sitting there, legs crossed, a glass of wine at his elbow, able to watch the hotel's wide glass doors swing open, bringing new arrivals in a swirl of silk gowns and top hats, along with a gust of fresh air, a swell of conversation, a burst of laughter.

Sam was gone most evenings as well, often not returning until morning. In case he did come back, Belle had given Margaret instructions to have a bed made up and waiting on the parlor sofa. They no longer slept together.

Even when Sam was present, he was poor company, Belle thought. She began to suspect that he actually enjoyed complaining about his time in Forrest Hall. She knew its reputation as the very worst of the Federal prisons, cold, damp, and rat-infested, with food barely fit for humans. Its nickname, the Last Ditch, was in recognition of the fact that it was considered one step short of the grave. She had only to look at Sam to see that his health *had* suffered. But she felt no sympathy for him because he had none for her. He rarely kept her company. He never asked how she felt in the morning, or at the end of another long, tiresome day.

Sam never gave any thought to what Belle's life had been like while he was gone. She had tried to tell him how difficult it was. To be alone. To discover she was pregnant, to pawn her jewelry, to be asked to leave her hotel, to have to reveal her situation to Mr. Sala, a total stranger. These humiliations had felt like hot needles pushed under her skin. Belle had carried off each one with bravado, but still they rankled. Sam had not shared in her worries and privations. He hadn't been there when she needed him. And he was supposed to be. *Isn't that what marriage is about? Through better and worse?* He had returned to London only after Belle had solved their financial difficulties through her own ingenuity and hard work. Without any help at all from him, her husband. She had forgotten that it was she who had sent Sam away in the first place.

One evening, he surprised Belle by staying in and dining with her in the parlor of their hotel suite. The evening began pleasantly enough, but by the end of the meal, Sam had clearly had too much wine. He pushed his chair away from the table, filled his glass yet again, and said, "I'm thinking of writing a book myself. I've spent as much time in prison as you, under far worse conditions."

Belle said nothing.

"Then we'd have two writers in the family. I'd like to give readers the benefit of my version of events."

"Would it differ from mine?"

"Only in a few particulars." Sam declined to elaborate.

"What will be the title of your book?" Belle asked.

"I was thinking of calling it *The Wreck*." He said this with a dramatic sweep of his arms. "Don't you think that's a good title? You, the writer?"

"What does it refer to?" Belle asked, though she was sure she knew.

"Me, of course. Your husband. Samuel Hardinge. Former Captain in the U.S. Navy. Dismissed for—let's see if I have the words right—for 'neglect of duty.' Yes, that's it."

"You're talking rubbish," Belle said sharply. "You do nothing but drink from morning till night. Look at you! You can barely hold your head up. Your shirt front is dribbled with food."

"So you agree. I *am* a wreck!"

"Oh, Sam."

"You don't even try to understand, do you? You never did. What it's been like for me. In this whole city, the greatest in the world, I am known only as Belle Boyd's husband. No one here knows anything about me except for what they refer to as 'events aboard the *Greyhound*.' Women say it with a sort of simpering delight, the men with sympathetic scorn. They knew I was ruined, even before I knew it myself. They understood that I had thrown everything away. Everything that mattered. My country. My family. My honor. I threw it all away. And for what? A woman who doesn't respect me."

"How can I respect you? You should see yourself! Wallowing in self-pity."

Sam poured more wine.

"I'm moving out." He stood up, swaying unsteadily, and stumbled from the room.

❧

In early May, George Sala dropped off five copies of *Belle Boyd in Camp and Prison* and reported that it was selling briskly. Belle spent several satisfying days reading it and admiring the handsome blue cover. With her name at the top. Right where it belonged.

George also delivered a royalty check—for more money than Belle had expected. Before her confinement, she had found a larger apartment that she had hoped to be able to afford. With Mr. Sala's assurance that her book's strong sales would continue, she sent Margaret off to see the manager and give him instructions to have the apartment ready in two weeks' time. Surely by then, this baby would have put in an appearance.

Obligingly, Grace Hardinge was born the following week, after fourteen hours of agony. "A healthy baby girl," the midwife kept saying. As if that was all that mattered. Not a word of praise about Belle's bravery during her hours of torment. Eliza would have praised her.

Afterward, the doctor told Belle she was lucky the delivery had been an easy one. As if she should thank him. When it was Belle who had suffered. Belle who'd done all the work. How could women endure such pain? How could Mama have done this eight times?

Dear Mama. Belle missed her terribly. Mama and Eliza both. They would have fussed over Belle. Cossetted her. Prepared all her favorite foods. Taken care of her in just the ways they knew she liked. It seemed that all anyone cared about was Grace. Belle had hired a wet-nurse. So at least that was taken care of.

One thing she was absolutely sure of. She would never have another child.

❦

In a matter of weeks, Belle's life had changed completely. She was now a successful author and a mother and the head of her own household. A self-made independent woman! She was fiercely proud of what she had achieved. And it seemed her independence would be permanent. Sam had written asking her to send his things to a London address, in care of a certain Mrs. Annabelle Sinclair.

Belle tried not to think about the fact that her husband had deserted her. That her marriage had lasted less than a year. She told herself that Sam Hardinge was not the man she had thought him to be. That he was a useless drunk. A weakling. She told herself that she was well rid of him, choosing not to remember how much they had once cared for each other. She could not think of that now. Being an independent woman meant she had no one to rely on but herself. She must look to the future. Belle sent Sam his things, along with a note telling him he had a daughter. He wrote back his congratulations but expressed no interest in meeting Grace.

❦

Belle's friends, who had avoided her in recent months, flocked back, filling her new apartment with their congratulations and best wishes. She decided she must forgive them. The awkwardness of an early pregnancy combined with her money embarrassments along with obvious marital problems really had been too much! And Belle wanted their praise. She craved it. She was proud of her book. And of Grace, too, of course.

The visitors often arrived in groups, and Belle was always pleased when she saw one of them carrying her book, wanting her to write a message inside. It felt like years since she'd been the center of attention this way. The object of everyone's admiration. More than anything, she loved it when a guest opened the book to a favorite passage and read Belle's own words out loud to her other visitors.

"'A Federal shell struck the ground within twenty yards of my feet; and the explosion, of course, sent the fragments flying in every direction around me. I had, however, just time to throw myself flat upon the ground.'"

Then someone would exclaim, "How could you have been so brave?"

Or, "How did you feel, knowing you might be killed at any moment?"

Belle shrugged with becoming modesty. "When I think back on it, I am amazed myself at some of the things I did."

"The dress with the bullet holes? Do you still have it?"

"I meant to save it. But in the end I cut it up so my servant could make shirts for two wounded Rebel soldiers. Their need was greater than mine."

More sighs and exclamations.

"Yet here you are. A mother with a new baby!"

They asked to see the infant. If Grace was not sleeping, the nurse brought her in and handed her to Belle, who held her daughter somewhat awkwardly while the visitors continued their flattery. Eventually their conversation passed on to other things. Belle didn't mind. After all, what was there to say about a baby?

In any event, there was so much else to talk about. One dramatic development after another. The war had ended unexpectedly a month earlier, with Robert E. Lee's surrender to Ulysses S. Grant at Appomattox Court House. Five days later, on April 14, Abraham Lincoln was assassinated while attending a play at the Ford Theater in Washington D.C. Andrew Johnson succeeded him as president.

⁐

On May 29, 1865, President Johnson issued a Proclamation of Amnesty, pardoning those who had fought against the Union. For so many years, Belle had dreamed of going home, but now she decided to wait. She had consulted a London lawyer and told him she wanted a divorce. He said he had never heard of a woman divorcing her husband, but that, under certain circumstances, it was possible to do so. As long as one did not care what other people thought. Which, of course, Belle never had!

One major difficulty still remained. Belle had to find a reliable way to support herself and Grace. She knew her book would not always be so popular as it was now, with the Civil War just ended. Since she had no plans to remarry, she had to be able to support herself and Grace indefinitely. She needed a dependable income.

What work did respectable women do? They were maids and governesses. She could hardly be a servant! What else was permitted? A woman might own a shop or an inn, but that required capital, which she did not have. And owning a business might not provide her with enough income. She did not mean to live in poverty! There did not seem to be an answer unless she married, which she simply would not do! It was all very difficult.

Perhaps though, the problem was in that one small word—"permitted." After all, Belle had spent her entire life doing things that were not permitted.

⁐

"Margaret, I am making a list of my talents," Belle declared one morning. She sat at her desk, pen in hand. Margaret was walking back and forth, Baby Grace in her arms.

"Here's what I have so far. Horsemanship. Singing. I am a gifted storyteller, or so I'm told. And a graceful dancer." She frowned. "I've always thought of myself as very accomplished, but it's quite a short list. Can you think of anything I've forgotten?"

"You are always elegantly dressed, madam. And you stand and walk beautifully. You have perfect posture. Almost like a queen. Also you have a lovely speaking voice."

"Hmm." Belle stared moodily at the list, then her lips curved into a smile.

"Storytelling. A lovely voice for singing and speaking. Graceful movement. Elegant appearance. What do all these gifts suggest?"

"I have no idea."

"I shall become an actress!"

*Martinsburg, West Virginia*

*Dear Miss Belle,*

*I was helping out at your mama's when your letter came yesterday. She read it to Mary with me in the room so I could hear it too. We was all surprised you and your husband is not living together anymore. That you got a divorce. Sounds like things has been hard for you. And with a baby to care for. Your mama cried some, but Mary was mad as a wet cat. Says it's scandalous. Says not a single person in all Martinsburg ever got a divorce. Maybe even in all West Virginia. She says if people find out, it could keep her from finding a husband. Then, when your mama read about how now you is an actress on stage—well, Mary near had a fit. Your letter told how you hired a famous actor to teach you. And that when he said you were ready, you went on tour.*

*Later, your mama and me talked about it. I think she didn't want to talk to Mary because your sister gets so angry at you. Mary doesn't try and understand. Your mama will always stand by you, even if she don't like what you do. She says you told her you has to earn money to support Grace. That you don't want to get married again. That your Sam didn't take care of you anyways, so why not take care of your own self? I guess that makes sense.*

*Me and my Sam have our own place now, but I still help out your mama sometimes. She pays me wages. I have a daughter now myself. Named Lee Laura. My Sam adores her. John lives with us. He's sixteen and works in the livery stable. Sam does barbering and I deliver babies. Everything's just like I said it would be.*

*—Eliza Hopewell*

*P.S. Be careful, Miss Belle. So later on you won't have no regrets. You can never undo the past.*

*Martinsburg, West Virginia*
*January and February 1868*

# Chapter 40

W hen Belle finally returned to Martinsburg, she arrived in the middle of preparations for Mary's marriage to a Baltimore lawyer named Oregon Wentworth Rowland. The advantage of arriving at such a busy time was that all the talk was about the upcoming wedding. The disadvantage was that Belle was expected to spend each morning in the sewing room with Mama and Mary, stitching sheets and hemming pillowcases for Mary to take to her new home. Both her mother and her sister knew that Belle had no skill with a needle, but sewing a wedding trousseau was a female ritual. Belle must be part of it.

In spite of everything that had happened, everything Belle had done in the years she'd been away, her mother welcomed her with the same love and affection she'd always shown. Belle had been dragged off to prison, released, exiled to England, married a stranger, divorced, become an actress, had a child. Mama forgave it all. Perhaps the reason was Grace herself, Mama's first grandchild. Or perhaps it was as Eliza said, that Belle's mother would always make allowances for her wayward daughter, even now that she was a grown woman.

At any rate, Mama was enchanted by Grace, frequently commenting on how much her granddaughter was like Belle at the same age. Now almost three, the little girl spent her days running between the kitchen and garden, reporting her adventures later to a captivated audience. How her Uncle Will had given her a ride in the wheelbarrow. How he'd helped her climb a tree. How they'd found a bird's nest. How Delia taught her to make pies.

Mary also doted on Grace, often cuddling her niece on her lap at the end of another busy day. Yet her warm affection was reserved for Grace alone. She did not seem at all pleased to have Belle home. *Divorce* was not mentioned. The word *actress* was never spoken. Yet it was always there. Belle thought it was typical of her sister not to say what she felt, but to make her feelings known just the same.

☙

One sunny morning, the three Boyd women sat together as usual in the small sewing room, Belle's mother and sister chatting contentedly as they worked. Belle had taken on a special task that day. She was sewing lace on the dress Mary had made for Grace to wear in the wedding. The little girl was ecstatic at the prospect of being a flower girl. She adored the pink satin dress and was impatient for it to be finished. When Belle asked Mary if she could sew on the lace, her sister had raised her eyebrows and handed her the dress without saying a word. Now Belle worked at it with grim determination, anxious not to spoil the pretty gown with her poor sewing. The lace could not be crooked! Her stitches must not show!

With the windows closed and the sun shining brightly, the room was much too warm. Belle was miserable. She could feel a headache coming on. Her fingers were cramped from clutching the needle too tightly. Glancing out the window, she wondered what time it was. Sometimes, after lunch, she managed to escape to Eliza's, her excuse being that Grace enjoyed playing with Lee Laura. The real reason was Belle's need to flee her sister's disapproval.

Belle held her sewing up to the light to see if the lace was straight.

Would she have to rip out her stitches again? Grace had come in several times already to check her mother's progress, sighing with exasperation when she saw how much work remained. Belle knew her daughter was eager to try on the dress so she could practice tossing flower petals from an imaginary basket.

This time, Grace lingered by Belle's chair. "When will you be finished, Mama?"

"Soon, I hope."

"That's what you said before. Aunt Mary would be finished by now."

"Mary has her own sewing to do," Belle said, speaking more sharply than she intended.

"Run along to the kitchen, darling," Mary suggested. "Ask Delia for a biscuit."

Grace scampered away, and the room settled into silence. Belle's fingers tightened on her needle. Would Mary now criticize her for how she had spoken to her own daughter?

Instead Mary said, "I've written to Rowland. He says he is pleased to have Grace come to live with us. I've told him how charming she is. And I'm sure when Rowland meets you, he'll realize you're still a lady. In spite of everything."

Belle knew she must hold her tongue. She was depending on Mama to take care of Grace so she could continue her career as an actress. But it turned out that Mama had planned to move to Baltimore after the wedding, taking Will with her. So now Rowland was also opening his home to Grace. It was very generous indeed. And it was generous of Mary as well, though Belle was sure her sister's offer had little to do with helping Belle and everything to do with keeping Grace.

"I think it is good of Rowland to be willing to overlook . . ." Mary paused delicately. ". . . your circumstances."

Belle just could not keep silent. "You mean the fact that his future sister-in-law is a divorced actress?"

"Yes, if you must be so . . ."

"Honest?" Belle interrupted. "If I must be honest?" She stopped pretending to sew. "Would you rather I lied?"

"I was going to say, if you must be so direct. You act as though you are proud of what you do."

Belle jumped to her feet, Grace's pretty dress sliding to the floor.

"Why should I be ashamed? I've done nothing wrong. My husband was unfaithful to me. It is not I who was unfaithful to him. I divorced him, and now I must earn a living. As an actress. Think about it, Mary. If a well-bred lady chooses not to marry, what kinds of work are open to her? Would you rather I was a servant? Or worked in a tavern? I could be a school mistress if I didn't mind starving. What would you have me do?"

Mama flapped her hands in the air. "Stop!" she begged. "You're sisters. You must learn to be friends. Fannie and I were always close. We depended on each other. I can't tell you how I miss her now she's gone. One day I'll be gone too. But you'll still have each other. To turn to in difficult times."

A wave of shame washed over Belle. Hadn't she caused Mama enough unhappiness? She must not let Mary provoke her.

Belle dropped to her knees next to her mother's chair.

"Forgive me, Mama." Turning to Mary, she said, "I'm sorry. Truly I am."

"This should be a happy time," Mama said, her lip trembling. "Papa is gone. Grandmother is too. But our Mary is getting married. We have Belle home. And then there's Grace!"

*You're a trained actress, Belle. Surely you can do this! For Mama's sake.*

Belle crossed to where her sister sat and embraced her.

"I wish you every happiness, Mary. I'm sure you'll be much better at marriage than I ever was." *That much at least is true!* "You will make a wonderful wife. And mother."

"And I promise to be a second mother to Grace. While you are away."

Belle returned to her chair. No one said anything more. One by one, they picked up their sewing and began to stitch, Belle thinking guiltily that never before had there been such an argument under Mama's roof.

*Perhaps now is the time to tell them the rest of my plans, as long as Mary and I are already disagreeing about the life I've chosen.*

"I've decided to take a stage name. To avoid embarrassing the family. I truly do not wish to cause either of you distress. Or Rowland." Belle paused. "I shall be known as Nina Benjamin." With a glance at her mother, she asked hesitantly, "Do you approve?"

"Benjamin for your father, and Nina for the baby who died after Gettysburg." Mama smiled sadly. "Of course I approve. Though it does seem strange to change your name."

"I'll never forget who I am."

Another silence fell. Then Mary asked, "What are the rest of your plans, Belle?"

"I've accepted a position as a starring actress with a theater company in New Orleans. I'll leave from Baltimore. Right after the wedding."

"Louisiana!" Mama exclaimed. "Why that's practically a foreign country!"

"What is it like there?" Mary asked. To Belle's sensitive ears, she sounded curious. Nothing more.

"New Orleans is unlike any city I've ever visited," Belle said. "I was there during the war. It's very beautiful. There are gardens everywhere. Most people speak French. Their cooking is full of strange spices. Even the coffee tastes different. They mix it with hot milk. It's called *café au lait.*"

"*Caffay-oh-lay,*" Mama repeated with a smile. "Such a pretty sounding word."

Mary pressed her lips together in disapproval. "I have never understood how you can enjoy traveling to so many different places. Especially one where they don't even speak English."

"You and I are so different, Mary. I like not knowing what to expect. To me, the same thing day after day is . . . Oh, I can't explain it." Belle waved her hand, brushing aside introspection. "Let's talk of something else." Turning to Mama, she asked, "What will you do with the house when you go to Baltimore?"

"I've found someone to rent it. The Osbournes. Remember how they took you and Mary to visit Papa at Harper's Ferry? They left Martinsburg shortly after and moved to Charlottesville. Their house here stood empty all through the war. It was badly damaged. Floors and staircases ripped out. Heaven only knows why. Frances and Felix will live here while it's being repaired."

"You would never actually sell the house, would you, Mama?" Belle's voice wobbled. She knew she sounded like a child, but she didn't care. Her whole life, this house had been waiting for her. If she needed it. "It's my only home!"

"And you were hardly ever here," Mama said, touching Belle's cheek as if to soften the words.

⌘

Two days after Mary's wedding, Mama and Grace accompanied Belle to the train station to see her off to New Orleans. As the conductor called "All aboard!" one last time, Belle knelt to give

Grace a final hug. Her daughter buried her face in Belle's chest and burst into noisy tears.

Looking at her mother over Grace's head, for a moment Belle's resolve weakened. Should she take Grace with her? Could that work? What about her plans to return to the stage? No, it was impossible. Anyway, Belle would soon be irritated with Grace's crying. And even if the child did stop, there would be the rest of the day for them to fill. And not just one day. One day, and then another.

Belle eased herself out of her daughter's arms, then took out her lacy handkerchief and used it to wipe Grace's tears. "Look, darling! Mama's going to give you her prettiest handkerchief. You can use it to wave good-bye. Won't that be nice?"

After hugging her own mama one last time, Belle stepped aboard the train and found her seat. By the time she lowered the window, the train was already moving slowly out of the station. Belle leaned out the window and waved until the white flash of Grace's flapping handkerchief had disappeared.

As the engine gained speed, Belle settled back in her seat with a sigh of satisfaction. She always enjoyed setting off on a journey, even one that promised to be long and challenging. It would take her more than three days to reach her destination. First she would travel south to Lynchburg, Virginia. Then west to Grand Junction, Tennessee. Then south again to New Orleans. Three trains. Six states. Fourteen hundred miles.

She did not mind having to sleep sitting up. Perhaps because of her time in prison, small inconveniences didn't bother her as they would most women. The padded seats were comfortable, the car well heated. She was wrapped in a warm wool traveling cloak. Mama had sent along a large basket of food, a necessity on such a long trip. Belle felt certain she would have everything she needed.

It was a relief to leave Baltimore behind. The wedding had been a trial. Although she was happy for Mary—who had never wanted anything more than to be a wife and mother—Belle had not much enjoyed her role as the divorced sister of the bride. And an actress, no less! Somehow many of the guests had seemed aware of her "unusual situation," as they tactfully phrased it. Mostly though, they chose not to speak with her at all, satisfying themselves with curious glances and excited whispers, all of which Belle did her best to ignore.

Then there was Grace, who refused to stay at Belle's side during the wedding luncheon, constantly running off to be with the bride and groom. *She's just a child,* Belle had told herself, *enjoying the excitement of being in a wedding and wearing a pretty dress. I should be happy she and Mary are so fond of each other. It gives me the freedom to pursue a life of my own.* Still she remembered the ache of seeing the two of them together. Her daughter and her sister—both of them glowing with excitement and happiness. Truthfully, it had seemed to Belle that the day would never end.

Now she gazed contentedly out the window at the changing scenery. She realized she had always been interested in geography, remembering the military map she had drawn in the early months of the war. Perhaps it came from her days as a horsewoman, when she had only a few seconds to judge the firmness of the ground or the height of a jump. Geography was easier to see in winter, with everything stripped away. Fields and forests were laid brown and bare. Hills rolled smoothly into the distance. Streams and rivers flashed blue, ice sparkling along their banks.

Everywhere she looked, there were signs of recovery from the war's devastation. New outbuildings. Mended fences. Plowed fields. Once in a while, in the middle distance, she would see a large, gracious home. Or sometimes the ruins of one, which was always a shock. Belle had traveled through this landscape while these lovely houses still stood. It pained her to see the leaning chimneys and blackened timbers. So much beauty gone!

Belle did not want to think about the war. It was over. It was not good to look back, she reminded herself. She must think about the future. *Her* future. The steady forward motion of the train helped her relax and think. Really, she did some of her best thinking on trains.

Everyone in Baltimore had been happy. So full of new beginnings. Every one of them. Mary, Rowland, Grace, Mama, her brother Will. They were all beginning something new. Without her.

*Don't worry,* she told herself. *Don't be sad. You will have you own new beginning.*

*New Orleans, Louisiana*
*March 1868*

# Chapter 41

"Nina! Nina!" A chorus of voices greeted Belle as she walked into David Bidwell's drawing room.

David was the owner of the New Orleans Theater, and the evening's host. He gave a party every Saturday night for everyone in the company and whatever guests they chose to bring. It was a good night for merrymaking, since the theater was closed on Sunday and they could all sleep late the next morning. He'd promised Belle a lively gathering of actors, artists, performers, and musicians. As if she needed persuading. The fact that the party began at the thrilling hour of midnight was reason enough to attend.

Belle responded to the welcoming shouts with an exaggerated curtsey, her head bowed. The truth was she did not want her new friends to see that their warm greeting had nearly brought her to tears. How long was it since she'd walked into a room full of people and been greeted with such enthusiasm? When she was seventeen, she'd always felt she had to entertain guests with singing and storytelling to be sure of her welcome. Here, there was no need. These people had accepted her immediately. Belle did not have to work to win their affection. She was one of them. She belonged.

One of the actresses glided up and took Belle by the hand. It was Adeline, a tall, blonde beauty, much quieter than the others in the company. Yet Belle had watched how she bloomed onstage like a flower opening to the sun. Adeline had been kind to Belle since the moment they'd met.

"Sit with me a while before we join the others," Adeline said. She led Belle across the room to a settee in the corner, detouring past several guests gathered around a man doing card tricks.

"Is it always like this?" Belle asked after they sat, lifting her chin toward David, who sat at the piano surrounded by a group of singers.

Adeline nodded. "You've seen how he is. David loves people. His father was a riverboat captain, and from the time he was a little boy, David would entertain the passengers with singing and dancing. You should see him dance the flip-flap!" She laughed. "Back then, they threw him pennies. Now he owns two successful theaters. David is a happy man."

Before Belle had a chance to wonder if everyone knew so much about David Bidwell, her new friend asked, "How are you settling in?"

"I've rented rooms near the theater. The furniture is a bit worn, but I've done my best with it. My apartment overlooks a courtyard with ferns and a fountain, even a palm tree. Every morning I drink my coffee and watch for a certain bird who comes to bathe in the fountain. Then he perches in a sunny spot and sings me an aria."

"It sounds charming."

"Will you visit me tomorrow, Adeline? You would be my first guest." Belle smiled. "I can offer you coffee. And a concert."

෩

The next morning, Belle's Creole servant, a sixteen-year-old girl named Lisette, opened the door to Adeline, then slipped past her and hurried to a nearby café for coffee and beignets. Belle had discovered the powdered sugar donuts on her first day and was already much too fond of them. While Belle and Adeline waited for Lisette to return, they toured the apartment, walking arm-in-arm like old friends.

"How clever you are at disguising your furniture with shawls and pillows. You're much better at that sort of thing than I am."

"I've had no choice. I've led the life of a gypsy ever since I was a young woman, making a home for myself wherever I was."

Belle did not say more. She liked Adeline, but it was too early to tell her any details about the past. She had resolved that New Orleans would be a fresh beginning. She would try to follow Eliza's advice. She would be careful. Certainly she would not tell Adeline about her time in prison. Or that she had a child. David thought she was a widow. This was what everyone at the theater believed. It wasn't true, but Belle didn't care. She told herself that Sam Hardinge might well have managed to drink himself to death by now.

Soon Lisette returned from the café. Belle and Adeline settled themselves at a small table near the windows, sipped their café au lait, and nibbled pastries. The promised bird appeared, splashed in the fountain, and broke into song.

"I love New Orleans," Belle confessed, patting sugar from her lips. "It's so different from other places. The rules are not so strict. A woman can walk wherever she likes without a gentleman escorting her. You and I can be friends even though our mamas didn't grow up together. I know I will be happy here."

Adeline smiled and sipped her coffee. "You don't mind living alone?"

"I find I rather enjoy it, although I've never truly lived alone before." *Not quite true, but near enough.* "When I was a girl, I always had my family around me. Later my husband." There—Belle had at least mentioned him.

Tactfully ignoring Belle's confession, Adeline said only, "You're right about New Orleans. In most cities, people would think it indecent for a woman to live alone. With no one to protect her honor."

"I am perfectly capable of defending my honor without help from any man."

"So I see," Adeline said, nodding her head toward the small pistol Belle wore in a pretty belt at her waist.

Belle looked down at the gun. It was the same one Papa had given her during the war. When she returned from London, she'd been so pleased to find it among the things she'd left behind in her room. She'd taken it to Baltimore and carried it in her purse when she boarded the train for New Orleans. Tucking it into her belt before she arrived, she decided she would wear it always. It would help her remember who she was. Belle Boyd. Not Nina Benjamin.

"Are you a good shot?" Adeline asked, still smiling.

"Yes."

Adeline blinked at her curt response while Belle sat motionless, lost in the past. After a few minutes, she roused herself to ask, "And you. Do you also live alone?"

"Not alone, no." After a pause, Adeline added, "I live with one of the company."

Belle realized her guest was as reluctant as she was to burden a new friendship with too many confessions. Yet she couldn't resist asking, "Who?"

"Can't you guess?"

Belle thought back and finally said, "David."

Adeline's cheeks turned pink. "We're not married."

Belle shrugged. "No one cares."

"At any rate, no one we know."

Belle heard a note of sadness in Adeline's voice. One day she was sure they would tell each other more. But not today.

# Chapter 42

After the actors took their final bows, Belle lingered on stage while the others scattered to their dressing rooms. The audience had departed too, taking their applause with them. The theater sat dark and silent. At times like this, the cavernous space felt smaller to Belle. She felt smaller too, as if she were diminished without an audience to mirror the emotions she displayed on stage.

Something was wrong with her, but she didn't know what. Perhaps it was her holiday visit to Baltimore. She had spent most of December there and vowed she would never stay so long again. Every minute, she had felt like an outsider. Mary had not yet had a child, much to her disappointment. She and Rowland treated Grace as if she were their own. Belle's daughter did not seem to have missed her mother at all.

She knew she should feel grateful to Mary. Thankful that Grace was so happy. After all, wasn't freedom what Belle wanted? A wave of melancholy swept over her. She shouldn't stand here any longer on the empty stage. It wasn't good for her mood.

Forcing herself to walk briskly, she found her way to the narrow stairs that led down to a warren of dressing rooms. By now, the backstage was shrouded in darkness, and she had to walk carefully to avoid ladders, stacks of lumber, piles of folded canvas, coils of rope, and bright red buckets of water. More than anything, theater owners dreaded fire.

When she opened the door to the dressing room she and Adeline shared, she found her friend pinning on her hat, about to leave.

"There you are! David wants to speak with you." Adeline kissed Belle's cheek on her way out the door. "He wouldn't say what it's about. A secret! You can tell me tomorrow. Good night, my dear!"

Belle took off her costume, slipped into a dressing gown, then sat in front of the mirror to remove her makeup. She was nearly finished when there was a knock at the door.

"Come in, David!" she said without turning from her reflection.

"Good evening, Nina." He made a mocking bow to her graceful neck and shoulders, partly revealed by her robe as she arranged her hair. "A good performance tonight."

"Thank you."

He perched on the edge of a table, an actor's pose. "Belle, how long have you been with me?"

"Nearly a year."

"You have become quite popular. People enjoy your performances. One audience member in particular." He pulled a calling card out of his pocket and looked at it. "This gentleman claims that he came to the theater on a whim three nights ago and has been here every night since. He wants to meet you." A pause. "For goodness sake, turn around, Nina. It's not every day that a wealthy coffee merchant sends me to an actress's dressing room to arrange a personal introduction."

Belle allowed herself a small smile but did not turn around.

"What does the gentleman propose?"

"Luncheon tomorrow at the Hotel Dauphin."

"I would be delighted to meet him. What is his name?"

David handed Belle the card. She turned it over, appreciating the feel of the paper. It was excellent quality, thick and smooth, the creamy surface engraved with elegant script.

"Colonel John Swainston Hammond," she read. "A Yankee?"

"Perhaps. His accent is hard to place."

"No matter," Belle said, reaching for her drawstring purse and dropping the card inside. "You may inform the colonel that I would be pleased to meet him tomorrow."

✍

Belle stood for a moment in the arched entry of the hotel dining room as if searching for someone. Which indeed she was, but she also knew she made a charming picture framed in the doorway, a slim-waisted figure in a blue silk dress with yellow beaded trimming that almost matched the butter yellow walls. She had dined here before and chosen the dress deliberately.

As Belle scanned the room, her head with its stylish feathered hat turning from left to right, she had the satisfaction of seeing all the gentlemen in the room shift their eyes in her direction. How she loved this city! Where women were not so bound by convention as elsewhere, and men were so frank in their appreciation of the female form.

A tall man in a well-tailored suit jumped to his feet and rushed toward her, eager to claim this lovely prize in front of an august company of diners.

"Miss Benjamin!" A small bow and a light kiss applied to the back of her lace-gloved hand. "I cannot tell you how I have looked forward to this." Then a hand gently placed at her back to guide her to a table in the corner, which sat amid a wonderland of flowers in shades of rose and pink. A waiter hurried forward but was waved away as the gentleman seated Belle himself.

"Camellias!" Belle exclaimed, leaning forward to smell their faint fragrance.

"I have always appreciated camellias," the gentleman said. "They are the only flowers I know that bloom in winter. But what I like best is how they travel in disguise. They masquerade as roses, yet if you look closely, they are something quite different." He looked at her and smiled. "Like you, Miss Benjamin. Beautiful. Unexpected. Not quite as you appear." Another smile. "If you are willing, I would know you better."

Belle was used to being admired, but it had been years since she was courted. She had returned from her visit to Baltimore feeling lonely and unhappy. And now here was this handsome gentleman with his camellias and suggestive conversation.

They regarded each other silently until Belle laughed and murmured, "Sir, I have accepted your invitation to lunch. Perhaps you would care to introduce yourself?"

The colonel took this opportunity to jump to his feet again, bow over her hand, and press another kiss onto her fingertips.

"My apologies! Colonel John Swainston Hammond, madam. At your service."

Belle waved him to his seat, saying, "If you and I are to become better friends, as I think we shall, you should know that my true name is *not* Nina Benjamin."

"Mr. Bidwell mentioned this, though he would not tell me your name. To be honest, I did not want him to, wishing to hear it from your own lips."

"My given name is Belle Boyd," she said, then waited.

The colonel reared back in amazement. "Why, you are famous! A celebrated heroine of the Confederacy."

Because they had just met, Belle did not know if his surprise was real or pretend. But she had already made up her mind about one thing. She liked Colonel Hammond—his flattery, his lively conversation. He was very agreeable company. She decided to reassure him about her past.

"I hope you did not believe everything you read about me. I may have done a few things in my youth which were reckless and unladylike. In fact, I *have* done such things. With pride, I might add. But I assure you I have never been anything less than virtuous."

"Of course, dear lady. But let me say that it's your boldness, your fire, which makes you so attractive on stage. And I suspect in person as well." Colonel Hammond shook his head, saying, "Belle Boyd. Belle Boyd. I had no idea. These last few days I have been infatuated with you. Yet the object of my obsession has been a beautiful actress named Nina Benjamin. And now you tell me that's not who you are!"

"Nina Benjamin is an illusion, Colonel. Seated before you is the reality. Belle Boyd, born Maria Isabelle. From Martinsburg, Virginia, now West Virginia. Once a heroine of the Confederacy, now a proud citizen of these re-united States of America. You see how reality shifts under our feet."

"Not just a heroine but a philosopher!"

Silence descended. A waiter, standing nearby, leapt at the chance to fill water glasses, deliver menus, make recommendations, and relay their order to the kitchen. During this interruption, Colonel Hammond continued to gaze at Belle, a smile on his lips.

When the waiter had left, the colonel leaned forward and whispered, "By the way, Miss . . . Boyd. Is that a pistol I see in your belt?" She nodded. "Do you wear it always?"

"I don't wear it on stage." Belle's eyes sparkled with mischief. "Mr. Bidwell says it makes the other actors nervous."

"I should think so!"

"You see, I live alone. I like to have it close by. It's a comfort to me. Should I ever feel in need of protection." She said this primly, with an artful lowering of her eyes.

The waiter delivered their turtle soup, and as they picked up their spoons, Belle said, "Now, sir, it is my turn to ask questions." A sip. "Did you fight in the war? Your card declares you to be a colonel, but in what army? I detect an English accent."

"Quite right. I was born in England, attended Oxford, then fought in the Crimean War. A terrible conflict. The Russians our enemies. The Turks our allies. Savages on both sides."

He fell quiet and for a moment gazed unseeing at the starched white tablecloth. Then his eyes lost their faraway look, and he spoke again.

"Eventually I left England and settled in Boston. But it seemed war would follow me. In the early days of the Civil War, I enlisted as a lieutenant in the Massachusetts infantry. Another brutal four years."

*And another Yankee!* Belle thought, but she decided she did not care.

"Yet now the war is over," she said, perhaps as much to herself as to her companion.

"Yes. The nation has begun to rebuild. And what better place to do so than in this lovely city?" Colonel Hammond motioned the waiter to fill their wineglasses, then raised his. "To New Orleans, a city filled with beautiful women, but none more fascinating than Belle Boyd."

*Martinsburg, West Virginia*

*Dear Miss Belle,*

*I was sorry to read about your visit to Baltimore. That you felt there was no place for you there. But I am very glad to hear New Orleans is to your liking.*

*So you are spending time with a gentleman! I can't say I'm surprised. You never did have a lick of trouble getting a man interested. Are you thinking of getting married? I know you said you never would. But you often change your mind.*

*Colonel John Swainston Hammond. A nice sounding name. As you know, I always been fond of the name John. I wish I could meet your colonel. I hope he's not too handsome. You've always put too much store in how a man looks.*

*Things here is the same. Everyone healthy. Lee Laura growing up before our eyes. Our own John has started walking out with a girl. They seem to like each other just fine. I'm thinking they'll get married soon, and then I'll be a grandma.*

*Yours,*
*Eliza Hopewell*

*P.S. I think of you every day, Miss Belle. And remember you in my prayers.*

*New Orleans, Louisiana*
*February to Mid-March 1869*

# Chapter 43

At first, Belle had been certain that her friendship with the colonel would not lead to marriage, even if he suggested it, which she was certain he would not. There were any number of men who would consider a romantic interlude with an actress, but few who would be willing to marry one.

Belle had forgotten how pleasant it was to have a man by her side. John enjoyed her friends and seemed comfortable with their unconventional ways. He had not been at all shocked when she told him Adeline and David weren't married. Belle began to think she had found a kindred spirit in Colonel Hammond. Like her, he was intelligent, educated, well-traveled, and broad-minded. He was willing to look at things and ask, *Why?* This was something Belle was always wondering. *Why must things be as they are?*

The colonel wooed her with lavish bouquets and romantic dinners, horseback rides and carriage picnics. Like Belle, he was easily bored, so he was always arranging interesting outings. An excursion on a brightly painted Mississippi riverboat. Or a visit to an old cemetery, where they stood with other onlookers and watched voodoo priestesses perform strange rituals.

On another afternoon, he took her to the coffee roasting warehouse on Magazine Street, where he worked as an importer and sales agent. Belle insisted on inspecting the rough burlap sacks and reading the stenciled labels. Haiti, Martinique, Cuba, Colombia. And other far off places. Standing in the middle of the huge space, she spread her arms and closed her eyes. After a deep inhale, she said, "I do believe, John, that I like the aroma of roasted coffee better than anything in the world." She opened her eyes. "Although I do confess to being quite partial to the pomade you use on your mustaches."

Belle relished the freedom of New Orleans. More French than American in flavor, the city had a looser set of moral standards than elsewhere in the South. Here it was perfectly acceptable for John to join Belle for intimate late-night suppers in her apartment. They feasted on shrimp in cream sauce, steak and mushrooms, with exotic fruit pastries for dessert. The food was delivered from a nearby hotel and served by Lisette.

Belle was always ravenous after a performance, and John teased her for how much she could eat. In response she would delicately pat her lips with a napkin and remind him that soldiers were known for their hearty appetites.

"I was made an honorary lieutenant in Stonewall Jackson's regiment for my service to the Confederacy. Someday I will show you my uniform. I look quite dashing."

"I'm sure you do." He untied the napkin from around his neck and tossed it to the floor. "Come here, my love. I want to caress that tiny waist of yours. It seems even more miraculous now that I've seen how much you eat."

Belle curled herself onto his lap, and he stroked her side.

"We are so comfortable together, you and I," she said.

John kissed her neck just behind the ear. And the base of her lovely throat. She would not permit him to go lower.

"Hmm. We should get married." He held her away from him, to look into her eyes. "Don't you agree?"

Belle had been expecting this question, but she did not have her answer ready. She had told John about her first marriage, that it had been unhappy, but not that it ended in the scandal of divorce. She had also told him about her daughter, Grace, living in Baltimore with Belle's mother and married sister.

Belle slipped from John's arms and began to walk back and forth. It helped her think. The truth was she did not know if she wanted a husband or not. For the first time in years, she was completely happy. She had her own money. And work that she loved. She had friends. And she had her freedom. She was answerable to no one.

Belle knew what Adeline would say if she asked her. Her friend's dearest wish was to marry and have a child. David Bidwell wanted neither marriage nor family. He was perfectly content with things as they were. He knew Adeline would never leave him. Adeline had all the freedom in the world. Yet David was still her master.

*But that's Adeline. What about me? I do care for John. He is an interesting companion. We are well matched. But do I love him? Truly I have no idea. I thought I loved Sam, and marrying him was a terrible mistake. I do not want to fail at marriage a second time.*

While Belle paced, the colonel sipped the last of his wine, following her with his eyes.

"I hope you would bring Grace to live with us. You've often said how you want to give her a home. I would consider it an honor if one day she called me Papa."

"May I give you my answer in a few days?"

"Of course." He held out his arms. "Meanwhile, let me hold you again. Come and sit."

And so she did.

❧

Torn by indecision, Belle spent a sleepless night. More than anything, she wished Eliza were there to advise her. Or even Mama. Then she thought of Zeferina, a fortune-teller who was famous in the French Quarter. Belle knew that many respectable whites visited her, from bankers to housewives. Adeline sometimes consulted her.

The next morning, Belle walked to Jackson Square, intending to search for Zeferina and ask her advice. In the end, it was the fortune-teller who found Belle. Suddenly the woman was standing in front of her, as if she had appeared out of nowhere.

Tall and imposing, Zeferina was what was known in the city as a "Creole of color," with skin the shade of café au lait. Her strong features and black eyes were set off by a spotless white cloth elaborately wrapped and knotted around her head.

"Come," the woman said. She led Belle through a wrought iron gate and into an overgrown courtyard. Unlike Belle's own sunlit garden, this space was dark and brooding. There were cats, lots of them, silent shapes gliding ghostlike in and out of the shadows. Under a palm tree sat a small round table covered by a purple cloth with two threadbare upholstered chairs pulled close. The woman gestured Belle to one, then sat in the other, pulling a shawl over her shoulders against the damp chill. Belle shivered. The garden was unpleasantly cold, and she already regretted coming.

Still silent, Zeferina reached for a well-worn pile of picture cards. An inch above the deck, her hand stopped and hovered, as if taking a message from the air.

"Hmm. I think we will get a clearer reading from your hand."

With some reluctance, Belle reached out. The woman frowned, and Belle realized she must remove her glove. *Of course!* She peeled it off, then offered her hand.

The woman took it roughly, and Belle's fingers curled involuntarily into a fist. An annoyed shake of the head from Zeferina, and Belle forced her hand open. The woman studied Belle's palm for a long time, sometimes tilting it left or right. Belle felt her hand grow warm in Zeferina's strong grasp, and she began to relax.

"Your future will be eventful," the woman said, then paused. "As your past has already been." The seer looked at her and smiled for the first time. "There will be more travel. More adventure. A second husband. And a third." Belle tried to snatch her hand away, but the woman held fast. "Don't worry. Your first marriage was brief and unhappy. Your second marriage will last many years. Your colonel adores you." She stared more closely at Belle's palm. "There will be more children. In addition to Grace."

Belle shivered. Was it because Zeferina knew Grace's name? Or because she'd mentioned other children?

"You will have many trials, though. I see you in a kind of prison." Zeferina traced a line with her finger. "Not a true prison this time. But still, a place you cannot leave. Or perhaps you do not want to leave it. And I see you on a stage. People applauding."

Zeferina released Belle's hand.

"I should marry the Colonel, then? The marriage will be happy?"

The fortune-teller shrugged. "No one can escape her destiny. That is foolish. You do not seem like a fool to me. Have you never looked at your hand? Go ahead. Look!"

Belle was pulling her glove on, but she stopped and stared at her palm.

"The lines of your life are deeply etched. You have a powerful destiny. You are strong, but there will be times when Fate overwhelms you. There is nothing you can do to change that."

Now it was Zeferina who held out her palm. Belle dropped a coin into it.

Afterward, Belle chose not to think about the details of what the woman had said, instead remembering only that her marriage would last many years. And the words, "Your colonel adores you."

❧

The next two weeks were as happy and busy as any Belle could remember. First a trip to the jewelers to pick out a ring. A large ruby, which Adeline gazed at wistfully before kissing Belle on the cheek and wishing her every happiness. John arranged the ceremony and planned their honeymoon trip to Baltimore, where he would meet Belle's family. When they returned to New Orleans, Grace would come with them. Belle ordered a bouquet and planned the wedding luncheon. This time, instead of invitations printed on silk ribbon, she wrote out two dozen notes on excellent stationary and delivered them personally to her friends. She ordered a new hat with long feathers, blue and cream and black to match the blue silk gown she planned to wear on her wedding day. It was the same dress she'd worn when she and John first met. He claimed it was his favorite. Belle could still recall posing in the entrance to the hotel dining room. It seemed impossible for so much to have happened in three short months.

❧

A week before the ceremony, Belle and John took a walk through one of the public gardens. It was early March, one of the first days of fine spring weather. As they strolled arm in arm, Belle was supremely happy.

"My parents had a loving marriage," she said. "I hope ours will be the same."

"I promise to take good care of you, Belle." John patted her hand where it rested in the bend of his elbow. "By the way, has David found someone to replace you? You haven't mentioned it."

Belle's feet stopped moving. Very slowly, with enormous effort, she turned her head and looked up at him.

"What do you mean, John?"

"David Bidwell, he knows you're leaving the company."

"I did not tell him that," Belle said slowly, still trying to understand what John was saying.

"Surely you understood that I want you to retire from the stage. I wish for my beautiful, talented wife to belong to me alone. Any man would feel the same."

Belle tried to speak, but her lips refused to form any words. Shaking so hard she could barely stand, she clung to John's arm like the stunned survivor of a shipwreck.

"Belle, you're unwell! It must be a fever. I'll take you home. Lisette will put you to bed. Thank goodness it's Sunday. Just the same, I'll send a message to David that you can't perform tomorrow."

$\infty$

An hour later, Belle was lying in her bed in the dark when Adeline slipped into the room.

"What is it, dear? What's wrong?"

Belle clutched Adeline's hands. "John wants me to give up acting. I didn't realize. I thought he was proud of me. That he enjoyed seeing me on stage. Having people admire me." As the words tumbled out, her voice rose to a thin wail. "Zeferina said my marriage would be long. She said John adores me. She saw me on stage. There were people applauding. Could she be wrong? She mentioned the colonel by name. And Grace too. Tell me, is she ever wrong? I must know!"

Adeline pushed Belle back onto her pillow, smoothed her hair, rubbed her icy hands.

"She's never wrong," she said slowly, "but sometimes a person might misunderstand what she says. Or the meaning isn't clear until much later."

Belle rolled her head from side to side on the pillow. "That doesn't help. I have to know. I'm nearly twenty-five! I thought that if I ever intended to marry again, this was my chance. Grace could live with us. I could have a husband and a family and a home and still be an actress. I don't know what to do. Adeline, help me decide!"

❧

The next morning when John arrived, Belle was sitting at her breakfast table by the window, wrapped in a silk dressing gown, drinking coffee as she watched a pair of birds pursue each other from branch to branch. It was spring.

"I'm all right now, John." She lifted the coffee pot and smiled at him. "Will you join me?"

Belle had made her decision. She would not look back.

*New Orleans, Louisiana*
*Late March to June 1869*

# Chapter 44

"I do," Belle said without hesitation, her voice ringing through the small chapel. The wedding guests looked on with nods and smiles.

The luncheon afterward was lengthy and festive. Belle's theater friends enjoyed celebrations, and a wedding was a rare occasion. During the toasts, John kept reaching for Belle's hand and raising it to his lips. As she looked around the room, catching the eye of one friend and then another, she felt a warm sense of belonging. She looked forward to the future. She and John would bring Grace back to New Orleans. This would be their new home. They would be happy here. She was sure of it.

Following the wedding, Belle and John visited her family in Baltimore and stayed for a month. When the time came to leave, Grace did not want to go. For more than a year, she had lived in the house on Mount Vernon Place with her grandmother, Will, Aunt Mary, and Uncle Rowland. There had been only a single visit from her mother in all that time.

Belle tried reminding Grace of their years together in London, living in a series of apartments and hotels. It was clear that her daughter could barely remember that time. Next Belle described all the attractions of her adopted city—its beautiful buildings, lively markets, and colorful riverboats. She told Grace about the fountain in her garden and the bird that came and sang every morning. She talked about the open-air cafes that served creamy hot chocolate and powdered sugar donuts. Grace could take riding lessons. She could learn to speak French.

Belle's headstrong daughter was not interested. Grace had a special playmate in Baltimore named Anna. Could Anna come? She did not want to leave her behind. She did not want to leave her grandmother either. Or her uncles. Most of all, she did not want to leave Aunt Mary.

Belle told Grace that there were people in the city who kept small monkeys as pets. She had seen one of these tiny creatures walking down the street at the end of a thin silver chain. She'd seen another that sat on its owner's shoulder, dressed in tiny clothes, like a miniature person. Enchanted, Grace said she wanted a monkey. Belle promised she would have one.

On the day Belle, Grace, and John left Baltimore, the rest of the family chose to say a subdued farewell at the house rather than escort them to the station. Rowland stood in the front hall, looking grim, one hand in his pocket, the other around Mary, who leaned against him, pale and mute with grief. Mama alone tried to be cheerful, insisting that everything "would come right in the end." Whatever that meant.

Belle could not help being moved to pity when she said good-bye to her sister. She held Mary in a long embrace, saying, "I will write often and send you news of Grace. We will come for Christmas. I promise. I pray that by then you will be expecting a child of your own. It's bound to happen soon."

❧

After they returned to New Orleans, John insisted they move into his rented house.

For some reason Belle had not anticipated this. *Of course! My apartment is too small for the three of us. Grace must have a bedroom of her own. It's the only sensible thing.*

The colonel's house had large, airy rooms, but the garden was not at all inviting. Instead of a sparkling fountain, and shrubs filled with birdsong, it contained a collection of statues afflicted by a dark creeping moss. Belle felt that the frozen shapes would move if they could, step into the sunshine and stretch their limbs. Sometimes she felt the urge to speak to them, to acknowledge them at least, standing stiff and silent, for Heaven only knew how many years.

"Hire a gardener if you like, my love. You should have a project. I think you must leave the statues, though. The house is rented, after all."

Belle found a grizzled African to pull up the paving stones and plant trees and vines. For a while, she was satisfied. Then she called him back.

"There are no birds."

"No, missus. Takes time for the birds to come. And sometimes they don't. They chooses where they wants to be."

"Find me birds in cages then."

So the man returned with small wicker cages and hung them in the trees, but the birds were mostly silent.

"Why won't they sing, Mama?"

"I don't know."

One morning, Grace walked into the garden to see her mother opening the doors of the cages. They stood together and watched the birds fly off one by one.

☙

Belle took Grace in search of the monkey she had promised. The market was one of Belle's favorite places, an exotic swirl of color and motion, a Babel of languages. Stallholders sang out their wares in accents of French, Spanish, Irish, German. Housewives and maids inspected guavas, papayas, and mangoes, haggling over prices. Creole women in bright dresses walked through the crowds with swaying hips, baskets of banana fritters balanced on their heads.

"There is everything here, Mama!" Grace exclaimed, eyes wide.

Belle bought her a spear of sugar cane and told her to chew the end until the sweet juice ran over her tongue. They followed their noses to the livestock area, where goats, pigs, geese, ducks, and chickens added their complaints to the din. Grace stared in mute amazement at a baby alligator in a cage, all jaws and teeth. She leaned forward to study the fierce looking creature, her hands clasped safely behind her back.

"It's a squirrel monkey you want for your daughter," the alligator's owner told Belle. "I haven't had one in a while. The little girl will have to wait."

"She's not good at waiting."

The man shrugged. Belle gave him her address, and he promised to send word when he had a monkey.

⁂

Mother and daughter spent every day together, and every day was the same. At nine o'clock, after John left for the warehouse or the docks or wherever he was bound, Belle and Grace met Adeline at their favorite café. The ladies sipped café au lait, Grace drank hot chocolate, and they shared a plate of beignets. Grace had learned to ask for them in French—*"Ben-yay, see voo play."* The waiter would bow and say, *"Charmante, mam'selle."*

Adeline praised her accent. "On your next visit to Baltimore, your family will be surprised to hear you speak French so well."

"I miss Baltimore," Grace said with a frown, dropping her do-nut back onto the plate and crossing her pudgy four-year-old arms. "I miss my friend Anna. I wish you had a daughter, Miss Adeline, so I could have someone to play with."

"So do I, little one."

Each day, as soon as the bell of the St. Louis cathedral chimed ten, Adeline stood up, said, "I must go," kissed them on both cheeks, and hurried away to the theater. With the air still stirring from the flurry of Adeline's departure, a heavy silence descended on the table. Belle stared after her friend.

*Adeline has a life, and I have none. No, that's not quite right. I have a life too. And I know Adeline would trade places with me in an instant. I should be grateful for what I have. And not always be wishing for more.*

Turning to her daughter, Belle spoke in the most cheerful voice she could manage, "What would you like to do today?"

"I don't care, Mama. You decide."

Belle looked at Grace. The past month had changed her. She was no longer full of songs and chatter. Now that New Orleans was familiar, nothing interested her. So it was Belle's task to fill another long day. With a visit to the market or a walk in the park. When it wasn't too hot, they would go all the way to the levee to watch the paddleboats and barges making their way up and down the Mississippi.

Somehow they filled the hours, but every day ended the same way, with Grace napping in her room and Belle reading on the verandah. Both of them waiting for the colonel to return, bringing the world with him, telling them stories of all the things he'd seen and done that day.

One night, as a special treat, the colonel took them to the New Orleans Theater. It felt strange to Belle to sit in the audience, watching the actress who was her replacement say the lines she herself had so recently spoken. She was quiet on the way home, thinking of everything she'd given up.

Grace was enchanted by the theater. The lights. The music. The scenery. But especially by seeing Mama's friend Adeline on stage.

"You used to do that, didn't you, Mama? Why did you stop?"

The colonel answered for her. "It's not something mamas do."

Belle missed her old life much more than she had expected to. Without something to occupy her mind and make use of her body, she felt lost. She hadn't quite understood all that she was giving up. The variety of the theater had suited her perfectly. There were always new roles to assume, fresh lines to learn, scenes to rehearse. The daily rituals of putting on and taking off makeup and costumes. Not to mention the thrill of performing. The rapt, upturned faces of the audience. The applause. The satisfaction of an extra curtain call. The audience's approval reflecting herself back to herself. Or another self. Selves.

Belle felt her days stretching endlessly into the future. One after the other. In the daytime, when she had Grace to entertain, Belle managed to keep herself steady. But sometimes at night, she woke in a panic, feeling like she was suffocating. She would jerk upright, staring wide-eyed into the darkness, gasping for air, willing her heart to stop hammering, while her husband slumbered peacefully at her side.

❧

"It's the heat," the colonel declared, taking off his wide-brimmed straw hat and drinking off a glass of chilled lemonade before kissing Belle's cheek. "And it's just the beginning. We should have left the city until the weather cools."

"People in the market are saying there are fever outbreaks, John." Belle thought longingly of Mary's house in Baltimore with its cool, high-ceilinged rooms. "Let's go north."

"It's hard for me to get away just now. Why don't you and Grace go without me?"

"I don't feel up to traveling alone. It's such a long way. Won't you come with us?"

The colonel gave Belle a puzzled look.

"That's not like my brave girl. What is it, darling?"

He pulled her onto his lap. When she leaned over and whispered in his ear, he pulled back almost immediately, eyes wide, a smile growing on his face.

"A child! That's wonderful news. How long have you known?"

"About two months."

"Why did you wait to tell me? I would never have planned for us to stay in the city if I'd known."

Belle's pale face had taken on a little color at the colonel's reaction to her news. She smiled mysteriously. "This is women's business, dear husband."

Her heart, which had been so heavy, suddenly felt lighter. She realized now that she had been afraid. In her first marriage, to Sam, she had also become pregnant after just a few months, and Sam had been away when she found out. She remembered how dreadful it had been. She was alone, facing the ordeal of childbirth in a city thousands of miles from home, desperate for money. Now she was pregnant again. And again too soon. Again far from home. She had been so worried about telling John.

This time would be different, she realized. Her colonel was here, by her side. He seemed pleased about the baby. Even though, once again, it had happened much too quickly. Belle ought to have asked Eliza how to keep a child from getting started in the first year, until she and her new husband knew each other better. Perhaps she could manage to have Eliza with her when the baby came. Perhaps she could have the child in Baltimore. Or Martinsburg. Perhaps Grace's birth had not been as harrowing as she remembered. Everyone said second babies were easier, didn't they? Still, the important thing was that John was here. He would take care of her.

Belle put her arms around his neck and said, "I love you, Colonel Hammond."

*Dear Eliza,*

*By the time you receive this letter, I will be on my way to California. I'm heartbroken to leave New Orleans. To travel even further from you. Mama. Mary. I'm having a baby. To be born in December or January, I think. I'm not ready to have another child. I feel so alone. John doesn't know how I feel. Of course <u>he</u> wants a child. A son. What man does not?*

*I still don't understand why we must leave New Orleans. I've been so happy here! For the first time I have friends. Of all the places I've lived, this is the only one where I truly feel like I belong. And now John tells me we must leave.*

*I asked him why we could not move to Baltimore instead. He says Baltimore and New Orleans are old cities with old ways. He asks, why should we stay in the East? I answer, because your wife is happy here. And he tells me I will be happy in San Francisco. That the climate is pleasant. That there are flowers everywhere. He reminds me how I love the ocean. Sometimes he does ask me what I'm thinking, but then he doesn't listen to what I say.*

*I do not want to go but know I must. I've learned the hard way that for a marriage to succeed, the wife must follow the husband. This is what it means to be married. I remember reading once that out West there are horses that run wild. When one is caught it must be "broken." Taught to obey the command of its rider. That horse and I are one and the same.*

*Your Belle*

*P.S. I do love him*
*P.P.S. For the first time in my life, I am afraid of the future.*

*San Francisco, California*
*September 1869*

# Chapter 45

The house John rented was newly built, a tiny whitewashed cottage that still smelled of fresh sawdust. With just two rooms downstairs and two rooms upstairs, it was situated in a part of the city called Potrero Hill. There was a high white wooden fence around the scrubby backyard to give them privacy. Tangles of bougainvillea in flaming reds and purples grew near the fence. Hummingbirds flitted about. Small lizards sunned themselves on rocks. The day they arrived, John carried two kitchen chairs outside. He and Belle sat in the overgrown yard and watched Grace run in circles, her chubby fingers outstretched toward moving drifts of butterflies.

John took Belle's hand. "I was told this neighborhood is sunnier than the rest of the city. I want you to be happy here."

She smiled and nodded. Anything more was too much effort. She wished she were still on the train. They'd had their own compartment. With seats that turned into beds at night. During the day John took charge of Grace. They explored the train together, leaving Belle free to gaze out the window. She had spent hours looking at unbroken expanses of nothing. Nothing at all. She remembered how safe she'd felt in that little room. Shut away from the rest of the world. It had soothed her to sit and look out at the vast, empty country. It lulled her. Put her to sleep. She felt like she was asleep even now. Or perhaps she only wished to be.

Belle realized John was talking to her. She must try to listen. Why was she so sleepy all the time? Was it just the baby growing inside her? The baby. Forever growing. She tried not to think about it.

John's mouth was making more words. "I know I appear wealthy, Belle. But that's only true as long as I work. As I'm sure you know, I don't own any property. Even my house in New Orleans was rented. I'm a salesman. Coffee, tea, cotton, indigo, land. It doesn't matter. San Francisco is full of opportunity. A man can get rich here."

Belle's thoughts drifted away.

That night it was John who cooked their dinner of bacon and eggs. John who unpacked the trunks until he found Grace a warm nightdress because when the sun went down the night was colder than anyone expected. Belle sat at the kitchen table. And smiled. Somehow she knew if she smiled, no one would ask anything more of her.

෴

The next morning, there was a knock at the door.

"That must be Nan," John said.

"Nan?"

A look passed over John's face, then was gone. "Please tell me you remember, Belle. She's the Scots woman I hired to do the cooking and cleaning. And help look after Grace. Her name is Nan. I told you about her. Several times."

Belle said she remembered, even though she didn't.

John answered the door and showed a woman into the parlor. A scrawny woman with sharp bones and red hair that looked like knives.

"Mornin', missus."

In the silence, John cleared his throat and looked at Belle. The thin woman's eyes moved back and forth between them.

"Why don't you go upstairs, Belle, and get dressed? Grace, you too. When you're ready, Nan can take you to the market."

*Nan. Nan. Sounds like a goat.*

John's mouth was still moving. "Nan will introduce you to the baker, the butcher, and so on. It will do you good to get out, Belle. While you're upstairs dressing, I'll talk to Nan about her other duties."

When Belle returned to the parlor, everyone was waiting. Three pairs of eyes looking at her.

"Mama, your buttons are all wrong!"

Giving the colonel a glance, Nan asked, "Shall I?" and took a step toward Belle.

"No. I'll do it."

Belle stood in the middle of the parlor while John rebuttoned the front of her dress. After he stepped away, he opened the leather purse that hung at his hip and drew out three one-dollar bills. He looked at Belle, hesitated, then handed the money to Nan, who folded it and put it in the pocket of her apron.

"Help my wife set up accounts with the butcher, baker, and dairyman." His eyes narrowed. "If necessary, Grace can help answer any questions. She's only four, but bright for her age. Use the cash for everything else. Flour, sugar, tea, lard, etcetera. There might be other things my wife requires. Use your judgment. I shall expect a strict accounting. I will return at four o'clock."

He started to leave, then turned to face the woman. "You see how things are."

"I'll take care of everything, sir. The little girl too."

The colonel looked at Belle, his lips pinched in a frown. Then he blew out his cheeks, grabbed his walking stick, and took his look of worry out the door.

დ

When John returned from the city, he found Grace playing in the garden and Nan busy at the stove. He hurried past them both and ran upstairs. Belle was in the bedroom, seated in front of a mirror she'd brought from New Orleans. She was brushing her hair. John put his hands on her shoulders, bent and kissed the top of her head. She met his eyes in the glass and smiled.

"Did you have a good day?" he asked.

"Yes. I met all the shopkeepers. Nan organized the kitchen. Then she helped me unpack our clothes and put everything away."

That was more words than Belle had spoken in weeks. A look of happiness flashed across John's face.

*I must try harder. Really, I must.*

"I feel . . ."—she paused— "better." Another pause. "It's better when I'm busy, John."

"I know," he said, still smiling. "Stand up a minute, dear."

When Belle stood, he took her place in the chair, pulled her onto his lap, and wrapped his arms around her. As she leaned back against his chest, the chair gave an ominous creak.

She laughed. "Oh dear. Perhaps our new furniture is not as strong as it needs to be."

Nestled contentedly in John's arms, Belle wondered why she kept wanting to freeze moments like this. Why she wanted so desperately to make time stand still. *Am I afraid of giving birth? Is that it? How can a man understand what it feels like to face such an ordeal? And possible death. To face it alone. As every woman must. But I am more alone than most.*

"Do you think you can be happy here, Belle?"

"The house is fine, John. The yard too. It's good to have a place for Grace to play outside. A safe place."

They sat for a long time.

"Are you worried? About the birth? Is that why you're so quiet?"

"A little."

"I know nothing of such things. We will make sure to find you a good doctor, though. Or a midwife. When the time comes you shall have whatever you want."

*Eliza!*

⁂

Each morning John left and was gone all day. When he returned, he brought the city with him. It came in on his clothes, the smells of fish from the waterfront, cedar and tea and spices from the warehouses. He brought Grace toys from China. Intricate wooden puzzles of interlocking links. Trick boxes that unlocked only when the panels were slid open in a certain order.

And how he talked! The words poured out like a torrent until Belle felt she might be swept away. The geography. The neighborhoods, each one different. How the Gold Rush and the railroad had brought immigrants from all over the world. How the land along the Bay was being filled in and the famous hills leveled by armies of men and mules and noisy machinery. John said it was as if someone had kicked open an anthill. This was progress!

"I've been meeting with some men who know about land speculation. San Francisco is full of opportunities. Why, in comparison, New Orleans is just a backwater."

*So many words.*

She tried. But after a while, Belle felt herself fading again. During the day she would stand for a half hour at a time, staring out the bedroom window at the sweeping view of bay and hills. John had told her the view was magnificent. Full of promise. She saw dusty brown hills. A misty vagueness surrounded her. It was inside her too. She did not know where it came from. Where it began. Where it ended. Where she began. Every day the mist descended without warning, and Belle could feel herself dissolving, like a ship sailing into a low bank of clouds and gradually disappearing, until it seemed that it had never even been there.

☙

One morning, as Nan was clearing away the breakfast dishes, John announced, "I've decided we should all go into the city today. Both of you must change into your prettiest dresses. I'll show you the sights." He looked at Belle. "You'd like that, wouldn't you?"

Belle nodded. Smiled.

"Where will we go, Papa?"

"Montgomery Street. Where all the stores and fine hotels are. We'll have lunch there. But first we'll visit the harbor and see the fishing boats and the seals."

"What does a seal look like, Papa?"

"Hmm. I'd say it's like a cross between a dog and a fish. The head is very like a dog. And they bark like dogs."

"They sound very ugly."

"Not at all. In fact, they're rather charming. Like puppies. You'll see."

John reached for Belle's hand and squeezed gently. She felt the warmth of it as if from a distance. She wanted to press his hand back, but it seemed too difficult. As did the thought of dressing

herself. Doing up her corset, putting on her hoopskirt and petticoats, her dress, her stockings, her shoes. So many hooks and
buttons! But of course, she would do whatever John asked. She was
his wife.

He pushed back his chair, the sudden scraping making Belle
wince.

"Grace, put on that yellow dress your Aunt Mary made. And
perhaps your mother will comb your hair. Or would you like Papa
to do it?"

"I can do it myself. Papas don't know how," Grace said with a
giggle as she ran up the stairs.

In their bedroom, John handed Belle a dress of lavender bro-
cade and asked, "Shall I send Nan up to help you?"

Belle wrinkled her nose and shook her head in quick, small
jerks.

"No. I don't like her touching me."

"Why?"

"I don't know why." She told herself to make a smile. "Don't
worry. I can manage on my own."

"Then I'll see how Grace is doing. Or I might go into the garden and have a smoke."

Belle stepped into her corset, pulled it over her hips, and began to fasten the tiny hooks that ran down the front. After that,
she'd tighten the back laces. But not too much. She looked down at
herself, pressed her hands against her belly, just beginning to swell.

"It's not your fault," she whispered. "Something's wrong with
me. I don't know what."

*I just want to be still. I want everything to be still.*

Belle discovered there was a secret to getting dressed. She must
keep her hands moving, even when they seemed like they belonged
to someone else. More than once she noticed that her hands had

gone still. Then she made them move again.

John's face lit up when he came back and saw Belle was ready. He crossed the room in two strides and cupped her face in his hands.

"How well you look!"

Belle made herself smile. Then she stepped away and offered him something she had been holding behind her back.

"Here. You should take this." It was her belt and the pistol she always wore. When he looked at her with a question in his eyes, she said, "Until I am myself again. The belt doesn't fit now, anyway."

☙

At the harbor, Grace asked about the seals.

"Where are they, Papa? I don't see them."

John pointed. "There. On the rocks."

She stared for a long moment, then jumped in surprise.

"Oh! I thought they *were* rocks. Until one of them moved. They're so brown and round. I can hear them barking. Just like you said." Grace clapped her hands. "They *do* sound like dogs."

"Like dogs," Belle repeated. John glanced at her. She was holding her arms away from her sides. "I've always loved feeling the wind. It's almost like you could lay against it, and it would carry you away."

John took her hand and tucked her arm inside his. "Come. I'll show you the fishing boats."

They walked along the dock to where rows of small boats bobbed in the water below them, masts swaying like trees in a forest. Fishing nets were spread everywhere, drying in the sun. Men in canvas aprons stood at wooden tables, cleaning their catch with flashing knives. Odds and ends of fish littered the ground. Heads.

Tails. Shimmering strings of guts. Over the heads of the men, the sky was thick with gulls that screeched and wheeled in the wind, taking turns diving in and swooping back up. The birds frightened her with their harsh screams, their sharp beaks clamped tight onto glistening bits of fish. Belle closed her eyes. That was better. Now she could feel the wind on her face. As it rushed through her, the other noises faded away.

Grace pulled John away for a moment. When he looked back, Belle had taken off her hat. It lay by her feet on the filthy ground. She'd torn the pins from her hair, and it blew around her head and shoulders. She stood like a statue, eyes closed, face tilted toward the sky.

# Chapter 46

John took Belle to see a man. A doctor, he said. The man was big, with thick brown whiskers. Like a bear.

The doctor made sure she was seated comfortably, then sat himself and asked, "How are you feeling, Mrs. Hammond?"

Belle didn't say anything. There was nothing to say. She didn't feel anything at all.

"Your husband tells me you're expecting a child."

She thought about that. Finally she nodded.

"But not your first?"

She looked at him, put her head on one side, trying to remember.

"You have another child. Isn't that right, Mrs. Hammond. A daughter?"

Belle thought again. Nodded again.

"Your daughter's name is Grace. Isn't that right?"

Belle kept her eyes on the man's face, watched his lips move. But the noises coming from his mouth had stopped making sense.

"Your husband says you were married in March. Perhaps your pregnancy comes as a surprise?"

Belle didn't answer. She had drifted back to the harbor. The seals that made her laugh. The gulls were too loud, and their beaks too sharp. She liked the wind, though. Now she could feel it rushing through her hair. She smiled. She liked the wind best of all.

"A welcome one I trust?"

She opened her eyes. A strange man was leaning across his desk toward her. Too close. She didn't want to look at him. He had a face like a bear. So she looked down at the desk. It was beautiful dark wood. She remembered the name. It was called mahogany. Such a strange sounding word. Is that what the man's lips were saying? *Mahogany. Mahogany.* She tried whispering the sounds, trying to fit them inside the shapes the man's mouth was making. *No, that's not it.*

The furry lips said, "Mrs. Hammond, are you afraid?"

Belle understood "afraid." She pushed the word away. She didn't like that word. It was better to sit quietly and listen to the wind.

When they came out of the room with the books and the desk, John was waiting. He dropped his newspaper and looked at her, but she knew her face was blank and empty. Like the wind. She sat and folded her hands in her lap, waiting for whatever would happen next. The man and John stood in the doorway and talked with their heads almost touching. They kept their voices low. They didn't have to. Belle wasn't listening. What did she care what they said? It was just words. *Mahogany. Mahogany.*

"Is Mrs. Hammond always so passive?"

"God, no!" John said. "If you could have seen my wife when I met her. So full of life. You can't imagine! Now she is . . . a shadow. A ghost." He took an uneven breath, then continued. "My wife is fearful of being pregnant. I'm afraid I've added to her fears. I became involved in a land deal in the city. Without sufficient knowledge of my partner's honesty. The whole thing went bust. Now we have less money than before. In one of Belle's lucid periods and a weak moment of mine, I confessed to her what happened. She is more fearful now than ever."

"You mustn't blame yourself, Colonel."

"We are far from home and family. I've hired someone to help, but Belle says the woman frightens her. Poor Grace can't understand what's happening to her mother. Neither can I. What should I do, doctor? I don't know where to turn."

"Do you know the town of Stockton?" the man asked.

"It's about eighty miles up the San Joaquin River."

"The State of California has built an asylum there. For the insane." John turned his head away. The man took his arm. "Don't be alarmed. I know the word is frightening."

John lurched backward. "I could never put Belle into an asylum. One hears terrible stories about what goes on in such places."

"You are correct. Many asylums are indeed dreadful. But there are others that are more humane and up to date in how they care for patients. They provide wholesome food and activities. Patients can spend time outdoors. I assure you, the place I mention achieves impressive results. Most patients are released in less than a year."

"Then there's hope?"

"Indeed there is. As you said, your wife has no family or friends in the city. She is expecting a child. For many women, fear of childbirth can cause temporary insanity."

"Temporary, you say."

"I believe so. In any case, given your circumstances, it is the only place for her."

ℰℛ

They traveled up the San Joaquin River on a small paddleboat, a journey of two days. Grace dragged her stepfather all over the boat, sharing her discoveries, pointing out interesting sights on shore. Boys swimming, men fishing, women washing clothes. When the boat made one of its frequent stops, the two of them would stand at the rail to watch passengers getting off and on, sacks of mail being exchanged, crates of goods loaded and unloaded.

All the while, Belle sat in a deck chair under an awning, wearing a loose jacket to hide her advancing pregnancy. Most ladies would not be seen in public in such a state, but she did not care. She lay with the weight of the baby pinning her to the chair. She tried not to think about the baby. Did not wonder if it was a boy or a girl. Had chosen no names. She gave no thought to the future. She did not wonder where they were going. Or why. She left that to John. He would tell her what to do. Sometimes he came and sat with her for a few minutes, stroking her hand, the only part of her she would let him touch. Even that she could not stand for long. After a while, she would slide her hand out from under his and hide it in her lap. John would leave her then.

In Stockton, they found a room in a small boarding house. The next day, they took a walk that brought them to a large brick building near the edge of town. John carried Belle's carpetbag. She had seen him put her things in it that morning. A loose dress, underclothes, two nightgowns, a shawl, her brushes and some extra combs for pinning up her hair. She didn't ask why he was packing her bag.

As they entered the building through the frosted glass doors, Belle asked John the name of the hotel. He looked at her with a frown and didn't answer. Once inside, he disappeared, saying he had business to take care of. He left Belle and Grace in a lobby filled with green plants. Everything was quiet. Someone brought them chilled lemon water.

John and another gentleman walked out of an office together. The words on the door said ASYLUM ADMINISTRATOR. Belle didn't know what the words meant. It didn't matter.

The men stood and talked with their heads together. Belle

remembered this happening before. John and another man, standing and watching her. She knew they were talking about her. It didn't matter.

"You have done the right thing, bringing your wife to us," the man was saying. "I believe she'll recover after the baby is born."

John and the man shook hands. The man patted John's shoulder. John walked toward where they sat and held out his hand to Grace.

"Are we leaving now, Papa?" she asked, jumping down from her chair.

"You and I are leaving. Your mama is going to stay here for a bit. She needs to rest."

John looked at Belle. "You don't mind staying?"

Belle shook her head, made herself smile. A woman in a plain gray dress with a white bibbed apron appeared and took her by the hand. She let the woman lead her away. They climbed the stairs together. Belle did not look back.

The room had white walls and a narrow iron bed with a white coverlet. Everything was white. There was no rug on the floor or pictures on the wall. It felt blank and empty. Like Belle. She stood by the window and stared out at the grounds.

"Do you like flowers?" the gray and white woman asked.

Belle understood "flowers" and nodded. The gray and white woman took her into the garden and said she could pick flowers for her room. When she reached for the scissors the woman was holding, the woman said she must point to the flowers she wanted, and the woman would cut them for her. The woman gave Belle the basket to carry.

The woman asked if she knew the names of any flowers. Belle shook her head. She thought maybe she had known the names once. She wanted to tell the woman this. But she didn't know how.

Anyway, she couldn't remember the names anymore. So it didn't matter. When the basket was full, the woman took her to a small kitchen, where they put the flowers in a jar of water.

That night, Belle had trouble sleeping in the white bed in the white room. She could feel the baby growing, its weight dragging on her flesh. When she finally slept, she dreamed she was Rose Greenhow, drowning with a heavy purse hanging around her neck. Somehow she knew there was a baby in the purse, tiny but very heavy. She woke with her heart drumming in her chest.

ↄ

Belle never saw any male guests. The gray and white maids told her they lived in another part of the hotel. The maids never left her by herself. They took her to meals. And to hymn singing.

Belle did not sing. She liked listening, though. Music was the only thing that made the wind stop blowing inside her head. She thought maybe once she had known the words to the hymns. That she had known the words to many songs. She thought maybe she had known how to play the piano. Sometimes she looked down and saw her fingers moving with the notes.

In the dayroom, the other ladies did embroidery. Belle would sit and watch their hands move, watch them poking the needles in and out of the cloth, the needles trailing long threads. All the threads were gray.

Sometimes the maids took the guests to gather flowers in the garden. Something was wrong with the flowers, though. They were gray too. No one else seemed to notice. Belle didn't want gray flowers. She always shook her head, no.

Some days everyone walked to the river that flowed past the hotel grounds. This was what Belle liked best. Then the maids stopped taking her to the river. A man with thick glasses came to see her. He asked why she tried to throw herself into the water. Belle wanted to tell him that the river had been whispering to her. She had only leaned forward to hear what it was saying. Another time, the man asked about a knife she had taken from the dining room. He said a maid had seen her. Belle didn't remember any of that.

The days passed, and she felt herself drifting further away. She did not speak anymore. Even inside her head, there were no words. The wind had blown everything away.

Every day, a man and a little girl came to sit with her in the dayroom. The man would try to hold her hand. Belle wouldn't let him. He was just a stranger with a sad face. The little girl sat in her chair and kicked her legs back and forth, like she was on a swing. Or maybe she wanted to run away somewhere. Maybe she wanted to run to the river. Maybe that was it.

*Stockton, California*
*Late November 1869*

# Chapter 47

The baby came in the night. The room was crowded with people. Hands. Voices. One voice saying over and over. *Push. Push.* The word sounded like the rushing wind that was always in Belle's head. Only this wind was stronger than ever. This wind was a gale that twisted right through every part of her. It was like a furious storm, and then it passed. When it was gone, she was still here. Still here.

Belle must have fallen asleep afterward because the next thing she knew it was morning, and the sun was streaming through her window. She looked down at herself and saw she was wearing a clean nightgown, and someone had fixed her hair. It lay on her shoulder in a thick brown braid. Everything was peaceful and quiet. When she listened, she could hear voices outside her room. Speaking softly. One of them saying that the birth had been quick because the baby was so small.

A gray and white woman came into the room. A nurse. Not a maid. Belle knew that now. The nurse helped Belle sit up, gave her a drink of water, fluffed her pillow, and asked if she was comfortable.

"A boy," the nurse was saying. "You have a baby boy. Should I bring him to you?"

Belle nodded. She still had no words. But she knew they would come.

The nurse returned and placed a tightly wrapped bundle in Belle's arms. When Belle took the baby, the warm, solid weight made Belle feel solid too. She folded back the blanket to see him better. A small wrinkled face. Eyes screwed tight. She touched his cheek with the tip of her finger.

*I was so afraid. I don't know why.*

Still standing by the bed, the woman asked, "Would you like to nurse him?"

*I never!* thought Belle, but she nodded.

The nurse showed her how to settle her baby at her breast. Belle gasped when the baby began to suck. Such a strange sensation. When she first took him, his body was straight and rigid inside his wrappings. Now she felt him relax and curl against her.

"He . . ." Her voice was faint. The nurse leaned close. ". . . is small."

Belle wanted to say more. That her first baby had not been so small as this one.

"He came a month early," the nurse said softly. "Maybe more." She glanced at the tiny creature. "Oh, dear. He's stopped sucking. I should take him back to the nursery."

Belle searched for the right words. "May I . . . longer?"

"A little longer."

Belle hugged the baby closer. She hummed to him. Her son. Names came into her head, slipping in from the past. Her past. She remembered.

*Jackson. Davis. Lee.*

~

Later that day, a man walked into her room. Belle knew him right away. It was John. Her husband.

"How are you, dear?" He kissed her forehead.

"Better. Colonel." She remembered she used to call him that. It made him smile.

A nurse peeked around the door and said, "There's a young lady here who wants to say hello to her mama."

Grace crept into the room, eyes wary, but at the sight of her mother, brushed and smiling, she broke into a grin and ran the last few steps.

"I . . . missed . . . you," Belle said, pulling her close. She looked up. The nurse had reappeared in the doorway, holding the baby. "Would you like to see your brother?"

Belle took the baby from the nurse and folded back the blanket. Grace leaned forward to see.

"He's very small."

*He's perfect.*

"What's his name?"

"Arthur Davis Lee Jackson Hammond," she announced, then looked up at her husband. "Is that all right, John?"

He barely glanced at the baby before saying, "Whatever you want, Belle."

༄

Arthur Davis Lee Jackson Hammond died three days later, and once again Belle drifted away.

*Stockton, California*
*March and April 1870*

# Chapter 48

Spring came, and the garden outside Belle's window burst into bloom. When she saw the colors, she turned her face away. She did not want to see them. She did not deserve another spring. Not when Arthur had not lived to see even one.

Once Belle started crying, she could not stop. She sat in her room with her back to the window and wept, tears trickling down her cheeks, dripping from her chin. She did not brush them away or make any sound. After two days, her skin was raw. One of the maids came in twice a day to bathe her skin in cool water and smooth it with a salve of almond oil and honey.

Arthur was dead.

A man came to her room and sat across from her, clasping her limp, cold hands in his. His voice was kind but firm.

"Please look at me, Mrs. Hammond." When she showed no signs of hearing, he said, "May I call you Belle?"

She turned her head.

"I think you're carrying a heavy burden. A secret. Something that makes you feel ashamed. I think that's why you're so sad. Can you tell me what the secret is? I think it would make you feel better to tell someone."

Belle shook her head. Ever so slightly. And looked away. The man waited patiently. Finally he stood, pressed his handkerchief into her unresponsive hands, and left the room.

The man came back again the next day, and the next, and the day after that. He sat across from her, held her hands, and spoke in the same gentle, insistent voice.

"There is no reason for you to carry this burden alone."

"I can help you."

"Trust me."

Until one day, Belle spoke. Through cracked lips, in a voice like rust, the words came, even though she tried to stop them.

"I did not want my baby."

The man said nothing.

"I did not want Arthur to be born. I tried to want him. But I couldn't. That's why he died. It was my fault."

She put her face in her hands.

The man touched her shoulder. "It wasn't your fault, Belle. Babies are small and weak. Sometimes they die. It's sad. But it's no one's fault." He stood. "I'll come again tomorrow. We'll talk more. I'm glad you told me. I think you'll start to feel better now."

❧

Little by little, Belle found her way back. Every day John and Grace visited her, and they walked together through the garden, across the lawn, down to the river. Everything was different. Belle's feet moved without her needing to tell them to. The sun felt warm on her skin. There was no menacing whisper at the river's edge. The water sparkled and chattered over the rocks like any other stream. The bright colors of the flowers no longer hurt her eyes.

The day came when Belle could remember the names of the flowers. She said them out loud for Grace, enjoying how the words felt in her mouth. How they sounded when she spoke them.

Cosmos. Dahlias. Alstromeria! Grace didn't listen. She wanted to chase squirrels, birds, butterflies. She was not interested in listening to her mother slowly recite the names of flowers.

John went inside the building to ask for a basket and scissors so Belle could pick a bouquet. When he came back, she held out her hand for the scissors. After she had cut enough flowers, she led her husband and daughter back inside to the small kitchen, where she put the flowers in a jar and filled it with water. The simple pleasure of doing, of knowing what to do and how to do it, flooded through her.

*So this is the world!*

She handed the flowers to John and said, "These are for you. And Grace." Her eyes filled with tears.

"Don't cry, Belle. Please don't cry. You've cried enough."

"I'm not crying because I'm sad. I'm crying because I'm getting better." She touched his cheek. *When was the last time?*

"Yesterday I walked down to the bottom of the driveway. I read the sign, John. It says 'The Insane Asylum of California.' I know now where I've been. All this time."

The world had come back to her.

❧

The doctor said it was too soon. Too soon for Belle to leave the quiet and order of the asylum. She must re-enter the world gradually. So one day she went with John to visit the boardinghouse where he and Grace had been living all these months. The same boardinghouse where Belle had spent a night she couldn't remember. She was shocked to see it. A small wooden building in need of paint.

"John, could you find nothing better?"

"It was important for us to be close to the . . . to where you were. So we could visit."

Belle thought of those visits. How dreary they must have been. For him. For Grace. Sitting in a room with a woman who was a ghost. A ghost who didn't even know who they were.

"And we needed to save on expenses," John was saying. "No. No! Don't look like that. You mustn't worry. It took a while to find a job, but I'm making good money now."

He told her about his work as a broker for some local ranchers, transporting and selling their cattle downriver to the San Francisco market.

The landlady, Mrs. Murphy, was kind, looking at Belle with eyes that were curious, but not prying, as she served them tea. The woman had taken a liking to Grace. She sent the little girl to fetch things from the kitchen and let her pass the plate of gingerbread.

"If you have everything you need, I'll leave you now. So you can enjoy your visit."

"No! I want you to stay," Grace said.

Mrs. Murphy shook her head. "That wouldn't be right. Not with your mama here. It's not just the three of us anymore."

Grace looked mutinous, but said nothing, only swung her legs, banging her shoes on the rung of the chair until John gave her a penny and sent her to the store for a stick of candy. She took the penny but let the screen door slam shut behind her.

"It's been hard for Grace," John said.

Belle felt a sudden weariness. She pushed it away. Down into that gray pit that lived inside her. The pit was smaller than it had been, but it was still there. Still waiting. Still filled with dark thoughts. She knew she could tumble into it again at any time.

*Will it never go away?*

The panic must have shown in her face because John grabbed her hand and said, "No. You're not to worry. We've been fine, Grace and I. We've missed you very much. We both have. But it was a long time for a little girl to be without her mother."

Belle believed him.

*He's right. I mustn't worry. All I have to do is get well again.*

*Martinsburg, West Virginia*

*Dear Miss Belle,*

*Now I knows why you haven't written in such a long time. Things sure has been hard for you. I was truly sorry to hear about your baby boy. It is a cruel thing for a mother to lose a child. I think you wanted Arthur more than you knew. You was just scared, is all. I wish I could have been there.*

*I was surprised you would write that you envy my life. You're right that I'm lucky. That delivering babies is important. That I live in a place where I belong. I know how blessed I am to have Sam and the children. I try to be Worthy. And I thank the Good Lord every day. But you wouldn't want my life, Miss Belle. My life is small. It fits me fine, but it wouldn't fit you. You'd be restless in no time. Flying out the door.*

*You asked if we're friends. Now we are, but we wasn't always. Before Freedom came, we was close, but we wasn't friends. You can't be friends with someone that owns you. I know it was your papa that had the papers on me. But you was the one I belonged to. Maybe you didn't always think about how that was. Maybe you forgot about it most of the time. But I never forgot. I thought about it every day. I thought about it just as soon as I woke up in the morning. And every minute after.*

*You say you might come back east with your family and live in Baltimore. Visit me if you can, Miss Belle. It's not far. Not for someone like you, who's been everywhere. I'd like to see you. It would be like old times. Only better.*

*—Your Eliza*

*Various U.S. Cities*
*May 1870 to December 1881*

# Chapter 49

At the end of May, Belle was discharged from the asylum. She and John and Grace went to Baltimore, where they moved into the Rowlands' big house on Mount Vernon Place. After almost three years of marriage, Mary and her husband still had no children. Mary was more than pleased to take over Grace's care. With Mama's help.

John found a position as an insurance salesman, undemanding work that allowed him to spend time with Belle every day. Her greatest pleasure was riding with him in Druid Hill Park. She still made an impression on horseback, turning heads when she passed by. Even so, she felt quite different than she had as a girl. She was no longer tempted to shout out a challenge to her companion and gallop fearlessly into the distance, jumping every obstacle in her path. Now she was content to ride sedately at her husband's side.

❧

In 1874, Belle and the colonel left Baltimore for Utica, New York, taking Grace with them. The next years took them to St. Louis, Dallas, then Philadelphia. John changed jobs often, trying his hand at selling clocks, sewing machines, pianos. Belle never questioned her husband's restlessness, but eventually Grace tired of their wandering life. When she was fourteen, she insisted on returning to the Rowlands', where she could lead "a normal settled existence."

It was during their years in Philadelphia that Belle gave birth to a healthy baby boy, John Edmund. After so many years, she had finally given the colonel a son.

The child, whom they called Eddie, was born in August 1881. That Christmas, Aunt Mary insisted that Grace spend the holiday in Philadelphia so she could meet her new half-brother. It was not a successful visit. At sixteen, Grace was as outspoken and independent as her mother had ever been. Unlike Belle, who had been pleasant and lively at that age, Grace seemed perpetually sullen and angry.

Grace held the new baby only once, saying loud enough for Belle to hear, "Maybe your mother will buy you the monkey she once promised me."

"My goodness, Grace!" Belle said. "That was so long ago."

Grace looked up, her eyes cold and unforgiving. "I still remember, Mother. I remember everything."

The atmosphere in the house grew even more strained after Belle's attempt to talk to her daughter about her conduct in Baltimore, a conversation Mary had asked her to have. It seemed that Grace spent much of her time with a group of friends her aunt and uncle had never met. Mary had written that the young people visited amusement parks, beer gardens, bowling alleys, and other places of "dubious entertainment." When Belle finally nerved herself to broach the topic, Grace's first response was humor.

"So Aunt Mary has mentioned this to you. I'm not surprised. I love her dearly, but she is so very old-fashioned. The places I go with my friends are quite harmless, Mother. In fact, they are filled with families. Although I must admit that they are mostly large German families. But I assure you the beer they give their children is always well-watered." She grinned, clearly enjoying Belle's shock. "Now that you are nearly forty, Mother, you may not know that it is no longer considered improper for groups of young people to go places unchaperoned. Times have changed since you were a girl."

*But I am only thirty-seven!* Belle tried not to be hurt by her daughter's words. Maybe she deserved them. She knew she had been a poor mother to Grace. But she had promised Mary to have this talk, and so she persevered.

"What about your reputation?"

Grace gave a harsh laugh. "Reputation? You never cared for *your* reputation. They said you were a prostitute, Mother. Don't deny it. I found Aunt Mary's clippings hidden in the attic. It's the worst possible insult, isn't it? To say a woman has lost her virtue. If people said that about you, why on earth would you care what anyone says about me?"

⁓

The next morning, Belle took one look at Grace's grim face across the breakfast table and realized she could not possibly spend another day indoors with her daughter. Assuming a determinedly cheerful expression, she proposed leaving Eddie with his nurse for a few hours, so she and Grace could enjoy a morning out.

As they threaded their way through the crowds of holiday shoppers, Grace said, "I don't know how you do it, Mother."

Her daughter's voice was pleasant for once, and Belle turned to her with a careful smile. "What do you mean?"

"I don't know how you manage so well with so little money."

"Grace, what a thing to say!"

"Don't deny it. You can't have much. I once overheard Rowland say that John made some poor investments in San Francisco. And he's always changing jobs. Even your house is rented. But somehow you manage to keep up appearances."

"Don't be spiteful, Grace."

"I mean it as a compliment. Your house is pleasant. You set a fine table. The servants seem content. You have your share of pretty dresses. There are gifts under the tree. It's all very well done."

Belle had stopped listening, her attention focused on a one-legged veteran half-lying on the cold pavement, propped against the wall of a church, He wore the tattered remnants of a blue uniform and had tied a ragged scarf around his head. No one else seemed to notice him. Without looking down, altering their stride, or interrupting their conversations, people avoided him as if by magic, stepping around his one healthy limb as if it wasn't attached to a human being.

Belle dropped some coins into the man's mittened hands, then clasped them in hers and leaned down to ask, "Where were you wounded, soldier?"

His faded eyes squinted up at her. "Gettysburg, ma'am."

"I'm sure you fought bravely, sir. You have my wishes for a Happy Christmas."

"The same to you, ma'am. Bless you." His eyes shifted to Grace. "And your family."

As they continued on their way, Belle took out her handkerchief and wiped her eyes.

"Should you have given him so much?"

"It's Christmas, Grace."

ɔ

The miserable visit ground to an end, and Grace returned to Baltimore. Shortly afterward, Belle and the colonel moved to Chicago, and from there to Dallas, where they had lived once before. John took a position as vice president of the Commercial

Travelers' Protective Association. This time, it seemed that the Hammonds might prosper. The railroad had been completed the year before, and the city pulsed with energy. The colonel insisted on renting a large house in one of the city's best neighborhoods. Belle liked the house, though she told her husband it was much too big for just the three of them.

Belle was happy for a while, buying furniture and carpets, filling up the rooms in the new house. Even so, there were times when she felt her mood slipping, and it frightened her. Mama had died the year before. She had been a loving mother and a faithful correspondent to her gypsy daughter. Belle missed her terribly. In fact, she missed everyone. Eliza especially. But also Mary. Belle's brother, Will, wrote to her now and then from Cincinnati, where he managed a hotel. Belle even missed Grace, who never wrote. It seemed that her daughter hated her.

*I must do better with Eddie. I want him to love me always.*

ಌ

On Sunday mornings, Belle would dress her son in his white linen sailor suit for a walk to the park, where he enjoyed feeding the ducks. Belle felt proud of her family on these weekly excursions. She knew the colonel did too. They made a handsome picture. Belle carried her parasol, her other hand tucked into the colonel's arm. Her husband held one of Eddie's hands. In the other, the boy clutched a paper bag of stale bread the cook had saved throughout the week.

"What would you think of me giving elocution lessons?" Belle asked on one of these outings. "I think I would have no trouble finding students."

The colonel did not hesitate. "I think it's a fine idea. I never liked the thought of you being on stage once you became Mrs.

Hammond, but I know you'd like to have something to fill your days."

In just one week of advertising in the newspaper, Belle acquired four students, young men planning to enter politics who wanted to improve their speaking skills. Twice weekly she met each one for a private lesson in her study on the first floor of the house. She taught them all the things she herself knew instinctively, as well as what she had learned from her acting days.

"Don't speak through your nose," she said to one student in particular, though they all seemed to do it. "Make your voice come from lower down." And she would place her hand at the young man's waist and press lightly. "You have a muscle here called the diaphragm. Use it to push the sound out. It will make your voice sound strong and commanding."

The touching was perfectly innocent, of course, though it always brought a flush to her student's cheeks. And her own. It had been a long time since Belle had flirted with the bounds of propriety in this way. She had forgotten how much she enjoyed it.

One evening, sitting in the parlor after the nursemaid had taken Eddie up to bed, John put down his newspaper and asked, "How are your students progressing?"

Belle laughed as she put aside the letter she was writing.

"I've just been describing them to Mary. Such throat clearings, coughs, and *ahems* you have never heard in your life! A veritable orchestra of sounds. Nor can they stand still. They sway constantly, like trees in a strong wind."

Belle jumped to her feet and performed an imitation, wringing her hands and rolling her eyes. John laughed and reached for her. When she went to him, he circled his arms about her.

"It is wonderful to see you so lively again. My clever, talented wife!"

Belle kissed his cheek and returned to her writing table. She paused after picking up her pen.

"One of them has a stutter. Poor lamb. He's the one I give my most special attention to. The rest would do well to remove their cigars when they speak. Can you imagine? So far they have all refused, each one telling me his cheroot is the only thing that will keep him from running off the speakers' platform entirely."

*Dallas, Texas*
*August to October 1884*

# Chapter 50

Three years after the Christmas visit to Philadelphia, Grace wrote to Belle that she was coming to Dallas. Not for a visit this time. She intended to live with them!

"Why?" Belle asked, before her daughter's bags were even unpacked. "I know you care for Mary more than you care for me. And she has more money to spend on you."

"As long as we are being so frank, Mother, I shall tell you. Aunt Mary is a dear. But her rules are stricter than yours. Since I care for her a great deal more than I care for you, I find it harder to disobey her."

*She moves into my home and announces that she intends to defy me!*

The fighting began almost immediately, noisy battles that raged throughout the house. Doors were slammed. Pitchers thrown. As a precaution, Belle told the housemaid to hide the most fragile objects in drawers and cupboards.

"I don't know what to do with her!" Belle complained to the colonel, coming into their bedroom one night after another argument.

"She's what, nineteen? Weren't you just like her at this age? You've often said so."

"I was."

"How did your mother manage you?"

Belle eyes narrowed as her fingers worked her hair into its nighttime braid. "As I recall, she was always quite mild with me. Then the war came, and I was off doing my patriotic duty. Serving the South. But I was never in danger of losing my virtue." *No matter what Grace might have said!* "Because I wasn't man crazy." She sighed. "I wish Mama were alive. Mary would probably have good advice too. She usually does! Though I hate for her to know what's going on."

"Wait!" John interrupted. "Is she? Is Grace man crazy?"

"I think that is what's at the bottom of it all," Belle said, slipping under the covers.

"She should be married by now," John insisted. "We must find her a husband."

Belle crossed her arms and scowled. "Why is it that whenever a woman shows some spirit, the solution is to marry her off?"

"Don't tell me you approve."

"Of course not. And yet . . . I understand. As you said, I was once that way myself."

John was not listening to her. "We're still newcomers here. How can we be sure Grace meets the right sort of man?"

Belle knew this was a tactful reference to her past. A divorce, two marriages, and her career as an actress made Belle unacceptable in the most exalted of Dallas's social circles.

"Perhaps you might introduce her to one of your students. Aren't there eight of them now? And several well-to-do bachelors?"

"Are you serious?"

"Why not? From what you say, they are all a bit older than she. Enough to steady her. Some are ranchers, with money and property. Perhaps one comes from a family that might consider marriage with a genteel, educated girl from outside Dallas society."

Belle spoke slowly, thinking out loud. "I doubt ranch life would suit Grace. But young Mr. Rawlings is a lawyer. Let me think about this." She sighed unhappily. "I wish now that when I first advertised for students, I had not used the name Belle Boyd."

"You wouldn't have found students so quickly if you had used Hammond."

Belle moaned. "My head hurts. I'm blowing out the lamp. We can talk tomorrow. Unfortunately, this problem will still be with us in the morning." She kissed her husband on the corner of his mustache, fretfully punched her pillow into its preferred shape, and lay her head on it with a sigh of irritation.

"I know I shall never sleep."

"Good night, Belle."

⁊

In the end, Grace was not introduced to any of her mother's eligible bachelors. One day when Belle was working with a student in her study, John walked into the room without knocking, something he had promised never to do. He was agitated over another of Grace's indiscretions and pushed the door open without thinking. It took a moment for him to comprehend what he saw in that brief instant before the two figures in the middle of the room leaped apart. His wife. Young Mr. Sheppard. Then he was striding toward them, his face red, his hands bunched into fists.

"What? You sir! You stand close enough to my wife to allow her to touch your face?"

"Colonel! I was merely helping him to shape his mouth properly in order to . . ."

John turned on his wife, spitting the words, "In order to receive a kiss from your lips?"

"Sir!" Mr. Sheppard protested. "I am afraid you have m-m-misunderstood."

In two strides, the colonel was across the room and towering over the younger man.

"Oh shut up!" he roared and punched Mr. Sheppard in the nose.

Belle's student howled in pain as blood dripped onto his white shirt. She pushed him from the room, then through the front door, all the while offering endless apologies.

"What is the meaning of this?" Belle demanded when she returned to her study, where the colonel stood in the middle of the carpet, rubbing his knuckles. He wheeled on her.

"I might ask you the same thing! It's bad enough that your daughter allows herself to be seen with all the wrong sorts of men. Now you, you . . ." Unable to finish, he ran his hand through his hair, a wild look in his eye. "I can't believe you would behave this way."

"And I can't believe you would suspect me of such vile behavior as apparently you do. Be assured that you are mistaken in what you think you saw."

❧

After Belle received the colonel's divorce papers, she countered with papers of her own. She charged Mr. Hammond with seeing other women. *Was this true?* And making false accusations that were injurious to her reputation as a wife and mother. *That much at least was true.* They had been married more than fifteen years. Belle chose not to think of it, instead focusing on her determination to keep her son. She would at least have Eddie!

For the next several weeks, the colonel was rarely home, leaving the house before Belle was up and returning long after she was in bed. A bed they no longer shared. It reminded Belle of the final days of her marriage to Sam, when the love between them had steadily withered and died. Once again she had failed at marriage, but she could not think of that now. She was too worried about Grace.

Her daughter was behaving strangely. She had stopped going out. She avoided calls from her current beau, one James Collier. Even though she went to bed early every night, she came to breakfast in the morning with dark circles under her eyes. She would sit at the table with her dressing gown carelessly tied, her braid half undone, staring listlessly at a cup of tea or nibbling on a piece of dry toast.

Fearing the worst, one morning before Grace was up, Belle steeled herself and knocked on her bedroom door.

"Go away!"

Belle went into the darkened room and sat on the edge of the bed.

"What do you want?"

"I want to help you."

Grace rolled over, sat up a little, eyed her mother suspiciously. "Why?"

"It doesn't matter why."

Belle wanted to reach out and touch Grace, smooth her tangled hair. "Tell me. Are you in trouble?"

Instead of asking what her mother meant, as Belle had thought she might, Grace shook her head wearily from side to side. "I don't know." Then, more softly, "Maybe."

At that moment, Belle felt nothing but tenderness for her daughter. *Will she let me help her?*

Resisting the impulse to put her arms around Grace, she said briskly, "We must take steps. Write to Mr. Collier and ask him to visit tomorrow evening. Your father will be out. Of course. When is the last time he spent an evening at home? At any rate, it gives us a chance to settle this unfortunate business once and for all."

"James might not come."

"I think he will. And you will spend today and tomorrow getting ready. You must have a bath and wash your hair. Come to my room and take whatever lotions and powders you need to make you feel like a pretty girl again. I have a new shawl I can lend you. And you may borrow my coral necklace." Belle let herself touch Grace then, lightly placing a single finger under her daughter's chin. "How does that sound?"

"Go-od," Grace said, drawing out the word, not trying to hide the caution in her voice.

Racking her brain for other useful advice, Belle added, "You should go for a long walk too. The exercise and fresh air will put color in your cheeks. And it will help you calm yourself and order your thoughts. Walking has always been a great help to me."

After she left the room, Belle stood in the hallway and leaned her forehead against Grace's closed door.

*Am I somehow to blame for all of this?*

❧

The next evening, James Collier appeared at the appointed time. Belle had given the servants the night off, so it was she who greeted the pale young man with a sparse moustache who stood on the doorstep, nervously crushing the brim of his hat between two fists. Belle seated Mr. Collier in the parlor and poured him a glass of wine from the crystal decanter, trying to put him at ease.

Grace looked beautiful when she walked into the room, her

skin like porcelain, her golden curls gathered in a ladylike knot at the back of her neck. The pale blue dress she had borrowed from her mother was very becoming. As Grace made her entrance, Belle watched Mr. Collier closely, trying to guess his feelings. She was pleased to see how he jumped to his feet and bowed, his cheeks reddening.

"Miss Hardinge. How well you are looking."

Grace, instructed by her mother to say little, merely smiled, sat, and accepted some wine.

Belle started, "Mr. Collier, you have been spending quite a lot of time with my daughter."

He nodded.

"I'm sorry, I did not hear what you said."

"Yes, ma'am!"

"That's better. I assume therefore that you find her company agreeable?"

"Very agreeable."

"She is gently raised, well-educated, and quite pretty. Am I correct?"

"Indeed, ma'am."

Mr. Collier took a long swallow of wine. Quickly followed by another.

"Did you know my daughter has been unwell of late?"

"I am sorry to hear it."

Belle stopped firing questions and sat back in her chair, regarding the young man intently. As the silence grew, Mr. Collier looked at Grace. She smiled sweetly and said nothing.

"The reason you are here, Mr. Collier, in case you do not know, is to give you an opportunity to act honorably and ask my daughter to be your wife."

"My wife!"

"Yes, that is correct."

"But I don't . . . that is to say . . . I have no intention of marrying at this time."

Belle leaned forward, eyes narrowed.

"Please explain."

"I'm too young. My parents would never allow it."

"But, James, you said you cared for me!" Grace cried.

Suddenly, Belle was on her feet and reaching for the pistol in her pocket. When Mr. Collier saw the gun, saw Belle's steady hand, his eyes widened. With one last, wild look at Grace, now sobbing in her handkerchief, he ran into the hall and sprinted for the front door. Belle followed, raised her pistol. Fired. Collier staggered and grabbed his right arm. Somehow managing to open the door with his left hand, he ran down the front steps and up the street.

*Martinsburg, West Virginia*

*Dear Miss Belle,*

*What has you gone and done now? There's a story in the Martinsburg paper, reprinted from the Dallas paper that says you shot somebody again. A man that got Grace into trouble? The paper says you was trying to get him to marry her. I guess that didn't work out too good. At least this time you didn't kill nobody. And now Grace has run off. Maybe to California? But you don't know who she's with?*

*I keep thinking that if I'd been with you in Dallas, I might could have stopped you. Why you still carrying that gun after all these years? It's brought you nothing but trouble. But you never did listen to me. So I guess there's nothing I could have done. Still, I'm sorry for you. And for Grace. What's going to happen to that poor girl? You said you don't know for sure if she's pregnant. How could you not know? Grace was only in Dallas three months. How did things go wrong so fast?*

*The newspaper also says you just got another divorce. Where will you and Eddie go? Baltimore? It's hard to imagine you living with your sister. You two hasn't got along in years. Not since Mary growed up. You just ended up being too different.*

*—Eliza*

*P.S. Stop and <u>think</u> next time before you go off and do something so foolish. You're not a girl no more. You're a forty years old woman. It's about time you got some sense.*

*P.P.S. I hope you can read my writing. I'm so mad I'm shaking, and the pen is like to jump right out of my hand.*

# Chapter 51

Belle was hurt by the way Grace had left. Her daughter had disappeared in the middle of the night without even leaving a note. She took only a small carpetbag. Along with all the money Belle had saved from three years of elocution lessons.

*I would have given her the money if she'd asked me.*

Belle had no answer to Eliza's question about what had gone wrong with Grace. She would probably never know. As for the future, there was only one thing she knew for certain. She and Eddie would not go to Baltimore. Eliza was right. Belle could never be happy living in Mary's house. Not Baltimore. No indeed. Belle had other plans. She was getting married. For the third time.

She had first met Nathaniel Rue High after a performance he gave in Dallas. He was a young actor whose rugged profile and deep voice earned him leading roles with a touring company based out of Toledo, Ohio. When Belle went backstage to compliment his performance, they found they had much to talk about. Nat was sixteen years younger than Belle, though neither of them knew it at the time. It did not seem to matter. She remembered her acting days with great fondness. It was pleasant to talk with someone who understood the pleasures and frustrations of life on stage.

Nat's company moved on from Dallas to other towns in Texas, and he and Belle began to write each other. As her family troubles mounted, she confided in her new friend. When she slipped a newspaper clipping announcing her divorce into an envelope and addressed it to him, she was not sure herself what she wished to happen. Nat's response was immediate and emphatic. A marriage proposal.

> *You must know I adore you! I could scour the country and not find another woman like you. Please say you will be my wife. The three of us can live together, you and me and Eddie, and be perfectly happy.*

Just two months after her divorce from Colonel Hammond, Belle married Nat High. But this time she decided to keep her name. It was the only one she had ever thought of as truly hers. From now on, she would always be Belle Boyd.

Belle and Nat agreed that he would continue to tour, as this was his only means of earning a living. Belle intended to teach again. Money would be tight. But she and Nat were in love. Somehow they would manage.

Since Nat's company was based in Toledo, they moved there. This would allow him to be home as much as possible between tours. Fortunately, Eddie had taken to Nat immediately. Belle's young husband was a born performer, charming the little boy with birdcalls and sleights of hand. After all, what four-year-old could resist having a shiny penny pulled from behind his ear?

As Belle watched Nat making shadow pictures on the wall in the darkened parlor, telling Eddie a story with his clever voice and hands, she felt herself relax. She decided that she had been unhappy for years. She looked at Nat fondly. She remembered the fortune-teller, Zeferina. The woman had mentioned three husbands, but not a fourth.

Belle looked younger than her age. She had kept her graceful figure. Her skin was unlined, her hair the same lustrous chestnut as always. Men still noticed her when she entered a room, as she was well aware. She was vague with Nat about her age, and he did not press her. He knew she was older and claimed he did not care. They were soulmates.

☙

For over a year they tried to make it work, but they were always short of money. The simple fact was that Nat could not support Belle and Eddie on his salary as a young actor. Expenses were so much greater with a family. Before, he had lived in a furnished room when he returned to Toledo between engagements. Now they had a house, a maid, furniture. The boy always seemed to need new shoes.

On one of Nat's visits, after Eddie was in bed, they discussed the problem late into the night. In the end they agreed that the only solution was for Belle to return to the stage.

"I hate to ask it of you, but I don't see how we can manage otherwise. You are better known than I and will command a higher salary."

"Oh Nat! Just thinking about touring makes me feel like a girl again. I assure you, I am quite excited."

"You will always be a girl to me," Nat replied gallantly, as Belle had known he would. He sat on the arm of her chair. "Do you have any ideas of what you'd like to do?"

"I've been thinking about it," Belle confessed. "I have no desire to return to the stage and simply do whatever roles the manager thinks best. I intend to create something totally original. A new show which I will take on the road with you as my manager." She paused dramatically. "I will be a *diseuse*."

"Which is?"

"A diseuse is a dramatic storyteller. I will recount my adventures, reenacting scenes from my career as a spy. I can wear my Confederate uniform, or I might design a new one. We'll have an army tent set up on stage for the camp scenes. Perhaps I'll ride onstage on a horse. I've seen that done. We can have military music. Bugles and drums. A scene in the Old Capitol Prison would play well, I think. Picture it. A gloomy cell, me wearing a white dress and standing by a barred window, singing sweetly for the men as I used to do."

Belle was walking about the room now, indicating where the tent would be, the prison cell, hopping onto the arm of an upholstered chair to sit sidesaddle and hold imaginary reins. Nat stared with his mouth open.

"You are a genius, wife! This will be a sensation. Audiences will love it." He scratched the back of his head and asked, "What about Eddie?"

Belle slid from the arm of the chair into the seat. "For now, it will be easy for him to travel with us. When he's older, he will go and live with Mary. There are many fine schools in Baltimore."

"Has Mary agreed? I know you don't always see eye to eye."

Belle shook her head. "No. But she will. Mary disapproves of the life I've led. *Had* to lead. But she adores children. It's her weakness where I am concerned. She and her husband always wanted a large family, but they only have the one boy. When the time comes, I'm sure they'll be pleased to have Eddie live with them."

"So we can count on her?

"Absolutely."

Pacing in front of the fireplace, Nat said, "It sounds like it will work. And best of all, you and I will never be apart."

ço

Belle continued to plan every detail of the show, reporting her progress to Nat whenever he was home. He was her manager now, and she trusted his opinion completely.

"I want to call it *'Dark Days, or Memories of the War'*. A double title. What do you think?"

"Excellent."

"The name was suggested by a group of veterans from the local chapter of The Grand Army of the Republic. I took their advice because, and this is another good piece of news, they have agreed to sponsor the debut performance."

"But the G.A.R. is made up of Union veterans! Why would they sponsor a famous rebel?"

"Because I am no longer the Rebel Spy. I have told them I intend to be a new Belle, a wiser Belle, who has grown to love the Union I once worked so hard against. We are one nation again. My story will represent the courage and sacrifice of both sides in our recently reunited republic."

Clutching his forehead, Nat mimed his response to these dizzying developments.

"This means the show should do well in both the South and the North," Belle explained. "Especially if we get the G.A.R. to continue their sponsorship. They've already booked the auditorium for the opening here in Toledo. It's to be the People's Theater."

"The People's?"

"I know. Not a first-class playhouse, but it's right downtown, and the stage is large. The backstage, too, in case we decide to include a horse. Which I think we must."

"The People's will do nicely."

"Now, I need your help with my costume. Let me show you my Confederate uniform. You've never seen it." Her eyes twinkled. "Stay here. I'll put it on and be down directly."

"Do you require assistance," Nat asked. He had been away four weeks.

Belle smiled but shook her head. "I don't want you to watch me put it on, piece by piece. You must see it all at once, the way the audience will. I wish you to be astounded."

A short time later, Belle swept into the room in a long gray skirt and matching jacket whose fitted waist showed off her figure. In every other detail, the jacket was military in style, with a stand-up collar, a double row of gold buttons, and two lengths of braid looping across her chest from shoulder to shoulder. Black leather gloves with stiff gauntlets reached halfway to her elbow. To complete the outfit, she wore a cavalry hat whose upturned brim was decorated with swooping black ostrich feathers.

"I pronounce myself astounded. How fine you look!" Nat cried. He circled Belle, admiring every detail, then stood in front of her, came to attention, and snapped off a crisp salute, which she laughingly returned.

"Now, for the accessories. I have a riding crop, of course. But also this." Unrolling a length of threadbare red velvet she'd placed on a nearby table, she drew out a sword and held it by her side. "What do you think?"

"The sword. Most definitely the sword. Your audience will be thrilled."

"I agree. Now, the skirt can be improved upon. I thought of adding a long train. It could be absurdly, inconveniently long. Part of the act. With me having to sometimes kick it out of the way and say something not quite ladylike. It would add a touch of humor, which audiences always enjoy. And after I've done it more than once, they will have the fun of waiting for me to do it again."

"Darling Belle." Nat took her in his arms. "You were born for this. Your instincts are so . . . well, I don't know if there's a single word for it. But you are an artist for certain."

Belle wriggled free. "So, you like the notion of the train? I did have one other idea. Quite daring, really. I was thinking . . . that perhaps . . . I might wear trousers."

Nat threw back his head and hooted with laughter. "A woman on stage. Not just any woman. My wife! Wearing trousers and carrying a sword." He took her in his arms once more, and this time she did not pull free. "Truly, there is no one like you in all the world."

A lengthy kiss followed, after which Belle murmured, "I think perhaps I will require some assistance upstairs after all."

# Chapter 52

*D*ark Days was a resounding success. Belle and Nat were able to settle their overdue bills and for the first time ever had something left over. Belle wrote to Mary, claiming to be happier than she had ever been.

> *I know you do not like to hear it, but I do feel I was born to be on stage. Not pretending to be someone else, though. I want only to play myself. For better or worse, I will tell my own story. In my own way. Let the audience judge my actions. Unlike the colonel, who denied me this outlet, Nat supports everything I do in this regard. He is the dearest husband in the world.*

Mary wrote back immediately. While she was pleased to hear that Belle was happy, her real interest was Eddie. What were Belle's plans for him?

> *Why not leave Eddie with us? Our Robbie and he are only a year apart. Nothing would make Rowland and me happier than to have Eddie live with us. We still hope for more children, but that may never happen. What do you think?*

Belle decided that Mary's suggestion made a great deal of sense. Really, it would be better for everyone if Eddie were settled in

Baltimore right away. Wouldn't it? They could stop in Martinsburg on their way to Baltimore. She would put flowers on Mama's grave and then visit Eliza, whom she hadn't seen in nearly twenty years. It would be a surprise.

c/s

Standing in the cemetery, Belle stared pensively at the lettering on the white marble headstone. MARY REBECCA REED BOYD, BORN 1826, DIED 1880.

"You don't remember Mama," Belle said, keeping hold of Eddie's hand, wanting him to stay with her. "She died just before you were born. But she would have loved you very much."

Eddie wasn't interested. He was leaning sideways, all his weight pulling on Belle's arm. He straightened finally, now hopping on one foot and tugging at the collar of his shirt. He had been very proud of his new suit when he put it on that morning but had tired of wearing it almost immediately.

"Only a little longer." Belle looked down at the tight grip she had on her son's hand, and then she glanced around at the cemetery with its rows of quiet stones. They were the only ones there. "All right, then. You can walk about if you like, but you must stay where I can see you."

In an instant, Eddie was running up the hill, picking up a heavy stick along the way and thrashing energetically at the tall grass. Belle looked after him. Now that he was gone, she was glad. Why had she tried to keep him with her? All she wanted was to stand by the grave and try to feel her mother's presence. The one person in her life who had always forgiven her for everything she had done. Or not done. Or done poorly. Belle touched the cold headstone, as if that could somehow bring her mother closer.

*I miss you so much, Mama! If only I could tell you the life I've lived in the years since you left me. All the places I've been. Of course you know, I've had my share of tragedies. The worst was poor little Arthur. I know you understand what it's like to lose a child. Now it seems that Grace is lost to me as well. She's in California. I hope she's happy there. I never was. Thank goodness I still have my little boy. Eddie. John Edmund. But we've always called him Eddie. I'm sorry you never had the chance to meet him. To hold him. I wish you were alive, Mama. I always felt it was you and Eliza who loved me for myself alone. The good news is that I do think I've found a loving husband at last. Nat adores me, and I him. I feel like I've reached a safe harbor with him at my side. I believe that things will be better for me from now on. I truly do.*

When she had run out of words, Belle took a deep breath, dabbing at her eyes with a handkerchief. Eddie didn't like to see her cry. When she was ready, she looked around for her son and saw him at the top of the hill, chasing squirrels in and out among the gravestones. She climbed part way after him.

"It's time to go see Eliza!" she called.

Eddie yelled back, "I like it here."

Belle took a few more steps. "You must listen to your mother." When he didn't budge, she added, "Come. I'll buy you a peppermint stick."

❧

On the way to Eliza's, they passed Papa's store, which had been closed since Mama's death. The door and windows were boarded up, and weeds grew through the wooden steps. It hurt to see it looking so rough and neglected. Papa had been proud of his store.

She remembered the day she and Mary had stood on the porch, watching Jackson's men set fire to the depot. It was the beginning of the war. Before anyone knew how long it would last. What the cost would be. So much time had passed since then. She had been seventeen. And now, somehow, she was past forty.

Belle gave her head a shake and crossed the street to the rebuilt railroad station and the little shop inside. It sold all the things Papa's store once sold. Tobacco, matches, needles, thread, soap, hairpins, headache powders, and all the other things travelers might need. Belle bought the promised peppermint stick and a bag of lemon drops for Eliza's family.

They continued walking, Eddie sucking on the candy he clutched in the handkerchief Belle had given him to keep his shirt clean. In his other hand, he gripped the bag of lemon drops, which he had insisted on carrying. As they walked, Belle wondered if she should have written Eliza that she was coming. Then she began to worry if anyone they passed would recognize her. *Surely not. It was so long ago.*

When they drew close to Eliza's house, Belle saw a crowd of people gathered in front, everyone dressed in their finest. It was easy to pick out Eliza. Even at a distance, Belle knew her. Something about the way she stood, with both feet planted firmly on the ground, solid and reliable. *It must be an important occasion.* Belle had never seen Eliza in anything but a plain cotton work dress. Now she was wearing a stylish navy-blue outfit trimmed in gray braid with a short matching cape. She held a baby in a long white gown that could only be for a christening. When Eliza looked up from the child in her arms, it took a moment for her to register Belle standing there.

"Miss Belle!"

"Hello, Eliza."

In the awkward pause that followed, Belle regretted coming. This was not the reunion she had imagined. Too many people were standing too close. Surely there were inquisitive neighbors peering out their windows. Belle felt foolish.

Eliza turned and put the baby in the arms of a tall young man standing beside her, then hurried forward to take Belle's hands.

"It's fine to see you. This is my grandson's christening day! We're getting ready to walk to the church. I'll introduce you in a moment. But first I want to meet your son."

Eliza leaned over. "You must be Eddie."

The boy nodded, widening his eyes at her, but kept the candy clamped firmly in his mouth. Eliza chuckled and tousled his hair. She raised her eyes to Belle's.

"Why didn't you write you were coming?"

"We're on our way to Baltimore to see Mary." Belle did not mention that she was taking Eddie to live with her sister. "I decided to visit Mama's grave." She was aware of the curious stares from Eliza's family. "I'm sorry I came at an inconvenient time."

"Nonsense!" Eliza protested, but Belle knew she was only being polite.

Even so, Eliza insisted on making introductions. It was clear that she was proud of her family and wanted Belle to meet them.

"Of course, you know Sam."

A gray-haired man in a dark suit touched his hat and gave a slow smile that Belle remembered with a pang. "Hello, Miss Belle."

"You're looking well, Sam."

"And this is John," Eliza continued.

"John! I would never have known you."

"It's been a few years." John still held the baby, jiggling him expertly when he began to fuss. "Thank you for the china bowl you sent when Louis was born. With alphabet letters. It was kind of you to remember us."

Eliza was moving on again. "This is John's wife, Lucille." A plump woman in an extravagant hat nodded formally. "My daughter-in-law has a millinery shop in town." Before Belle could think of a response, Eliza said, "And this is Lee Laura. Do you remember her? She's all growed up now." No longer a shy little girl, the young woman gave a dazzling smile, and Belle felt a stab of regret. Lee Laura and Grace had played together. *Where is Grace now?*

But Eliza was continuing her introductions. "Here are my other grandchildren. This is Young John, John's oldest. And this pretty girl is Anna. Louis is the baby. I think he looks just like John at this age."

There were more smiles and nods, with Belle at a loss for how to navigate this uncomfortable reunion. Then Eddie stepped forward, his arm held out stiffly, offering the bag of lemon drops to Anna. The little girl blinked at him but did not reach for the bag. Eddie shook it, producing an enticing rustle. Finally, he took the peppermint stick out of his mouth and said, "Candy. It's good," before popping the stick back in.

They all looked at Eddie, his hand and face and Belle's handkerchief a mess of melted green sugar. Everyone laughed, and for a moment the situation felt less awkward. It gave Belle a chance to remember herself. Surely she ought to be able to take command of the situation. This was not the hardest thing she had ever done!

She took Eliza's hand in hers. "We've kept you long enough. Please accept my congratulations. We'll come again another time." Knowing, as she knew Eliza did, that this would not happen.

Belle looked down at her son and smoothed his hair to give herself something to do.

"Eddie, make a proper bow, at least."

She ached to embrace Eliza, to throw her arms around her as she had when she was little. To feel Eliza's arms circling her, holding her close, steadying her. This is what Belle had imagined. This is why she had come. It would have been possible, if they'd met privately, inside Eliza's house. They could have talked then. About the end of her second marriage. About Grace. About Nat, and how Belle thought she finally had a chance at happiness. But none of that could happen. Not now. Not here on the street. With the whole world looking on. It would not happen today. It would never happen.

Giving one last smile and nod to Eliza, as she would to any casual acquaintance, she took Eddie by the hand and marched back up the street with her head held high. She couldn't bear to think that anyone might feel sorry for her.

*Various Towns and Cities*
*1886 to 1894*

# Chapter 53

Belle took her show on the road. As her manager, Nat arranged bookings, fees, accommodations, and every detail of the performance, including hiring a horse if Belle chose to enter riding astride, which called immediate attention to the fact that she was wearing trousers.

The show varied, according to her audience. As they traveled from one town to the next, even the name might change. It might be called *Perils of A Spy* or *North and South.* In Norfolk, Virginia, the title was *Dashing Deeds and Daring Exploits* and featured Belle's story as the thrilling centerpiece of a series of skits about the war. The important thing was that Belle Boyd was always at the center, her usual flamboyant self, telling her story with verve and passion.

Her closing number never varied, a rousing cheer from the entire company of "One Country, One Flag, One Sentiment—Union!" followed by the singing of *Hail Columbia!*, during which the audience would stand and join in. Belle Boyd was no longer a controversial, defiant, unwomanly Confederate patriot. Chameleon-like, she had managed to refashion herself into something entirely different. A universal figure who represented the sacrifice and heroism of both the North and the South.

❧

As the years went by, Belle and Nat began to have money problems once more. *Perils of a Spy* continued to be popular, but traveling with a troupe of actors was expensive and ate up most of the profits. Nat managed to trim the show in small ways. He simplified the staging. There was no longer a horse. They used fewer musicians. There were times when the two of them toured alone, Nat rounding out Belle's show with performances of magic tricks and comedy monologues. Even then, they sometimes ran up hotel bills they couldn't pay.

In the town of Little Falls, New York, a hotel manager knocked at their door early one morning. Nat was at the washstand, shaving, his suspenders dangling around his knees and his face full of lather. Belle was in her dressing gown. Never one to stand on ceremony, she called, "Come in!" and was instantly sorry. The manager carried a paper in his hand. Belle knew what it was. Without a word, she took the bill from the clerk and read it.

"This can't be right. The amount is much too high. We never ate all these meals. I'm sure of it. Half the time we go elsewhere. Your food is not very good, you know."

"This is the rate we agreed on when you checked in."

"Well, it's too much. You must reduce it."

"Here, let me see." Nat wiped the last of the lather from his face and read through the bill quickly. "My wife is quite correct. The figure is too high."

"I can't reduce it. I don't have the authority. You will have to pay."

"We won't," Nat replied firmly. "And there's the end of it."

Belle ordered the manager out of the room, but he stood his ground.

"My wife has asked you to go," Nat said, placing his hand on the man's chest.

The manager was short but solidly built. He knocked Nat's hand away and took a swing at him. Nat fell, hitting his head on the edge of a table. In a moment, Belle had snatched up her pistol and was pointing it at the manager.

"Leave us!"

The manager retreated but shouted over his shoulder that he was going for the police. By the time the officer arrived, Belle and Nat were dressed, their bags packed. They announced their intention to move to a different hotel. However, there was still the matter of the bill. The manager had given the policeman his version of events. Now the officer listened to Belle and Nat, whose bruised forehead was used to corroborate their story.

The policeman sighed unhappily. "The judge can't decide this case until Tuesday. Meanwhile," he said to the manager, "I will allow this couple to leave the hotel without settling their bill. But," he added, turning to Nat, "you must leave some of your luggage behind as security."

"She threatened me with a gun!" the manager said, glowering at Belle.

"Yes, well, that is something that will not happen again." The policeman turned to Belle. "If it does, Miss Boyd, I will place you under arrest for disturbing the peace."

Someone, either the manager or the policeman, reported the incident to the editor of the local paper. It was a front-page story, the most exciting thing to happen in Little Falls in some time. Belle was unhappy when she read it. She was still newsworthy, and stories about her were often reprinted in other papers. This report could appear anywhere. Including Martinsburg or Baltimore.

In the end, the story turned out to be a blessing. On reading it, a group of Union veterans raised twenty-five dollars and presented it to Belle. It was more than enough to pay both hotel bills and avoid the embarrassment of a trial. Before she and Nat boarded the train to the next town, Belle visited the newspaper office and insisted they print a notice that the charges had been dropped and the bill paid, that the local veterans continued to cherish their favorite "Rebel Spy."

*Griffin, Georgia*

Dear Eliza,

I'm afraid your Belle is a very poor correspondent, but it's not because I wish to be. You see, Nat and I are such gypsies these days that I often do not know where to tell you to send your letters. Yet when I arrive in a town and find one waiting for me, my heart overflows. I read each letter over and over until the pages wear out. Your words are such a comfort.

I am in special need of comfort after our Christmas visit to Baltimore. Which it turns out will be our last. While we were there, Mary shocked me by announcing that she and Rowland are moving to Parsons, Kansas. And taking the boys with them! Rowland says he is tired of lawyering and wants to open a business. A hotel. Or maybe he'll try ranching. Oh, he and Mary are full of plans!

The boys too. Eddie and Robbie say they want to be cowboys. What fourteen-year-old boy does not? Rowland ordered them both expensive cowboy hats for Christmas. Stetsons, naturally. And lariats. During our visit, they spent all day outside, roping the shrubbery behind the house. I can't blame my boy. Of course he's excited. But it hurts that he's so ready to go off and leave me. It's a bitter thing that they have all been planning this, and kept it from me. Nat tries to cheer me by saying we can include Kansas in our touring from now on.

For years, I thought of Mary's house as my home. Now I've lost that as well.

I am quite heartbroken
—Belle

*Various Town and Cities*
*1898 to 1900*

# Chapter 54

The touring continued. Belle, now well past fifty, was exhausted. Fortunately her marriage was happy, Nat as loving as ever. Still, she was reluctant to admit to her young husband that her famous stamina had finally deserted her. She didn't want to confess the tiredness that went so deep her bones ached.

As a new century beckoned, little interest remained in the great civil conflict of Belle's youth. The size of her audiences steadily dwindled. The pace of touring; the poor food; the third-rate boarding houses with their drafty rooms and sheets that had often been put on the bed still damp; the worry over selling enough tickets, even at reduced prices—all this was unendingly wearing.

By the time they paid the cost of renting an auditorium, plus room and board and transportation, there was never any money left. Belle had no choice but to continue. On and on. Notices began appearing in the local papers warning hotelkeepers about the couple. She came to rely on these dreadful snippets to rally local veterans into organizing a collection for her. No matter how grateful she was for the devotion of these old soldiers, it was still a humiliation. She was glad now that Mary was far away and unlikely to see the notices.

Yet somehow, with Nat's support, she would recover during the ride in a second-class carriage on whatever whistle-stop train took them to the next small town on their schedule. Each time, she managed to make something of an entrance when she arrived at the station, walking gracefully in her threadbare clothes with her head high, as if she were stepping into the spotlight. No hint of tiredness or worry in her voice or manner.

෭෭

In May of 1900, Belle and Nat were touring Wisconsin. Just the two of them. Belle was in poor health, and Nat spent money they did not have so a doctor could examine her. The doctor warned that Belle's heart was weak and ordered her to rest. She and Nat made plans to move into a cheap furnished apartment in Evansville. They would use it as their base, touring only locally until she had recovered. Meanwhile, she and Nat had no money to speak of, so they traveled to the small resort town of Kilbourn, where Belle was scheduled to appear under the sponsorship of the ever faithful G.A.R.

"Miss Boyd! Miss Belle Boyd!" cried a young male voice brimming with enthusiasm. "I'm Johnny Murphy." He removed his cap. "The hotel sent me to help you and your husband with your luggage." He looked around in confusion. "This is it? Just these three bags?"

Belle nodded. "This seems a charming town, but we will only be here a few nights."

"Folks are looking forward to hearing you speak. I'm coming. Wouldn't miss it for anything. And the hotel staff is thrilled. No one famous ever comes here."

Carrying their luggage as they walked, young Murphy was soon speaking to them over his shoulder. He slowed and said, "My apologies. I do tend to walk fast. It's not far now." He looked at

Belle. "I could fetch a carriage if you'd like?"

Hiding her breathlessness, she said, "Why don't you go on ahead, Mr. Murphy?" She gripped Nat's arm tightly. "We'll follow at a slower pace. It will give us a chance to see more of your lovely town."

Belle gave two readings to modest audiences at the local Methodist church. After the second one, she and Nat returned to their room, where she collapsed on the bed as soon as she walked through the door. She had never felt so tired.

"Belle?"

"I'll be fine. Just help me undress."

Nat unbuttoned her shoes and slid them off her aching feet. He unfastened her heavy wool costume and gently lifted it off her. He unlaced her corset and peeled it away from her skin. Finally he slid her nightdress over her head.

When he had helped her into bed and she was sitting propped comfortably against the pillows, she sighed. "That's better."

Her eyes were closed, but she smiled at the sound of Nat pouring a glass of wine. When she opened her eyes, he was standing over her, the wine in his hand, a look of worry on his face.

*There he is. My dear, sweet husband. What would I do without him?*

"Do you need help?"

Belle shook her head and reached for the glass. "I can do it."

"Small sips, darling."

After a few cautious swallows, she felt better. "I thought the reading went well. The audience was small but appreciative."

Nat sat on the edge of the bed and smoothed her hair.

"It went very well. You seem tired, though. Shall I order us some supper?"

She shook her head again. "Not for me. But you should

have something." She took another sip. "You are so good to me, husband."

Nat chewed his lip.

"Is it your heart again? Shall I find another doctor?"

"I'm fine now. The last doctor said I should rest, and that's exactly what I'm doing."

"You're sure you don't want to eat? Even a little soup? A piece of chicken?"

Belle made a face and pressed her lips together, shaking her head. "Not tonight. It's a waste of money to order food I'm not going to eat. Don't worry. I'll be fine in the morning."

He stood by the door, watching her reach under the pillow and then frown.

"Ah, there it is."

"Your pistol?"

"Yes." Belle smiled as she pulled it out. "I always feel better when it's close by. Run off and get yourself something to eat. I'm not going anywhere."

☙

Belle had vivid dreams that night, disjointed visions that smeared and dissolved, then coalesced into something new. She saw herself sitting at a desk, and she knew, the way one does in a dream, that she was writing to Grace. And she knew too that all she wanted to say was, "I'm sorry."

Next Belle was in a store, and the merchant was holding out his hand for his money, and she was counting it out, coin by coin. The man's face twisted in anger, and Belle knew she didn't have enough. She began to cry.

Then she was outside again, and people on the sidewalk were

pointing at her ragged clothes and laughing. *If I can ever get ahead, I will buy new ones. I promise!* Although she formed the words, no sound came.

Now a train station, but the train was pulling away. Belle ran beside it, trying to keep up. She stood and watched the train disappear in the distance, and she was alone on the platform. Suddenly there was a smell of roses and honeysuckle, and Eliza was there, reaching for her hand. *What happens now?* Belle asked. Again her words made no sound, but she knew Eliza understood because she smiled and lightly tapped Belle's chest, right over her heart. And then a whisper.

*Rest.*

# Epilogue

Union veterans in Kilbourn, Wisconsin gave Belle a military funeral. The six pallbearers included four Union soldiers and two who were sons of Union soldiers. The Ladies Relief Corps of the Grand Army of the Republic, a Union organization, collected funds to purchase a suitable dress for her to be buried in. Belle's grave at Spring Grove Cemetery is still decorated every Memorial Day.

# Discussion Questions

*Dear Readers,*

*Thank you for reading* A Rebellious Woman. *I hope you enjoyed Belle's story. If you are part of a book club or just like talking about books, here are some questions that might be fun for you to consider. If you're interested in more information about the real Belle Boyd, including original letters and photographs, please visit* **www.clairejgriffin.com**. *Thanks again for reading. You are why I write!*

*—CJG*

1. Overall, what do you think of Belle? Do you admire her? Disapprove of her? At what places in the book do you have these (or other) feelings?

2. What are some adjectives you would use to describe Belle?

3. How would you describe Eliza?

4. How would you describe the relationship between Belle and Eliza? What bothers or surprises you? How does their relationship change over time?

5. What do you think are Eliza's reasons for protecting Belle?

6. Take a look at the Etiquette Rules at the beginning of the book. Which ones surprise you the most? Why do you think there were so many rules about women's behavior?

7. How does Belle respond to these restrictions? How does that affect how you view her?

8. How would you have dealt with the limits that were placed on women in this time period?

9. How do these rules compare with what you know about how women are still controlled in certain sects/religions, both in America and abroad?

10. How do these rules compare with the types of restrictions the typical woman faces in American society today?

11. Belle was a product of her Southern upbringing. If she had been born in the North, do you think she would have been an Abolitionist?

12. How would you describe Belle as a wife and mother?

13. Why do you think Belle was reluctant to marry again after her divorce from Sam Hardinge? Was this a smart decision?

14. How would you describe Belle's relationships with each of her husbands? Why do you think she chose them?

15. How would you describe Eliza's and Sam's relationship?

16. When they are together, Sam has his own name for Eliza. What does this tell the reader?

17. What do you think led Belle to lose her sanity and end up in an asylum?

18. There is no record that Belle ever threatened to sell Eliza or her family, but most of the events in the book really happened. What real event surprised you the most?

19. Census records from 1880 show Eliza and Sam still in Martinsburg and living in a house they rented from Eliza's brother. Do you think Eliza is satisfied with how her life turns out?

20. Do you think Belle is satisfied with how her life turns out? Would she say she lived her life "exactly as she chose"? Do you think she has any regrets?

21. In the course of the book, Eliza and her family prosper, and Belle's fortunes decline. This is a historical fact. Did this part of Belle's and Eliza's story surprise you? Do you think it's an important aspect of their story? What does it teach us about our understanding of history?

22. How does Belle change throughout the book? How do your feelings about her change?

23. Do you think Belle deserves the reader's respect? Why or why not?

24. As I was writing *A Rebellious Woman*, one of the themes that emerged was freedom. What different aspects of freedom are explored in the book?

## About the Author

**CLAIRE J. GRIFFIN** has rowed competitively, traveled to seven continents, kayaked below the Antarctic Circle, camped in Africa, driven across the Sahara, eaten bugs, and been stung by scorpions two separate times. She has always said "yes" rather than "no" to adventure; this is likely why she identifies so strongly with Belle Boyd. Claire and her husband of forty-five years live in Brooklyn, New York, where Claire remains a fan of ethnic food, street art, and overheard conversations.

CPSIA information can be obtained
at www.ICGtesting.com
Printed in the USA
FSHW011702010521
80904FS